THE FLINTLOCKS

TORTURED Tones

The Flintlocks Rockstar Romance Series - Book 3

by

Tania Joyce

TORTURED TONES by Tania Joyce
Published by Gatwick Enterprises 2023
Brisbane, Australia.

TORTURED TONES
The Flintlocks Rockstar Romance Series – Book 3
EPUB format: ISBN: 978-0-6455547-4-8
Paperback: ISBN: 978-0-6455547-5-5
Hardback ISBN: 978-1-7635962-9-0
ASIN: B0C2P19SSZ

Cover Photography by: RafaGCatala
Model: Jorge Del Rio Romero
Artwork: Gatwick Enterprises
Edited by: Creating Ink

For more information on the author please visit: www.taniajoyce.com

Keywords and Subjects
Rockstar romance, drummer romance, enemies to lovers romance, bodyguard romance, celebrity romance, Hollywood romance, secret baby romance, secret child romance, protector romance, single dad romance, single mom romance, rocker, band, musician, music, new adult romance, contemporary romance.

To unconditional love.

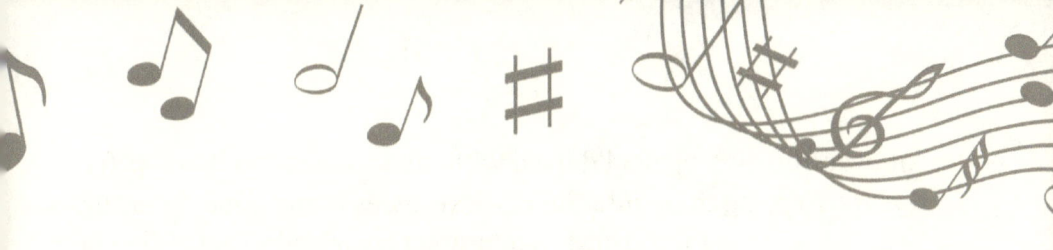

Chapter 1

COLE

It had been six hours, thirty-two minutes, and twelve seconds since I'd read the letter that changed my life. Downing another mouthful of vodka straight from the bottle, I stared at the page lying on my coffee table. Bile mixed with the bucketload of booze swirled through my belly. The Christmas party nightmares and hazy memories that had haunted me for years had turned out to be real. But I'd never expected to land in a living hell.

I had a kid.

A three-year-old daughter. *Charlotte.*

Her mom was my best friend's ex . . . Shelby.

But she'd been killed in a helicopter crash and named me as the biological father in her will. Blake, my band's manager, had given me the notice from her lawyers last night after our gig.

She'd wanted me to take care of the child.

What the fuck?

I didn't want a kid. I was too young. I loved being single. I was about to tour the globe with The Flintlocks. How the hell could I look after a toddler?

Was there any way out of this mess?

I needed my lawyer to perform a miracle.

I clutched the bottle to my chest and closed my eyes. Pain shot through my chest, sinking into the depths of my heart, stabbing it over and over again. I'd lived with my torment and demons for years. Burying them into the black recesses of my mind, ignoring them, had been for the best . . . to protect my friends, my family, my band, and our music. I'd been doing okay.

Coping.

Now . . . *I wasn't.*

I'd fucked up too many people's precious lives and had played my undeniable part in the death of two close friends—Phil and Aidan. How could I take on the responsibility of being a parent?

I wasn't father material. I was no role model. I never would be.

I lived and breathed for my band. Flint, Slip and newcomer, Lewis, kept me sane, stopped me from drowning in guilt, and prevented me from spiraling into the depths of depression. Everyone had their own problems. I never wanted to burden them with mine.

I'd made some stupid mistakes during my time, lived with some heartbreaking regrets, and prayed they'd disappear with time—not land on my doorstep. Now I'd have to live with them for the rest of my life.

Fuck.

The doorbell rang. I didn't move, opting for another mouthful of vodka instead. A few seconds later, the huge frosted-glass door swung open. In walked Flint, my best friend, and the lead singer and front man of our band.

I sucked in a deep breath. It shuddered through my chest. The concern and plethora of questions darkening his ice-blue eyes stirred the nausea gnawing in my gut. He ambled across the huge expanse of my foyer into the living area and sank onto the modular sofa beside me. Leaning forward, he rested his elbows on his knees. His black, long-on-top hair fell forward over one eye as he tilted his head toward me. "You look like shit."

"Wouldn't you be in the same situation?" I hadn't been to bed since our gig at Hayley's Bar last night. My mind wouldn't stop racing.

"Probably." He nodded, then stretched out his hand before him. His knuckles were red and raw. "I'm sorry for punching you."

"I deserved it." My cheek still ached from where he'd clobbered me after our show. Shelby's death, and the news of her child, had shocked the shit out of everyone. Especially Flint. Adding in the fact I'd betrayed him. "Flint, I don't know where to begin." I fought the sting in my eyes. "I'm sorry. I should've told you about that night. It's killed me for so long."

"I'm not gonna lie. It fucking hurts you didn't tell me. You've been my best friend for sixteen years and can talk to me about anything. *Anything.*" He swiveled to face me. "I'm devastated that Shelby was killed. But what I can't get my head around is this happened almost four years ago, right? Shelby and I weren't together. I was dating Lena. Why did you keep this a secret?"

"We had the dibs rule, man." My insides twisted and tightened. "She was your ex. We don't touch each other's girls, exes, or their friends. There's always feelings and baggage. Shelby was a no-go zone." After the ball-busting fight Flint got into with Phil—his now deceased brother—over Shelby in senior year, the rule had been made. It was our band's bro code. I'd sworn to never break it. But . . . I had.

"But we weren't dating." Confusion edged into his tone. "Why couldn't you tell me?"

Shame crept through my veins, seeping into every pore and sickening my stomach. I tightened my hold on the vodka and lowered my head. "Because I was never one hundred percent certain it happened. Not until Tia told me a couple of months ago. She saw the two of us . . . together."

Flint pinched his brows, forming a deep groove between them. "You don't remember being with Shelby?"

Gutted, I shook my head. "That night was such a blur. Do you remember your Christmas party after our last tour?"

"Bits of it. It was a long time ago."

Old wounds on my heart tore open as the murky memories and hazy nightmares came to life. "Aidan had died two weeks prior." My first lover, my boyfriend in high school, had committed suicide. "Our tour had ended." The exhaustion after a six-month grueling schedule across the US had taken its toll. "Priah had just dumped my ass." The love of my life had shattered my heart, ending our almost two-year relationship to return home to India. "I was a mess. Such a fucking mess. That night, I got so fucked up on drugs and alcohol, I couldn't even remember my own name. Shelby was upset, drunk, high, and jealous you were with Lena. We weren't in a good place. The more wasted we got, the more lines blurred. Really blurred." I sank deeper into the sofa, sifting through the fog in my head but only tiny flashes and snippets came to me. "I have a vague recollection of her dragging me into the laundry room. Doing it on the counter. But I clearly remember waking up the next day in one of your spare bedrooms . . . next to Yvette."

"Yvette Chang?" He raised an eyebrow. "She's freaking hot."

"Yeah. She is." I still hooked up with her occasionally. "But something about that night didn't *feel* right." I struggled to make sense of everything. "These visions of being with Shelby kept haunting me. When I called her a few days after that party, she denied everything. She told me to never call her again. So, I didn't."

That should have put the matter to rest. But the images in my mind never went away. I'd had too many sleepless nights, too many guilty nightmares, and had questioned my sanity about what had happened too often. "That's why I never told you." My voice scraped the back of my throat. "Shelby was my friend too. In a maddened moment, we obviously fucked. Being with her was a mistake. Now I'll be paying for it for the rest of my life."

Geez. I was a complete fuckup.

How could I be a father?

I sure as shit didn't want to be like my parents. They'd had little do with me and my sister, Tia since we were born.

"Cole." Flint grabbed the bottle from me, took a sip, then wiped his mouth on the back of his hand. "I loved Shelby. I really did. But we were over. Lena was my world until that relationship died in the ass too. Now I've found Sutton. She's my one. Don't be so hard on yourself." He handed the bottle back to me. "You shouldn't have let this shit about Shelby, Aidan, and Priah . . . and no doubt Phil, fester. I don't care you slept with Shelby."

"Hmph." I shot air through my nose. "You say that now. But things were different back then." *Way different.* "Phil had caused havoc during our tour, trashing rooms, picking fights with people at parties, and experimenting with stronger drugs. I came so fucking close to quitting to be with Priah. You were in the thick of taking flack in the media for our wild gigs. Slip was pissed at you for not honoring the dibs rule. We were at each other's throats. Do you honestly think we'd still be together if I'd told you *'I'm not sure but I think I slept with Shelby?'"*

"Yes." He didn't hesitate. "How could you think otherwise?"

Shit! Now, I felt even crappier. *But no.* I'd lost too much; I couldn't have risked losing someone else I loved. "I wouldn't jeopardize our friendship on uncertainty. After losing Aidan, and Priah leaving, I needed you guys more than ever. I'm nothing without our band."

"I'll admit things were shaky. But we've stuck together. We've always survived. This band is my life too."

I took a sip of vodka then rested the bottle against my thigh. My issues were insignificant compared to everyone else's. Priah had been my tipping point. Never again would I lose my head and heart to someone like that. I'd come so close to giving up music for her. Hell, I'd contemplated moving to India. But Priah hadn't wanted me to. Her culture and family came first. Not me. Turned out she had some guy waiting to marry her back home. She'd known about him for years. I was just temporary. Used and tossed aside.

Everyone lied.

Love destroyed lives.

I'd contributed to more than one trail of destruction.

I hadn't been able to love Aidan like he'd wanted me to. I'd learned quickly I loved women more than men. He hadn't handled our breakup well. I'd ignored his calls, his texts. I'd thought a clean break was for the best. I'd failed to see he wasn't well. His suicide tore my soul in two. He might still have been here if I'd just picked up the phone.

Shelby and Flint had loved each other so fucking much. But

study and music had pulled them in different directions after school. I'd never wanted to tarnish what they had.

Priah and I had been so in love . . . but her family had torn us apart.

And Phil? . . . I'd loved Flint's brother like he was my own sibling, but I hadn't stepped in to help him fight his addiction in time.

I hadn't stopped him from getting in that car that night.

What I'd thought was the right thing to do, to keep everyone happy, had turned out to be wrong. Phil's death had been my fault too.

I didn't want to destroy any more lives.

I didn't want to fuck up a kid's life.

All I wanted to do was go on our tour, play music, be with my friends, and enjoy being with women I didn't have to care about. I wanted to have fun and never be hurt or hurt anyone else again.

But how the fuck could I do all those things with a child? "Flint, what am I going to do?"

"I don't know, man. We'll work it out together." He rubbed and patted my knee. "But one thing you need to do is set in your mind that being with Shelby wasn't a mistake. We weren't together. She was smart. And beautiful. And funny. You were there for each other in a time of need. If it's your kid, you have to find a way to accept what happened. For the kid's sake."

"I don't want to be a father. I'll suck at it."

"You're wrong. You care for everyone. You're the glue that keeps us together."

Resting my head against the back of the sofa, I stared at the ceiling. "I don't know anything about being a parent."

"There's nothing like been thrown in the deep end." Flint sighed as he leaned back next to me. "You've got to learn to swim, real quick. But I'm here for you. So is Sutt, Slip, Lewis, and Tia." He turned his head in my direction. Concern darkened his gaze. "If she's yours, it affects all of us. With the tour coming up, we're going to have to take extra precautions. You saw the crowd at last night's show. It was wicked but insane. When I stormed out of the bar after decking you, there were tons of fans waiting in the parking lot. Sutt and I got swamped. It was scary. If it wasn't for Molly's security, we wouldn't have gotten out of there so easily. I called Blake on the way home. He . . . and I . . . want us to have full-time security from now until the end of the tour. Like you, I want to keep everyone safe."

I moved my head in some form of a nod. "I'm okay with that. There's been more paparazzi hanging around outside my front gate."

"Mine too. They make Sutton nervous. She's worried someone will jump our fence and get a picture of us walking naked around the house."

I chuckled, low and gruff. "That's not a picture I ever want to see."

"True." His eyes glinted as a small smile touched his lips. "We've had enough compromising photos of us posted online over the years, and I'm sure there will be more in the future. But let's stick to the ones taken at events and after-parties, not in our private homes. Blake's arranging security with Ashlem. They have a contract with Sam's Security Services. They provide Everhide's security and have a team here in LA."

Our friends in Everhide had used private security for years. But they were global mega stars. It was hard to comprehend that we were on the bottom rung, heading toward that level.

"Sounds good." If this kid was mine, she'd be thrown into the thick of this crazy life. I'd have to ensure her safety too. But one thing about this whole situation still confused me. Shooting forward, I placed the bottle on the coffee table and rubbed my eyes. My ribs constricted and punched my heart. "Why didn't Shelby ever tell me I had a kid?"

Flint sighed and rubbed my back. "Knowing Shelby . . . she wouldn't have wanted to hurt anyone. She probably regretted being with you too."

Damn. Shelby and I were more alike than I'd imagined.

"I hope this is a huge mistake." Tomorrow, I'd have to meet with my lawyer and have a paternity test. I'd know the results a day or two after that. But deep down in my gut, I already knew the outcome. Shelby wouldn't have gone to all this trouble to lump me with a kid for any other reason. Surely, Charlotte was mine. "I never wanted this to happen."

"Nobody does, man. I didn't want to lose Phil, or Aidan, or Shelby. But after the darkness there can be light." Flint clutched my shoulder and gave me a gentle shake. "I found Sutton. Maybe you'll find your something good as a dad."

I closed my eyes and shook my head. "I like my life the way it is. I don't want anything to change."

"Sometimes life throws shit at you that you just have to deal with, no matter how much it hurts or how hard the changes will be." He shuffled forward on the sofa and stared toward the bottle of vodka. "I made it through my grief after losing Phil thanks to you and Slip." His tone took on a hard edge. "If the child is yours, you're going to have to make some massive adjustments. So, man the fuck up. You will be responsible for her for the rest of your life."

Me? Responsible? That was a fucking joke.

My head throbbed like a bass drum being walloped with a beater. I turned to Flint and sucked in a shaky, deep breath. "Will you do me a favor?"

"You know I will."

"Will you come with me? To the paternity test? To the lawyer's?"

"Yeah, bud, of course." He drew me into a hug. "You got this. I promise."

Fuck. I didn't deserve such friendship, love, and loyalty. He seemed okay about me being with Shelby all those years ago.

But I knew better.

I wasn't convinced everything between us was right. But I was hell-bent on making it so.

On Monday, I went from the medical center to my lawyer's to rehearsals.

The hours passed too quickly.

Three days later, I got the results of my paternity test.

The kid was mine.

Fuck.

Anxiety and nausea took up permanent residency in my gut.

I wasn't ready to be a father.

Surely there was some way out of this.

I needed a miracle.

I needed a miracle *now.*

Chapter 2

COLE

In Downtown LA, sweat beaded on my brow as I walked toward the boardroom at the legal firm representing Shelby's family with Patrick, my lawyer, and Flint, my moral support. For the past two days, I'd met with Patrick to run through my options. They were less than limited since the child was mine. But I held onto a sliver of hope. Hope that Shelby's grandparents had changed their mind and wanted to contest the will. They'd be much better candidates than me to take care of the kid. They'd been looking after Charlotte since the accident. I didn't want to rip her away from the family she already knew.

Behind those mahogany doors, my future would be determined.

The receptionist led us into the meeting room and spun to face us. Her cheeks flushed as she eyed Flint and me up and down. Guessed it wasn't every day two rock stars walked through your office. If I wasn't so anxious about what laid ahead, I'd have chatted and taken selfies, packed on the charm and met everyone there. But my mouth was dry, and I could barely form a word.

She waved us through the doorway. "I'll let Usher know you're here. He won't be long."

"Thank you." Patrick nodded.

We entered the boardroom full of dark wooden furniture,

high-backed leather chairs and huge windows that overlooked Wilshire Boulevard. The three of us took seats on one side of the table. Patrick opened his laptop and leather folder containing a pile of documents.

Flint nudged his arm against mine. "Hey? Everything will be okay."

I half-heartedly nodded. I wished I shared his confidence.

Five minutes later, the door opened. In strode a man full of Matt Damon confidence, flecks of gray in his groomed beard, and dressed in a black pinstripe suit. *Definitely a lawyer.* He nodded in our direction, holding the door wider for a short woman with a kind smile that formed deep crinkles at the corner of her eyes, and an elderly man with snow-white hair in a wheelchair—Shelby's grandparents, Paul and Hannah Lane.

As I stood to greet them, a new truck overloaded with distress slammed into the center of my chest. Since when had Mr. Lane been in a wheelchair?

But what hit harder than that was the grief draining the light from their eyes. It seemed like a lifetime had passed since Flint and I had seen Paul and Hannah. Six years at least. They'd lived not far from our childhood homes in Pasadena and had raised Shelby after she'd lost her mom to some rare heart disease. Her dad had never been in the picture.

Patrick held out his hand to greet their lawyer. "Morning. I'm Patrick Lopez." He waved me forward. "This is Cole Tanner and his friend Flint Glover."

"Good morning. I'm Usher Weeks." He shook our hands then introduced Shelby's grandparents. "This is Hannah and Paul Lane. Cole, my understanding is you already know each other."

"Yeah." Nodding, I stepped over to them. "Hi."

"Oh, Cole." Sadness, confusion, hurt, and something I couldn't put my finger on ... oh, wait ... was that disappointment ... welling in Hannah's tear-filled eyes? She wasn't the first parent or grandparent who'd looked at me like that. "I wish we were catching up under better circumstances."

"Me too," I said. She held out her shaky hand, but I gave her a hug instead. After turning to Paul, I clutched his hand and gave it a friendly squeeze. He hadn't aged a bit since I'd last seen him. "How are you, Mr. Lane? Still surfing? What's with the wheels?"

"Hey, Cole." He wrapped his crooked fingers around the joystick on his wheelchair. "My surfing days are over. I've been in this damn wheelchair for two years. MS is a bitch."

Fuck. Multiple sclerosis? I didn't wish a degenerative disease on anyone, but would that change things for me? A dull ache thudded deep inside my head. *No . . . no, it couldn't.* However, I couldn't expect them to look after a kid when he was so sick.

I kept the mood light, play-punching him in the arm. "Bet that doesn't stop you from causing havoc around the town."

"Oh, there's none of that anymore. I'm trying to live my best life, but unfortunately, this shitty disease is beating me."

Crap. That's not good.

Hannah held out her arms to Flint and embraced him. "Oh, my goodness. It's been so long. Haven't you grown into a fine young man. How are you?"

My heart twanged. They'd always liked Flint . . . and me, Slip, and Phil when we'd hung out with Shelby and her friends at their house before going to gigs or parties. Hannah had always made us sandwiches and baked treats for our shows and had always said we'd be stars.

I was glad we'd proven her right.

"I'm good, Mrs. Lane." Flint stepped back, then clutched Paul on the shoulder. "Sorry to hear about Shelby." Too much emotion quivered through his voice.

Damn. This was hard on everyone. Not the reunion anyone could've anticipated.

Paul patted his hand. Water welled in his eyes. "It's been a rough couple weeks."

"Shall we get this meeting under way?" Patrick waved toward the table.

My stomach knotted and swayed. My blood pressure spiked. But I let out a jagged breath and nodded. "Sure."

We settled around the eight-seat table and Usher opened his

leather portfolio of notes and documents. "We're here to discuss the final will and testament of Miss Shelby Lane, and the custody of her daughter, Miss Charlotte Anne Lane, born on September sixteenth. The will left by the deceased indicated that Cole Tanner is the biological father of the child. Recent paternity results confirm this fact. It was Miss Lane's wish, in the event of her death, or the incapacity of herself and her partner, Mr. Keith Walker, that Mr. Tanner be notified and given legal custody to raise the child."

"Cole." A lone tear slid down Hannah's cheek. She splayed her shaky hands across her chest. "We never knew you were Charlotte's father. I'm so sorry. If we'd known, we would've insisted she tell you. You should've known you had a child. We assumed it was Keith's baby."

Keith had gone to the same local high school as Flint and Shelby while I'd gone to a private one. I didn't really know much about Keith other than he was Shelby's friend and had gone to law school with her in San Francisco. He'd been killed in the helicopter crash too. *Fuck.* Hannah and Paul had lost Shelby's mom, Shelby, and Keith, and had found out that I'd fathered their great-grandchild. There were too many devastating blows.

I'd had more than enough myself.

Hannah grabbed a tissue from her purse and dabbed her wet lashes. "Shelby and Keith were so happy. They'd gone away for the weekend to celebrate Keith's birthday. We were minding Charlotte for them. But they never came home." Hannah fidgeted with her tissue as more tears welled in her eyes. "Keith was a good man. He loved Shelby and Charlotte so much. But it breaks my heart they kept her from you."

I lowered my chin, fighting back the sting in my eyes. It still hadn't sunk in I had a kid. I didn't want it to. "It certainly has come as a shock, Mrs. Lane."

Once Shelby broke up with Flint, a year after high school finished, we'd rarely seen her. She'd come home to catch up with family and friends and to attend random parties during vacation. But after my night with her, and our phone call, I hadn't seen or heard from her since.

"Please, call me Hannah." Hannah's chin trembled. A nervous curiosity softened her tone. "It's none of my business, but can you tell me how this came about? Shelby never mentioned you'd been together."

My chest constricted as I stared at a scratch on the table. With a snag in my voice, I relayed to Hannah and Paul what I'd told Flint, leaving out the details about how messed up on drugs we'd been. I didn't want to tarnish their memories of Shelby in any way.

"She loved catching up with you guys. I always wondered why she'd stopped." Hannah sniffled and placed her quivering hands on her lap. "Cole, now I know you're the father, I see it so clearly. Charlotte looks just like you. Losing her will break my heart." She closed her eyes and shook her head. "She misses her mom and dad so much. We're all she knows."

My heart lurched. I didn't want to break that bond. Not ever. I wasn't an asshole. "I don't want to take her away from you."

"That is correct." Patrick straightened. "My client is here to discuss an agreeable arrangement regarding custody of the child that will be accepted by the court."

Usher's expression remained neutral. Linking his fingers, he rested his hands on the table. "We appreciate that. Charlotte's welfare is everyone's priority. But Mr. and Mrs. Lane don't want to contest Shelby's wishes. While they are the only close living relatives the child knows, they have concerns about their failing health."

"Health?" Patrick glanced up from his files. "Is there something notable other than your MS, Mr. Lane?"

"Yes." Paul clutched Hannah's hand. "Han has Parkinson's." *Shit!* I'd thought her shakes were just nerves. "It's getting more noticeable and harder to manage."

I slumped back in my chair. They were the nicest people struck with horrid illnesses. But as I closed my eyes, the pounding in my head grew louder and louder. My leg jiggled faster and faster. Where did that leave me? With Charlotte? *Fuck.*

"Cole." Patrick leaned toward me and whispered in my ear, "High care and degenerative medical conditions will be taken into account during the assessment of your case. Their health is not in your favor."

He wasn't telling me anything I hadn't already worked out. There had to be some other solution.

Usher's poker-perfect gaze drilled into me. "The Lanes want to honor Shelby's wishes and support you taking custody of Charlotte. Their age, health, and financial strain are considerable hurdles. They will only pursue legal guardianship if you're unfit to meet your parental obligations."

I placed my elbows on the table, dropped my head into my hands, and clutched my short hair. My breath ripped through my lungs. This was not going to plan. I wanted them to look after the kid. Not me.

Calm authority slid through Patrick's tone. "My client has concerns about taking the child into his care. His music career, constant travel, and lifestyle may not be deemed a suitable environment for the child."

"The Lanes think otherwise. There is no such thing as a normal family these days." A thin smile slid across Usher's lips. "We'd like to come up with a solution that suits all parties concerned and won't be rejected by the court."

"Cole, we love Charlotte with all our heart." Paul's eyes grew glassy. "But Hannah looks after me full time. If you honestly want nothing to do with your daughter, of course we'll take care of her. But we want you to have the chance to be her father. You were always a good kid. Yes, this will be a huge change, and it won't be easy. We know you have the financial means and capacity to give her an amazing life. You're her best option."

My heart stalled. No, I wasn't. I didn't want to use my music as an excuse, but I wanted what was best for the kid too. "Can't I just pay for support? Hire help?"

"Yes, you could do that." The disappointment in Hannah's tone punched me low and hard, right in the center of my balls. "But don't you want to respect Shelby's wishes? Charlotte is *your* daughter. You have a chance to be part of her life, see that she grows into a beautiful woman, and give her everything she needs."

I shook my head and puffed air through my nose. "I'm the kind of guy parents want to keep their daughters away from."

"I know what it's like to be a young man who loves women and parties and having fun." A small all-knowing smile curled the corner of Paul's mouth, but it was quick to disappear. "But before you make a decision you may regret, we'd like you to meet Charlotte."

Meet her? I already had enough regret and guilt eating me from the inside out. I wanted to forget the past, not live with a constant reminder of my mistake and the heartache I'd caused every day for the rest of my life. I didn't want visions of my child stuck in my head. "You think that's wise?"

"Maybe this will help your decision." Usher pulled out an envelope from his folder and handed it to me. "Hannah found this letter in Shelby's personal belongings along with her will."

The last letter I'd read had shattered my life. This one couldn't do any worse.

I opened and unfolded the page. *Shit . . .*

The page trembled in my hands. I sucked in a deep breath and read it:

Cole,

If you're reading this, myself and my partner, Keith, are no longer able to take care of our gorgeous daughter. I'm so sorry I could never bring myself to tell you about her. You were on the rise with your music. I didn't want to disrupt either of our lives. I didn't want to risk losing her.

I had a good life in San Francisco. Keith and I were good friends and fell in love. We were happy. A family. Please don't hate me. I did what I thought was best for us at the time.

That night you and I were together, you were the friend I needed. You mended my broken heart by giving me something magical to live for . . . a baby. For that, I will be forever thankful. Keith loved and raised Charlotte as his own child. I could never ask for more than that.

Charlotte has always and will always be loved. But knowing my grandparents' health is on the decline, I'd love that responsibility to come from you.
You've always had a good heart and soul. I know this news will come as a shock and be difficult to process, but please give our daughter all the love and care she needs.

It breaks my heart that I won't be there to see her grow up. I pray you can do that for me. I miss you guys. But I was happy. Whatever circumstances have led to this, know that I found peace for my mistakes and surrounded myself with people who loved me and our daughter.

Forgive me for not having the courage to tell you. I love her so much.
With all my heart, I'm sorry.
Promise me you will give her a million kisses and hugs every day.

Love always,
From here or afar,
Shelby

Fuck.

I handed it to Flint to read. I wiped my hand down my face and swiped the sting from my eyes. This was so surreal. Still heartbreaking. But new guilt twisted my stomach. How could I deny a dead friend's wishes? *Thanks, Shelby . . . Not!*

"Shit, Cole." Flint rubbed his cheek. "This is her handwriting. No question."

I'd had an agenda when I'd walked into this meeting to not

tear Charlotte away from the family she knew and do everything I could to give her the life she needed, but that outcome had taken an unforeseen turn. Hannah's and Paul's health, and this letter, changed things. I didn't want the courts to rule either of us unfit or for Charlotte to go into foster care . . . or be put up for adoption.

That left me with no option.

Fuck.

I was backed into a corner. Legally, I was screwed. Emotionally, I was torn between doing the right thing and wanting to be selfish. But how could I put myself first when a child's future was at stake?

I rubbed the back of my neck, kneading the tension in my muscles. "Um . . . I'd like to avoid drawn-out legal nightmares, or Charlotte being put into the system, so if . . . and only if . . . I do this, what's next?"

Usher nodded. "If you wish to take custody, there is a process, as I'm sure Patrick has discussed with you." He had; I just hadn't wanted to venture down that road. "You will need to respond to the *Petition to Determine a Parental Relationship* issued by the court with your paternity results and register your name on Charlotte's birth certificate. We found that it had no father named on the document. Then, you'll need to be assessed by Children's Services to ensure you can provide financial support, and a safe, loving, and caring environment for your daughter. If all is in order, and with no contention of the will, this should be processed quickly. After that, we'll come up with a plan with the Lanes to manage Charlotte's transition into your care."

A ringing erupted in my ears. My breath came in short, sharp shudders. The blood drained from my face. *Shit. I'd have a kid.* "But I'm going on tour for nine months. Can we do this when I get back?"

"This isn't a do-it-when-it-suits-you situation, Mr. Tanner." Usher looked down his nose at me like I was a piece of chewing gum stuck on the sole of his shoe. "We're talking about your child. We need to ensure she suffers minimal distress and avoids ongoing disruption after the traumatizing events she's been through. We need to get her settled into her new family as soon as possible."

"Cole, this is your kid," Flint mumbled. "Do you honestly want to leave her in limbo for that long?"

Fuck. Fuck. FUCK! "No. But how can I take a kid on tour?"

"Hire help." Flint shook my shoulder. My head spun through a list of people I knew, who I trusted to look after my kid. No one came immediately to mind.

"Cole." Hannah smoothed her hands over her skirt. "Paul and I have talked about this with Usher. We can stay here with friends in the interim and bring her over every day at a time that suits you. If you're open to the idea, I could come on the US leg of your tour. It would provide Charlotte with some familiarity while you both adjust."

"Come with us? You know it's three months of living on a bus or out of hotel rooms?"

"Yes, I assumed that. We've done several trips around Europe. I'm not going into this blind. Charlotte has traveled a lot with Shelby and Keith. They often went on incredible vacations. Our neighbor has agreed to look after Paul while I'm away. I'd love to come with you. I can live out my teenage fantasies by traveling around the country with a rock band."

I scratched at the heat burning in my chest. Could I take Hannah and a kid on tour? Was that possible? "Is that really an option? Take Hannah and Charlotte on the tour?" I asked Usher and Patrick.

Patrick nodded. "Your tour kicks off in about seven weeks. If we can get the initial assessments done, come across no hurdles, push this through the court, and Hannah goes with the two of you, yes, it's an option."

"If we present a strong case and both parties agree, I don't see why not." Usher gathered and straightened his documents into a neat pile.

As I glanced at Paul, my shoulders slumped. "Are you okay with this?"

He dipped his chin. "I'd do anything for Charlotte. So yes."

"But Cole. . ." Hannah placed her palm on the table. "I can't go overseas. I can't be away from Paul that long."

"Fair enough." My head wobbled with a nod. I'd have to hire a nanny. *God.* I was just like my parents. They'd always put their careers and travel before me and Tia. I'd never wanted to be like them . . . yet, there I was.

But I wouldn't let this kid change my life.

I loved my parties, my women, my music. Those things were solid. I wouldn't give them up for anyone. Not even a child. "This makes me sick to the stomach. I'm terrified. But fine. I'll take her."

"This shouldn't be viewed as a try-before-you-buy situation, Mr. Tanner."

Shit. Was this really happening? *Yep.* "I know."

"You seem like a respectable man." Usher glared at me as if he thought anything but. "Don't prove me wrong. If you are granted temporary custody, you will be reviewed and assessed by Children's Services to make sure Charlotte is safe. Your final assessment will be performed in a few months. After that, hopefully you are awarded full-time care. Hannah will play an integral part in providing reports on your behavior. I'd hate Children's Services to take your daughter away from you, Mr. Tanner."

"They won't. I'll get things into order." *How? I don't know.* "Hannah, if it's easier, you and the kid can stay with me. I have a guesthouse or you can use a room downstairs. My schedule is crazy. I don't have set times to work around."

"Oh." Hannah played with her tissue. "That's very kind of you. I don't want to impose, but I'd love that. That way you'd get more time with Charlotte."

"Yeah." My stomach swayed, dipped and dived. I couldn't form spit to save myself. "So . . . when do I have to meet her?"

"Let's do this formally." Usher grabbed his cell phone and scanned his calendar. "If Patrick can submit documents by the end of this week, I'll call a friend of mine in children's services who owes me a favor. We should be able to schedule a meeting for next Wednesday. Does that suit everyone?"

Fuck. A wave of nausea washed over me. I had a week of freedom left.

"Fine." But I turned to Flint and spoke low so no one else could hear. "Before I do this, guess what we have to do?"

A wicked smile inched across his face. "Hit the town hard?"

"Too fucking right. You'd better be ready for some big nights out."

"Always am."

"We're gonna party like there's no tomorrow."

"I'm down for that."

I'd ensure my kid had everything she needed and wanted. But she'd have to fit into my schedule and my plans with minimal to no disruption.

She wouldn't change my life.

Nope.

Not. One. Little. Bit.

Chapter 3

AVA

I stormed through the rotating door into the London Hotel in West Hollywood where I had to meet my security team and our new clients, The Flintlocks. My polished black shoes clopped loudly on the glossy tiled floor as I dashed across the lobby to the elevator bay. With my extra-large strong black coffee in one hand, I pressed the call button with the other. I glanced up at the LED floor counters above the doors. The tickers hadn't moved.

All four elevators were stuck on level ten, the second top floor. *What the fuck?*

I pressed the button again and again. "Come on, you stupid things."

After an already long afternoon, I didn't need this crap this evening. As I closed my eyes, I took a deep breath, searching for some calm, but the crushing ache in my chest overruled everything. The day hadn't gone to plan. No matter what suggestions and compromises I'd put forward to my ex-husband, Luther, he wouldn't agree to change our parental agreement. Mediation hadn't worked. Our lawyers had gone round and round in circles and had gotten nowhere.

Now, I'd have to take Luther to court. *Again.*

I was over fighting him at every turn.

I loved my son, Josh. He was my world. I wanted more time

with him. No, not just more time; I wanted full custody. The reality of that wasn't likely, but I held onto a sliver of hope.

I'd turned my life around. I'd made every change necessary and taken every step possible laid out by the court to prove I was a fit mother. I always had been. Luther could no longer use my past against me. *Conniving son of a bitch.*

Justice would be served.

As I leaned against the marble wall, a young couple wheeling carry-on luggage joined me waiting for the stupid elevators. They cuddled and kissed. *Ergh!* No wedding rings decorated their fingers. I should do them a favor and tell them never to go down the aisle. Marriage would be fun for a short while, but then it'd just fuck you over.

Like Luther had done to me. He wanted no part in being nice. He just wanted to keep hurting me, like I'd supposedly done to him. Money was all he cared about, and he loathed that I'd taken what was rightfully mine during our divorce. So he'd retaliated in the lowest possible way. When I'd been going through one of the worst times of my life, he'd used my job and my emotional vulnerability against me. He'd used the legal system to take the majority hold on the only thing I cared about . . . Josh.

Asshole.

I'd lost everything. My mother to cancer. My place on the force. My son to my power-tripping ex.

Total freedom from Luther wasn't likely, but more time with Josh would be a win.

The elevator doors opened, and I stepped inside. Draining my cup of coffee, I stepped out on level two and headed to one of the large meetings rooms where my team was gathering.

I loved working for Sam's Security Services. I loved these assignments. We'd been contracted to provide personal security for each member of The Flintlocks. We'd be their shadows during the final five weeks of their rehearsals and promotional appearances here in LA, then travel with them when their tour kicked off toward the end of November.

After the hell and heartache I'd experienced during my short time with the LAPD, I'd found my feet as a private bodyguard. This position had saved my soul . . . and my sanity.

With caffeine coursing through my veins, I entered the room and took a seat beside my best friend, Beckett. Wyatt, Sloane and Riley, the other members of the team, sat around the table chatting. At least I'd made it here before Wells, our boss, arrived.

"Evening, Ava." Beckett swiveled toward me. A big grin lit his face as he waggled a finger at my new black business suit, shirt, and necktie. "Nice threads."

"Yeah?" Smugness swayed through my voice as I tugged on the cuffs of my jacket. "You like it? It's one of a kind. Designer wear. Custom-made just for me."

He let out a low chuckle and straightened his shirt collar. "How bizarre. Mine too."

Something resembling a giggle escaped me. His uniform was the same as mine. Standard, company-issued work attire for tonight's outing. From the day we'd met at our security training course two years ago, we'd shared the same weird sense of humor. "You're such a buffoon. But you know I love ya."

"Love you, too." He hooked his arm around my shoulders and gave me a squeeze. But the tension from the day had me sitting stiff as a board.

He jerked his chin at me. "What's got you all wound up?"

I slumped in the chair and crushed my takeout coffee cup into a twisted mess, wishing it was Luther's neck. "Fucking Luther. Mediation failed, so I have to take him to court. In February. That's so far away." Four months seemed like forever.

"I'm sorry, Av." He clutched my hand resting on the table. "Luther's an asshole."

"You got that right."

Luther didn't want Josh. To him, our son was an inconvenience. But Josh was his tie to me. Luther had always said that if he couldn't have me, nobody could. He had no issues there. Who'd want me? A scorned woman, hell-bent on getting her son back? Nobody, right?

It was my fault for falling for the heir to Layk Studios, one of Hollywood's biggest film production and distribution companies.

I hadn't known who he was when we'd met at college. Becoming pregnant at twenty-years-old hadn't been part of the plan. While there were days when I wished I'd never laid eyes on Luther, I wouldn't change having Josh for anything.

"Is there anything Opal and I can do to help?" Beckett asked. His wife was a sweetheart. They'd both become good friends over the past couple of years. That was another thing I loved about this company and my team. We'd become a family. We had to trust each other—our lives literally depended on it.

"Nah. Thanks for offering, but I'll be okay." Once my blood pressure came down ten notches.

"Are you alright for tonight?" Worry and sadness hovered low and raspy in his tone. "Are you ready to start your last gig?"

I stitched on a brave smile. "Yeah, I am. I wouldn't miss my final assignment with you for anything . . . except Josh." After this tour, I'd be stuck behind a desk, taking on administration for our company's office here in LA. I loved being out in the field, on duty protecting people and working with Wells coordinating our team, but a month before mediation, I'd decided to give that up and show I could be a responsible parent. I had my family's support to take care of Josh when I traveled, and I'd been prepared to start my new job immediately. Those things hadn't helped me this time, but they would when I took Luther to court. As of February, I'd be home full-time. Luther couldn't use my job against me again. There'd be no more working insane hours at events or traipsing across the country with clients. There'd be no more thrills, elements of danger, or adrenaline in my future role. But for my son . . . my handsome little soccer star. . . yeah, I'd give up anything for him.

"Josh is one lucky kid to have a mom who loves him so much." Beckett gave my arm a friendly pat, then took a sip of his water. But as he put his glass down, a new glint simmered through his dark blue eyes. "At least this assignment will be a good one to end on. We get to travel and have some fun. It's not hard to keep our eyes on a bunch of rock stars."

Let's hope so. These gigs weren't always easy. They were often long, tiring, and demanding. Past clients had ranged from nervous, shy sheep to arrogant jerks to over-the-top divas. Constantly being on guard was never relaxing. But I loved ensuring they were safe. I was good at my job and lived for the excitement and variety in each day. Tilting my head to the side, I arched an eyebrow and sprinkled a touch of skepticism into my tone. "Did you read the briefing notes and profiles on these guys?"

"I sure did."

"We'll know what we're in for after tonight." From reading the security intel, The Flintlocks seemed to like their wild parties and excessive drinking, and had a huge, growing fan base that followed them everywhere. They weren't anything we hadn't dealt with before. "I might be glad I'm only doing the US leg of the tour."

"I can't believe you're ditching me early. I'll miss you overseas."

"I wish I could go, but Josh is more important. I couldn't go that long without seeing him." Even during this gig, I'd fly back on my rostered days off—my scheduled times to see Josh—so I could spend our time together. I wouldn't miss one day that could be spent with him. Not ever.

"Totally understandable." Beckett flicked a finger toward me. "So are you gonna keep this band's drummer in line?"

"Oh, you know I will." Cole Tanner would learn quickly that I wasn't one to be messed with. I took my job seriously. He needed to respect that. "No client has ever gotten the better of me."

"True, but if he gives you any problems, you let me know. We can swap guys. You can mind Sebastian . . . um, Slip . . . and I'll cover Cole."

"Thanks." I folded my arms and rested my elbows on the table. I loved that Beckett and the rest of team looked out for me, but it wasn't necessary. "Cole won't be any trouble." And he'd be easy on the eye while I had to protect his ass. "He seems to like his women, so things won't ever get boring."

Beckett chuckled. "Oh, this job is never boring."

"True. That's why we love it."

Wells walked into the room with Ramona, my other bestie and fellow team member. She'd been banging our boss for the past few months. Only I knew. But with her necktie off-center and those I've-just-been-shagged hooded eyes, anyone with half a brain could work it out.

She came to sit beside me. Her cheeks were as red as Dorothy's ruby slippers. Lucky her for getting some. I hadn't had sex in more than six months. Soon I'd forget what it was like. The place between my legs would be like a lost, overgrown temple. No one would ever find their way down there again.

I leaned toward her and spoke softly, just so she could hear. "You're late."

A mischievous smile slid across her lips. "Worth it."

Standing at the front of the desk, Wells cleared his throat. With his square jawline, hard gaze, buzz cut, and menacing black suit perfectly tailored to his big six-foot-three frame, he gave off an air of intimidation. He was a stickler for following the rules—that was why we got along so well. "Evening, folks. Hope you're ready for the long months ahead. I'm excited to work with these guys."

We'd had several meetings over the past couple of weeks with Blake, their manager, Falcon, their tour manager, and April, their personal assistant and publicist, to discuss every detail of this assignment. They certainly kept the boys on a tight schedule.

"But before you meet them, does anyone have any questions?" Wells asked.

"Nope." I shook my head.

No one else had any questions either.

"Good." Wells clutched and rubbed his hands together. "I trust each one of you has studied our intel material and know these guys' moves inside and out. You've memorized the way they walk, talk, and hold themselves. You know every measurement and detail of their physique. They've raised concerns about the increased number of people and paparazzi hanging around outside their homes. I read your reports after you went to assess their houses for security and surveillance upgrades. No issues were found, which makes our life easier. Correct?"

We all nodded.

Beckett and I had visited Cole's and Slip's house up in Laurel

Canyon to evaluate their home security. Neither of the guys had been present. April had shown us around. That woman was a marvel. How she coordinated four guys' lives and managed their publicity and promotional schedule was beyond me. I thought I was efficient, but April was organized on a whole new level I didn't know existed.

"Ava? Did you sort out a schedule with Mr. Tanner to shadow him on his runs?"

"Not yet. But I will after I meet him." I looked forward to exercising. Running helped clear my head. After the day I'd had, I needed to run a marathon . . . maybe two.

"Make sure that happens. We don't need someone knifing him on some unknown track."

I'd go down before my client. That was what I was trained to do. "That won't happen on my watch."

"Excellent." Wells straightened and buttoned his jacket. "So tonight, we're escorting the band to The LA View Bar on Sunset." We'd taken other celebrities to the popular joint before and knew the layout well. "It's going to be busy as always. I've contacted the venue's security team. They know we're coming." He glanced at his watch. "The band should've finished their photoshoot by now. If there are no other issues, it's time to meet The Flintlocks."

When we did one-off events or escorted a high-profile person or celebrity to a function or outing, we rarely had much interaction with them. We were just assigned to the job, sometimes with a driver, and took them wherever they needed to go, watched them, and returned them home. But for an assignment like this where we would be shadowing someone for months on end, we always met our clients.

"Alright." Wells waved toward the door. "Let's do this."

I wished I could catch his enthusiasm. I was sure once I met the guys, got them to the venue, and focused on the job at hand, I'd be fine. I'd stop wanting to taser every asshole that came across my path. Easy, right?

After checking our gear, plugging in our earpieces, and making sure our comms connected, we filed out of the room.

We piled into the elevator and headed up to their suite . . . on level ten. *That'd be right.* The floor that had held up the elevators before. The tangled knot that had been twisting in the base of my neck all day tightened. The tension in my jaw ached. What had they been doing to hold up four elevators? *Ergh.* I didn't want to know. I'd seen a lot of shit in my time. I was sure I was about to see a lot more while touring with the band.

Wells knocked on the door to the suite. Seconds later, Blake, their manager, opened it and waved us inside. "Evening. Nice to see you again. Come on in."

The seven of us shuffled into the room and took position, standing in a row along the main wall. After studying our intel material, I knew everyone present. The band—Flint, Cole, Lewis, and Slip—and two stunning women—Sutton, Flint's girlfriend, and Tia, Lewis's girlfriend who was also Cole's sister and one of the band's sound engineers. They lounged on the sofas, drinking alcohol. April was on the phone, pacing in front of the doorway to one of the bedrooms.

But the moment I laid eyes on Cole Tanner, the hairs on my arms stood on end. His electric green eyes drilled into me as he swigged a mouthful of vodka from the bottle, then handed it to Flint. *Great.* Those fuckers were drunk before we'd even stepped outside.

I straightened my stance, clasped my hands behind my back, and lifted my chin. I was on duty. Time to focus. But there was no denying that Cole was much better looking in real life than in the pictures and videos I'd studied.

Blake rested his butt against the arm of the sofa chair. "Hi y'all." His Texan drawl was as smooth and sleek as his expensive gray suit. "We're looking forward to having you work with us over the months ahead. I hope the guys don't cause you any grief, but their safety is top priority."

Standing with his feet shoulder-width apart and ramrod straight, Wells nodded. "Understood. That's why we're here. "

"You ready to match these folks up?" Blake jerked his head toward the band and the girls. "They're getting edgy, so let's make this quick."

"Certainly," Wells stepped toward the band. "Evening, everyone. Your safety is paramount. So please, follow my team's directives, and be mindful of your surroundings, and if you have any concerns you can contact me directly." He waved at us. "These men and women are half your security detail; you'll met the rest on our next roster rotation. They will be with you for all work-related matters, travel, and special circumstances we've discussed. From the time you step out of your front door to the time you go back through it, they'll cover you. During the tour, that means to and from your hotel room or tour bus, and to the venues and publicity appearances. Ultimately, for the next ten months, you do not shit without these guys knowing about it. Got it?"

"Loud and clear." Flint raised the bottle toward us, then took a sip. The other guys grumbled and nodded.

Wells continued. "Based on your profiles and requirements, Flint, you are assigned Sloane Sturgess." Sloane dipped his chin. Flint half-heatedly waved. "Sebastian, Beckett Rivers is your man."

Beckett bowed.

"It's Slip." Their lead guitarist's lips twitched into an almost there smile. "Don't ever call me Sebastian. Got it?"

"Understood, sir." Beckett dipped his chin.

"And no fucking sir shit either." Slip growled.

"Yes, sir . . . Slip." Beckett's eyes glinted as he nodded.

I pursed my lips, trying not to laugh.

Wells just drew his shoulders back and let out a deep breath. "Lewis, you've been allocated Mr. Wyatt Johns."

"Hey, man." Lewis threw Wyatt a wicked smile. "You can watch me and Tia anytime. She likes that."

Tia smacked him on the arm. "I only like watching you."

"No, you don't." He hooked his arm around her shoulders and kissed her cheek. "Wyatt's hot. He can watch."

Tia grazed her teeth across her lower lip as she eyed Wyatt up and down. "Yeah . . . okay. He can watch."

Wyatt's cheeks reddened as he shuffled on his feet. The shit we had to put up with was not for the fainthearted.

"And Cole? You have Ava Matthews."

His brow drew into a deep furrow. "Why the fuck do I get a chick?"

My back stiffened. "I beg your pardon?" I was out of line to snap at a client, but who did this guy think he was?

Cole held up his palm. "No offense, but seriously? You're half my size." I wasn't. I was five-foot-nine compared to his six-foot-two build. "How will you keep the fans off me? I'll be protecting your ass, not vice versa."

I drew my shoulders back. As I sucked in a deep breath, my nostrils flared. I was damn good at my job. I'd proven that fact on more than one occasion, and I wasn't going to let some arrogant rock star question my skillset. "Want to make a bet?" My voice sliced through my teeth.

Wells just chuckled. So did my teammates.

"Cole?" Warning flashed in my boss's gaze. "I can assure you, Ava is best suited to your needs. Do not underestimate her strength, her fitness, or her training. You'll end up worse off. Trust me."

"I doubt it," Cole mumbled.

Wells pointed to Ramona. "Ramona is part of our secondary team that will cover you on the days this team has off. Sutton and Tia, you are under our protection when you are with the band. I'll be coordinating our efforts with Ava, my second-in-charge, and I'll be keeping an eye on April and Blake with Riley. Any questions?"

"None." Cole snarled. He leaped from his seat, and stormed toward the exit. "Let's get the fuck out of here. It's time to party." He opened the door and disappeared.

I gave Wells a curt nod and took off after Cole. "Mr. Tanner."

Cole didn't stop heading for the elevator.

"Mr. Tanner."

He kept walking. *Asshole.*

Halfway down the hallway, I caught up to him. I grabbed him on the shoulder and spun him 'round to face me. "Do you have a problem, Mr. Tanner?"

He eyed me up and down as the corner of his lip curled into

a sneer. "No. Just stay out of my way and everything will be fine."

He turned to walk off. But I grabbed his arm, bent it behind his back, and drove him into the wall. "My job is to protect you," I hissed toward his ear. "Don't be cocky, smart, or a dick, or I'll take you down. I know what I'm doing. I'm damn good at my job. Don't ever question my ability. Deal?"

He jerked his hips backward, ramming his butt into my pelvis. He swung his shoulder up high and twisted to face me. Okay, I should've held him tighter, but I wasn't out to hurt him—just put him in his place. But he clearly knew some defensive moves, I'd give him that. He grabbed the lapels of my jacket, pushed me back a few steps, and pinned me against the opposite wall.

Towering before me, he growled, low and husky. My heartbeat quickened with a mix of intrigue and spite as his electric green eyes speared me to the spot. Pure adrenaline shot through my veins. It had been too long since I'd had any man this close to me other than during combat training. I didn't need Cole in my space. *But holy fuck.* He smelled good. A mix of earthy woods and spice . . . and alcohol.

His eyes narrowed as his lips hovered a few inches from mine. "Don't touch me again or I'll have you fired."

In an easy defense move, I drove my fingers into his jugular notch and pushed him backward. He gasped and gagged. *God.* I didn't even push hard. This guy was all show, not as tough as he made out to be.

The moment his back connected with the opposite wall, I stopped toying with him and pointed at his face. If I'd really wanted to hurt him, he'd be on the floor or unconscious by now. I was no fucking pushover. "Touch me again, and I'll break those precious hands of yours. You need them to drum, don't you? . . . And for looking after your daughter?"

Yeah, the details of him finding out he had a child had been in our briefing notes too. It wasn't every day you found out you'd knocked up some girl and had to take responsibility for your actions. I, of all people, understood consequences. I prayed that despite the life-altering change he'd been dealt, Cole was a decent person who'd take care of his daughter who'd suffered too much loss. That he wasn't just this half-drunken ass-wipe that loomed before me.

Surely there weren't two Luthers in the world.

The light in his eyes disappeared, but within a blink they flashed with jade fire. "Stay out of my business."

I stepped in closer and stabbed my finger against his rock-hard chest. "Your safety *is* my business. Got it?"

The air between us warped as his breath hit mine. The alcohol fumes were enough to intoxicate a college frat party. We stood there, glaring at each other. Where was my professionalism? This was not the way I wanted my first meeting to go. My rough, shitty day wasn't his fault. I shouldn't be taking my personal crap out on him.

The others walked down the hallway toward us. Wells and Beckett had huge grins on their faces. Blake nodded, and Flint burst out laughing.

"Oh, Cole." Flint smiled, shaking his head as he walked past, holding Sutton's hand. "Looks like you shouldn't piss off your security guard. Ava? I like you already."

I grabbed Cole by the shoulder and gave him a hard pat. "We have an understanding now. Don't we, Cole?"

His heated gaze burned into me, stirring something hot and angry inside my chest and in the pit of my stomach. *Oh, yeah* . . . that fire was my self-control, restraining me from punching him in the face.

He shrugged his leather jacket straight. "Fuck you. Don't ever touch me again."

"Don't give me a reason to."

"Don't worry. I won't." He stormed off to join his friends.

Becket fell in beside me as we gathered in groups by the elevators. "Oh boy. You're gonna have fun with that one."

I nudged my arm against his. "I might take you up on your offer to swap guys."

"I think Slip will be just as much trouble as Cole."

The band, Tia, and Sutton took turns at the bottle of vodka.

34

Blake and April talked to Wells and Riley. The rest of us stuffed our ear pieces into place, ready for our outing.

I did like a challenge. Cole would no doubt be one. As the elevator approached, I stepped into position in front of the doors. Time to work. I threw Cole a sideways glance. "Are you going to play nice, now?"

"I'm always nice." His tone certainly wasn't.

I'd thought my day couldn't get much worse after my meeting with the lawyers and Luther, but then I'd met Cole Tanner. *Ergh!* But I'd handle him. I'd dealt with worse. Hell . . . I'd been married to the worst.

Cole just had to learn the ground rules. Hopefully he was a quick learner otherwise this was going to be a very long tour.

The elevator arrived.

Here we go.

After the all clear, we stepped inside.

Here was to night one, on duty for The Flintlocks.

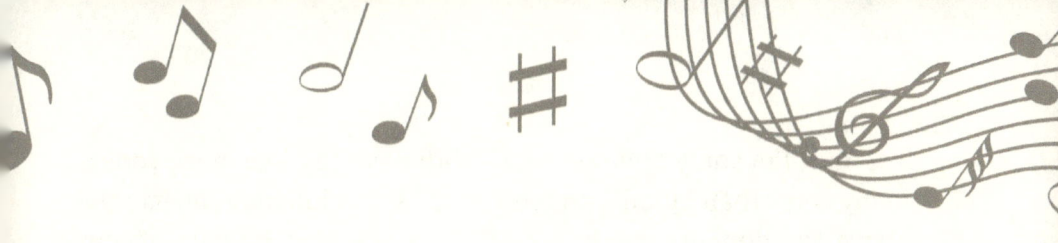

Chapter 4

COLE

There was a first time for everything. I'd never had a female bodyguard before. With dark brown eyes that had burned me from the inside out and more attitude than Christina Aguilera, Ava had certainly put me in my place. She didn't take any of that just-because-I'm-a-woman crap.

I liked that. I hadn't meant to be rude. Having a colossal amount of chaos cantering through my head was no excuse. I'd apologize. I hadn't been myself lately. Not sure I ever would be again.

In the hotel's driveway, I climbed into the first SUV and rested my head back against the plush leather seat. Lewis and Tia joined me while Flint, Sutton, and Slip went in a separate vehicle. Tonight, I just wanted to get shit-faced, pick up some hot chick, and get laid. I needed to do something, anything, to take my mind off tomorrow. The anxiety of meeting my daughter had lodged firmly in my chest. Every breath hurt my lungs. A big night out was the only thing that would alleviate the stress, the panic, and the fear from crippling my veins.

Just as we were about to head off, Wyatt, Lewis's bodyguard, jumped into the front passenger seat next to the driver. Ava slipped into the seat beside me.

Shit. Best to man up and get this over and done with.

"Ava, I'm sorry about earlier." With what felt like more vodka in my veins than blood, I swayed on my seat, clutching the handle above the door to steady myself. "You wouldn't be part of our security detail if you weren't good at your job. I didn't mean to piss you off."

"Apology accepted." She gave me a curt nod. "Let's hope I don't have to prove my point again."

I brushed my fingertips over the hollow in my neck. "My throat is still sore. Good hit."

The subtle grin that quivered across her lips held too much satisfaction. Yeah, I couldn't mess with her. She'd take me down. Was it wrong that I thought that was kinda hot?

But stupid.

I'd seen that flash of heat in the depths of her eyes when I'd held her against the wall. In my current state, I hadn't been able to tell if it was attraction or pure hate. It'd better have been the latter. I had enough shit to deal with without adding her to the list. She had a job to do. So did I. Mine involved drinking and hooking up. I didn't care in what order they happened.

"Ava, if you need any tips on babysitting my brother, just ask." Tia wedged her crutches beside her, then tapped my foot with her moonboot. She had a few more weeks of recovery left after ankle surgery. She'd been as bad as me, keeping secrets from everyone. Hers had recently surfaced and changed our lives. But she was happy now. I couldn't wish for anything more . She was the best sister a guy could have.

"He'll keep you on your toes," Tia continued to talk to Ava like I wasn't right there. "He's like a puma: sleek, smooth, and seductive. Girls readily offer themselves as prey, but he has a weakness for the supermodel types."

I shrugged my shoulder. What could I say? Tia was right. But there were more to my preferences than just looks. Most girls I hooked up with were regulars. They were career-oriented chicks who constantly traveled across the globe, chasing fashion shows, movies, and photoshoots. They didn't want commitment. Neither did I. We were friends with benefits without any complications.

My only other stipulation was no blondes . . . not since my night with Shelby.

Ava was blonde. Despite being tall and okay in the looks department, she was my bodyguard . . . so I had to stop eyeing her in that suit. *Hmmm.* There was something about a woman in uniform that warmed my blood. *Shit. Stop. Don't be a dick.*

"Supermodels. Noted." Ava's expression was impossible to read, all neutral and set in stone. "As we will be working together, let's get the rules straight. You stay in the venue. Stay in the designated VIP sections. Stay out of trouble."

"I can't promise that." I threw Ava a sorry-not-sorry smirk, then stared out the window as we drove off. But that was the truth. The guys and I didn't always start problems when we went out, but we often attracted them. Usually, it was from other men getting jealous of their girlfriends talking to us . . . or getting too friendly. We'd been in more fights than I cared to remember. But now Flint was with Sutton, Lewis was with Tia, and Slip had toned down his antics for some reason. Our outings had been different, less disruptive. Incident free. That was kinda nice. I couldn't deny that. Plus, I liked my face the way it was. I didn't miss cut lips, bruises, or black eyes—the one from Flint had almost disappeared. I didn't need to risk damaging my hands from fending off jerks. I needed to drum more than I needed oxygen. We still drank, danced, and had a shit load of wild fun. And I was more than happy to entertain the ladies. "We do like a good time."

"That's fine." Ava dipped her chin. "My job is to ensure you can do that without being mobbed, knifed, drugged, or hurt in any way. My team and I have your backs."

I half-grinned, swayed toward Ava and raised my eyebrow. "Hmm. I'd like to see you on your back."

Her gaze hardened, prickling my skin. Her tone cut sharply. "When? When I throw you onto the floor in a self-defensive maneuver? Or when you're asking for three broken ribs?"

I chuckled. "Well, it certainly wouldn't be when fucking."

"I'm glad we're on the same page, Mr. Tanner." A muscle ticked in her jaw. "I am your bodyguard. Not one of your hookups."

My sister slapped me on the knee. "Cole, be nice to Ava. Her job may involve taking a bullet for you."

Fuck! The reality of that hit me hard. We had some overzealous fans. Our recent gig at Hayley's Bar had highlighted that fact. Flint and Sutton could've gotten hurt. It was one element of being famous we all struggled with. We loved meeting and greeting our followers, but I'd hate to ever be in a situation where someone's life was endangered. "Would you do that? Take a bullet to protect us?"

Ava didn't miss a beat. "There is an element of risk in being a bodyguard. I pray it never comes to that. But yes. So don't give me a reason to step out of the way."

Being shot would be one way to avoid the meeting tomorrow. *But no.* I wasn't that fucked up. I just wasn't ready for the change. The hours were ticking by too quickly. *Fuuuuck!* This was my last night of freedom. I had to enjoy every damn second of it.

Ten minutes later, we arrived at the club. The rest of the band pulled up behind us. Bypassing the long line of partygoers waiting at the door, we followed security into the huge venue. Summoning my party mode, I pushed my worries to the back of my mind, rubbed my hands together and hollered at my friends, "Let's fucking do this. Bring on the shots. The girls. The party!"

As we weaved through the packed crowd, people's faces lit up, mouths gaped, cell phones cameras flashed in my eyes. Being recognized still gave me a rush. It validated the fact that we were good at what we did. Sometimes I needed that reminder . . . but not tonight. Loud music thudded through the speakers and thundered through the center of my chest. The dance floor overflowed with gyrating bodies. Disco lights flickered across the crowd. The electric energy pulsing through the air took over me, mixing with the buzz from alcohol already coursing through my entire system.

Oh yeah. Tonight will be good.

Upstairs in the VIP area, we took seats in our reserved section of navy and red velvet sofas and chairs. Tia and Lewis rejoined us after taking the elevator. She tossed her crutches aside and sank onto the seat opposite me. "I can't wait to get rid of those things."

"In three weeks you can." I said, then smiled and waved to the girls at the table next to us. *The evening just got better.* Our security stood nearby. Ava and Beckett were at the front of our area by the stairs. Sloane and Wyatt were behind us, by the wall. *Good.* I didn't want them to cramp our style.

Slip fell onto the sofa beside me and was quick to order a bottle of vodka and bourbon from the cute waitress wearing metallic pink hot pants and a black tube top. But I didn't look twice. My mind kept drifting to tomorrow.

Slip nudged my arm with his elbow. "You feeling okay?"

"Yeah. Why?" Other than a little more drunk than expected at this hour of the night.

"Normally, you'd be all over that chick."

"So would you." I clipped the back of his long blond hair. "What is with you lately?"

A big grin inched across his face. "Wouldn't you like to know."

"Yes. I fucking would."

He lowered his chin, nodded, and fidgeted with the leather bracelets around his wrist. "Um . . . yeah. I have to come clean. I've been meaning to tell you something for a while." He rubbed and rolled his hands together. "I'm seeing someone. It's only casual, been on and off and up and down. But with the tour coming up, and with our new security detail, we can't keep it under wraps any longer."

I jerked my chin back. This *was* news. "Who?"

"Maddy."

"Oh, fuck. Are you serious?" *Shit.* That didn't come out right. "I mean, that's awesome." I loved Maddy. She was fun. An actress like Sutton. But concern slammed into my ribs. "Do Sutton and Flint know?"

The last time Slip had dated somebody's best friend, it hadn't ended well. But that had been Flint's fault, not his. I prayed that Slip hooking up with Maddy, Sutton's best friend, didn't end in the same hot, fucked-up mess as Slip's last serious relationship.

"Yeah. I told them on the way here. They seem cool about it. Lewis and Tia have known for months. Since your birthday."

"Since April?" My voice pitched high. *Shit.* Why was I always the last person to know what was going on? I'd been the last to know Lewis was screwing my sister. The last to know my ex, Priah, had no intention of staying in America. The last to know how much love could fucking hurt you and make you do stupid things . . . and sometimes those stupid things left you with no choices.

Like taking on a kid.

Somehow I had to find the strength to face tomorrow. Be a father to a child I hadn't known existed until ten days ago.

Ergh! I needed more vodka.

The waitress returned with our drinks and glasses and placed them on the table. *Perfect timing.*

But before I drank more alcohol, I threw my arm around Slip's shoulders and gave him a big hug. He and Flint had been my best buddies since we were nine. Nothing would ever change that. I was happy for him, and I'd be there for him if hooking up with Maddy all turned to shit. "I'm stoked for you and Mads. She's a great chick. But damn . . . have I lost my wingman?"

"I'm not going anywhere." Chuckling, he elbowed me in the ribs and pushed me aside. "You've never needed me to be your wingman."

"Yes. Always. We have a lot of fun hooking up with women."

"I'm just sticking with Maddy for now. You can have every other chick."

"Good thing I don't have a problem with that." *Wow.* I was the only one single in our band. There was another change I hadn't seen coming.

"I'll still party with you like a crazy motherfucker." He poured a round of shots and held one out to me. "Now get this into you, Daddy."

"Fuck you." Laughing, I play-punched him in the thigh. God, I loved these guys, but the word *Daddy* speared my chest. As I sucked in a deep breath, panic shuddered through my lungs in jagged waves. *How many hours did I have left?* I glanced at my watch. *Fourteen. Shit.* I wiped my hand down my face to erase my worries. After grabbing the shot from Slip, I downed it. The ice-cold vodka slid down my throat. The burn settled in my stomach, seeped through my veins, and soothed the tension in my temples. Just for a second. Then it was back. *Fuck.* I slammed the glass onto the table, swiped the bottle from Slip, and topped up my shot. I picked up my glass and waved it toward my friends. "Okay, assholes. Let's drink." I raised my vodka a touch higher. "To new directions. To one I didn't see coming."

"Cole, you'll be a great father." Tia gave me a reassuring smile as she held up her bourbon.

"I'm freaking out." That was an understatement. "Did you see the crap I had to buy?" Two days ago, I'd gone shopping with our housekeeper, Mackenzie. She had two young kids. After burning a hole in my credit card, I'd come home with clothes, toys, bedding, sippy cups, booster seats, and a ton of other junk. Shit I'd never wanted to purchase.

"Yeah. But I bet you buy more booze in a week." Lewis teased. I shot him a glare, then grinned. I did like my vodka.

"Here's to changes." Flint waved his glass at me. "We've all been through them—the good, the bad, and the fucking awesome." He gave Sutton a quick kiss on the cheek. She giggled, blushed, and curled her hand around his leg. "But whatever life throws at us we'll get through everything together. Even kids."

"Thanks, man," I held my shot forward. We chinked glasses. Flint had been too forgiving, but I'd hurt him. I'd never forgive myself for that. Every time he looked at me there was a new distance in his eyes. I was sure he wasn't looking forward to having the constant reminder of his ex in the form of my kid in our lives either.

"Hey. We have so much to be grateful for." Lewis entwined his fingers with Tia's and kissed the back of her hand. "We have each other. We're going on fucking tour. We'll always be family."

I had to remember that. I'd survive anything with this group of people. I had to.

We drained our glasses, drank more, and fell into conversation about the tour, cracked dirty jokes, talked about Sutton's second season of filming *Angels in LA* and the show's up and coming launch party, and had each other in fits of laughter. It was just what I needed to take my mind off tomorrow . . . even if the diversion only lasted for a few minutes at a time.

Needing more of a distraction, I stood and mingled with the other guests in the VIP section, mainly the girls I'd noticed when we first arrived. My friends were quick to join us. We swallowed more alcohol and had a few selfies with the ladies, but after talking to them about their college studies, I lost interest.

As I topped up my drink, a tall leggy Asian girl came up the stairs with two girlfriends. I swayed on my feet and did a double take. *Was that? Yep. Min fucking Liang. What was she doing here?* With her long, black hair cascading down her back and her short party dress barely covering her panties, she was the distraction I needed. One of the girls I'd hooked up with on more than one occasion.

I waved to her and her friends to join us.

But once they reached our VIP section, Ava and Beckett blocked their path. Ava turned to me and raised a questioning eyebrow.

No bodyguard would cockblock me.

I stepped over to Ava, squeezed between her and Beckett, and took Min's hand. Remaining wedged between Ava's and Beckett's bodies, I edged in closer to my bodyguard. "Hmm . . . is that your gun or are you happy to see me?"

Her eyes narrowed into sharp slits. "That's pepper spray. Want me to use it on you?"

"Nah. Not tonight." I tugged Min toward me. "These girls are with me."

Ava dipped her chin. With no hesitation, she stepped back and let the girls through.

How did she do that? Stay so rigid? The woman needed to lighten up. It wouldn't kill her to crack a smile, would it?

I led the girls over to our table, snaked my hand around Min's waist, and drew her against my chest. "I didn't expect to see you tonight. What are you doing here?"

A saucy smile touched her lips as she played with the tips of my button-down collar. Her glittery eyelids sparkled in the bright disco lights. "We've just finished Fashion Week in New York. We're here for two days, then off to London. We were at this wicked party at Layk Studios earlier tonight." She waved her long pink fingernails toward her blonde friend. "Isla is friends with this nanny who works for some guy who's high up in the studio. We've been to some wild nights, but that was insane. There were drugs, booze and sex, all on offer."

"Sounds like my kind of party." Except for the drugs. I didn't touch them anymore.

Min introduced Isla and Natalia to me and my friends. I gave each of the girls a quick kiss hello on the cheek. "Evening, ladies. Would you like a drink?"

"Oh, yes, please." Isla's sexy German accent flitted through the air as she clapped, jingling the silver bracelets on her wrists. "I'd love some champagne."

"Sounds good." I waved down the waitress and ordered a bottle.

Min slid her hand around my waist and drew my hip against her side. "I'm glad I ran into you. It's been a while."

"It certainly has." I draped my arm around her shoulders and whispered in her ear, "Last Fashion Week, if I remember."

"That was fun." She turned in to me, ran her hands up my chest, and linked her fingers behind my neck. "Anna always put on a good party."

"That was a hot night." A pool party with hundreds of girls in skimpy bikinis—what was not to like? Hooking up with Min had been a bonus.

"Pity Anna's not putting on another fab get-together while I'm here." She inched a touch closer. "I wouldn't mind a repeat."

Min kissed the side of my neck and licked the edge of my earlobe. A shiver ran down my arm, and the hairs on my skin stood on end. But it wasn't from Min's warm breath. I glanced over her shoulder. Ava stared at me. Her face, set in stone.

Crap. Did she have to watch my *every* move?

Ergh! Not going to happen.

I cupped Min's cheek and gave her a quick kiss. "Let's have another drink and see how the night pans out."

I turned my back to Ava so I could chat with our friends. But Ava's eyes were still on me. I could feel them drilling into my back. I couldn't shake the weird sensation. I'd had bodyguards before, so why was she bothering me? Why tonight? I downed another shot of vodka and did my best to ignore her.

After a few more drinks, I took Min downstairs and we danced in the middle of the crowd, gyrated our bodies together, getting hotter with each beat that boomed through the busy club. A few songs later we were back up in the VIP area, making out on the sofa. As she sat sideways across my lap, I ran my hands over her bare legs, teasing her skin just beneath the hemline of her dress. My dick ached. I was drunk. I'd partied. Now there was only one thing left to do . . . without Ava looming in the background. I slid my fingers an inch higher underneath Min's skirt. "You wanna get out of here?"

She played with the open top buttons on my shirt then popped another one undone. "I'd love to, but I can't leave." She leaned in and kissed my exposed throat. "You wanna sneak off somewhere? Restroom maybe?"

Not ideal, but . . . "Fuck yeah. Let's go."

I lifted Min to her feet, stood, and tapped Flint on the back. "I'll be back in a few minutes."

Flint's eyes glinted as he nodded. "Have fun."

"Planning on it." I led Min out of our section in the VIP area and veered toward the restrooms on the other side of the mezzanine floor. But just as I passed our security, a hand caught my arm. *Ava.*

"Mr. Tanner? Where are you going?"

I smirked. "You really want to know that?"

"Yes."

I got up in Ava's face. She didn't flinch at the stench of vodka on my breath. "I'm going with Min. Somewhere to . . . you know . . ." Did I really have to spell it out?

Ava dipped her chin.

Good. No spelling required.

I hooked my arm around Min's shoulders, and we staggered across the floor. But Ava followed. *Crap.* She really was my shadow. They hadn't been lying about that. *So be it.*

My hazy eyes struggled to focus in the dimly lit corridor that led to the restrooms. We passed the men's and ladies' toilets and stopped in front of the handicap bathroom. But just as I swung the door open, Ava tapped me on the shoulder and stepped in front of me. She peered inside the restroom as if she was making sure it was safe. She then nodded and stepped outside.

I threw Ava a smirk. "Won't be long."

"Fine." She dipped her chin again and didn't even flutter an eyelash as she turned and stood on guard.

I shut and locked the door behind me. *Fuck. Focus. On Min.*

Before I had the chance to gather my wits, Min pinned me against the side wall, undid my jeans, and fell to her knees. *Oh. God. Yes.* This was what I needed to let off some steam. Closing my eyes, I rested my head back against the tiles. Min took me in her mouth and worked her magic. *So. Fucking. Good.*

But Ava's voice drifted through the door. "Becks. I'm just down the corridor . . . I'm outside the handicap bathroom . . . Yep . . . The joys of the job . . . He better not be a noisy fucker . . . I don't want to hear it."

I winced as I concentrated on Min. I swirled my hair through her silky hair, thrust into her mouth. Min's hot, wet tongue licked, lapped and sucked me. *So hot.* I clenched my jaw, trying not to make a sound. For Ava's sake . . . *Fuck.* She was a few feet away on the other side of the door. Why was she messing with my mind?

Shit. Hissing my breath through my teeth, I pulsed my hips, driving my cock into Min's mouth time and time again. Heat coursed through my veins. My pulse quickened. Tension tightened my balls. "That's it, baby." She took me deeper and sucked harder as she massaged my nuts with one hand and pumped my dick with the other one. *Oh, shit yeah.*

I spilled into her throat, throbbing and quaking with my release. Stress dissipated from my body in slow delectable waves, but then it slammed back into place with a thump. *Fuck . . .* I didn't feel any better.

I thudded my head against the wall, twice.

I glanced at my watch. *1:24.*

Less than twelve hours until I got my kid. *Crap.*

I needed more vodka.

But first… I helped Min stand, spun her 'round and pinned her against the wall. "Baby, that was hot." I slipped my hand beneath her dress, stroked the front of her panties, ready to get her off and fuck her hard, but she stepped away from me.

"You're always fun." She wriggled her dress straight. "But we'd better go. The girls will be looking for me."

"But I want to make you come." I always reciprocated. *Always.*

"I'm okay. Next time." She stepped over to the basin, rinsed her mouth, then combed her fingers through her hair. I zipped up my jeans. She slinked toward me, grabbed my hand, and opened the door. "Let's go."

Ava stepped to the side, giving us a clear path. Her mouth twitched with a that-was-quick smirk, but it rapidly returned to a flat line.

Hand in hand, I led Min back to our seats. The minute we joined her friends, Min laughed, giggled, and hugged them. Who was I to complain if she was happy?

But then she glanced down to the main bar. She pursed her lips, then gave me a quick kiss on the cheek. "Thank you, but we have to go. Our dates have just arrived."

"Your dates?" The words punched me in the guts.

Cute wrinkles formed on the bridge of her nose. "Yeah. What goes on tour, stays on tour." She linked arms with Isla and twinkled her fingers at me. "Love you. I'll call you next time I'm in town. Bye."

Damn! She just blew me and was off to meet some other guy? I loved one-night stands. I had a cell phone full of girls I could call for casual hookups. I didn't care about sleeping with chicks who just wanted to live out their I've-slept-with-a-rock-star fantasy. I was happy to oblige. But I rarely was with more than one girl on any given night. Min was as bad … or as good … as me. I'd gotten a blowjob. I should've been stoked. Why wasn't I?

I sank onto the seat beside Slip and drank a mouthful of vodka straight from the bottle. He was busy texting somebody. Was it Maddy? Flint and Sutton sat nearby, talking to other partygoers. Lewis and Tia were mingling too. Me? . . . *Fuck.* I was alone.

That had never bothered me before. So why now?

I loved my life.

I wasn't ready to settle down.

Why did I feel like crap?

As I finished the bottle and hung out with my friends, the night disappeared.

Just after three a.m., I staggered out to our town cars with everyone in tow.

"You okay?" Flint swayed on his feet.

"Yeah, man," I slurred. "Fucking peachy."

He chuckled. "You want us to come with you tomorrow?"

A throbbing pain erupted in my temples. "No. Tia's coming."

"Okay." He draped his arm around Sutton's shoulders. "Call us if you need anything. Otherwise, we'll see you at rehearsal day after tomorrow."

"I'll be there."

Flint and Sutton jumped in their town car. Then I waved goodbye to Slip, Tia, and Lewis, who were heading back to Slip's house.

I sank into my town car. Just me. By myself. In the back. Ava and the driver sat up front. As we took off, I stared out the window. The streetlights turned into blurry, hazy, glowing, fuzzy balls. The road passed by in a monotonous endless loop. The void in my chest threatened to return. I wouldn't let it.

At my house, I clambered out of the car and stumbled toward my front door. I tripped up the step. But Ava caught my arm. She'd come out of nowhere. "Let's get you inside."

"I got it." But I slumped against her hold.

"Clearly." She punched in her access code and opened the door.

She half-carried me over to the sofa. I flopped onto the long seat, lay down and covered my eyes with my arm. "Thank you."

"You're welcome."

I peered at her from beneath my arm. She straightened, but before she turned, I reached out and caught her hand.

I lowered my voice, trying to inject some playfulness into my tone but failing. "Min was something, wasn't she?" *Ain't that the truth.*

Ava tugged her hand free. "Not my place to judge or have an opinion, Mr. Tanner."

"But don't you? How can you just watch us and not form an opinion?" Was I looking for a fight? Someone to argue with so I could vent about Min not staying with me tonight, my world that was about to change tomorrow, my future that would never be the same? *Fuck!* I'd bottled shit up for so long—now wasn't the time to crack. I was too drunk to be reasonable.

Ava grabbed a throw off the end of the sofa and unfolded it. "You pay me a lot of money not to."

"So you do have one—you're just not telling me?"

"Something like that."

"Do you hate us? Celebrities?"

"No." She draped the throw over me. "I know this life isn't easy."

"How?" Why was she taking care of me?

"I used to be in that world with my ex-husband. His life is similar but different to the one you're in."

"What world?"

"TV and film production."

"And you're divorced?" I sat upright. My head spun like a turntable set on 45 RPM.

"Yes. I have been for three years."

"Fuck, you must have been married young."

"We all make mistakes."

I slumped back against the seat. "Don't I know that."

Ava walked over to the fridge. My gaze fell to her ass. I could barely see straight, think straight, or sit straight, but damn, she rocked a business suit. She grabbed a bottle of water, returned to my side, and handed it to me. "Drink this. I'll be back here at midday to pick you up."

"What for?" I took the bottle.

"You're meeting your daughter at one."

"Fuck." My heart lurched. I clutched the bottle against my chest, hoping it would stop my ribs from constricting. It didn't.

I closed my eyes. For a few hours I'd forgotten about tomorrow.

Now the day blazed before me.

"Good night, Mr. Tanner." Ava headed for the door and disappeared outside.

The door clicked shut.

My huge empty house loomed around me. The massive atrium sat deathly still and silent. I closed my eyes. In my world of music, and loud concerts, and problems, I didn't like the absence of sound. With Tia spending more time with Lewis at Slip's place, I had my home to myself . . . for just a few more hours.

I should've savored this moment. The quiet. But I didn't.

The back of my eyes stung. I sucked in a shaky deep breath.

Tomorrow I'd meet my daughter.

I'd be a dad.

Was I prepared?

Nope. Not at fucking all.

Chapter 5

COLE

Late the following morning, my dull headache reminded me of the copious amounts of vodka I'd drunk the night before. Showering didn't make me feel any better. Nor did the Advil I'd swallowed. On the drive to meet my daughter, I fidgeted with the satin bow on the fluffy cream teddy bear I'd bought and twisted it around my fingers. My heartbeat slammed against my ribs. Life was about to change . . . forever.

Tia placed her hand on my knee and gave it a rub. "Aren't you a little bit excited to meet Charlotte?"

"Do I look excited?" My palms sweated as I tightened the bow tails around my thumb, cutting off blood circulation.

"Cole, I know this is scary." She softened her tone. "But you're doing the right thing. Not just because you have to, but because you have a huge heart. You're one of the most caring people I know. You've been there for everyone who's struggled through some tough times over the last few years, including me. Now you need to be there for your daughter. Charlotte needs you to take care of her."

The ache in my head turned into a thudding drum. "I don't know how to do that."

"You will. Just be you." She rested her head against the seat. "Life can change in the blink of an eye. We know that. After we lost Phil and I had my accident, it took me a long time to find my way forward. But I did. I came home, found a new career, and fell for Lewis. Charlotte is your new path. Her future depends on you. This isn't going to be easy. But please give her a chance."

"I'm here, aren't I?"

I didn't miss the subtle shake of Ava's head. She sat in the front passenger seat like a steel statue, but she'd heard every word. What was her fucking problem?

"Yes, you are." Tia clutched my hand. "Charlotte's your flesh and blood. She might be the best thing that has ever happened to you. But promise me one thing—maybe two." She lowered her chin and closed her eyes. An anguish I knew all too well settled in her soft tone. "Don't be like our parents who were never around when we were growing up. Don't risk losing her because you didn't make an effort."

Both things scared me. I never wanted to be like my parents. They'd put their careers before us. They'd given us everything money could buy but rarely their time. We'd been forced into extracurricular activities at school, handed off to nannies, or left in the care of neighbors while they jetted their way around the world climbing corporate ladders. With my band about to tour, was I destined to be the same? *Yep.* That crushed my soul. Charlotte deserved better than that.

But what hit me harder, though, was I never wanted to risk losing someone I loved again. What if I liked the kid, connected with her, then the court ripped her away? I honestly don't think I'd survive that. I'd lost too many people I cared about already. I had to keep my guard up. Remain emotionally detached. Was that even possible? *God,* I hoped so.

The car pulled into the parking lot outside the children's services building. The two-story white complex looked more like a medical center than a corporate office.

Ava jumped out of the front seat and opened the SUV's door for me. As I stepped out of the car, concern flashed in her eyes, but she straightened, and it quickly disappeared. "Good luck, Mr. Tanner."

No amount of Xanax would lower my blood pressure, but I nodded. "Um. Thanks."

Tia shuffled along on her crutches as Ava led us over to the glass front doors. I didn't think security was necessary on this occasion, but Blake had insisted.

We headed up to the second floor and were shown into a private meeting room. Standing by the large window, I closed my eyes and sucked in a deep, shaky breath. A fierce dizziness swam through my head. My heart raced too fast. Nausea bubbled in my gut. I glanced at my watch.

Shit.

Time was up.

The door opened and my heart stopped.

Hannah stepped inside. "Hi Cole."

I quickly scanned behind her, but there was no sign of the kid, only Paul.

Hannah gave me a heartwarming hug. The worry in her eyes did nothing to alleviate my nerves. "How are you doing?"

"I've been better." I clutched the teddy bear around its neck to stop my hands from shaking.

Paul zoomed into the room on his wheelchair and shook my hand. "You made it."

"Yep. I'm on time, too." I was usually the last one to turn up to places I had to be at with my band. Time management wasn't my forte. But Ava had dragged my ass here, almost literally. I tilted my head toward my sister. "Do you remember Tia?"

"Yes. I sure do." Paul's eyebrows shot skyward as he shook her hand. "You were always running around with the guys. I've seen you on that TV show, *Through the Smoke*. I've watched nearly every episode."

"That's very cool, Mr. Lane." Tia straightened on her crutches. "I'm glad you like the show. The seasons I'm in are still running, but I've left acting behind me. I broke half my leg on set. This is a second attempt at fixing my ankle." She wriggled her foot, showing off her black moonboot.

"I'm sorry you got hurt, dear." Hannah gave her a kiss hello on the cheek. "But it's lovely to see you. What are you doing now?"

"I'm working for the band on their sound and lighting team."

"Oh." Hannah splayed her hands across her chest. "I love that. Family sticking together."

Tia flicked the back of her hand against my arm. "Well, Cole and I do. Mom and Dad are still floating around the world somewhere."

"Lucky them." Paul's lips quirked into a lopsided grin as he pointed to his wheelchair. "I won't be going anywhere in this thing."

"You're fine, honey." Hannah kissed Paul on the head. "We'll do that road trip to the Grand Canyon soon. I promise."

I tried to summon a warm smile but failed. They still seemed so in love. That was cool. But it was a path I never wanted to venture down again. It was rare to find a love that lasted. Most of the time it just fucked you up. I wanted to avoid it like another pandemic.

I half turned and thumbed toward Ava, standing by the far wall. "This is my new addition. Ava is my bodyguard. She, or one of her team, will be with me nearly twenty-four/seven. I won't be able to jerk off without someone watching me."

She glared at me. The corner of her lips twitched. "Trust me. I will not be watching you do that."

I let out a low chuckle. I liked her quick comebacks. But something about her was still off. I couldn't put my finger on it. Maybe it was just me. I wanted to mess up her perfectly slicked-back blonde bun, see a crease in her impeccably ironed shirt, and put a scuff on her shiny polished black shoes. No one needed to look that prim and proper at this hour of the day. Oh wait . . . it was after noon.

"Be nice." Tia play-punched my arm. "You need her."

"Fine." I stuffed my hands into the pocket of my hoodie. But I liked a good challenge. Getting Ava to show some form of emotion might be it.

Hannah fidgeted with her beaded necklace, twisting it around her shaky fingers. "Cole, are you sure about this? I don't want you to meet Charlotte if you really don't want anything to do with her. Charlotte has had enough disruption, heartache, and trauma after losing Shelby and Keith. We don't want her to go through the process of getting to know you, bond with you, only to have that ripped away."

"Me either." I dug my fingernails into my palm. "I promise you—I'll do my best to ensure that doesn't happen." I would. I just didn't know how to do that or where to start.

"Remember she's a child." Hannah tone turned motherly and wise. "She will sense your feelings. So just be honest and genuine."

Fuck. I was in trouble. This might be a lost cause already. "Fine."

"Alright then, Cole." Paul turned his wheelchair to face the door. "Are you ready to meet your daughter? She's in one of the other offices with the social worker. Shall we?"

My breath shuddered through my chest as I forced myself to nod.

Tia gave me a reassuring smile. "I'll go grab a coffee then wait in the reception area. I'm here if you need me."

"Thanks."

Hannah and Paul led me down the hall to a meeting room with a glass wall. I couldn't see anyone inside as Hannah knocked on the door.

My heart clambered to my throat. My pulse thudded in my temples. *Crap.*

Is it hot in here?

From behind the oval oak table, a curvy Black woman, dressed in navy dress pants and a white blouse, rose to her feet. She came over and opened the door.

"You showed up. That's a good start." She lifted her chin and scanned me up and down. She thrust out her hand. "I'm Arilla McCarthy. I'm the social worker assigned to your case and will be assessing you over the coming months."

"Hey." I shook her hand. *God.* My palm was sweaty, but there was nothing I could do about it. "Cole Tanner. Nice to meet you."

"Do you have any questions about the oncoming process, Mr.

Tanner?"

My lawyer had bombarded me with emails and information overload during the past few days, but I understood what had to be done. "No." I grimaced. "I've got it. Take care of the kid. Check in with you via Zoom before I go on the tour. Show up to the final review hearing in a few months. Any other issues, call you."

"Good." She nodded as if impressed. "You aren't the first person to find out that you've fathered a child. I'm sorry about the unfortunate circumstances. But I'm glad you are taking responsibility and want to be part of your child's life. How long for and at what capacity is now up to you. Don't give Hannah or me a reason to submit anything other than a glowing report at your final custody hearing, Mr. Tanner. The court will ultimately decide what is best for your daughter's future. Her care and well-being are our priority."

That may or may not be with me. My eyebrows pinched together. "Mine too." I squeezed the teddy bear's neck, hoping and praying my head would stop spinning, but it didn't work.

"While we have no reason to be concerned, for your first meeting and to ensure the child's safety, I'll be watching you through this glass window." Arilla flicked a finger toward the glass wall.

"That's fine. I'm used to being watched." I sneered at Ava, lingering in the hall beside me. She mimicked the gesture.

"Well then, Mr. Tanner." Arilla stepped to the side. "It's time to meet your daughter."

"Thanks." But I couldn't move. Couldn't breathe. This was it. *Shit.*

Arilla's tone softened with a subtle hint of compassion. "Just remember she's more terrified than you are."

I doubted that.

"We'll leave you to it." Arilla weaved around me to head out of the office. "Just remember, we're watching."

"Okay." My head jerked with an awkward nod as I took a couple of hesitant steps into the room. Arilla shut the door behind me. *Crap!*

My heart thundered like a herd of elephants were charging across my ribs. My head throbbed and ached. I glanced toward the glass wall. Arilla, Hannah, Paul, and Ava stood in a line like they were the firing squad, waiting for me to make one false move.

Fuck. I swiped my hand down my clean-shaven face.

Movement behind the desk caught my attention.

From behind the chairs, out she crawled. She plonked onto her bottom and stared up at me.

I lost the ability to breathe.

Two big green eyes, identical to mine, locked onto me as if assessing if I were a friend or foe. The shape of her tiny pink lips and chin were the same as mine. But her flawless fair skin and blonde hair that fell in soft waves to her shoulders were just like her mom's. I covered my mouth. Tears welled in my eyes. Oh my God . . . she was my daughter.

I blinked the tears from my eyes and took a slow step toward her. "Hi, Char-Charlotte." My voice snagged in my throat. "I'm Cole."

She grabbed her toy pink pony off the playmat beside her and combed its hair.

Shit! Now what? I had no idea how to talk to a kid.

I took another few steps toward her and squatted. "What's your pony's name? She's very pretty."

She didn't look up. "*His* name is Sullivan."

I pursed my lips, unable to contain my grin. *Cool.* We had a queer horse. I was down with that. "He's got a very pretty mane. Do you mind if I sit and play with you for a while?"

She shrugged. I took that as not a no. I sat on the floor and crossed my legs. "I have a present for you. Do you like teddy bears?"

She nodded.

I held out the bear I'd bought. "This one is for you."

She eyed the bear but didn't take it. She was far from settled. Neither was I.

"Don't you like him?" What was wrong with it? "I can get you a different one if you like."

She resumed brushing her horse's tail. "Are you looking after me now?"

The lump in my throat grew to the size of a football. I cuddled the bear against my gut. Maybe I was the one who needed the toy for comfort and security, not her. "Yeah, I am."

"I want *my* daddy." Her lower lip quivered. "But Mommy and Daddy are in Heaven."

The sadness in her trembling voice tore my heart in two. "Yeah. I have some friends in Heaven too. I miss them every day. Do you miss your mom?"

She nodded. Tears pooled in her eyes.

"Your mom was very cool. She was so beautiful. And kind." I couldn't say a bad word about Shelby . . . except for the fact that she'd never told me I had a kid.

"Ma said you play moo-sic."

I winced. "Is Ma Grandma Hannah?"

Her little head bobbed.

"Cool." Now I knew who we were talking about. "Yes. I play drums. A big set. Maybe we could play sometime."

"Ma doesn't like loud noise."

I chuckled softly. "Well, I do. Noise is my thing. We can play loud music. And sing. And dance. I could teach you to play the drums or the guitar or the piano. Would you like that?" I couldn't play the piano or the guitar to save myself, but luckily my friends could.

Charlotte sucked on her bottom lip and glanced toward Hannah. Then she shook her head. "Ma won't let me."

A sly smile curled across my lips. "I'll work on Ma. Okay?"

"'Kay." A flash of excitement flickered in her eyes.

I picked up the small plush white unicorn off the floor. "This guy's cool. What's his name?"

"Martin."

I pursed my lips again, trying not to laugh. I loved the names of her toys. "Do you think Martin would like a friend?" I held out my bear again. "I have this teddy who needs a buddy. Do you think they could play together?"

"What's his name?"

"I don't know." I looked at the cream fluffy bear. "What would you like to call him?"

"Barney."

"Barney it is."

"Thank you." She took Barney and placed him on the floor beside her. "Can we play ponies?" She picked up a comb and handed it to me along with Martin. "Brush his tail, please. Can you braid it?"

Fuck. I didn't know how to plait. "Can you teach me how to do that?"

She shook her curls. "Ma always does it."

"My sister might be able to teach me. She's got long hair."

We sat on the floor for ten minutes, playing with her pile of toys. The ponies lived in a magical forest and had to run away from the big bad bear . . . Barney. For a three-year-old, she had a wicked imagination. Whatever ideas I suggested for the story were wrong. She immediately went off into a different tangent that made my mind spin. I couldn't keep up. Maybe I shouldn't have drunk so much last night.

Then she tossed her pony aside, grabbed her pink backpack and slide out a book. "Will you read me a story?"

"Sure." I held out my hand to take it.

"No." She clutched the book to her chest, scooted over to me, and crawled into my lap. I held my arms out wide as she wriggled against my chest. *What the fuck?* I hadn't expected this. That she'd trust me so soon. She had no reason not to. But still . . . my mind was completely blown. She picked up Barney, tucked him underneath her arm, and opened the book. "I turn the pages. You read."

My heart melted a tiny fraction.

I glanced toward my onlookers. Hannah had tears in her eyes; her hands were fanned over her heart. Paul gave me the thumbs-up. Arilla glared at me like I was under police interrogation . . . which I kinda was.

But Ava . . . nodded. Her shoulder-width stance was still rigid as a rock and her hands were clasped in front of her body, no doubt posed, ready to strangle me or anyone who got in her way, but . . . *whoa!* Were those tears welling in her eyes? Surely not.

I was just trying to be nice and not scare the fuck out of my kid. I sucked in a deep breath and let it out slowly. This was pretty cool. The back of my eyes prickled again. I smoothed my hand over Charlotte's soft silky curls that smelled of bubblegum. Her tiny body was light as a feather. Every time she looked at me, her big green eyes weakened my knees. Thank God, I was sitting down. *Yeah . . . she's my kid.* I took a deep breath and read the first page of *Alice in Wonderland.*

But Charlotte groaned, tossed her head back, and smacked it against my shoulder. "No. That's wrong. You've got to do funny voices. Just like Ma does."

"Oh. Sorry." I chuckled. "This is a first for me, kid. Shall we start again?"

"Yes. Alice has a *pretty* voice. But Rabbit talks really fast, like I'mlateI'mlateI'mlate."

Oh boy! What was I in for? For someone so little, she had one of the biggest personalities I'd ever seen. I cleared my throat. "Got it."

By the time we got to the Mad Hatter's tea party, Charlotte's body had slumped against my chest. Guessed she was getting tired. I certainly was. "Hey?" I closed the book. "Let's finish this later. Why don't we go have something to eat. Do you like ice cream?"

"Uh-huh."

"Well, how about we head home?" Since Arilla hadn't stormed into the room, I assumed I'd passed the initial test. The next step in transitioning Charlotte into my care was to spend the afternoon together with Hannah present to make sure Charlotte didn't freak out. *Or me.* I'd had Mackenzie buy a stack of toddler-appropriate food. I had no idea what to feed a three-year-old. "I have vanilla and chocolate. Are they okay?"

"Rainbow is my favorite."

Why did that not surprise me? "We can mix the two together for now. But I will make sure I get some rainbow ice cream next time I shop."

"Okay."

We packed her toys into her bag, then I slung it over my

shoulder. Taking Charlotte's hand, we headed for the door.

Hannah wiped a tear from her cheek. "Oh Cole, that was wonderful."

I was still shaking all over. Charlotte hadn't cried or screamed or cringed in the corner screaming bloody murder, so that was a bonus. But I'd wanted to do those things.

I knelt beside Charlotte and pointed to my sister, who'd returned. "Charlotte, this is Auntie Tia. She's gonna be like a big sister."

Tia bent down. "Hi Charlotte. Nice to meet you."

Charlotte tucked in beside my arm and clutched Barney tight under her elbow as if she were shy and unsure of Tia.

"Geez, Tee." I packed on the sarcasm. "Maybe I'm better with kids than you are."

"Fuck you." She sneered at me, then smiled sweetly at Charlotte. "We'll become best of friends. I guarantee it."

"Hey!" I shook a finger at Tia. "No swearing around my daughter." But then I winked at her. I was sure my kid would be the first one in her class at kindergarten who taught others to swear. *God.* This parenting thing was already daunting. Then I swiveled on my knee toward Ava. "And Charlotte, this is Ava. She's my bodyguard. She's like a cop who has to make sure everyone around us is being good."

Charlotte whispered in my ear, "She's pretty but looks mean."

I brushed my fingertip down the length of Charlotte's cute little nose. "Yeah, so we better not upset her."

Ava raised a questioning eyebrow, no doubt wondering what Charlotte had said. But then she stepped forward, bent down on one knee, and held out her hand. She smiled a soft, stunning, warm smile, and her eyes sparkled. *Fuck! Where did that come from?*

"Hi Charlotte. I'm honored to meet you. Are you going to help me look after this guy? He's so tall, we have to make sure he doesn't hit his head on doorways"—her eyes sparkled as she scrunched her nose and patted her head—"or trip over his big feet." She pointed at my Nikes.

Charlotte giggled as she clutched the front of her dress and twisted from side to side. "Yeah. He's like a giraffe with big shoes."

"Watch it, kid." I ruffled the top of Charlotte's head, then stood, as did Ava. I threw Ava a saucy grin. "You know what big feet mean."

"I don't ever want to find out what's in your pants."

"That wasn't an invitation."

But Ava's gaze dropped to my crotch, then she raked it upward over my chest and met my eyes. The outer edge of her eyebrow arched upward. "Good."

Heat rippled across my skin. My pulse jumped a notch. What was wrong with me? *Fool.*

"Ahem." Arilla drew her shoulders back. "Excellent work, Cole. You seem to have a connection with Charlotte already. From here on in, it's up to you and Hannah to follow the plan and get support in place for your tour. Enjoy your first afternoon together, and I pray you'll have many more. Call me if you have any concerns. Otherwise, I'll talk to you and Hannah in a month."

"Thank you." I shook Arilla's hand. "Catch up with you soon."

Charlotte's arm curled around my leg and she tugged on my jeans. "Ice cream."

I cradled and rubbed the back of her head. "Okay." I turned to Hannah and Paul. "You cool to head off?"

"Yes. Charlotte will need a nap." Hannah smoothed her hands over the front of her cardigan. "She'll probably fall asleep in the car on the way home."

"A nap?"

"Yes. I'll run through her routine with you later."

"Routine?" I couldn't do routine. I had no regularity in my days.

"Yes. Meals. Naps. Playtime. Bath. Bedtime. Children need routine."

I laughed and shook my head. "Oh, Hannah. Whatever routine you had, that's all about to change. But we'll find a way to make it work."

I had to. Charlotte had to fit into my life, not the other way around. I wasn't going to change my ways for her.

I glanced down at Charlotte. "You ready to see your new

home?"

She held up her tiny arms. Holding Barney by the leg, she flapped her little fingers on her other hand at me. "Up."

Confusion rippled through my head. *What?*

"She wants you to carry her," Paul said.

"Oh. Right." *I'm such an idiot.*

I picked up Charlotte and cradled her on my hip. *So weird.* I'd never held a kid before. None of my friends had children, and nor did my relatives. I was the first.

Charlotte rested her head against my shoulder and sucked on her thumb. Barney dangled from her tiny fist.

Something warm and strange swelled inside my chest. I hated to admit it, but my daughter was fucking cute.

Tia fluttered her eyelashes at me, pouted and teased. "Oh, Daddy. You're so sweet."

I glared at her and mouthed, *"Fuck off."*

I had no idea what I was doing or how to be a dad.

I was used to winging my way through life.

I prayed that would work with a kid.

But right then . . . it was time to take my daughter home.

How fucking surreal was that?

Chapter 6

AVA

Friday morning, at five-thirty a.m., I headed to Cole's house, which was just under thirty minutes from my dad's house in Los Feliz. Joining Cole on his occasional morning runs was one thing I wouldn't mind doing. I loved exercising just as the sun was coming up. The fresh air helped clear my head and me to face the day. Running five miles was nothing, I normally ran ten.

The band had a big day ahead, attending a photoshoot, then rehearsal. It'd be a long shift, but I was set.

I had warmed to Cole a fraction. As private security, we were supposed to avoid any form of emotional attachment with our clients. Say nothing. Keep our opinions and thoughts to ourselves. Stay diligent. Be on constant lookout for any sign of a threat. We were there to keep them safe—that was it. But watching him meet his daughter two days ago had woven a thread of warmth into my heart. I wished Luther had been that attentive with our son. Cole, taking his time with Charlotte, making sure she wasn't scared, had been a surprise. The guy wasn't pure asshole.

Ahead of schedule, I drove up the bendy road toward his home, high in Laurel Canyon. As I hit his street, I gaped. I tightened my grip on the steering wheel. Half a dozen paparazzi stood on the sidewalk with long telescopic lenses posed toward his house. *What the fuck?* It was too early for this crap.

I inched past them, continued around the bend and parked my Range Rover just past the house. A flash of headlights in my rearview mirror caught my eye. A white Camry pulled up on the curbside fifty yards behind me. Was that another photographer? Just one of the neighbors? No one got out of the car. I sat, waiting. Two minutes later, a young woman in a gray hoodie and jeans hopped out of the vehicle and disappeared up the steps into a nearby home. *Good.* No issue there. Time to go.

In stealth mode, I entered my access code into Cole's side gate and slipped into the garden unnoticed.

Once I reached the glass back door, I dropped my bag at my feet and draped my uniform over the nearby outdoor sofa.

I peered through the huge glass windows. The TV was on, showing some cartoons, but I couldn't see anyone. I knocked on the sliding glass door. *Nothing.* I tried the handle. *Locked.* But then movement caught my eye. Charlotte sat on the floor in the living room playing in front of the TV, sucking on a colored marker. Her mouth was covered in ink that trickled from her lips in dark purple streams down onto her pink pajamas. My heart skipped ten beats. She raised her other hand holding a yellow felt-tipped pen toward her mouth.

I slapped the glass. "Charlotte. No."

Cole's daughter stopped and looked at me but then sucked on the marker.

"NO!" *Oh my God!* "Put the marker down. Put it down."

She didn't.

Shit. I rushed to the front door, entered my code, and ran into the living room. "Charlotte, sweetie." I tried to keep the panic out of my voice as I knelt and gently eased the markers from her fingers. "These are for coloring. Not eating. Yucky." *Damn.* Had she tried every shade in the twelve-pack? Luckily they were safe watercolors, but still. *What the hell?* Just as I packed the markers away, Charlotte shrieked. Her cry echoed throughout the huge room, and she burst into tears.

"Hey." I rubbed her arm. "It's okay. We can color soon. Are you hungry? How about we clean up and get something to eat?"

Charlotte screamed even more. Tears rolled down her cheeks. Snot ran from her nose.

Shit.

Taking her in my arms, I gave her a cuddle and headed to the kitchen to find a cloth or something to clean her face with. "Shh. Shh. Shh. It's okay."

I grabbed a handful of tissues out of the box on top of the microwave and wiped her cheeks and mouth. Gently. Softly. Just like I did when Josh was upset. "Where's Cole or Ma?"

Her little lips trembled as she flopped forward, cried, and tried to wriggle out of my arms.

"Cole?" I called out. *No answer.* I yelled louder. "Cole?" *Where the hell is he?*

Seconds later, Hannah came rushing out of the guest room and down the hallway. "Oh, my. What's happened?" She tied her robe and dashed forward to take Charlotte.

"She was here on the floor, eating the markers. Where's Cole?"

"I don't know." Hannah cuddled and kissed Charlotte's ink-stained cheek. "I heard him up with Charlotte earlier. I took the opportunity to stay in bed for a little longer but must have dozed off. I woke up when she cried, and you called out."

"She's okay." I rubbed and patted Charlotte's back. "Just not happy I took her coloring markers away."

"I've got her." Hannah nodded gratefully. "Thank you. You go find Cole."

I rushed upstairs and knocked on his bedroom door. There was no answer. I eased the door open. The huge king-sized bed, covered in a tangle of black bed coverings, was vacant. So were the bathroom and closet.

I zoomed around upstairs and checked every room. There was no sign of him. Returning downstairs, I checked the rest of the house. Games room, home theatre, music room . . . then, the gym.

Found him. By the window, with earbuds in, he sat on the rowing machine, pulling on the cable and sliding back and forth on the seat at pace.

I clenched my teeth and my fists and took a step toward him, but then froze at the distant darkness clouding his eyes. The anguish slammed into my chest. I'd never seen someone look so . . . lost. So sad.

Well, I was about to give him something else to worry about.

I stormed over to him. "Cole?" No response. *Ergh! Damn earbuds.* I waved in front of his face, then clipped him on the head. "What the fuck?"

He ripped out his headphones and clutched his chest. "Jesus Christ!" He raked in heavy breaths. "You scared the shit out of me."

"What are you doing?" I flicked my hand at him. "You left your daughter alone in the living room. What were you thinking?"

He groaned and rose to his feet. After swiping his workout towel off the floor, he wiped his damp hair, brow, neck, and arms. Jolted from my concerns for his daughter, I sucked in a sharp breath. I scanned the sweaty red shirt that clung to his chest and outlined his corrugated abs, toned arm muscles that were carved with perfect definition, and sculpted legs that were long and tanned. If I wasn't so mad, I'd take more time to appreciate the view. There was no denying he was the best-looking client I'd ever had.

He jammed his hands on hips. "She's not alone. I'm here. So is Hannah."

"Hannah was asleep. Charlotte's three. She can't be left unattended."

"She has toys. She was coloring. She's fine."

I took a step toward him, lifting my chin. "Are you fucking stupid? I found her eating markers. She was covered in ink."

"Shit." He hooked his towel around his neck and took a step toward the door. "Is she okay?"

"Yes." I caught his arm, stopping him in his tracks. "She is now. Hannah's with her. But in the future, you can't leave a three-year-old alone. Not ever."

"What would you know?" He pulled free of my hold, snatched his water bottle off the weights bench, and downed a few mouthfuls.

I drew my shoulders back. He didn't need to know anything

about me, but I was a mother. My anxious regard was for his daughter. "I have a child."

He blinked and jerked his chin back. "You do?"

"Yes." An ache shuddered through my heart. I missed Josh so fucking much. "A boy. He's six."

Cole slumped and rubbed the back of his neck. "Sorry, I didn't know. I'm new at this parenting thing and have no idea what I'm doing."

"Well, learn quick." I folded my arms. "You're lucky it was only coloring markers. What if she'd swallowed something, or choked, or had done God only knows what? She could've gotten hurt."

He winced. "Fine. I'll make sure Hannah is with her next time."

"Good." I nodded. "Someone has to be with her always. She's young. I know this is a shock to your system, but you have to be more careful. Charlotte comes first. Hannah has to report to your social worker too, remember? You don't want to lose your daughter over silly mistakes."

I'd paid the price for mine; I'd hate for Cole to do the same. I'd do anything to clear my wrongdoings and get more time with my son.

"Well thank fuck I have you to help when needed."

I narrowed my eyes into sharp slits and shook my head. "No. I'm security, not a nanny."

"You're more like a drill sergeant," Cole mumbled. "You'd have my kid doing military exercises before breakfast."

I arched one eyebrow and injected some sass into my tone. "No. Just you. Now get your ass into gear. We have a big day ahead."

He puffed air through his nose and headed for the door. "Let me check on the kid and Hannah, then we'll go for a run."

"Deal."

"Are you sure you'll be able to keep up?" A glint shimmered through his eyes as he held the door open for me.

Hmph. He could be a gentleman . . . *nice.* "I'm positive."

A handsome smile curled across his lips, too devilish for his own good. "We'll see about that. You know I run, work out, and drum for about six hours every day."

He didn't know I ran half-marathons for fun and liked cross-fit training. "I like endurance." I sailed past him and glanced back over my shoulder. "Show me what you've got, drummer boy."

"Oh . . . it's on."

The challenge was set.

After checking on Charlotte, we headed out the front pedestrian gate into the fray of paparazzi. Cameras flashed, blinding my eyes in the soft morning light. *Great.* Duty had started. I stepped in front of Cole, blocking him from the small crowd. But he just smiled and waved at them.

"Morning all." Cole stood on the curbside, stretching his quads, undeterred by the photographers. "So you get your facts straight for your news headlines, this is Ava. My bodyguard. Not my latest hookup."

Didn't the company logo on my black T-shirt and leggings make it obvious who I was? *Probably not.*

"Why do you need security, Cole?" a man with a black baseball cap asked. "Has something happened? Has there been an incident? A threat?"

"Yeah. You pricks are hanging 'round my home too much." A playful grin slid across his mouth. He walked off, waving over his shoulder. "See you soon."

We headed down the road, side by side. I met his quick stride, step for step. "You talk to the paparazzi?" Most clients I'd worked with couldn't stand them.

"Yeah. Be nice to them, they usually reciprocate. They don't get crazy or disrespectful. They're just doing their job."

Hmph. This guy continually did my head in. He was nice one minute, horrid the next. Arrogant but caring. Fun-loving but troubled. *Damn.* He was more messed up than I was.

He took off at a steady pace, jogging toward Fryman Canyon Park. As we veered left up the incline, he sped off at a sprint. Was this a test? How far should I let him get ahead before I chased him down? *Nah!* I'd let him have his fun, thinking he'd gotten the better of me.

At the top of the ridge, he waited, pacing back and forth across the dirt track, sucking in deep breaths with every step. "What happened to keeping up?"

"I can go all day, Cole. You, in that state? I doubt it." I continued along the trail at a constant stride. "Come on. Move it."

"Too easy." He fell in beside me.

We fell into sync. I let him set the speed. He ran a bit slower than I normally did. He didn't have to go light on me. For five minutes, just the sounds of our breathing, the gravel and dirt crunching beneath our running shoes, and the random squawk of a bird flying overhead filled the air.

As the path disappeared behind us, Cole turned and ran backward. "So, do you come here often?"

I threw him a *that's pathetic* glare.

"Come on, Ava. This is new to me." He turned and ran forward. "I usually run by myself. I'm not exercising with you if we can't talk. I'm not a diva."

"Jury's still out on that one."

"Fair call. We didn't get off to the best start. I'm sorry about that. I've had a fucked up couple weeks." He skipped over a tree root protruding from the uneven track, not missing a beat in his stride. "Finding out I had a kid hasn't been easy. The preparations for the tour are a whole new level of crazy. The hype we're causing is fucking incredible. We've never needed full-time security before. This is a first for us."

"That's great, but remember why I'm here." I pumped my arms in time with my gait. "I'm on duty to make sure someone doesn't mug you, stab you, beat you up, or harm you in anyway."

"I get that. But do you think you could lighten up a little?"

"I'm doing my job, Mr. Tanner."

"Come on, Ava. I'm trying to be nice."

"Fine," I moaned, keeping in time with his long steps. "Have I been here before? Yes. I've run this track a few times over the years."

"Do you live nearby?"

"Los Feliz, near Rowena Reservoir."

"Is the reservoir where you normally exercise or are you a

gym junkie, treadmiller?"

"Both, but I mainly run in Griffith Park."

"I love running through the hills. It's the only time I get to myself these days. The fresh air and listening to music help me deal with all the shit that's going on."

As I stole a glance at him, a flash of darkness shimmered across his eyes, but it was gone within a couple of strides.

"You okay?" I wasn't totally unempathetic.

"Yep. Always." He smiled thinly and waved me forward to head up a narrow section of trail through the trees ahead of him. He may have been a performer, but he was a horrid liar. Or maybe I just saw through his bullshit. I'd learned to do that thanks to my ex.

As I jogged in front, I felt him checking out my ass. He could look all he liked, but there was no way he was getting a piece of it.

He rejoined my side when the track widened. "Thanks for helping with Charlotte this morning. I'm still getting my head around having a kid, how to handle it, and what the fuck to do."

"Understandable." But to avoid going down an emotional path, I threw him some smack. "Are you sure you've only fathered one child? Going by your reputation, you might have more kids land on your doorstep."

"Fuck! Don't freak me out. One is more than enough."

"Sorry. I shouldn't tease."

"I don't mind that—just not the reality."

"There's only one way to stop the possibility of having more babies."

"Yeah, well, I'm not about to give up fucking women."

"So I've noticed."

He chuckled. "I don't know how you do your job."

"I'm all for you having fun and can turn a blind eye when necessary. But I've also seen a lot of bad shit in my time. Keeping you and your friends safe, in all situations, is all I care about."

"Have you always been in security?"

"No." I kept my eyes focused on the path ahead, but my tone dropped. "I used to be a cop."

"You did?" His toe stubbed a stone. He stumbled a step but kept running. "What happened?" He winced. "Wait, I'm sorry. You don't have to tell me."

"It's okay." I was in a much better place. Most of the time. What didn't kill you made you stronger, right? "Ever since I was a kid, I wanted to be a cop like my mom and dad. But when mom got sick with cancer and died, I didn't handle it well. I went through a rough patch and had a few ugly incidents at work that led me to leaving the force." I didn't need to go into all the heartbreaking and horrific details. "But I still wanted to look after people. I found Sam's Security and have never looked back. The team I work with is amazing. They have my back more than the force ever did. We've only been together for two years, but they've become my family."

"I'm the same with my band. We've been best friends for sixteen years."

"That's awesome you've become successful together."

"It hasn't always been easy."

"Life isn't. Trust me. I know."

"But this run is. *My* jury is still out on whether you can keep up with me or not." Just as we entered a clearing of dry grass, he shoved me on the shoulder. "See you back home, slow coach."

I stumbled sideways but didn't fall.

He took off at a sprint.

Ergh! Men! They had to learn the hard way.

Fire licked through my veins. Like a gridiron player, I charged after him and tackled him into the short grass beside the dirt path. As he landed on his back, shock flared in his eyes. I dropped my knee into his shoulder and pinned him in place. "Are we going to have this argument again, Mr. Tanner? Do you think I can't protect you or keep up?"

"Fuck," he hissed, raking in deep breaths. "Are you trying to kill me?"

I tilted my head to the side. "I can if you want me to." I had a concealed knife tucked in my sock.

"Get off." He pushed me to the left as he rolled to the right.

Before he could stand, I lunged for him again, pushing him

forward onto his stomach. I drove my knee into the back of his ribs, grabbed his arm, and bent it behind him. Clutching a handful of his hair, I pinned his face against the ground. He wasn't going anywhere. "I can do this all day, Cole. Do not run away from me. It is for your safety, remember?"

"I'm the one in danger here." He wiggled but didn't break free. "Alright. Alright." He slumped and slapped his hand on the ground. "I surrender. This is not the type of rolling around in the grass I like to do with a woman."

"Then be nice." I play-pushed his face into the grass again, then let go of his hair and stood. "Now get your ass off the ground. It's time to head back to the house." I held out my hand to help him up.

He clambered to his feet and dusted himself off. With a huge grin on his face, he puffed and panted. "I've never met a woman like you."

"What?" I brushed the dirt from my leggings. "Someone who won't fall for that charming smile of yours?"

He straightened. "You think it's charming?"

"You have a nice smile. Don't push it."

"Shit . . . a compliment. That's a first." He took off at a jog.

I followed. "Maybe you should run alone so I don't have to put up with your shit or your talking. I thought you were supposed to be the quiet one."

"Maybe the others are just louder than me."

"Good point. Now . . . can we just run?"

With a nod, he took off down the hill. But he didn't race. *Win.* We slipped into his yard via the side gate and warmed down, stretching by the pool.

After entering the house via the laundry room door, we ambled down the hallway. He nudged me in the arm with his elbow. "Glad you kept up."

"Next time we'll run at my pace." I wiped the sweat off my brow with the back of my hand. "Um . . . any chance of grabbing a towel? The other day, April said it would be okay for me to use your guesthouse to shower and change in. I've left my gear outside to do so." Getting ready here rather than heading home or to the office to do so would save me a ton of driving time, and I was a stickler for never being late.

He stepped in front and spun to face me. Crashing into his chest, I jerked to a halt. Inhaling his musty, sweaty scent combined with the wave of heat radiating off his body fuddled with my head. A mischievous smile curled across his lips. "You want me to join you to wash your back?"

I swallowed hard.

Him. In the shower. Licking the sweat from his body. Fucking against the tiles . . . Oh no. Don't go there.

"No, thanks. I can manage." My voice may have remained level and calm, but my knees wobbled. That smile of his *was* dangerous. "You need to check on Charlotte, then get ready so we can make your photoshoot on time. I don't like being late. I'll call our driver to make sure he's running on schedule."

"Fine. You can use the bathroom by the games room rather than the guesthouse—that's full of crap. There are plenty of towels in the linen cupboard."

"Thank you."

But he didn't move. He just stood there, staring at me with a puzzled look on his face. With our gazes locked, my pulse thudded a touch too fast. Did I have a dirty mark on my forehead from tackling him on the ground? A smudge of colored marker on my mouth from Charlotte? Blotchy patches of heat in my cheeks from our run . . . or from him standing too close?

God. He had the most stunning green eyes I'd ever seen. If I wasn't careful, I'd melt into a puddle on the floor.

But then he nodded. A soft but raspy '*hmm*' rumbled low and deep in his throat as he turned and dashed toward the living room.

I slumped against the wall.

Fuck. He was so nice at times, then a complete jerk at others. What would it take to find out what the real Cole Tanner was like? But that was against protocol. Light chitchat when we ran was fine but anything else wasn't an option.

I had to stay focused.

I was only on this gig for four months, then I was out of there.

Cole Tanner was my client.
Nothing more. Nothing less.
Yep. I'd better go shower. And I'd better make it icy cold.

Chapter 7

AVA

After lowering my body temperature in the shower and dressing into my casual uniform of black pants, T-shirt, and bomber jacket, I headed out into the kitchen. But my skin prickled. Cole sat on the living room sofa, leaning forward. His head rested in his hands. His palms covered his eyes.

The tension radiating off him warped the air.

In this job, we sometimes saw things no one else did. Those moments when your client was away from the spotlight, their friends, and the public, where you caught a glimpse of their true colors, their vulnerability. Those moments where the pressure simmered to the surface.

Like now.

It was hard not to feel for the guy. He was dealing with a lot of issues—the tour plans, rehearsals, an overloaded promotional schedule, Charlotte. Maybe he was having an off day. I'd only met him in person three days ago. But I knew what it was like to pretend everything was fine when it wasn't. It had cost me my son. It was hard not to care and be concerned about someone who seemed to be struggling. If my worries escalated, I'd talk to his manager—otherwise, I wasn't supposed to get entangled in his personal life.

I dropped my bag gently on the kitchen counter. I didn't want to startle him. "Hey. You ready to go?"

"Yeah." He bobbed his head. "Hannah's just left with Charlotte. They'll be back later tonight." He straightened and rubbed his brow. "When Paul goes back to San Fran at the end of next week, they'll be staying here full time."

"You ready for that?" I clipped my comms radio onto my belt, then threaded my earpiece wire underneath my shirt and hung it around my neck.

Cole's intense gaze followed my every move, but then he closed his eyes and pinched his brows together. "Nope. It just seemed like the easiest option with my schedule. I won't be here much, so we won't be in each other's way."

"You're supposed to be making room for your daughter." My voice came out too sharp for my liking. Responsibility took effort; he had to make changes, not just rely on Hannah.

"How the fuck do you do it?" The desperation in his voice slammed into my chest.

"How do you work full time and take care of a kid?"

Pain tore through my chest. I lowered my chin and leaned back against the kitchen counter. The wounds to my heart had never healed. "I do have a son, but I don't have full custody. Luther, my ex, has him the majority of the time." It crushed my soul every second Josh wasn't with me. "When I have Josh, if I have to work, I have my dad or my sister around to help. When you're a single parent, you've got to have family and friends . . . or a nanny . . . who support you."

He swiveled on the sofa to face me and slumped against the back of the seat. "My sister and my friends work with me. My parents spend most of their time overseas. Finding someone I trust and can rely on is hard to come by."

"True." I zipped up my jacket. "But you'd better find someone sooner rather than later. Hannah is only a temporary solution."

"Don't remind me," he mumbled.

"Oh, I will." I could give him a certain amount of tough love. "Your child comes first."

"Nope. Music does."

"Don't kid yourself, Cole."

"Maybe I am, but right now . . ." A playful glint returned to his eyes. Gone were the shadows of stress that had plagued him seconds ago. "It's time to work and play."

"It's just work for some of us." I smirked as my cell phone beeped. Our driver had arrived. "Time to go."

We grabbed our bags and headed out the door.

An hour later, I escorted Cole across the parking lot at Venice Beach toward the band's trailer for their scheduled photoshoot. On the drive there, he'd been glued to his cell phone, texting and making calls to people, but I hadn't caught on to whom. Not that it was any of my business.

Sloane pulled up at the same time as we did and joined us with Flint. Every person strolling past on the sidewalk stopped to gawk at the guys. Flint turned on his sexy, seductive smile and waved. Cole just grinned and strode along. He didn't need any flamboyance; the man commanded attention with his presence alone.

Wyatt had texted me five minutes ago. He and Beckett had arrived with Lewis and Slip. Wyatt stood guard by the trailer door. With his eyes hidden behind mirrored aviator sunglasses and a small curve playing across his lips, he was no doubt enjoying watching the small group of girls and guys gather 'round. Beckett was grabbing us coffees from the mobile van parked on the curbside.

"Where's Wells?" I asked Wyatt as I scanned the street.

"On his phone." He pointed across the lot. "Over there by the motorbikes."

No doubt texting Ramona. "Fair enough."

We stopped by the steps to the trailer. The door flew open. April leaned out of the doorway in her tailored shorts suit. With cell phone in hand and stress lines embedded around her eyes, she flicked her Jennifer Lawrence blonde hair over her shoulder. "You're late, guys. Hurry up and get in here. We have a tight schedule."

Cole swiveled toward me. A devilish glint shimmered through

his eyes. "You gonna come in and watch me dress?" His sultry how-about-it tone had returned.

I ignored the flutter in my belly. "You can keep your fantasies to yourself. You've got nothing I haven't seen before. Besides, the view out here is much better."

Who was I kidding? If I went inside, it would be impossible not to watch Cole Tanner rip off his clothes and redress.

He closed the gap, leaving less than a foot of distance between us. He chuckled, low and husky as his flirtatious gaze skimmed over me from my head down to my toes, then back up again. "I have to agree."

I locked my knees to stop them from buckling. *Ergh!* How could he switch from mopey and moody to seductive god with the blink of an eye? *Damn rock stars.* I didn't want a bar of it.

I stabbed the center of his chest and pushed him back a step. "You don't pay me enough to put up with your shit. Now get inside, and get this shoot over and done with so we can get to rehearsal on time."

"Gladly."

Flint shoved Cole on the shoulder, sending him up the stairs into the trailer. He leaned over to me. "Sorry about Cole. Just ignore him."

Believe me. I was trying to.

The moment the door to the trailer shut behind Cole and Flint, I leaned against the side wall, closed my eyes, and let out a deep breath.

"Hey? You okay?" Sloane asked.

"Yes. It's just been a very long morning." Spending more time with Cole had presented new challenges. His goofing around, suggestive glances, and sexually fueled comments made me want to swipe each smirk off his face with my fist. But witnessing his vulnerable moments, watching him with his daughter, hearing his deep laugh, and catching the smell of his seductive earthy cologne had left me needing all my strength not to grab him, pin him against the wall, and kiss him until we were both delirious.

What the fuck was wrong with me?

I'd never faltered in being professional, but Cole Tanner had gotten under my skin. His mix of arrogance, compassion, struggle, and charm made an intriguing yet lethal cocktail. One I never wanted to taste. I'd fallen for a charmer before and had sworn never to do so again.

I had to reset. Cole was my client. My paycheck. The last job before I got Josh back.

I was counting down the days until I saw my son again. The hours couldn't pass quickly enough.

Inhaling the fresh ocean air, I drew it deep into my lungs and erased the divine scent of Cole that had lingered in my head. I lifted my chin, savoring the sun on my skin and the warmth on my cheeks.

I loved being outdoors. I loved the wide stretch of sand leading down to the shoreline. The lazy waves hitting the beach. Clear, blue sky overhead. The palm trees catching the breeze.

I'd miss this when I had to work behind a desk. It was a gorgeous mid-October day. I was glad I didn't have to go into the water like the guys did for their photos. The ocean would be freezing. I'd only be diving in if I had to save Cole's ass if he couldn't swim—or his sexy comments went too far, and I wanted to fucking drown him.

What was with that?

The guy had more mood swings than there were colors in the rainbow. His world had been altered by taking custody of Charlotte—I understood that. He was terrified about being a parent. Who wouldn't be? But he had to step up. He'd been so good with Charlotte during their first meeting. He'd cared and taken the first step toward being a father, even though he probably didn't realize it.

Beckett came across the parking lot with a tray of coffee and handed me one. "Ava? You okay? It looks like you need this."

"You're a lifesaver." I grabbed the cup and took a long soothing sip. *Heaven.*

We stood on guard a few feet away from the trailer, surveying the crowd, monitoring movement, and were ready to jump into action to keep the fans at bay if needed.

The problem was, when we were on duty, dressed in uniform, we attracted as much attention as the band but for different reasons. We were like homing beacons. The minute people saw us, their interest piqued as they glanced around, often in a fluster, curious and hopeful of spotting a celebrity.

Beckett took a gulp of his coffee, then wiped the corner of his mouth with his fingertips. "Ava, is Cole giving you a hard time?"

"He's tried to but failed. I had to show him again during our run I'm no pushover. He gets up in my face, pastes on that fucking charming smile, and drops sexy innuendos like they're on tap. If he thinks I'm going to fall for it, he's got another lesson coming his way."

"You go, girl." He kept his eyes on the growing crowd as he talked to me. "But you don't need to put up with his shit."

"It's nothing I can't handle." I had this. *Yep . . . absolutely.*

"I'll swap if you want." Humor touched Wyatt's eyes as he grinned over the rim of his coffee cup. "Last night, Tia and Lewis invited me to join them for a threesome on the way home after they'd had dinner and way too much to drink. If it wasn't for our strict policy against getting involved with the client, I'd gladly join them." Wyatt was our party boy. He always went out on our days off and entertained us with tales of his hookups.

"You sly dog." I giggled but quickly stopped when a group of girls ran over to the edge of the parking lot. Guessed word was getting out the guys were here. "Crowd's growing. We'd better get into position."

"Yes, ma'am." Sloane drained his coffee. "At least you didn't have to put up with Flint fucking Sutton in the car on the way home like I did. The privacy screen wouldn't shut properly. I'm not deaf."

I laughed. Neither was I. Listening to Cole getting a blowjob at the club had been entertaining. We'd certainly seen and heard it all. We were paid a fuck-load of money to look the other way in some situations. Most of the celebrities I'd witnessed getting down and dirty weren't anything to get excited over. But after spending time with Cole, he might be a different story.

I finished my coffee and tossed the empty cup into a nearby trash can. "Never a dull moment, right?"

"No. Never." Sloane grunted. He was the quietest member of our team, but probably the most lethal. Like a special forces operative, he moved silently, blended into the shadows, and could take ten people down without drawing a breath.

April stepped out of the trailer. "Okay, folks, your mothers' meeting is over. The guys are on their way out."

"Copy that." Beckett straightened his baseball cap. "Let's go."

As we formed a line in front of the trailer, the guys emerged dressed in black clothing. All wore jeans but Slip had on a leather vest, Flint, a silky button-down, Lewis rocked a mesh T-shirt . . . and Cole? *Hot damn.* His ripped jeans clung to his long legs and a tight muscle tank top showed off his cut arms. Every drop of moisture in my mouth disappeared. I licked my lips and swallowed hard. Okay, I could see why he attracted so much attention. He had that whole good-boy-bad-boy vibe going on that made you look twice . . . or maybe just stare, unable to drag your gaze away.

I cleared my throat, straightened my sunglasses on the bridge of my nose, and stepped closer to him. My team and I flanked the guys and headed for a small portable gazebo that had been set up near the shoreline where the photographer and Blake were waiting. Behind us, the makeup artist, Penny, the wardrobe assistant, Cassidy, and a growing crowd of fifty onlookers and a handful of paparazzi followed.

For an hour, I stood beneath the gazebo with my team as the guys had photographs taken. Music blared from a portable speaker as Kris, the photographer, directed them to stand, sit, lie, run, or jump in the sand. Many shots resulted in the guys pissing themselves laughing as they shoved each other around, moved into position, and held their poses.

It was hard not to be caught up in their energy and fun. My line of work didn't accommodate much social time. When I had rare time off, I was with Josh, spent time with Dad, or hung out with my sister or my team. One good thing about having a desk job soon was that I'd have more time to catch up with my family and friends. No more shift work did have some merits . . . but I'd also possibly be bored to fucking tears. I'd miss the action and my team when they traveled. But Josh came first.

The guys ripped off their shirts and headed into the water. Buffed bodies glistened in the sunshine before me. *Oh yeah.* This job did have some perks. Flint outshone the others, performing and posing for the photographer, but my eyes were set on Cole.

"You okay, Ava?" Beckett nudged his shoulder against mine. "Need a cold drink? A fan?"

"Nope." I kept my tone neutral and stared straight ahead, but my insides were alight. Did my breath hitch? Could Beckett sense my pulse had jumped? *Fuck it.* I had to get something good out of putting up with Cole's shit. Admiring his picture-perfect body would do. As he flexed his arms, puffed out his chest, and slid his hands over his wet stomach, my thighs clenched together. *Damn.* "I'm just admiring the view."

"So is half of Venice Beach." Wyatt lowered his aviator sunglasses, keeping an eye on the growing cluster of fans and curious bystanders. "At least the onlookers are being well behaved. Makes our job easier."

"For now." I grunted. But keeping my hands off Cole Tanner was getting harder by the minute. Maybe I should swap who I shadowed with Beckett or Wyatt. *No . . . Don't be stupid. I am fine.*

After the guys finished having their pictures taken and they wrapped themselves up in warm robes, we lingered beside them as they talked to the group of fans, signed autographs, and had a ton of selfies.

But after ten minutes, Blake held up his hands to the fans and hollered, "Sorry, folks. The guys have to get to rehearsal. Hope y'all got to say hi, and we look forward to seeing everyone toward the end of next month when the tour kicks off."

Angsty cries filled the air as some fans rushed forward, reaching for the guys. *"Flint, we love you!" "Guys, wait! I want a photo." "Cole. Lewis. Slip. Come back."*

My team and I formed a line between them and the band. A

sea of cell phones waved around us as they tried to snap shots of the guys. One girl tried to push past Beckett, but the man was a concrete tower—she got nowhere. Some chick with long, pointed pink fingernails thrust her cell phone in front of my face, scratching the side of my cheek.

"Ow. Fuck." That hurt . . . and stung. I wiped my face. A lick of blood smeared my fingertips. *Son of a bitch.* But I held my ground. The band members didn't falter in their stride as we guided them away from the mass of people and back into their trailer.

Sloane called our driver while we waited for the guys to change. The moment the black Mercedes twelve-seat van with darkened windows rocked up, the guys jumped in, followed by us, and we whisked them off to rehearsal. When everyone was leaving from one place and traveling to the same destination, the van was a much easier option to move around in rather than our separate vehicles.

But at the first set of traffic lights, Cole swiveled toward me. He hooked his finger underneath my chin and turned my cheek toward him. "Holy shit. You got scratched."

"Yeah. Some bitch with nails got me." I pulled my chin free. "It doesn't hurt."

"It's bleeding. You don't need stitches, but still . . ."

"It's fine. Are you hurt?"

"No."

"Then that's all the matters."

"You should put something on that. You don't want it to get infected." He slid forward toward the front passenger seat and tapped Sloane on the shoulder. "Hey? You got a first-aid kit in here? Ava's been scratched."

"Yeah." Sloane dug into the glove box. "Here." He handed Cole the kit. "Ava, you alright? Didn't think a small scratch would bother you."

"It's not." Irritation clipped my tone. "Cole, I'm fine."

"Shut the fuck up." Cole grabbed the antiseptic cream out of the box and handed it to me. "Put this on it, or shall I do it?"

I snatched the tube from him. "I don't want your hands

anywhere near me."

"Why?" He lowered his voice. "Afraid you won't want me to take them off you?"

"No. It's so I don't' break every fucking bone in your fingers. Do you want to keep drumming?"

Slip laughed. "Damn, Cole. Ava's got you by the balls."

"No. She hasn't." Cole flopped back on the seat.

What did Slip mean by that? I wished I had him by the balls and at my mercy—then he might be more compliant and listen to me.

"Oh . . . yes, she has." Slip laughed. "I've never seen you give a shit about security before."

"I just don't want her to end up with some ghastly, puss-infected sore on her face." Cole sneered. "That okay?"

"Yep." As Slip nodded, he winked at me.

I unscrewed the cap and dabbed ointment onto my sore. I winced. *Damn.* That burned like acid. I recapped the tube and handed it back to Cole. "Thank you."

"You're welcome. See? I can be nice."

I wasn't sure if that was a good thing or not.

For my sanity, it'd be easier if he wasn't.

Chapter 8

COLE

Inside our secure rehearsal facility in Burbank, I hammered out a raw rhythm on my bass drum and hi-hats. Sweat dripped from my short hair, ran down my skin and soaked my T-shirt. My hands were a blur as I struck the snares, tom-toms, and cymbals with the drumsticks. The reverberations from each strike coursed up my arms and legs and settled in the center of my chest. *Fuck yeah.* Drumming was what I lived for.

At this end of the huge, brand-new 30,000 square-foot studio, our full stage had been constructed with hundreds of lights flashing overhead. Massive LED screens projected graphics and videos behind me. Booming amps and speakers lined the front of the riser or hung from towering metal frames. Stretched out across the floor in front of the stage lay a mass of equipment trunks, cables, and our control panel where Tia, Kieran, and Tristan oversaw our show.

Every time I walked through the doors to rehearse, butterflies took flight in my belly. This would be our biggest tour to date. I couldn't wait to hit the road next month. To take this show around the world and play in front of thousands of fans.

We were halfway through practicing our set list. Flint was flawless, singing and playing at his mic a few yards in front of my drum kit. Lewis added perfect rhythm with his bass to my left.

Slip was on point with his electric to my right. Our management team and crew watched us from the floor, tweaking and refining each element of our show. But every time the stage lights flashed, I could just see our security guards, sitting on a row of chairs in front of the stage. They were chatting and sipping coffee, but Ava's eyes were on me.

Something in her gaze intrigued me. When we talked, she kept details light and barely said anything. She taunted me, stirring something deep inside me that I didn't want to awaken. But I couldn't stop myself from going back for more.

I'd never been a show-off. I didn't think I was better than anyone else. But this morning, it had been fun to test her fitness. She'd kept up with my pace, put me in my place, and drilled me into the ground. Not a lot impressed me, but she did. Now I was paying the price. With the thrum of the music filling my in-ear monitors, my thighs burned, protesting each pound of the drum pedals. The fire blazing in my muscles was self-inflicted stupidity from overexerting myself up the hills. *Dick.*

But pushing Ava wasn't just about seeing if she was fit. I'd wanted to break her tough exterior and get her to crack a smile. After tragically losing friends, having my heart annihilated, and my band coming too close to collapsing too many times, I'd become hell-bent on ensuring the people in my life had fun and were happy. Life was too short to be serious all the time.

But fuck . . . now, I had to be.

Somehow I had to be responsible for a child.

How was I going to take care of Charlotte when this—playing music—was my life?

I had to find a nanny. Have the band over to meet Charlotte. FaceTime my parents to introduce them to my kid. The call with them last week hadn't gone well. They'd been less than thrilled, but that was nothing new. Still, it was better they found out via me rather than the press. Having a child just added another thick layer of disappointment to the endless discontent that Tia and I seemed to inflict on their lives. I wasn't surprised when they'd said they weren't rushing home from Paris to meet her. They'd wait until we were in Europe for the tour.

If I still had custody of her then.

Fuck.

I hated uncertainty. I hated the stress. I hated that my life had been turned upside . . . again.

I was about to stop at the end of a song where we normally paused rehearsal, but Jackson, our production manager, stepped onto the stage, circling his finger through the air. I tugged out one of my ear monitors to hear him.

He hollered and clapped. "Keep it going. Push through. Cole, don't stop. Roll out that new transition. Come on guys. Next song. Go. Go. Go."

Flint gave the thumbs up. Lewis and Slip nodded, not missing a note on their guitars.

I bobbed my head and stuffed my ear monitor into place. Taking a deep breath to refocus, I wound down the pace with long, drawn-out beats on my drums.

The stage lights dimmed, and a lone spotlight hit Flint.

We'd hit the slow section of our set.

Fuck. Why had I agreed to include this single on the tour? So what if it was one of our biggest hits?

Flint sauntered up to his mic, strumming his strings. His haunting, anguish-filled voice filled my ears as he sang:

Sometimes I feel like my world is spinning around
Somebody please help me off this merry-go-round
I can't see how I'm supposed to come back down
Without your love I'm falling toward the ground

Sometimes I feel like I'm struggling to breathe
My mind is racing so fast I cannot see
My heart is hurting so much it cripples me
Without your love I don't know who I'm supposed to be

You pulled me in, loved me hard, pushed me down, broke my heart

Took me high, made me fall, raised me up, but lied through it all

Sometimes I feel like I'm traveling a treacherous road
I'm down and out in this world, feeling all alone
I'm walking in circles facing every day on my own
Without your love I can't find my way back home

My breath ripped through my lungs, hurting my ribs. I slammed the cymbals harder than necessary, struck my snare with too much force. We'd written this song just after Flint had broken up with Lena, his second serious girlfriend. Every word he'd penned was an arrow through my chest. It was like he'd channeled my heartache over Priah leaving, my grief over losing Aidan, and my fear our band was falling apart. Flint and Slip had been fighting. Phil had been drunk and high all the time. I'd buried my anguish into the depths of my soul to maintain the peace. While Flint took the flack in the media for all the wild partying after our gigs, I was the one smoothing over our issues that weren't in the spotlight. I kept everyone talking, put out the emotional fires, and stuck Band-Aids on shattered hearts. But mine had been irreparable. I'd do anything for those guys. Anything. They didn't need to know I was broken on the inside too.

We'd come the closest we'd ever been to losing everything when Phil died. Flint's depression had put him on a path of self-destruction, and the pressure to write a new album had been at an all-time high. Thanks to ultimatums, we'd survived. Our love and friendship were too strong to fail us. We'd been through too much to quit. But those trying times had been rough. I never wanted to go through anything like them again.

But then . . . Charlotte had happened—a road I hadn't seen coming.

One I couldn't see the end of. One that didn't have an end.

Fuck.

We hit my solo that led to the end of our main set before our encore. My feet hammered the pedals. Clutching my sticks tight,

I swung and crossed my hands back and forth as I played each drum. Thrashing. Striking. Harder and faster. Harder and faster. The thundering beat and reverberations pummeled my soul and thrummed through my chest. But anger and frustration fueled the adrenaline surging through my veins. Every time I bobbed and flicked my head, droplets of sweat trickled down my face, fell into my eyes, and flew from my hair. But I didn't stop. *Slam. Slam. Slam.*

Why, when my band and I were finally in a good place, did everything have to turn to shit?

Why hadn't Shelby told me about Charlotte?

Why was Ava in my head?

Arrrrrgh! Fuck!

I hit, struck, and pounded each drum. Irritation poured through my sticks again and again. Again and again. With a crash on the cymbals, I smashed out the last beat. As the clang rang through the air, I stopped pumping the pedals. I sucked in huge lungfuls of air to catch my breath. My heart hammered my ribs with bone-cracking thumps.

The stage lights flared, shining down on me.

All eyes had turned in my direction.

Nobody moved. Mouths gaped.

A shudder coiled up my spine, prickling my skin.

Ava sat on her chair, leaning forward. Her lips were slightly parted. Her eyes glimmered with heat. She nodded and mouthed, "*Wow.*"

Flint swung his guitar behind his shoulder and rested his hand on his mic. A combination of concern and bewilderment swam through his eyes. "Where the fuck did that come from?"

I wiped my face on my shirtsleeve. "Guess I was just in the moment, man." Yep, drumming was my therapy. Had I resolved anything? Come up with any solutions? *Nope.*

"You gave me goose bumps, dude." Slip held out his arm, twisting and turning it this way then that.

"You need to do that every show." Lewis retied his sweaty hair into a small man-bun. "It was fucking wicked."

"Thanks." Not sure I could pull that off again. Not sure my

heart and head could take it, but I'd do my best.

After we ran through the encore, Blake, Falcon—our tour manager—and our crew cheered and applauded. Drained of energy, I joined the guys at the front of the stage. We grabbed bottles of water and sat or lay on the edge of the riser with Jackson, our stage and lighting crew, and our entourage discussing what went well, what needed working on, and what needed changing. As I stretched out my sore legs and winced, Ava cracked a grin full of twisted pleasure. *Oh yeah.* She liked seeing me in pain. I needed a good deep-tissue massage. Lesson learned. No more antics when running.

But I'd made her smile. I'd take that as a win. Mission complete.

Now I could concentrate. On music. Nothing else.

Across the weekend, we had grueling back-to-back rehearsals. We worked on refining our choreography, and our mash-up, but mastered the transition between each song. We were on a roll.

But thanks to the long days, I didn't get home until ten or later each evening. Charlotte was already tucked in her bed, asleep. Hannah was always sitting on the sofa reading a book and having a cup of tea. On Monday evening, I walked through the door and dumped my bag at the bottom of the stairs.

"How was your day?" Hannah placed a bookmark in her book and closed it.

"Awesome." I headed over and sank onto the ottoman, keeping a courteous distance. I stank of sweat and needed a shower. "We've been working on lighting for each song, slowly bringing everything together. We're about to push full run-throughs." We had to. The tour was only a month away, and we had a lot of publicity and events on beforehand.

She looked at me over the rim of her reading glasses. "When are you going to spend time with Charlotte?"

Was it wrong I wanted to avoid my new reality? *Yep.* But I couldn't. Grimacing, I rubbed the side of my face. "Maybe Wednesday? We have rehearsal in the afternoon. I'll have everyone over for lunch beforehand so they can meet her too."

"Good." She took a sip of her tea. "We're not here on a vacation,

Cole."

"I know. Just timing is hard."

"That's why I'm here."

"I can't thank you enough for helping out." I eased to my feet. "But I have another long day tomorrow, so I'm gonna hit bed."

"Sure. Me too. Have a good night."

Sleep was not my forte, but I gave Hannah a warm smile. "You too. See you in the morning."

I headed upstairs and peered through Charlotte's bedroom door to check on her. She lay curled up asleep with Barney tucked beneath her arm. Closing my eyes, I thudded my head against the doorjamb. How the fuck could I make this work? Find balance? I had no fucking idea.

I staggered into my room, showered, and fell into bed. But like most nights . . . after a couple hours sleep . . . I jolted awake. Sweat covered my body. I panted like I'd run ten miles at a sprint. My mind raced at a thousand beats per second.

Flashes of being with Shelby burned my brain. Her heartbroken tears over Flint stabbed my chest. Aidan's anguished pleas to stay with him rang in my ears. Phil's begging for drugs drummed in my head.

Fuck!

Shaking all over, I clutched my chest. The pressure in my skull throbbed.

When my nightmares hit, I'd usually get up, wash my face, go downstairs, and drum for hours, but with the tour coming up I needed to rest. So I collapsed against the mattress and stared at the ceiling. I begged the sun to rise so I could go running, rehearse, or keep busy to distract myself from the guilt that consumed me over fucking up people's lives or playing my part in their deaths. What if I hurt Charlotte too?

I sucked in a deep breath then let it out slowly. Closing my eyes, I repeated the process. *In. Out. In. Out.*

There . . . I was fine. This would pass. Everything would be okay. I fell asleep sometime around four, then woke at seven and was out the door by nine.

At rehearsal, we nailed our first full run-through. Every song in our set list had come together. Our transitions were getting smoother and smoother.

"Fuck yeah." I pumped my fist as Flint struck the last chord on his guitar.

"Woohoo!" he hollered into the mic, then turned to us. "That was fucking awesome, guys. Well done."

"Brilliant." Jackson clapped and whistled.

I joined the guys at the front of the stage for our post-run-through meeting. But just when Jackson began to speak, April's cell phone rang. As she spoke quietly, her worried eyes settled on me.

My stomach cinched. What had I done?

After a minute, she handed me her phone. "It's Hannah."

Shit. "What? Why is she calling?" Hannah had April's cell phone number; she was the best way to reach me if something was urgent. I never had my phone on me during a performance.

A chill ran down my spine.

Oh, fuck. What had happened?

Was Charlotte okay?

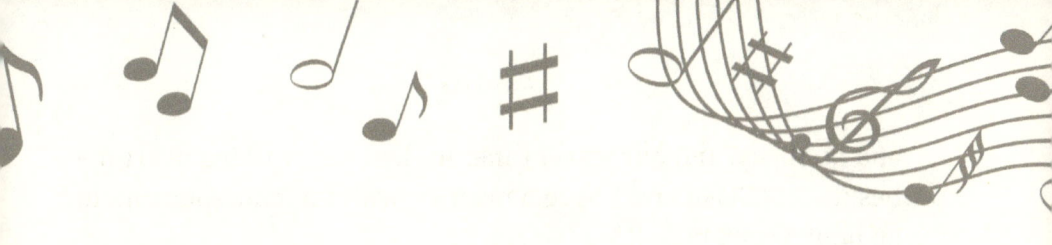

Chapter 9

COLE

I snatched the cell phone out of April's hand and held it to my ear. "Hannah? What's up?"

"Cole, I'm sorry to trouble you while you're rehearsing. Charlotte has a raging fever. I've called your home doctor. He's on his way but running behind schedule. I've got to take Paul to the specialist before he heads back to San Fran at the end of this week. You have to come home and take care of Charlotte."

"What? I can't. We've got another session to run through."

"Paul can't miss his appointment. Charlotte can't be there in this state. She's vomiting. She's burning up. I've given her some Children's Tylenol and I'm waiting for it to work. You have to come home and look after her."

"But . . ."

"Cole . . . this is your daughter. Come. Now."

"Fuck." I clutched my hair and tugged on it. I didn't need this shit.

April's face blanched. "Cole? Is Charlotte okay?"

"No. She's got a fever. Can you go to my place and look after her?"

"No." Irritation flickered across April's face. She was under just as much pressure as the band was for the tour. The time-consuming and exhausting task of coordinating all our promo and publicity, and our travel itinerary had her working overtime beside us. "Blake and I have a meeting with the tour sponsors in an hour. I can't miss it."

I glanced around at our road crew. Tia was still recovering from surgery; she was out. No one else had met my kid nor been to my house. *Fuck . . .* who else could help? I glanced at my watch. It was three o'clock. *Shit!* Mackenzie, my housekeeper, would be running around after her own children. I turned to Ava. "Can you go look after my kid?"

She hesitated for two seconds, then hardness set in her eyes. She tilted her head to the side and shook it. "Sorry. Not in my job description."

The tension in my temples tightened and throbbed. "Come on. Please?"

"Your daughter needs *you*." Her tone could have cut diamonds. *Ouch.*

"Cole?" Flint slapped me on the shoulder. "Go. It's fine. We've had a great session. Lewis, Slip, and I can work on choreography while you're gone. Ava's right. Your kid needs you."

"Shit." Pacing in front of my drums, I put the cell phone back to my ear. "Should Charlotte go to the hospital rather than just see the doctor?"

"I'm sure it's only a fever. But if she gets worse, yes, she'll have to go to emergency." The worry in Hannah's voice didn't ease the knots in my gut. "I have to leave in half an hour. Will you be home in time?."

I pinched the bridge of my nose. I couldn't believe I had to do this. "Fuck. Yes. I'm on my way." I handed April's cell phone back to her. "Thanks. I gotta go."

She arched a saucy eyebrow at me. "I haven't seen you rush off after a woman like this in years. Kinda cool that a three-year-old has you flustered."

"Fuck off." I stormed over to my drums and grabbed my bag, then waved at Ava. "Let's go."

Ava stood, straightened her jacket, and nodded. "Yes, Mr. Tanner."

Oh, now she moved! And why did I like her calling me that?

As my driver drove toward my home, I dug into my backpack and ripped out a fresh black T-shirt. I yanked my sweaty one off and pulled on the clean shirt. Sitting beside me, Ava scanned every inch of my chest, raised an eyebrow, then looked straight ahead.

She wasn't the first women to admire my physique. Most chicks did it with their hot mouths and hungry tongues. But Ava often looked at me like she wanted to skin me alive with the knife I was sure she had concealed on her body somewhere.

I slumped in the seat. "How do you do this?"

"Do what?" she asked.

"Drop everything and rush home to be with your kid."

"When they're your responsibility, you have to. No matter what you're in the middle of doing or working on, you have to stop and go to them."

"This sucks." I dropped my head back, hitting the leather headrest. "I need to be with the band." *Shit!* What if this happened in the middle of a show?

"No. You *want* to be with your band. You *need* to be with your child." She stared out the car window. "Some days being a parent can be hard and frustrating. Guilt can consume you."

I didn't need to be a parent for that. Guilt consumed me every day. She had no idea how much.

"It's okay to have a career, hang out with friends, pursue things that you love, but sometimes they have to be put on hold or pushed down the priorities list when you have to take care of your family."

"I can't do that." The guys would be joking around, working on coordinating their stage moves, and I was sitting in a car . . . missing out. *Shit!* I'd never suffered from FOMO before. I was always with my friends, invited to the hottest parties, out on the town. *Damn.* This was a first. "The tour is my priority."

"It is for now, but that won't last forever."

No, it wouldn't. But at this point in my life, it took up nearly every waking moment. "Paul goes home on Saturday." He'd been staying with friends in Pasadena. "Hannah will be around all the time. This won't happen again."

She swiveled her head toward me. "Don't be delusional. Your daughter getting sick isn't a one-time event, nor is having to put her needs before your own."

"Fuck." I thumped my head against the seat. "I don't have time for this."

"Time?" She sucked in a deep breath then let it out slowly. The muscles in her jaw tensed. Was she mad at me? What had I done? She closed her eyes and lowered her voice. "Then why did you agree to take Charlotte? Why not let someone who will love her take care of her?"

The anguish in Ava's tone caught me off-guard. She was usually so blunt and cold and full of tough love, but this was new. This was personal for her. She hadn't told me the full story about her ex and why she didn't have custody of her kid. I hadn't meant to upset her with my own messed up situation.

Why did I take Charlotte? It was the right thing to do. She was my reckless mistake I had to take responsibility for. "Because she's mine." My heart struggled to beat. I didn't want my life to change, but every time I was in the same room as Charlotte, something in my head and heart altered. I had no control over it and wanted it to stop.

"Then be the father she needs." Ice shot through Ava's tone. "If you don't spend time with her or show her that you love her, she'll grow up resenting you. Is that what you want?"

My heart twanged. I wasn't going to be like my parents. *No way.* "No. It's not."

"Good. Don't be an asshole. There's already enough of them in the world."

"Point taken." I liked Ava. Like my friends, she didn't kiss my ass. She wasn't trying to hit on me or get me in the sack. She wasn't part of my sphere of music. I didn't need a pity party. Not ever. I'd deal with my shit. She was the right dose of harsh reality I needed to keep me grounded in the middle of my chaotic storm.

I'd take this fathering thing day by day.

I could look after a sick kid.

At home, I rushed through the front door and headed straight into the living room. Ava followed close behind. My breath hitched, shuddering through my chest. Charlotte lay stretched out on the sofa in a yellow tank top and panties. Hannah sat beside her head, wiping Charlotte's brow with a damp facecloth.

I'd seen people passed out from drinking too much, flaked out on drugs, high to the heavens, but nothing freaked me out more than seeing my kid limp on the sofa.

Her little round cheeks were bright red. Damp strands of sweaty hair clung to her brow. Her eyes were closed, and her head had lolled to the side. *Shit!* I fell to my knee beside her and stroked her soft curls. She didn't even flutter an eyelash. The back of my eyes prickled. All I wanted was to see her better. "Hey, Char. I'm here."

"She's just fallen asleep." Hannah handed me the facecloth. "But her temperature has come down."

I touched the back of my hand against her forehead. Her blazing skin burned my fingers. *Fuck.* I had no idea how to deal with this. "Are you sure she doesn't need to go to hospital? She's so hot."

"She's better than before. Your doctor should be here in ten minutes. He'll tell you what to do." Hannah rushed over to the dining table and grabbed her purse. "I've got to go. Keep her cool and hydrated. I'll be back after dinner."

Just as Hannah took off out the door, Charlotte shivered. Her little teeth chattered together. "I'm cold. I need a blanky."

"Okay." I reached for a throw to place over her.

But Ava cleared her throat.

I glanced over my shoulder. She stood hovering by the bar, shaking her head. "No blanket. It's just the fever passing. She'll be okay."

"But she's shivering."

"She's not cold. Trust me."

It went against every bone in my body not to put the blanket over Charlotte's shivering body. "So what do I do?"

Ava sucked in a deep breath, then sighed. "Get a fresh cool

cloth. Put it on her forehead."

I rushed over to the kitchen and rinsed the facecloth under the cold water. "You should be doing this. You have experience with a kid; I don't."

"You have to learn how to take care of her at some point in time. Now is just as good as any. I'll wait until the doctor's been in case we have to take her to the hospital."

"So you're just going to stand there?" I didn't mind the view, but my attention had to be on Charlotte, not Ava.

"No." She waved toward the office down the hall. "I need to check in with the surveillance team."

"Is there an issue?"

"I hope not. I'll let you know if there is."

"Thank you." I jutted my chin toward the kitchen. "You're welcome to grab a coffee or a drink out of the fridge. Help yourself to food if you're hungry."

"Thank you." She dipped her chin. "But I'm okay."

Ten minutes later, my doctor arrived. Ava let him in via the security intercom in the office and met him at the door so I didn't have to leave Charlotte's side.

In long loping strides, Dr. Morley walked over to me and placed his bag on the ottoman. Dressed in a navy polo T-shirt, tan dress pants and loafers, he was one of the most casual, cruisy doctors I'd ever met. He shook my hand. "Hey, Cole. Good to see you."

"Hi Donovan. This time it's not me or one of my friends who needs your help." He'd been to a few of our house calls over the years for parties gone too wild, cuts that needed stitches, and general illnesses that needed attending to. "Um . . . this is my kid, Charlotte. She's burning up."

"Your daughter?" Donovan's bushy eyebrows shot skyward. "The lady on the phone didn't provide that information." *Shit.* That was another thing I had to add to my list. I had to meet with April and send out a press release about Charlotte being mine. It'd save the onslaught of speculation and gossip. "You guys always surprise me. I never know what to expect when I walk through one of your doors, but I hadn't anticipated this."

"We like keeping you on your toes."

"That you do." He chuckled as he squatted beside the sofa. "Hi Charlotte." Her big green eyes fluttered open. "I'm Dr. Morley. Is it okay if I check your temperature and listen to your chest?"

She nodded and closed her eyes.

As Dr. Morley examined her, checking her ears, throat, and glands, and listening to her breathing, I filled him in on the story of how Charlotte had landed in my life. Every time I'd retold it over the past two week or so to my parents, to my entourage, and to my band's road crew, nausea had swayed through my stomach. Nothing eased the guilt from what I'd done all those years ago. The only thing that made it bearable was how adorable my kid was. It was wrong to be glad that Shelby had died, but I would've never met or known I had a daughter otherwise. How fucked up was that?

"Has she been anywhere different or eaten anything unusual?" Donovan pressed her tummy, then scanned her skin, I assumed for rashes and unusual blotches.

"Um. No. I'd have to check with her grandmother who has been with her. On Friday, Charlotte did try to eat a dozen coloring markers."

Donovan shook his head. "No, they might cause a tummy ache or maybe diarrhea. Not this."

He asked more questions. I hated that I couldn't give him definitive answers. I'd only known her for six days, and for most of them I'd been at work.

Donovan took off his stethoscope and put it back in his bag. "Cole, I don't think it's anything more than a fever. Her temperature is still a touch high but not extreme. If it goes over 103°, and she gets delirious or unresponsive, take her to the hospital. But if she's had this for a few hours, let's hope the worst has passed. The best thing to do is to let her rest and sleep it off. Give her children's acetaminophen or ibuprofen every four hours if her temperature is still high, and make sure you keep her cool."

"Is that it?" Sounded easy enough.

"Yes. Call me if anything changes."

"Thanks, doc." As he stood, I shook his hand.

"You're welcome. I'll see you and the guys at my office in three or so weeks for final medicals before the tour."

"We'll be there." I never looked forward to blood tests, stress tests, or swabs of various kinds, but they were necessary.

After Donovan left, I sank onto the sofa beside Charlotte.

She stirred and licked her tiny lips. "Ma. Ma. Mommy." Her little voice whimpered.

My heart constricted. I'd do anything to have Hannah or Shelby here to help look after her. But I was all she had. I hoped we both survived. I leaned forward and stroked her hair. "Hi sweetie. I'm here. How you feeling?"

"Where's Ma? I'm hungry."

"Me too." I hadn't eaten anything since lunch. "What would you like? A sandwich? Some fruit?"

"Cookies and milk."

Did I have cookies? "Let me go see what we've got."

I headed into my kitchen and found chocolate-chip cookies in my pantry, and I grabbed the milk from the fridge along with a beer for me. I returned to the sofa and helped Charlotte to sit upright. As she nibbled on a cookie and sipped her milk, I sat beside her and savored a mouthful of beer.

Moments later, Ava returned from the office. If I'd blinked, I would've missed her gaze soften as she took in Charlotte . . . then me. Warmth meandered through my chest as our eyes met. But it disappeared when she lifted her chin, and steel reset in her eyes. "Just so you're aware, I'm monitoring a car that is outside your house again. I noticed it was there when we came home. I've aligned your neighbors and paparazzi friends to their vehicles, but this one has a female driver. There've been no women photographers by your front gate. Do you know if one of the nearby residents owns a white Camry?"

Shit. I would've never noticed an unusual car. I lived on a small dead-end street with six other houses owned by young wealthy property developers and business tycoons. I knew everyone thanks to some fucking wicked parties. "Not that I'm aware of.

They own Porsches, Maseratis, and Bentleys. Is she someone's housekeeper? Relative? Booty call?"

"We're still trying to piece information together. Once we left this morning, she walked past your driveway twice, but kept her head down. I saw the same woman go up to a neighbor's house last week. Do you know who this is?"

Ava handed me a tablet and showed me an image of a short women wearing blue jeans, a gray hoodie, and a red cap. Her long blonde ponytail fell halfway down her back. *Blonde? Nope.*

"She doesn't look familiar. She's not one of my neighbors."

"We'll keep an eye on her. If she's back tomorrow, we'll investigate further."

"Thank you." I handed over the tablet. "I don't need some fan breaking into my home. I don't want Charlotte or Hannah to get frightened or hurt."

"Your house is very secure, alarmed, and monitored. We'll keep you as safe as possible."

I nodded. "I know."

She tucked the tablet under her arm. "Is there anything else you need me for today, Mr. Tanner?"

Hmmm. Why did my name rolling off her tongue do strange things to my body temperature? Was I sick too? *Yep. Definitely.*

"If not, I'm going to take off," she continued.

"You going to get Josh?" Her ex had supposedly switched around the days she got her kid last week to tie in with his meetings and travel plans.

"Hopefully." A quiver of reserved excitement hovered in her level tone. "Yes."

Would I ever be excited about having a child? That hadn't happened so far. Not likely to happen anytime soon. "Okay. I'm good. Thanks." I half-heartedly waved. "See you tomorrow for rehearsal."

"I'll be here at two-thirty. Make sure you're ready."

"Got it."

Ava softened her tone and waved at Charlotte. "Bye, Charlotte. Be good for Daddy."

"Bye, Ava." She stuffed a cookie in her mouth. Crumbs and chocolate were scattered across every inch of the beige sofa around her. Was this kid going to ruin every piece of furniture in my home?

Ava took off and closed the door behind her.

It was just me . . . and Charlotte.

She looked up at me with her big green eyes, took a sip of her milk, then her face paled. Worry creased her brow and she frowned. "My tummy hurts."

Before I had time to blink, Charlotte threw up. Regurgitated milk and cookies coated her legs and clothes and dripped onto the rug in chunky blobs. She burst out crying. "Arrrrgh!"

Oh my God. I was not qualified for this shit. I shot forward and slammed my beer down on the coffee table. "Charlotte, what the fuck?"

She wailed even louder and dropped her sippy cup, spilling it onto the floor.

Shit. Clenching my teeth, I lowered my voice. "It's okay." It so fucking wasn't.

I grabbed my cell phone and called Ava. She answered within two rings. "What's up?"

"Get back here. Charlotte just threw up everywhere. I need help."

"No, you don't." A hint of humor hovered in her voice.

Was she smiling? Trying not to laugh? "Yes. I. Do."

"Cole. Stop." How could she remain calm when there was mess everywhere? "Use that instinct of yours and actually take care of your daughter. You'll be fine. You've got this."

She hung up. *What the fuck?* She hung up? On me? *Ergh!*

Tears streamed down Charlotte's cheek as she held her vomit-covered hands toward me. "Hold on, sweetie. Stay there."

Damn you, Ava. I didn't need tough love—I needed fucking help. I tossed my cell phone aside and rushed to the kitchen. I grabbed some dishtowels from the bottom drawer and returned to Charlotte. "Let's clean you up."

I wiped the tears off her cheeks, then the goo off her mouth, tummy, and legs. How could one kid produce so much spew? I'd only given her a small cup of milk and one cookie. But then I wrinkled my nose. My stomach swayed. *God*, puke stank.

I cleaned Charlotte as best as I could and wiped up the mess off the rug and sofa. They'd have to be professionally dry-cleaned later. I scooped up the bundle of rags and tossed them into the kitchen sink.

"Come on, kid. Let's get you bathed." I picked up Charlotte from beneath her armpits and held her at arm's length. But she stared at me with her big teary eyes and pouting lips. That wasn't fair. Not one little bit. She'd melt the evilest of hearts with her cherub face. "Fine. Have it your way." I drew her against my chest, ignoring her damp, dirty clothes. Halfway up the steps, her body went limp against my chest. Her head slumped against my shoulder. I touched her forehead. A new fire ignited her skin.

Fuck.

I hadn't signed up for this. *Wait. Shit . . . yes, I did.*

How was I going to do this? How could I take care of her and prove to the court I could be a father when I just wanted to devote my time to going out, partying, and my band?

What if, no matter what I did, I wasn't good enough and children's services took her away?

Fuck.

My head wouldn't stop spinning. My kid was sick.

But I could do this.

I'd bathe her. Cool her down. Have a crack at this fathering thing.

Oh Lord, give me strength.

Chapter 10

AVA

What was I thinking? I'd hung up on Cole. *Shit.* I bit my lip, not sure whether I wanted to laugh or curse more. He could fire me for hanging up on him and not returning to his house. Maybe he was used to people dropping everything and doing what he wanted, but I wouldn't be one of them. He needed to be a father. It had taken all my strength not to help Charlotte. But deep down, I didn't want Cole to turn out to be like my ex—someone who handed off taking care of his child to others. Cole was just nervous, anxious, and scared to learn. He'd be okay. I was confident . . . somewhat.

Leaving him had also been for a selfish reason.

It meant I could pick up Josh early . . . *cross fingers.*

It would be a waste of time driving all the way home to Los Feliz only to turn around and come back to Beverly Hills. But my stomach sank, twisted, and churned. Luther didn't like spontaneous change. He kept Josh away from me for every second possible just to be a prick.

I pulled up at the end of the street not far from Cole's house, wiped my sweaty hands on my pants, and called Luther.

"What do you want?" His surly voice hissed through the speaker.

"Hi Luther. Always a pleasure to talk to you." Snideness slithered in my words.

"I'm busy. Get to the point."

"I've finished early and was hoping it'd be okay if I picked up Josh now rather than later. I could swing by the house in twenty minutes or so."

"I'm still at the office. That's four hours ahead of schedule. What the hell? No."

An arrow shot through my heart. "Luther, could you be nice for once in your life? I was flexible and changed my dates with Josh to suit you; could you please let me collect him now? Zoe won't mind." I got along quite well with Josh's nanny. "It'd save me hours on the road since I'm in the area."

"Why are you in Beverley Hills?"

I closed my eyes and rubbed at the mounting tension in my forehead. "I'm not. I'm nearby. My client lives halfway between your place and mine."

"Who is it? Is it someone I know?"

"My clients are none of your business."

"Whatever," he snapped. Not knowing every detail of my life would be boiling his blood. Good. "But if you pick Josh up early today, I'll dock the hours off your next weekend with him."

My heart crumbled onto the floor in the car. "Luther. It's just for a few extra hours today. You're at the office, you won't even notice he's gone. There's no inconvenience to you whatsoever."

"That's the deal. Take it or leave it."

"Asshole," I mumbled as I pounded my fist against the steering wheel.

"What was that?"

"Nothing." I didn't care if he'd heard me. He was one. But I didn't want to argue. I grasped every opportunity to be with Josh. With all the recent changes to our schedule, it had been too long since I'd seen him. Two and a half weeks seemed like a lifetime. "Luther, I'm so over your shit." Fire curled through my veins in waves of hot rage. "You don't care about Josh. I can't wait for our court hearing and to put an end to these cruel games you want to play."

"We'll see about that." Smugness rippled through his gruff

chuckle. "Do we have a deal?"

I hated bending to Luther's demands, but I didn't want to give him any fuel to use against me. It crushed my soul having to give in. But each day I didn't fight with him was another day his hold on Josh grew thinner. It wouldn't be long now. There was only one way to win this battle and that was in the courtroom . . . and I was hell-bent on winning. "Fine. I'll call Zoe to let her know I'm on my way."

Luther hung up. No goodbye. No nothing. *Jerk.*

I called Zoe. But she didn't respond. I dialed Josh. He answered on the first ring and was so excited I was getting him early.

As I pulled into Luther's driveway, four sports cars were parked in front of the garage and by the entrance. I pulled up behind a Porsche and hopped out. Blaring music drifted from the house. Some lifestyle journalists had described Luther's monstrosity of a home, with its grand gardens, huge glazed windows, and gilded regal furnishings throughout the interior as old-fashioned elegance. But to me? It looked more like a cat had thrown up in a French parlor. I was glad I no longer lived there.

I rang the big gold doorbell. No one came.

I tried again. And again.

After the fourth ring, muffled laughter from inside the house drew closer. Zoe opened the door. With long wet blonde hair cascading forward over her shoulder, a silky pink robe wrapped around her boney body, and a glass of white wine in hand, she staggered on her feet. The stench of wine on her breath nearly knocked me backward.

"Shit." Her face blanched for two seconds, then she pasted on a bright smile. "Hey, Ava. You're early."

Zoe had been Josh's nanny for the three years since our divorce. She'd just turned twenty-two, had nearly finished her business management degree, and was way more than the live-in nanny. Josh had told me he'd seen Luther and Zoe *cuddling* on more than one occasion. I was convinced Zoe was doing everything possible to get Luther to give her a job in his family's film corporation.

I'd never been dazzled by Luther's parents, the famous people he knew, or the Hollywood circles he worked in. I was fucking Shania Twain . . . he didn't impress me much. I'd warned Zoe to be careful. Luther would promise everything and deliver nothing but heartache.

I prayed she woke up and left him before he broke her like he'd done to me.

Maybe he already had—she was drunk off her rocker.

I jutted my chin toward her drink. "You having a party?"

"No. Don't be silly." She swiped her hand through the air. "Some of the girls are over. We were just having a drink in the spa."

I arched my eyebrow. "One drink?"

"Maybe a few." She giggled.

"You're supposed to be looking after Josh. You can't be drunk when he's in your care." I'd be noting this in my diary of evidence to use against Luther in court. But I couldn't blame Zoe for wanting a drink. Living with Luther would push anyone to their limit. I'd been there, done that, paid the price.

"Isla's here. She's not drinking." She swept her wet hair back over her shoulder, then grabbed onto the door as she swayed. "Josh is fine. He's been watching TV. Come in. I'll get him for you."

"Zoe . . ." I sucked in a deep breath and stood my ground. Thanks to my ex's insanity, I legally couldn't enter his house. No issue there—I never wanted to put a foot inside the place ever again. "I'll wait here."

"Shit." She smacked her palm against her forehead. "God. I'm so stupid. I'm so sorry. Luther and his fucking rules."

Yep . . . "Trouble in paradise?"

She sighed, then took a big sip of her wine. "No . . . yes . . . it's just Luther's always working. I haven't had any time off in weeks. But it's nothing you need to worry about."

I wouldn't. I only cared about my son. "How's Josh been?"

She rested her head against the door. "He's such an angel. He's been counting down the days to see you."

My chest swelled. *Me too.*

Zoe loved Josh. I could never get mad at her. I just hated that she spent more time with my son than me.

Footsteps clambered down the wooden staircase, then raced across the tiles.

"Mommy." Josh charged past Zoe. He dropped his backpack at my feet and flung his arms around my waist. I hugged him so tight. Tears pricked my eyes. "Hi, baby." I kissed the top of his head. "I missed you."

"I missed you too." He squeezed me so hard, I struggled to breathe.

"You okay?" I smoothed my hand over his soft, dark hair.

"No." He spoke into my vest. "I want to get out of here."

"Okay. Let's grab your things, then we can head home. How's that sound?"

"The best."

I picked up Josh's bag and slung it over my shoulder. "Thanks, Zoe. Will you be right to get Josh from school tomorrow?"

"Yes. Always."

"Okay." Sadness flooded my chest. I wished it was me doing school runs every day, not her. "I'll see you in two weeks."

"I'll be here." She swayed with the door. "Hey? How's your new assignment? It's some rock star, isn't it?"

"Excuse me?" I never talked to Luther about my assignments. I hadn't told Josh who I was working for. No photos of Cole and me out running had hit the Internet. Or was she phishing for information to hand to Luther?

"Who is it?" Curiosity simmered through her intoxicated tone. "Is it a guy? Anyone famous and super-hot?"

Guy—yes. Famous—yeah. Hot—very. It wasn't confidential who I was working for, but I protected my clients as much as possible. "Sorry. I can't give out that information."

"It's got to be a good-looking guy. You'd spill otherwise. I bet you don't mind being in a crowd, crushed up against someone with a smoking-hot body. There must be a perk in the job."

"It's not fun in those situations, trust me." But Cole's body was smoking hot. That wasn't a lie.

Zoe laughed and waved her glass at me. "No matter what shit Luther says about you, I like you, Ava. Just watch your back, okay?"

"Thanks. I always do." What did she mean by *watch my back?* I always did. "It's my job to keep an eye on every angle."

Josh tugged on my hand. "Mommy, let's go."

"Okay. Okay." I waved at Zoe. "Bye."

I jumped in my Range Rover with Josh and headed off. As we drove home, Josh spoke at one hundred miles an hour, filling me in on every minute detail about school, his friends, and the homework he had to do.

"What about soccer?" I asked, peering at him in the rearview mirror before turning onto Santa Monica Boulevard. "How was your game on Saturday?"

"Ergh," he groaned, thudding his head against the safety seat. "I was late. Coach wasn't happy."

"Why were you late?"

"Dad had friends over again. Mostly girls. The party was really loud. He locked me in my room, so I stayed out of the way."

"He *what?*" My mind spun. What was Luther doing?

"He bruised my arm too." A chill ran down my spine as Josh lifted the sleeve of his T-shirt. He twisted his arm to one side. "See here?"

At the next red traffic light, I swiveled in my seat to take a closer look. Yellow marks in the shape of fingers discolored his inner bicep.

What the . . . ? "He hurt you?" Nausea flooded my gut.

"No. Not really." Josh shrugged.

That was the first mark I'd seen on Josh. Luther wasn't violent, but I'd have to photograph that for the court.

Josh lowered his sleeve. "Dad had a bad headache in the morning, so Zoe had to take me to the game. She wasn't happy about it."

I faced forward and tightened my hands around the steering wheel. Luther was supposed to take Josh to soccer, not Zoe. If he couldn't take Josh, he was supposed to call me. *Prick.* I'd be having words with Luther about both things later. The parties seemed to happen every weekend. If Luther wanted to hold wild get-togethers and socialize with his posse of friends, I was more than happy to take care of Josh. I'd switch into my new role at work quicker than Luther could blink. Josh's well-being and safety were my main concerns. I lightened my tone as we headed along the road. "I'm so sorry, J-bear. Your dad likes his parties. But how was the game?" I kept glancing in the rearview mirror to check on Josh.

His handsome face lit up. "I scored a goal."

"You did? Awesome. High five." I reached back with one hand, and he slapped his palm against mine. "You're a super star."

"You should've seen it, Mom." He animated every word with his hands. "I ran so fast. So fast. And then I kicked the ball, and it went in."

"Woohoo. That's amazing. I'm super proud of you."

"It was so cool. I was the only one who scored a point." Josh loved soccer. His favorite team was LA Galaxy. Luther had promised to take him to a game, but never had. Probably never would. I'd tried to get tickets several times to take Josh myself, but games had always conflicted with my roster. Once I started my new role, I'd be able to take him.

"I'm hungry." Josh flopped his head back against the seat. "Can you make chicken pasta tonight? It's my favorite."

"It's already cooked." I'd done the shopping and baking late last night, ready for Josh's stay. I loved cooking with him, but tonight, I just wanted *us* time. He was worth it.

"You're the best mom in the whole wide world." His face shone with a heartfelt smile, filling my chest with warm flutters. In a few months the court had to agree with him, right?

I was a good mom.

There was nothing I wouldn't do for my son.

I splayed one hand across my chest. My boy was perfect in every way. "Oh, that's so sweet. You're the best too. You and me, we're a team. Always remember that."

"I know, Mom."

Over dinner, we talked and talked. Every time Josh mentioned Luther, my heart ached. Luther came home late from the studios and headed straight into his office to do more work or had clients over to entertain. Zoe either studied or had friends around, often leaving Josh alone by himself. She'd help him with his writing, spelling, and reading, but never played with him. Meals were often home delivery. Josh wasn't in any danger, nor mistreated. He was just lonely and unhappy. I hated that we couldn't be together more often. Not yet anyway. I had to believe when I had my time in court, justice would be served. I'd done everything required— now I wanted more custody.

After snuggling on the sofa and watching *How to Train Your Dragon* for the fifth time, it was time for bed. Before I tucked him under his blankets, I gave him a big hug, breathing in the scent of his apple-scented skin and savoring his warmth. I treasured every hour, every minute, every second I spent with him. Having him here was the best.

"I love you, Mommy," he whispered against my neck.

Tears welled in my eyes. "I love you too. To the moon and back. Now hop in." He plonked down onto the bed. I drew the quilt over his shoulders and snuggled him. "Night. Have a beautiful sleep. I'll see you in the morning." I kissed the top of his head, switched off his light and headed to my room. After climbing into bed, I read on my Kindle for half an hour, and was about to turn out my light when my cell phone buzzed.

I grabbed it off my nightstand. My heart skipped a beat when Cole's name lit the screen. Why was he texting? Had some schedule or rehearsal time changed? But those details would come via April or Blake, not from Cole.

I swiped open the message:

> COLE: HEY. CHAR'S BETTER. NO MORE TEMPS. FINALLY

Ooooh. That was sweet. He was giving me an update. I'd been worried about her.

> ME: YOU SURVIVED. WELL DONE.
> COLE: BARELY. VOMIT WENT EVERYWHERE.
> ME: THE JOYS OF PARENTING.
> COLE: THANKS FOR NOT HELPING.
> ME: YOU HAVE A LOT TO LEARN. TODAY WAS ANOTHER

LESSON.

COLE: DO YOU LIKE WATCHING ME SUFFER?

I giggled. But no, I didn't.

ME: NO. YOU'RE GOOD WITH HER. DON'T BE SO HARD ON
YOURSELF.

COLE: TODAY WASN'T FUN.

ME: NOT EVERY DAY IS.

COLE: SO I'VE GATHERED. GOING TO BED. HAVE A GOOD
NIGHT.

I bit my lip as warmth touched my cheeks. Him in bed would
be a sight to see. No . . . don't go there.

ME: YOU TOO. SEE YOU TOMORROW. AT 2:30.

COLE: DON'T BE EARLY.

ME: YOU KNOW I WILL BE. XOXO

COLE: :-)

Oh shit! I sat upright and stared at my screen. I hadn't meant
to send hugs and kisses. *Fuck!* I always sent them to Josh. *Damn
it.* Cole wouldn't read anything into it, would he? *No. No . . . of
course not.* Most of the time we were at each other's throats. It'd
be okay . . . yep . . . absolutely fine.

Ergh! I flopped down onto my pillow. It was late. It'd been a
long day. Tomorrow would be even longer.

The best thing about the new day was I'd get to wake up and
see Josh. Those were the days I lived for.

If I could survive the next three and a half months with
Cole Tanner, and Luther's heartbreaking games, I could survive
anything.

Chapter 11

COLE

In half an hour, everyone was coming over for an early lunch and to meet Charlotte before rehearsal. This morning, Charlotte had run around the house like nothing was wrong. It was like she'd never been sick. Ava had been right. I'd survived looking after her. Charlotte's clothes, my sofa, and the floor rug had been the only casualties. I'd sent Ava an update on Charlotte last night since she'd been worried about my kid, even though she'd stood back. I hadn't expected a response, but the few messages we'd sent each other and scoring texted hugs and kisses from her had taken me by surprise. Had the ice queen melted toward me a fraction? *Nah . . . well, maybe a little.* She hadn't pummeled me to the ground yesterday, so that had been a win.

But Charlotte had slayed me. Yesterday, I'd never felt so helpless, scared, and willing to sell my soul to do anything and everything possible to make her feel better. What was with that?

She certainly was a fire-cracking, roller-coasting tornado that had swept into my life. Up until now, the idea of having a kid had been surreal, like I'd been stuck in one of my horrific nightmares. But yesterday, having to drop everything and come home to look after her had slapped me with reality.

April's press statement would cement it further.

With coffee in one hand and a dull ache throbbing in the back of my head, I sat in my office and reread her email. My fingers trembled as I scrolled over the touch pad. Once this announcement was posted, the news I had a kid would break across the Internet by the end of the day.

Fuck! Was I ready for this? The onslaught of media questions. More paparazzi outside my home. Everyone wanting to get a photo of Charlotte. *Nope.* But there was nowhere to run. Nowhere to hide. No one to blame for this mess but me. *Own it, dick!*

I sucked in a deep breath, held it, and replied to April's email with *"approved"* in the subject line. I closed my eyes and hit send. There was no going back.

That was one item off my long to-do list—onto another.

Introducing Charlotte to my friends was the next confronting task. The guys had been itching to meet her, but our schedules hadn't given us the chance.

They'd be here by eleven. Flint meeting Charlotte still worried me. He'd been beyond supportive, but fuck . . . Charlotte was his ex-girlfriend's kid. Meeting her would be hard. Maybe it was just me being weirded out.

I closed my laptop, then headed out to the kitchen. Mackenzie had ordered a ton of pastas, salads, and Italian dishes from my favorite restaurant. As I inhaled the aroma of garlic bread and dishes warming in the oven, my stomach grumbled, and my mouth watered. I needed the huge carb intake to burn off at rehearsal this afternoon.

Mackenzie had set the dining table and stocked the fridge with beer and wine just before she'd left. I didn't know how I'd survive without her. She'd be a great nanny but had bowed out of the running before I'd even had the chance to ask her. Mackenzie was married and had two young children and seemed to love working for me and the guys while her kids were at kindergarten. For nearly two years, she'd cleaned our houses, shopped, and run errands for us, and organized the catering for spontaneous get-togethers like today. She didn't want to work full-time or travel. This life, where the hours were irregular and every day was different, wasn't for everyone. I needed someone like her but who could look after Charlotte twenty-four/seven.

Did a nanny like that even exist?

I'd never been good at asking for help. I'd never needed it. How was I going to find someone suitable to take care of my kid?

I had plenty of time. Nope . . . No, I didn't. My calendar was full, from sunup to beyond sundown. I had to find someone. But when? How? *Ergh!*

I'd deal with it later, not today. To distract myself and to fight off my hunger, I grabbed the packet of breadsticks out of the pantry, ripped it open, and stuffed the contents into a jar. As I bit into one, Charlotte came scooting down the stairs with Barney tucked under her arm. She hadn't let go of that teddy bear since I'd given it to her. I must've done something right. Hannah had dressed her in pale yellow jeans and a navy top with butterflies on the front. She reached the bottom step and rushed across the living room to me. My chest swelled and my heart skipped to a faster beat. How could it not?

She crashed into my legs and raised her arms. "Up."

"Hey, munchkin." I scooped her off her feet and placed her on my hip. "You ready to meet some new friends?"

"Yeah." Her big green eyes twinkled as she rubbed her hand down my face. "You're hairy."

"I don't shave every day." A three-day growth was my normal.

"It's funny." She wrinkled her cute nose. "All soft and tickly."

"Is it okay if I keep it?"

"Yep." She pointed to the breadsticks. "Can I have one?"

I tickled her tummy. "Manners?"

She giggled and grabbed my hands. "Please."

"Sure." I pulled one out of the jar and handed it to her. She bit into it and crumbs fell onto her shirt, across the kitchen counter, and onto the floor. I shook my head. The mess this kid caused did my head in. In the six days she'd been in my house, she'd destroyed a rug, half my sofa, broken a plate, spilled ketchup all over the table, and left a trail of destruction wherever she went.

I liked things neat and tidy and spotless. *Note: nanny will need to be a diligent cleaner.*

The doorbell chimed, then it swung open. Lewis and Tia came in. Lewis carried a plush rainbow-colored llama under his arm and Tia hobbled inside on her crutches. She had just over two more weeks in her moonboot, recovering from her ankle surgery. I hope this fixed her injury. It broke my heart she couldn't do acting and stunt work anymore, but she'd moved on and seemed to have found her new calling working in our sound and lighting team. I loved my sister. It was great to have her home, and even better that we got to hang out again. For the first time in as long as I could remember, she looked truly happy. Lewis had been a big part of that.

That was all I ever wanted. I wanted people to be happy. To have fun.

But sometimes the best of intentions backfired. Some still haunted me. Some still lurked deep in my heart. As long as no one else got hurt, I'd be fine.

Tia and Lewis crossed into the living room, and aimed for the sofa.

I hoisted Charlotte up higher on my hip. "Auntie Tia and Uncle Lewis are here. Come say hello."

She nodded as she gnawed on her breadstick. Dribble and chucks of slobbered on breadstick covered her mouth.

Ergh! Just ignore it.

I walked over to the sofa, sat adjacent to Lewis, and placed Charlotte on the cushion between us. "Charlotte, this is Lewis. He plays the bass in our band. That's not as cool as the drums but still wicked."

"Hi, Charlotte. Welcome to the family. This is for you." He held out the llama.

"Fank you." She clutched it in her arm next to Barney.

He stroked her bouncy blonde curls. "I love your hair. It's as long as mine only curly."

Charlotte crawled over to him and patted his head. I pursed my lips, trying not to laugh at the gluggy crumbs that had been stuck to her hand and were now in Lewis's hair.

"I like yours too." Charlotte tilted her head to the side. "What's a bass?"

Undeterred by—or unaware of—the gunk in his hair, he tapped the center of her chest. "It's a very cool guitar."

"Ooooh." Her little mouth gaped as she nodded.

"Hello, Charlotte. How are you today?" Tia leaned over and waved.

"I'm good, fank you."

The door opened and in strolled Flint, Sutton, and Slip.

"Hey." Slip struggled to carry a huge brown teddy bear that was almost as big as he was. "We're here, so let's get this party started."

Charlotte's eyes widened at the sight of the bear. She crawled back to me and clutched my arm. I hoped Barney didn't have a size complex.

Slip sat on the ottoman in front of Charlotte and spoke in the softest tone I'd ever heard come out of his mouth. "Hi. I'm Slip. And this big guy is Cuddles." He pointed to the bear beside him. "He needs a home. Would you like to look after him?"

Charlotte clutched Barney and her llama against her chest and shook her head. Tears welled in her eyes as if she were terrified.

"Hey. It's okay." I rubbed her arm. "Don't worry about Cuddles. I'll look after him for now."

"Fuck." Slip ruffled his hands through his long hair. "Sorry. I thought the bear was cool."

"Maybe if you're a giant." Sutton clipped the back of his head. "I told you it was too big." She sat down next to Slip and gave Charlotte a gift bag of goodies—some clothes, a hairbrush, glittery hair clips and a doll. They were much better received.

Then I turned to Flint. He'd been standing back, hovering behind Sutton.

My stomach sank through the floor. Charlotte crawled onto my lap and turned to face him. She pointed. "Fhint."

What? My breath shot from my lungs. How did she know who he was? "Yes. That's Flint."

"Whoa." His eyes glazed over as he drifted toward us and sank onto the seat beside me. "She's a mini you. Hi, Charlotte. How do you know my name?"

"Mommy showed me pictures. And videos. You sing and play moo-sic." But she looked at me and my friends. "Where's one more?"

My breath hitched hard. My heart jolted against my ribs. "You mean Phil?"

"Yeah." She fidgeted with her toys.

Whoa! Shelby had told her about us! *Fuck.* "Um. Phil is with your mommy in Heaven. Lewis is with us now."

"Ooooh." Sadness swallowed the sparkle in her eyes as she fidgeted with the ear on her teddy bear. "Did he die too?"

"Yeah." I smoothed my hand down her hair and gave her a cuddle. "So we have to take care of each other. Is that okay?"

"I fink so." Worry quivered in her soft voice. Then she lifted her chin and sat three inches taller. "Where's Ava?"

"She'll be here later when I have to go to work."

"She's mean but pretty."

I chuckled. She was spot on. "Yes, but if you don't eat markers again, she won't have to get mad at you."

Charlotte pouted and looked up at me with big puppy-dog eyes. "I like coloring. You do some with me?"

"Ma can this afternoon. I have to go to rehearsal."

"What about tomorrow?"

I rubbed my hand down one side of my face, then the other. My schedule was overflowing. I had back-to-back rehearsals for the next few days and functions to attend. Once the tour started, I'd have even less free time. I only had an hour or two free in the morning, and that was filled with working out and breakfast. I barely had time to shower before I was out the door. "We'll do something together soon. Promise."

But that was a promise I wasn't sure I could keep.

"Hey?" Sutton stood and held out her hand to Charlotte. "Would you like to come help get lunch ready? Whatever is in the oven smells delicious."

"Yeah." Charlotte slid off my lap, took Sutton's hand, and skipped over to the kitchen. "I'm hungry."

Slip shot after them, depositing the big bear by the bar on his way. "I'll help."

"We'll come too." Lewis stood, and helped Tia to her feet, then they joined the others at the kitchen island.

I slumped back on the sofa, half-turned to Flint and dialed down my volume. "That went better than planned."

Concern flooded Flint's eyes as he tracked Charlotte's every move. "She doesn't look sick."

"Nope. She had mad fevers until about nine last night, then slept through to six this morning. She woke up like nothing had happened."

He nodded, then lowered his chin. Anguish swam through his voice. "Are you okay?"

I managed an awkward nod. "I think so. You?"

He puffed air through his nose. "How did you expect me to react? You have Shelby's kid. You have something I'd always wanted to have with her one day."

"Fuck." My heart tore in two. "I'm so sorry."

"Bah!" He burst out laughing. He picked up a cushion and smacked me with it. "I'm fucking with you, man. Get it through that thick head of yours. I'm not messed up by this."

I grabbed the cushion and beat him over the head with it. "You fucker. I've been worried sick."

"I know. Gotcha good though, didn't I?"

We always took the piss out of each other, but damn, I'd nearly had heart failure. I'd caused enough pain to last a lifetime—I didn't want to cause anymore. I rubbed my chest. "You sure did. Fuck. I almost died."

"Seriously, Cole." He chuckled, holding up his hands. Humor glistened in his ice-blue eyes as he flicked his long black hair off his face. "Stop stressing. Shelby will always be special to me. She was my first. But she left and we moved on. I am so fucking in love with Sutton now, more than I ever was with Shelby and Lena combined. You having Shelby's daughter will never be a deal-breaker. If anything, it's a fucking awesome way to remember someone we cared for."

Tears welled in my eyes. Guessed I was the only one still trying to find peace with what had happened. Still trying to slot Charlotte into my life. I was far from okay. But every day was a step in the right direction. "Are you sure?"

"Yes." He glanced over to Charlotte, sitting on the stool eating another breadstick. "How could you not love that kid? She's fucking adorable."

"Don't be deceived by her cuteness."

But then his tone turned serious again. "So . . . Shelby must have told her about us. Why? If she had no intention of telling you Charlotte existed."

"Fuck, man. I don't know. I can only speculate. Maybe she told Charlotte stories about her high school friends, and that you were her old boyfriend, along with a gazillion other stories you tell your kid about growing up . . . or maybe she did it in case something happened, so that we wouldn't be complete strangers. It sucks we'll never know the real reason."

"Yeah." Flint slapped his hand against my knee and gave it a gentle nudge. "Are you positive you're alright?"

I rested my head back on the sofa and stared up at the high ceiling. A dull ache loomed in the back of my skull. "My head hasn't stopped spiraling. I don't know what the fuck I'm doing."

"Cole." He swiveled toward me, placed his elbow on the back of the sofa, and rested his head in his hand. His gaze drilled into me, pinning to the spot. "It's okay to let down that guard of yours. It's okay to love your daughter. It's what you're supposed to do. Love her no matter what. When my parents wouldn't talk to me after Phil died, it broke me." The painful memory, and the concern radiating off him, slammed into my chest. I'd seen him hit rock bottom; it had taken everything Slip and I'd had to save him. "Don't ever do anything like that to Charlotte. I know you better than anyone—even Tia. You're trying to be cool, calm, and collected and pretend you've got everything under control. But you haven't. Not yet. And that's okay. It's only been several days. Give it time."

"I don't have time. Our schedule is overflowing."

He shook his head. "It's not just about hours in the day. It's about letting someone new in. You've avoided letting anyone else get close to you since Priah left. I get that. But now you've got no other choice. You have to love Charlotte. She's your daughter. You're all she's got."

I held onto the chains around my heart. How could I let go when there was no certainty? "It's so fucking hard to do that. This isn't a permanent thing yet." I didn't want to feel. I didn't want things to change. I didn't know how to take care of a kid.

"Then do everything humanly possible to ensure it becomes permanent. She's turned your world upside down. Mine did, too, when I lost my brother. You and Slip were there for me. Now, we're here for you. Don't risk losing her. Don't try and do everything yourself. I don't want to see you go down a path of self-destruction like I did. Let's not go through that shit again."

"I'm not that fucked up." Maybe I was worse.

"Thanks for that." He half-grinned and thumped me in the arm. "But like you did for me after losing Phil, I'm giving you an ultimatum."

My blood pressure spiked. "What? Why?" I wasn't bordering on being a raging alcoholic in need of rehab, was I? *Nope.* "I don't need an ultimatum."

"Yes, you do." He jabbed his index finger into my bicep. "Get your shit together and be the dad that kid needs. Step one—ask for help."

The mild ache in my head turned into a hard throb behind my eyes. "How can I do that when all I've done is lie and hurt the people I've loved?"

"The people who truly love you will stand by you through everything. Especially me."

I slumped deeper into the sofa, overwhelmed by how much he cared. "I just don't know where to start. I need help with *everything.*"

"Break it down. What's the biggest thing you need right now?"

"A full-time nanny before we go overseas." I could ask Min. Her friend Isla knew a nanny. Her network of contacts might lead to finding someone. But if they were anything like Min, that wouldn't be good. I'd end up with them in my bed. That's not what I wanted. I needed a nanny I wouldn't be tempted by.

"Well done." Flint slapped me on the shoulder. "You asked for help. Was it that bad?"

I sneered at him. "No."

"We've made progress." He waved toward our friends in the kitchen. "We'll ask these guys if they know someone. If they don't have anyone in mind, we'll start widening the circle. We know a lot of people. We'll find someone that will put up with your crazy ass and your kid."

"Okay. Let's do this."

Flint and I eased to our feet and joined the others in the kitchen. Sutton was pulling out the pasta dishes from the oven and placing them on the table. Slip was cutting the garlic bread and piling the slices into a breadbasket I didn't even know I owned. Lewis had poured the girls glasses of wine.

"Hey, everyone?" Flint grabbed a few beers out of the fridge and handed them out. "Cole needs a nanny for Charlotte. Anyone got any ideas?"

As I took a sip of my drink, warmth meandered through my chest. The only way to survive being a single dad was with help from my friends. I needed them—now more than ever.

I eased in beside Charlotte at the kitchen island and kissed her head. Something about her seeped through the cracks in my heart. I kept trying to resist it but couldn't. She sat on the stool, sang *"la, la, la"* along to the music playing through the speakers and drummed two breadsticks against the counter. *Yep.* She was mine. No question about it.

Lewis downed a mouthful of his beer, then clicked his fingers and pointed at me. "Actually, I might know someone. It's a long shot, but my brother wants to move to Cali. Lee's a school accountant but his partner, Mateo, is an elementary teacher. I'm not sure if being a nanny is something he or they'd be interested in, but I'll ask."

"Please do." I nodded. "That'd be cool."

"What about our cousin Harper?" Tia leaned against the

counter, tossing a salad in a big bowl.

Shit. Why didn't I think of her? "Isn't she in Nepal?"

Harper would be ideal. She taught English to Nepalese kids and loved traveling, painting, reading and watching old Hollywood films. I wasn't sure the offer to work for me would be enough to entice her home.

Tia picked out a cherry tomato from the salad, tossed it in the air, and caught it in her mouth. "Yep. Harper's in Kathmandu. She'd be fun to have on the tour."

"It's not just for the tour." I winced. "It's ongoing. Forever. Until Charlotte's like . . . eighteen." Anxiety hovered through my every word. *Fuck . . .* that was a long time.

Tia just giggled. "There's no harm in asking. Email her. That's the best way to track her down." She slinked sideways and nudged her hip against Slip's. "You'd like Harper around again, wouldn't you?"

He shook his head as he munched on a slice of garlic bread. "Um. No. I'm with Maddy."

A wary smile quivered across Sutton's lips, but it was gone within the blink of an eye. She pinched her eyebrows together. "Slip, did you used to date Harper?"

"Date? No." He licked breadcrumbs from his fingertips. "We just slept together."

I jumped in. "Slip was the first to break our dibs rule. He lost his virginity to Harper in senior year. He thought he was king shit because she was in college." She was three years older than us and quirky, and fun, but we hadn't seen her for almost two years. Not since Phil's funeral.

"I was the shit." Slip grinned from ear to ear. "We fooled around for a couple months. She wanted more. I never did. But she was a hot fuck. She has this tongue ring, and when she sucked on my—"

"Slip." I glared at him and covered Charlotte's ears. "We can't talk about sex in front of my kid. She's too young."

Lewis chuckled and slapped me on the back. "Oh, she'll learn a lot by hanging around us."

"That's what worries me." Was I destined to ruin her life too?

My kid had no hope. But my concern drifted to Slip. "So do you have any issues if I contact Harper and ask her to work for me? Any problems if she comes back?"

Slip shrugged a shoulder. "Nope. None."

Thank fuck for that.

Slip swiped the garlic bread off the counter and headed over to the table. "Let's eat. I'm starving."

"Time for lunch, kiddo." I picked Charlotte up and carried her over to her booster seat at the head of the table.

After Flint and I took the chairs adjacent to Charlotte, and everyone else found a seat, we dug into the dishes of food. Plates were loaded with pastas and salads. I filled a bowl with spaghetti bolognese for Charlotte and placed it in front of her. She, of course, ate it with her hands.

Flint held his beer toward me and jerked his head toward the others. "See?" he said over everyone's chatter and laughter. "Asking for help wasn't so painful. Was it?"

We chinked our bottles together, and I sighed. "No. I guess not."

"You got this. Everything will be fine."

"It will be once I know Charlotte's taken care of. I promise she won't be a problem." I had Hannah to take care of her for now. I'd find someone else before we headed overseas. "I assure you, I'm not going to miss one more rehearsal, or a show, or skip any of our appearances and parties or the events we have planned."

Flint dug into his carbonara. "Cole, I know you're as committed to the tour as the rest of us, but you're going to have to make some adjustments. You can't ignore Charlotte."

There was no way I could do that as she stuffed a handful of spaghetti into her mouth, dripping sauce everywhere. I grabbed a napkin and wiped her chin. *What a mess!*

Flint waved his fork at me. "You're going to have to come home earlier than normal, take the random afternoon off, start later, miss an after-party."

Miss a party? Never. Charlotte had to fit into my life, not change it. I'd do everything for her, but I wasn't going to stop doing what I loved. "We've worked too damn hard for this tour. I'm not going to miss one second of it. I'm not giving up anything and definitely not giving up hooking up with different chicks all the time."

He threw me a smug smile. "You'll change when you meet the right girl."

"I'm not in a hurry to do that."

"Maybe you've already met her." He tickled Charlotte on the tummy. She giggled and threw me a big smile, her mouth covered in sauce. She wasn't making it easy on me. Nor was Flint. "You hated your parents not being around. So, don't be a dick, and make sure you spend time with her."

"I do. I see her for an hour or two each morning. It's the only free time I have." That was more time than my parents had spent with me each day during my childhood years.

But was it enough?

Ergh! This was doing my head in.

I needed another drink, more food, and a hell session on the drums to hammer out the knots in my system.

Flint was wrong.

I could look after Charlotte and keep my current workload and schedule. Nothing had to give. I could go out. Party. Be with women. Come home to my kid. *Easy.*

Charlotte would be fine.

So would I.

Tomorrow night we had a function to attend. *Perfect!*

I needed a night out.

I needed to get laid.

I needed a stiff drink.

I had everything under control.

Chapter 12

AVA

For four nights in a row, Cole and the band went out after rehearsing—to a movie premiere, to a charity dinner, to a club and a bar just to party and be seen.

The guys didn't stop.

I didn't know whether to be in awe of their stamina or worried that they'd collapse with fatigue. These guys seemed to burn the candle at both ends harder than my other clients in the past.

By the end of three days straight, I was grateful for a night off, rotating my shift with my fellow team member, Kennedy.

But after a day's rest, I was back on duty.

On Monday, as the band ran through their tour set list, I stood at the side of the stage. Cole pounded on the drums, and for a few minutes, I stopped counting down the days until I saw Josh again. Every strike Cole made flowed with smooth style and gallant grace. Every thudding beat hit the center of my chest. The other guys were under his complete control, conforming to his rhythm and pace. As his body dripped with sweat and every sinewy muscle and vein bulged in his arms, his focus didn't falter . . . except maybe for a split second when he stole a glance at me. He winked and the space between my thighs clenched. *Fuck.* That wasn't good.

Beckett stepped in beside me, holding out his packet of peanut M&M's, his favorite afternoon break snack. "So . . . Cole, huh?"

My breath snagged against my ribs. As I took a green M&M—one wouldn't hurt while on duty—I drew my shoulders back, not breaking my poker face. "What about him?"

"Come on, Ava." He tipped the last five M&Ms into his hand, picking out the sole green one for me. "We've worked together for two years on gig after gig. He's the first guy who's had you flustered."

"I'm not flustered." I popped the candy into my mouth, then crunched on the chocolate-coated nut.

"You so are." He tucked the empty packet into his jacket pocket. "Your cheeks are flushed. You keep fidgeting with your hair. You can't take your eyes off him." He stuffed the M&Ms into his mouth, smiled brightly, and munched away.

Beckett was wrong. I wasn't into Cole. I wanted to murder him most of the time. He was easy on the eye and not as arrogant and cocky as I'd first thought. Without a doubt, he was emotionally messed up, like most people were, and he had a lot to learn about how to take care of Charlotte. But why my pulse jumped a fraction every time he looked at me did my head in. It was wrong and stupid, and had to stop. "He's just . . . nice to watch."

"Maybe. But you're my best friend. I'm looking out for you. Please don't do anything foolish."

"He's my client. I know the rules." Wells would kick anyone off this assignment in a heartbeat if we got involved with a client. Personal involvement clouded judgment, was a distraction, and put the team at risk. I'd never do that.

Beckett cocked his eyebrow and gave me a sly sideways glance. "What if he wasn't your client?"

I sucked in a deep breath and tucked my hands into my back pockets. Cole pounded out another beat. Something drew me to him; there was a fine line between wanting to slap sense some into him and tearing his clothes off. If he wasn't my client . . . I'd fuck him in a heartbeat. *Crap.* I couldn't go there. "He *is* my client, so there is nothing to discuss."

"You'd fuck him." Beckett chuckled. "You can play hardball with me all you like, but you have this energy around him that is hard to miss."

Panic skipped through my veins. Too much was at stake to consider anything but a professional relationship with Cole. "He's just like my ex, full of smooth talk and suave attitude. I won't jeopardize my job or compromise my team over some good-looking rock star. Getting Josh back is my priority." I needed a clean report from Wells for the court. I wasn't going to tarnish my chances in anyway.

"I know." Concern softened Beckett's tone as we tracked three road crew members realigning a speaker. Nothing seemed out of the ordinary. "But do you want to swap guys? I'll take Cole. You take Slip."

Maybe I should, but if I did, would that be an admission I was attracted to Cole? I couldn't have that. I was strong—everything would be fine. "No. There's no vibe to worry about—not a good one anyway. We don't exactly get along. I promise I'll let you know if anything changes. But I've got this. I can keep my pants on."

Cole tossed a stick into the air, caught it, then pointed it at me before slamming out another song. *Shit!* My clothes may have stayed on, but *fuck,* that didn't stop my panties from getting wet.

A small groove formed in Beckett's brow. "It's been a while since anyone has been in your trousers."

"Yeah, well. My last hookup was a turn-off." I'd only been on a few dates since my divorce. Every one had just been for the soul intention of getting laid. I wasn't sure I ever wanted a relationship again. I couldn't even contemplate the notion until the mess with Luther was behind me.

"Was that the guy with the crooked red dick?"

I pursed my lips to stifle my giggle. That was a memory I wished I could erase. "Yes. But I'm not interested in seeing anyone. Not until I get Josh. Even then it may not happen. I just want to spend time with my son."

He dipped his chin. "I know. I've got your back always. No matter what."

"Thanks, Becks."

The guys finished their session. As they wiped the sweat from their bodies on towels and had their meeting with the production team, Beckett and I joined our team on the floor.

April paced in front of the row of chairs with her cell phone to her ear. Four weeks out from the tour, permanent stress lines had etched into her face.

"So you can't accommodate us? Is that what you're saying?" She'd been on her cell phone most of the day, trying to find an alternative hotel in Portland that suited our needs and requirements. Falcon, the tour manager, had been onto his team as well. The place they'd booked had been gutted by a fire and had to be closed.

She hung up and tapped her cell phone against her forehead. "Fucking. Useless. Imbeciles." She spun to Blake. "Portland is a problem. No one can fit us in at such short notice. I can't have everyone staying in different locations. We might be staying on the buses for two nights."

"The guys won't like that." Blake groaned. His Texan drawl seemed to drone more than usual. "Neither will I."

"I'll find somewhere." She spun on her high heels. "Just give me another day or two."

Her stress levels worried me. Maybe I could help alleviate them. I'd managed large, last-minute team lodgings before. "Excuse me, April." I stepped over to her. "You need somewhere in Portland?"

"Yes." Exasperation burned in the tone. "Can you perform a miracle?"

"Maybe. It might not be five-star accommodation but it's secure." I scanned my cell phone for my contact. "If it's a viable option, I can call Kelsey at NorthWest Star Academy. He manages security training facilities. He should be able to get the crew into dorm-style rooms at one of his complexes and the guys and the main entourage into a nearby hotel or the manager lodgings at the grounds."

New life blazed in her blue eyes. "Oh my God, yes! At this stage I don't care if everyone camps in tents—I need a place booked. Falcon and I are beside ourselves trying to find somewhere. This is his job—not mine. Damn holiday season does my head in. We have a backup plan for everywhere, but Portland has fallen through. This would be a godsend."

I held up my phone. "Well, shall we call Kelsey?"

"Yes. If you pull this off, you are my bestie for life."

"I'm just happy to help."

With Falcon in tow, we headed over to the end of the stage and made the call. Twenty minutes later, accommodation was booked for the Portland dates—the crew were allocated to one of the training facilities closest to the venue, and the band and entourage and security team at a Comfort Inn on the outskirts of the city.

April gave me a big hug. "Thank you. You're a life saver."

"You're welcome." I nodded.

We rejoined the group as they were ending their meeting. Wells and my team were getting ready to escort the guys home.

"What was that all about?" Cole asked April as he rested his butt against the stage.

A sparkle had returned to April's eyes. Smiling, she waved her upturned palm up and down at me. "This woman is a savior. She just helped resolve our Portland issue. But it's nothing for you to worry about."

Cole ignored April, drilling me with his gaze. He hooked his towel around his neck and crossed his ankles. "Did you find us somewhere to stay?"

I liked that the band was aware of every element that went into pulling the tour together. Everyone seemed close, a true team, but each member played their part. It was a nice change, and they were more down to earth than some of the other celebrities I'd worked for. "Yes." I tucked my cell phone away in my jacket. "You'll be roughing it in a three-star hotel."

He waggled his sexy eyebrows. "As long as there's a bed and a hot shower, I don't care."

And no doubt room to bring home a girl. "That's about all you'll get in this place."

April pointed at Cole. "I don't want to hear any complaints.

You can thank Ava later."

"Oh, I'd love to." A sultry sexiness slid through his tone.

I sneered, giving him the evil eye.

"Wells, Ava is a true asset." Falcon slapped me on the shoulder. "She's a keeper."

"Oh, we know." Standing by Blake, Wells straightened his spine and folded his arms. "She's my second-in-charge for a reason."

Blake clapped his hands. "Well, I'm glad that's one less thing to worry about. Thank you, Ava."

"You're welcome."

He glanced at his watch, then lifted his chin toward my team. "But today, time is getting away from us. The guys are attending a friend's gig tonight. Let's get everyone home, have a quick turnaround, and we'll meet at Flint's at nine."

I scanned my messages and re-checked the confirmation email from our driver. "We're all set. The van will pick everyone up from there."

"Excellent. It will just be me and the guys." Blake half-hugged April. "This one's taking the night off."

"Yep." April nodded, unashamedly. "I have a date with a hot bubble bath and a bottle of wine. No one is to disturb me." She pointed at each of the guys. "I'm turning my phone off for a few hours. Blake can deal with any issues."

"We won't have any. Will we?" Blake threw a challenging glare at the band. "We have an interview tomorrow morning at ten. Remember that?"

"We do. But Duke's playing." Flint dialed up the party mode in his voice. "It's gonna be a big night."

Bring it!

I looked forward to listening to a different band for a few hours. After watching Cole play earlier, I needed to get my head off a certain drummer. I'd drop him home, head to the office to run over tonight's details, and refresh my comms gear. The battery on my radio was almost flat.

I'd done some hard assignments that had bordered on dangerous, had pushed me physically, and had driven me close to exhaustion. But this wasn't as demanding as those other gigs had been. The guys' schedule was hectic, but it was nothing I couldn't handle. They had their rest days, as did we. Regular medical checks, proper nutrition, and time management were essential to survive a grueling and demanding job.

But Cole seemed to ignore most of the rules.

For the next week, I'd turn up at his place at the designated time either for a run or to take him to his promotional duties or rehearsal. At the end of the day, I'd escort him home, where he'd rack up several shots of vodka, down them, then head out to some party or event.

Most nights he got drunk and brought home some tall, gorgeous supermodel. I doubted he got much sleep. I, at least, rotated my roster with Kennedy. Cole never had any downtime.

He pushed himself hard every day. He demanded the best of himself in every rehearsal, then went out every night.

Was it wrong to worry about him?

I knew what it was like to pretend everything was fine on the outside when on the inside you were about to crack.

Music was one thing, and so was maintaining his public profile, but what grated my nerves was that I hadn't seen him spend any quality time with his daughter.

Every morning when we were about to walk out his door, Charlotte's big green eyes followed him. The longing in her gaze for some love and attention hurt my heart.

I couldn't say anything. *Could I?* It wasn't my place to do so.

But what the fuck was he doing?

Yes, tour was close. Yes, the guys had some big events to attend before we'd hit the road. But would it kill him to spend a day with his daughter?

On Tuesday, following an interview and a full bump-in, bump-out rehearsal for the tour, I had to take Cole to a Halloween party, the second one since the weekend. Just him. The other guys had opted to rest.

At two a.m. in some swanky cocktail bar in Santa Monica, Cole stumbled over to me in his sequined Elton John Dodgers baseball costume with his arm draped around a gorgeous brunette's waistline. Her legs were as tall as palm trees, and she was dressed in shortest French maid's outfit I'd ever seen. The thing was, she rocked it.

"Home time. Let's go," Cole slurred, swaying on his feet.

I nodded, called our driver, and led them out to our car.

At his house, he and his hookup, Lola, staggered through the door. At the bottom of the staircase, she giggled, clutched the railing, and climbed a few stairs. But Cole turned to me. A lazy, sexy, very drunk smile curled across his lips. "Catch you later, Ava. Unless you want to join us."

I narrowed my eyes. I wasn't into sharing. "You wish."

"I have." He took a slow, swaggering step toward me. Lowering his glittery glasses, he pinned me with his gaze. Intensity sparked the air around us, prickling my skin. "All the time lately."

My knees buckled. *He what? No way.* Clearly, he was too drunk to think straight. I drew my shoulders back, sucked in a deep breath, and jabbed my finger against the center of his chest. "Keep dreaming, drummer boy. You couldn't handle me . . . and I'm not interested." I flicked my hand toward Lola, halfway up the stairs. "Go entertain your friend."

"Oh, I will." His vodka-infused breath brushed across my cheek as he leaned in to whisper in my ear, "But I will be thinking about you."

Oh Lord, give me strength. I closed my eyes, breathed him in. *No. Don't.* "Whatever does it for you, Mr. Tanner." I eased back, putting a foot of distance between us. But the charge between us remained. *Crap.* "Good night. I'll see you tomorrow at eleven."

"Don't be early." Grinning, he walked backward to the steps.

"I will be here on time." I nodded, then tilted my head toward the hallway. "I'll do a quick security check and be on my way."

"Knock yourself out." He waved toward the office. "You know where to find me if you need me."

As Cole joined Lola and headed upstairs, I ambled into the office. After closing the door behind me, I leaned back against the cool surface. Confusion and intrigue pounded my brain. Had Cole been joking or was he serious about thinking about me? *Me?* I was no supermodel. I brushed off his flirtatious comments and sexy innuendos as arrogance. The notion of him being into me was simply laughable. It was best to forget what he'd said. I had a job to do. Nothing could ever happen between us, so it was foolish to even play around with the idea.

I checked the security access logs—all good. Only Hannah and Mackenzie had been there today. But as I scanned the emailed report from our surveillance team, I paused at the enclosed videos of someone walking past Cole's driveway. *Shit.* It was that chick with blonde hair again. I skimmed through the attached footage. She'd walked past the gate three times just after Cole and I had left near noon and the paparazzi had dispersed. She hadn't been in exercise gear—just jeans and a hoodie.

This had happened too many times for her to be a random passerby.

I replied to the email; it was time to investigate who she was. Cole's safety was paramount. We didn't want any perimeter breaches, for Cole to be hurt . . . or his kid . . . or Hannah.

As I was about to leave, giggles and laughter drifted downstairs. At least someone was having a good time. But the loneliness in my chest flared. I'd almost forgotten what it was like to have fun in a relationship, short-term or otherwise. My life revolved around work and Josh. I couldn't remember what it felt like to be happy. Loved. Connected. But Cole Tanner was not one to fantasize over. He was nothing but a tempting piece of fruit—one bite would be dangerous. He'd banged more women in the past couple of weeks than I'd had men in the past two years. The only thing we had in common was we both didn't want a relationship.

Beckett was right.

It had been months since I'd been on a date. Maybe I should go on one or two before we traveled so I could make it through the next three months. It would be good for my sanity if nothing else.

I opened the door and headed home. Alone. At least one of us would be getting some sleep.

The following morning, at ten-forty-five sharp, I arrived back on Cole's doorstep. No one answered the doorbell, so I let myself in with my security code.

Hannah was making a cup of tea while Charlotte munched on a piece of toast at the table.

Hannah poured a dash of milk into her mug. "Oh, morning, dear. How are you?"

"Fine." I headed over to the table. I never had trouble sleeping once I hit the bed. This morning I was set to go. "Is Cole ready?"

"I haven't seen him yet."

Ergh. We had a long day of rehearsals ahead. He'd better get his ass into gear.

"Hi Charlotte. How are you, gorgeous?"

"Good. Fank you." She yawned and rested her head back against the chair. Had Cole and his guest kept her awake last night? "You taking Cole to work?"

It was cute that she called him *Cole*, but he was still a stranger to her and hadn't earned any other name like *Daddy*.

"Yes. We go on tour soon." I picked up a piece of dropped crust off the floor and placed it on the table out of reach. "Are you ready to go on a big vacation?"

She shot her peanut butter-covered hands up in the air. "Yeah."

"How about you, Hannah? Are you ready for the endless weeks of bus travel and quick hotel stops?"

"Yes. I can go anywhere with my trusty pillow and a heat pack. I'm looking forward to it." She came over and took a seat at the table. "But can I be honest with you?"

I dipped my chin. "Always."

"I'm worried about Cole, dear." She wasn't the only one. "He runs, then rehearses, then goes out, then brings girls home. He doesn't stop."

I knew—I shadowed him nearly every second of the day. But hey, the guy was young and having fun. "He's enjoying being single."

"Yes. But . . ." Concern threaded through Hannah's tone. "It's something more than that. Don't you see it in his eyes?"

My heart lurched. Old knots in my stomach tightened. I did.

I'd been there. The stressful mix of high-pressure work and looking after a child was never balanced. I'd pushed myself to do everything, but it had never been enough. Not facing my problems had only created more.

"Hannah, I can't get involved. If you have concerns maybe you should talk to his friends or Blake." Cole had medical staff, nutritionists, therapists, and friends at his fingertips. Help was available.

"Yes. I'm sorry." She stirred her cup of tea with a spoon, tapped it against the rim, then placed it on the saucer. "It's not just about his work; it's about Charlotte." The shake in her hand intensified as worry swam through her eyes. "I've kept my mouth shut, trying not to interfere with Cole's life, but maybe it's high time I did."

I liked Hannah. She was a fiery spirit indeed.

"I think he needs that. But right now, I've got to get his ass to rehearsal."

I walked over to the staircase, stood at the bottom, and called out, "Cole? Time to go."

The door to his room flew open. Dressed in dark jeans and a tight black T-shirt, he staggered downstairs. Lola tiptoed behind him wearing nothing but her skimpy bra and panties, clutching her shoes, dress, and clutch against her chest.

I sidestepped closer to the door to give them space.

"I'm sorry, Lola." Cole reached the bottom of the steps and turned to her. "I hate having to ask you to leave, but I've gotta go."

She rested one hand on his shoulder for balance and slipped on her stilettos. "Can't we have a coffee first?"

"Your Uber will be here in a sec. Maybe next time." Exhaustion swung through Cole's tired voice as he lowered her hand off his shoulder.

You wouldn't be like that if you took a break and got some sleep. Fool.

"It's okay." Lola shimmied toward him and fluttered her eyelashes. "There will definitely be a next time when I'm back in LA."

I rolled my eyes. I stood, feet shoulder-width apart, waiting for my client to get his ass into gear.

Lola handed Cole her clutch. She slipped her skimpy dress over her head and wiggled it into place over her hips.

Cole seemed to drink every inch of her body in. Even I could appreciate her hot figure.

"You have my number." Cole gave her purse back. "See you next time."

She giggled and kissed his lips. "I'll be in Europe for a few months. Might see you somewhere during your tour."

"I'd like that."

Charlotte shrieked, smacked her hand on the table, and tossed her sippy cup onto the floor. *Yep.* The kid was craving some attention too.

Hannah jumped up to retrieve the cup. Her angry eyes glared at Cole.

"Oh, shit," Lola whispered to Cole. "I didn't know you had guests."

"That's um . . . my kid. And her grandmother."

Lola's face blanched as she stepped backward toward the door. "You have a kid? Cole, why didn't you tell me? I don't do kids."

"What? Charlotte's fine." He rubbed at the deep lines forming on his brow.

"I'm sure she is. But I'm not." Lola's angelic mode switched to a harsh feistiness. "Kids aren't for me. Not even by association. I'm out of here." She gave Cole a quick kiss on the cheek. "I'll wait outside for my Uber. Thanks for a great night. But bye."

I opened the door for her. I knew that tone. She wouldn't be calling him in a hurry.

Smirking, I was a bit too quick to shut the door behind her. *Good riddance.*

But then I glared at Cole. What was he thinking? I didn't care that Lola had been here or that she didn't want to be around kids, but him letting her strut downstairs in her lingerie in front of Charlotte struck a nerve.

It wasn't my place to say anything.

But I didn't have to.

Hannah stormed over.

She pointed at the door and hissed in his face, "What the hell was that? You're bringing different girls home every other night and confusing Charlotte. She has had enough stress adjusting to a new home and new people—she doesn't need any more. I don't care who you sleep with. But don't parade them around in front of your three-year-old. Especially young ladies in their underwear, if you can call that piece of lace a garment."

"She was hot, wasn't she?" Smugness twinkled in his eyes.

Hannah's face reddened. "You find time to go out to all hours of the night and bring home women. You find time to run. Time to hang out with your friends. Yet again, you're about to rush off for the day. When are you going to spend time with your daughter? You've hardly spent more than a minute with her since we arrived."

"I have. When she was sick. And when everyone came over. And . . . and . . ." Yeah, he couldn't think of any other significant length of time. *Dick.* "That's what you're here for. To take care of her."

"No." Hannah took a step closer. "I'm here to help you and her adjust. I'm here to take care of her when you have rehearsals, events, tour obligations, and shows. But the rest of the time, she's your responsibility."

"Fuck." His shoulders slumped. "I'm trying to find a nanny."

"How about being a father?"

"I'm doing my best."

"You haven't even tried." Disappointment laced Hannah's tone.

Cole flinched and closed his eyes. "Ava, tell her I have."

Me? "I'm not part of this."

"Oh . . . yes, you are."

"Then, I agree with Hannah," I said, blunt and to the point.

"Fuck you," he sneered.

Hannah jumped back in. "Cole, I have a call with the social worker tomorrow. I'm not going to lie to her. You need to sort your life out. For Charlotte's sake."

"I will." He lowered his chin and rubbed his forehead. "Soon. Just give me some time."

"It's running out," Hannah snapped.

My heart cracked. She was right. Cole needed to make more of an effort.

He nodded, then turned to me. "Let's go. I don't want to be late for rehearsal."

But I wouldn't let him pass me.

"What?" he snapped.

I glared at him and pointed my hand at Charlotte.

"Ergh." Cole stormed over to his daughter and squatted in front of her. "Hey Char, I have to go to work. I'll be home late, and you'll be asleep when I get back. Ma's going to take care of you today. But maybe tomorrow morning I can take you to the park. Would you like that?"

She clapped. "Yes. Does it have swings?"

"Yes. And a climbing fort. And a slippery slide. And some spinning things. Does that sound like fun?"

"Yeah."

"It's a date."

He stood, hesitated, then kissed her on the head. He turned and stormed toward the door. He threw me an evil grin. "Happy?"

Hannah and I shook our heads.

I followed him. "Not even close. But it's a start."

Chapter 13

COLE

The following morning, I sat at my kitchen counter, drinking my double espresso, but my guts churned with every sip I swallowed. I didn't want to lose my kid. Scanning the calendar on my cell phone, I didn't know where, when, and how to add the task of spending time with Charlotte into my packed schedule.

Weeks out from the tour, we rehearsed nearly every day. We had interviews, photoshoots, events, and promotional activities leading up to kickoff. Our free time was minimal.

Was this what my parents had faced? Their careers consumed every hour of their day. But that was a good thing. Any time spent with them was always stressful and soul crushing. Vacations and Sunday dinners often resulted in arguments, tears, and someone storming off and slamming a door. That was often Tia, but I'd had my fair share of door-unhinging moments too. We'd grown up with one nanny after the next, telling Tia and me where to go and what to do as we lived our lives around our extracurricular school activities, music, and sport. Then, when I'd turned sixteen and the band had started to pull regular gigs, Flint and Phil had organized everything. I'd showed up with my drums, set them up, and played. Now April and Blake ran our lives. We had sponsors and road crews attending to our gear. I'd never had to take care of someone before—not even myself.

Now, I was responsible for my kid.

Hannah had been right. So had Ava. I hadn't spent any time with Charlotte.

I'd sworn not to be like my parents, and didn't want to be like them, so somehow, I had to make room for her.

Starting today.

Or was I too late?

Hannah had her phone call with Arilla, the social worker, this afternoon. My report card wouldn't be good. *Fuck.*

I had to step up.

I was.

I'd told the guys yesterday that I wouldn't be at rehearsal until after lunch. I didn't want to miss one second with the band, but I needed time with Charlotte. Somehow I had to find a balance. I just didn't know where to begin.

Hannah came downstairs with Charlotte and placed my kid's pink backpack on the counter. Charlotte stopped by the TV, distracted by whatever kids' program was still on from before she'd gone upstairs to get changed.

Hannah rested her tremoring hands on the top of Charlotte's bag, her eyes darkening with worry. "When was the last time you had eight hours of sleep?"

I puffed air through my nose and stared into the bottom of my empty cup. "Um . . . maybe when I was seventeen."

"Cole, you can't keep pushing yourself like this." She grabbed some snacks from the pantry and filled a water bottle for Charlotte. After placing them in the bag, she slid it toward me. She never let her condition stop her from doing anything, but her shakes seemed worse today. I hoped she was okay. "I'm not saying stop living life and doing what you love, but you need to pace yourself. Slow down and get some rest. You have this huge tour coming up. You must take care of yourself."

I didn't do slow. I didn't like sitting around doing nothing. I ate well. I exercised. I drank a bit too much. But I had to keep busy, and my brain occupied so I didn't have time to think about the mistakes I'd made and the pain I'd caused.

"I'm fine, Hannah."

"You're not. Maybe I'm the only one who has the balls to tell you that."

"No. You're about the third." Flint, Ava, and now Hannah had all voiced similar concerns. "I'm here, aren't I?"

"Yes. Just don't let it be a once-off occurrence."

"I won't. I promise."

"Good." Her dangling earrings jiggled as her shakes worsened. I didn't know much about Parkinson's disease other than it attacked the nervous system. Hannah's condition was mild, but her tremors became more obvious when she was concerned. *Fuck.* I didn't want to give her any reason to worry. She leaned against the counter. "Your world won't end if you take a break, smell the roses, and spend some time with your daughter."

"I'm working on it." Somehow. "I've got so much on, I don't know what can give, but I'll find the time. I will." I'd thought this kid wouldn't change my life, yet there I was, trying to find time in my schedule to be with her. *Fuck.*

"Excellent. Now enjoy your morning. Ava's just arrived." She pointed at the lit video security intercom on the kitchen wall. "I'm going to get changed and head out to see a friend. I'll be back here around noon in time for you to go to rehearsal."

"Thanks, Hannah. For everything."

"You're welcome."

Ava was another thing on my list I had to deal with. I'd been so fucking tired yesterday on the drive to and from rehearsal, I hadn't had the energy to apologize for what I'd said to her when I'd brought Lola home. But my drunken proposal still skipped through my mind.

What if Ava had agreed to join us?

What if she wanted a romp between my sheets?

A lopsided grin tugged the corner of my mouth. *Oh yeah.* I would've pushed Lola out of the bed, sent her home, and given Ava all my attention. It had been Ava's pussy I'd pictured licking when I'd gone down on Lola. Images of Ava had filled my head when I'd buried myself inside Lola. What was with that? Clearly, I was more fucked up than I'd realized and was obsessing over things I couldn't have. Shouldn't want. Needed to leave well alone.

But Ava walked through the front door in her casual uniform, and my dick jerked to life. What was it about her fitted T-shirt, tactical belt, baseball cap, and shiny heavy-duty shoes that turned up the temperature of my blood? Maybe I just wanted her to rough me up, throw on the ground again, and have her way with me.

I'd be down for that.

She stood by the door, holding her jacket and bag of gear in front of her. "Morning, Mr. Tanner."

A soft groan rumbled in my throat and reverberated through my chest. Every time she called me that, my pulse surged . . . and my cock hardened. The end of her eyebrow always flicked upward in a challenge I wanted to answer, and the saucy glint she got in her eyes raised my body temperature a fraction too much.

There was no denying there was a spark between us. It was just one that could never be ignited.

"Morning, Ms. Matthews. Come in. You don't have to wait by the door." I waved her over to the kitchen. "How do you always look so damn fresh in the morning?"

"I get sleep." She dropped her bag at the end of the island and leaned against the counter.

"Oh . . . that's why." I clicked my fingers and pointed at her. "I don't get much of that."

"I've noticed."

"About that." I winced. "Sorry about the other night with Lola. Asking you upstairs was inappropriate and out of line."

She shrugged. "You were just drunk and messing around."

Did anything ever faze her?

Why was I so compelled to apologize for having fun? *Oh, because I'd been a dick* . . . and I wanted us to get along. I wasn't about to change my ways, but I could be more considerate. "Yeah. That's all it was. It won't happen again."

Hopefully . . . maybe . . . no guarantees.

Easing off the kitchen stool, I grabbed the travel flask of coffee I'd made earlier and hooked Charlotte's backpack over my shoulder. "You set to go?"

"Always." Ava picked up her bag.

I turned off the TV, scooped up Charlotte from the sofa, and carried her against my chest. "You ready to go to the park?"

"Yeah." With Barney tucked under her arm, Charlotte and I headed into the garage. Ava followed, jumping into the front passenger seat of my Lamborghini SUV. The floral scent of her perfume made it impossible to ignore her, but today was about Charlotte. After I'd buckled her into the kids' car seat, we drove off.

But as I exited the front gate, a swarm of paparazzi circled my car. Flashes went off. Muffled voices slammed against the windows.

"Cole? Can we get a picture of you and your kid? How does it feel to be a father? Is the child's mother really dead?"

What the fuck?

As if I'd make up some story about Shelby being dead. But how did it feel to be a father? I eased the car through the gathering of people. How about beyond daunting. Numbing. Shit scary. Terrifying . . . but not as bad as it had been at first.

I peered in the rearview mirror. Charlotte stared at the flashing cameras and faces looming outside her window. Tears welled in her eyes.

She didn't need this shit. She was just a kid. She hadn't asked for this life. But I had. I'd never wanted anything else.

"Charlotte, it's okay." I reached back and rubbed her foot. "They're just taking some photos. Look the other way. They won't hurt you." I hoped that would always be the case.

She hugged her teddy bear and sucked on her thumb, but her gaze remained fixed on a huge camera clicking away on the other side of my window.

Through the dark tint, they wouldn't capture much, but I waved at them and took off down the street.

Ava remained silent for most of the drive to North Hollywood. That wasn't like her.

"Are you okay?" I asked.

"Yes." She glanced in the side mirror and checked over her shoulder. My pulse jumped as I did the same. We hadn't been followed . . . hopefully. She straightened and focused on the road ahead. "I'm just glad you're finally spending time with Charlotte."

"Yeah. I've messed up. I'll sort things out."

"Good."

I pulled up to the curb beside the Valley Village playground. It was quiet for a Thursday morning. There were only two other moms having coffee at a picnic table with babies in strollers.

"I'll wait here by the car." Ava pointed to the front of the vehicle as we got out.

"You don't have to."

"Cole, I'm on duty."

I glanced around the huge open parkland dotted with trees. There were two cars next to mine. No paparazzi had followed us. No walkers or joggers were around. There didn't seem to be any threat. "Ava, you can join us."

"Cole . . . go spend time with your daughter."

"I intend to. Come over if you get bored." I unbuckled Charlotte, placed her on the ground, and was about to take her hand when she rushed off, running toward the swings.

Shit. I raced after her. *Damn.* She was fast. Once we reached the playground, I lifted her into the toddler swing and swung her gently back and forth. "Hold on."

She clutched onto the chains and giggled. "I am."

"This okay?" How high should I push her?

"No. Higher."

"Alright. You asked for it."

As the swing soared through the air, Charlotte's laughter wrapped around my heart and squeezed it. How could this little person I barely knew affect me?

After ten minutes, she'd had enough time on the swings and raced over to the climbing fort covered in green shade sails. "Cole, follow me."

I was way too big and tall but how could I refuse? We climbed up the narrow steps, ran across the slatted, swaying bridge, and slid down the twisty slippery slide. She shrieked, screamed, and giggled as I chased her around the fort and through a flock of pigeons on the grass, sending them fluttering into the sky.

After half an hour of more swinging, climbing ,and running, we sat down at a picnic table next to each other. I handed her a drink and a cookie from the backpack. Her big green eyes watched my every move as I poured myself a coffee into the flask's cup.

"What am I gonna do with you kid?"

Charlotte shrugged. "I don't know."

"Do you like staying with me?"

She shrugged again as she sipped on her straw.

"Do you like your new house?"

"It's big. Ma won't let me touch anything."

I liked Ma. But Charlotte was a kid. She needed a play space. "How about we turn one of the spare bedrooms upstairs into a playroom?"

"Yay." She clapped.

"You ready to travel with me? There will be lots of bus rides, and a few plane trips, and we'll get to stay in some cool places."

"Can I bring some toys?" She crunched on her oatmeal cookie.

"Yes. As many as you want."

"Okay. Can I go play on the slides?" She pointed to the fort.

"Sure. Do you need help?"

"No. I can do it."

"Okay. I'll have some more coffee then come over."

Charlotte took off, zooming across the ground and climbed into the fort. She jumped across the chain bridge, then zipped down the slide. At a run, she clopped up the steps again and set the route on repeat.

Ava had remained by my car. She may have had sunglasses on, but judging by the small flutter in my stomach, she was watching us. Well, she could do that from here. "Ava?" I called out and waved her over. "Please. Come join us. I have coffee."

That lured her to the table.

I'd learned one thing about her . . . she loved coffee. Strong and black. Just the way I liked mine.

I poured coffee into the lid of the flask and held it out to her. "I don't have that many germs."

A small smile played across her lips as she slid onto the bench seat opposite me. "I couldn't care right now. I need caffeine." She took the cup and savored a sip. "Thank you."

"You're welcome."

As she took off her sunglasses and hung them from the neckline of her T-shirt, she glanced over my shoulder, across the park, then checked that Charlotte was in sight.

"Do you ever relax?" I grinned over the rim of the flask.

"Yes. When I'm not on duty."

"And what do you when you're not working?"

She always hesitated before talking. I guessed she wanted to make sure we weren't crossing any lines. But fuck lines. I wanted to know more about her. She had a kid; so did I. I needed to learn what I could from somebody.

"I don't get much time off, but when I do I read, run, do yoga, meditate, enjoy the occasional glass of red wine or two." A glassy sheen passed across her eyes as she followed Charlotte zipping across the bridge again. "And spend time with my son."

The wave of anguish in her voice hit me low in the guts. The only time she showed any form of vulnerability was when we talked about kids. She was human after all. So many questions popped into my head. "It's none of my business and you can tell me to fuck off, but you don't seem to see him much."

She placed the cup on the table and swiveled it back and forth, back and forth. "No. Only the second Tuesday and the last weekend of each month, with the random change thrown in to meet work obligations. That's more to accommodate Luther than me. "

"Why don't you have equal custody?" I winced. "Um . . . fuck. Sorry. You don't have to tell me."

"It's okay." She smiled a sad smile, but her hard glare prickled my skin. "Fucking up can cost you everything."

Been there. Done that. But she didn't seem like the type of person who'd screw up. "Can I ask what happened?" I grabbed one of Charlotte's cookies and held it out to Ava.

"Do you want the long or short version?" She took the cookie and had a small bite.

"Whatever you're comfortable with." I was a good listener—I'd own that.

"Fine." She shrugged her shoulder, just an inch. "My ex turned into a manipulative, vindictive asshole."

She took a sip of coffee. Put the cup down. Licked her lips. Folded her arms.

I waited for her to say more. But she said nothing.

I jerked my chin back. "Is that it?" Was that all she was going to tell me? *Damn.* She was a tough nut to crack.

"I wish." Her eyes glinted in the sunshine as she let out a puff of air. "But no. When Luther and I divorced, we had equal custody. But Luther always loathed our settlement and the amount he had to pay in child support." The hard edge in her voice, mixed with a touch of blasé attitude, didn't mask the underlying base of raw heartache. "He hated that I wasn't his anymore and became obsessed with revenge and control."

What the . . . ? An anxious tremor rippled through my gut. "Did . . . did he hurt you?"

"Not physically." She gave me a wicked, no-chance-in-hell smirk. "He wouldn't dare lay a finger on me. I think we both know how that would go down."

Yes, I'd learned that lesson, twice.

"He turned into an unreasonable, spiteful man. Everything worsened when Mom was diagnosed with advanced cancer six months after we divorced. She died shortly after that." The anguish in her tone stabbed my heart.

I lowered my voice and kept one eye on Charlotte swinging around a pole. "Loss messes you up." I had firsthand experience of that.

"Yes, but it's my fault I lost equal custody." She drew her shoulders back and tucked flyaway hair from her braid behind her ear. "I was on the force back then. The long days on the beat were tough; the bad outweighed the good. After losing Mom, Dad was heartbroken. My sister had a miscarriage. I drank a bit too much some days. Luther and I were always arguing over his insane inability to be flexible with Josh and having to go through our lawyers for every request." As if taking her time to carefully compile the words, she pursed her lips, then spoke in a tortured tone that tore my heart. "I shouldn't have let my personal life affect my work, but it did. I fucked up on the job. I didn't get help when I should've."

"Did you shoot somebody?" *Shit,* I shouldn't be flippant about something so serious.

"No. Luckily I've never had to do that." She fidgeted with the cup. "I just went too far when I shouldn't have. After I'd had this huge fight with Luther, my partner, Craig, and I were called to this house out in Elysian Heights. This asshole had beaten the shit out of his eight-year-old kid and young girlfriend. They were bloodied and bruised from head to toe." Her eyes glassed over as painful and traumatic memories no doubt flickered through her mind. I had a bucketload of those too. "He wouldn't calm down, kept kicking them and accusing them of taking his drugs. So we tasered him, restrained and cuffed him. But as we hauled his ass out to the cruiser, he wouldn't stop bad-mouthing me, saying I was his next whore, that all women deserved to be put in their place and disciplined. He reminded me of Luther. There was nothing but pure evil in this guy's eyes. I lost it." She winced. "I punched him hard several times, kneed him in the balls, and made sure he fucking hit his head when we put him in the car. It was all caught on body cam."

I didn't miss the strain in her voice or the regret.

I reached across the table and squeezed her hand. "Hey?"

She flinched but didn't pull away.

"What's wrong with that? It sounds like the guy needed more than a few punches."

"When you're a cop, you can't do that. I ignored Craig calling out to me to stand down." She shook her head and withdrew her hand from underneath mine. "The guy was restrained. I was out of line. It's against our code of conduct and illegal to hit someone when they can't defend themselves . . . at any time really."

"Fuck that. You're a total badass. That guy deserved every blow." I didn't condone violence, but sometime discipline didn't go astray. Nor the odd reminder that you'd been a dick, like Flint had done when he'd clobbered me.

"No . . . he didn't." She lowered her chin. The sorrow darkening her eyes speared my chest. "When Luther found out what had happened, he went straight to his lawyers." The quivering anger and disappointment in her voice sliced through the air. "Rather than support me through my grief and trauma, he used my personal life, my job, and my mental health against me. He filed for majority custody and won."

Only majority? "Why didn't he go for full custody?"

"This is Luther's game. He knows I'm not unfit. Therapy confirmed that. Taking Josh was his way of hurting me. He likes to keep me on a leash and knows I'll do anything for our kid."

"Fuck." I swiped my hand across my chin. "What an asshole." No wonder she was harsh, tough, brutal. She'd witnessed things I hoped I'd never have to in my lifetime. She'd lost loved ones, and she'd been more fucked over by love than me.

"Oh, he is." She set grit into her tone. "I had enough guilt over snapping at work and failing to do my job right, but being made out to be an unfit mom was the lowest of cruel blows. But it hit me with some realities too. I wasn't in a good place after Mom died. I wasn't enjoying my job. So I quit, got help, and found a new career. But Luther doesn't care. He throws his money and power around and defeats me every time I legally try to get more time with Josh. He's done it to me twice—I won't let him do it again."

"So he's a controlling, narcissistic prick?"

"That sums him up." She folded and rested her elbows on the table. "But next time we go to court, I will win. He's got nothing over me. I've passed every physiological assessment. I don't put a foot out of line. I'm changing roles at work."

That was news. "You're giving up being a security guard? I thought you loved it."

"I do. But Luther's lawyers have made my job sound more dangerous than being a targeted crack-loaded henchman for the

Mexican mafia. So to remove any contention, I'm taking on an office-based, admin management role for our company. I hate having to give up field work, active duty, and the travel, but it's what I have to do to make the court happy."

Wow. Changing careers for your kid was extreme. I could never give up music.

For someone who had been through so much, she projected nothing but strength. She seemed to have her shit together. There was nothing she wouldn't do for her kid. I admired that. Her love for her son blew my mind.

Would I feel that way about Charlotte one day?

I hoped so.

My kid ran around the fort, chasing small, yellow butterflies. She'd certainly made an impact.

"Is your new role the reason why you're not coming overseas with us?"

"Yes." She nodded. "This job helped me get my life back on track. It's enabled me to service and protect people in a new way, helped restore my confidence, and reaffirmed I'm a good mom." She threw me a saucy smirk "And they don't mind if you have to rough someone up who's been a dick every now and then... within reason of course." She made light of what had happened, but no doubt the scars ran deep.

"Like me?"

"I had to put you in your place to prove I'm good at what I do."

"I never doubted you." Maybe for a split second.

"I made sure you didn't." A hint of color touched her cheeks just before her gaze darted toward the street. A black Mercedes was parked beside my car. *Shit.* How long had it been there? We'd been so engrossed in talking, neither one of us had noticed it.

She snatched her cell phone out of her jacket and snapped a photo of the car side-on.

I appreciated the need for security, but sometimes it turned me into a nervous wreck. Excluding the last few minutes, I'd become more aware of my surroundings lately than ever before. More paranoid.

Charlotte was digging in the sand. The moms were feeding their babies. A man walked a dog across the park.

"Is everything okay?" I asked Ava.

The car took off and she nodded. "Uh-huh."

I stuffed my hands into my hoodie's pockets. The wind was picking up and held a chill. "Sorry, I didn't mean to distract you. But thank you for telling me about Josh. Now I understand why you're so hard on me about Charlotte. You and I are more alike than you think."

"How so?" She put her phone away.

My shoulders slumped, and my chest ached. "We've lost loved ones. We've made mistakes, big and small. Sometimes, no matter how much you try to do the right thing, be perfect, your efforts are never good enough. You hate failing and fucking up. You feel guilty over letting people down." No amount of therapy in the past had helped me. "But that doesn't stop you from doing everything possible to protect those you love and care about. You want to do what's right for your kid. I don't want the court to rule me as unfit either." But were my career and lifestyle cause for concern? What hope did I have?

"Only you can fuck that up, so don't." She handed me her now empty cup. "Your head is in the right place—make sure your heart is too."

"I will. It is."

"Good." A small smile crossed her lips.

I'd never met someone who was so different but so like me. Everyone was dealing with shit—just on different levels. I prayed everything worked out. Ava needed Josh . . . her family. And Charlotte needed hers. She needed to be in Hannah's and Paul's lives . . . and mine.

Charlotte ran over to me and handed me two sticks she'd picked up off the ground from a nearby tree.

"Can you teach me to play the drums?"

I took them and tapped them against the table. "Here? Right now?"

"No, silly." She tugged on my sleeve. "At home."

"We can do that." I glanced at my watch. Eleven-fifteen a.m. We had time. "Would you like another swing first?"

"Yes." She ran off before I had time to blink.

"Back soon." I swung my legs over the bench seat. I stood and turned to Ava. "I'm sorry you lost Josh and have to give up the job you love. You're a damn good bodyguard. You seem like a great mom. If you ever need anything, if I can help in any way, just ask."

"I will. Thank you."

I dashed after Charlotte. I couldn't deny playing had been fun. I guessed I was a big kid at heart. But finding out more about Ava had hit home hard. I also had to be an adult.

I had a wild history. The slightest mishap could be turned and used against me. I didn't want that to happen.

Charlotte needed me.

After another huge swing and run around the fort, we headed home.

Now I'd get to do something even better than playing in the park with Charlotte.

Play the drums.

That was something I could do.

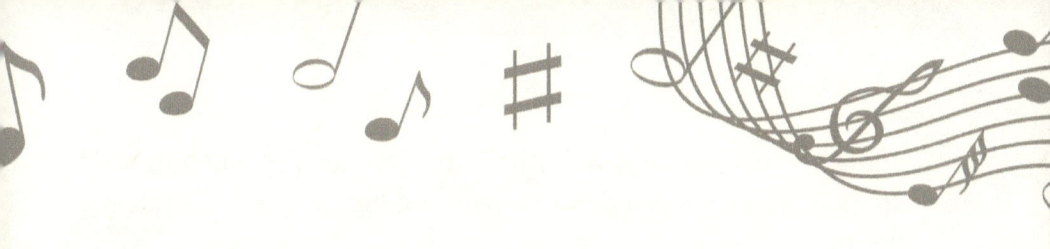

Chapter 14

COLE

As I carried Charlotte from the car into the house, holding her upside down with her legs hooked over my shoulder, she wriggled with giggles and fits of laughter. *Damn.* That was the best sound. Spending time with her had been worth the effort. And our day wasn't over yet.

Halfway down the hallway, Ava stopped by my office door. It was a pleasant change to see a soft smile touch her lips rather than her usual cold, thin sneer. "I'm going to check in with my team, then head off. I'll pick you up at one to take you to rehearsal."

"You can stay if you like. I have food. Coffee. A spare room if you want to rest."

"Thanks . . . but I've invaded enough of your personal time. Enjoy this hour with your daughter."

"Yeah. I will." I placed Charlotte onto her feet. But as I reached for her hand, she raced off down the hallway to my music room. Her energy was contagious. "I better go." I thumbed toward Charlotte, but something held me in Ava's orbit. She leaned her shoulder against the office door and caught her bottom lip between her teeth. *Mmm . . .* she shouldn't do that. My body tingled in places that it shouldn't.

We'd had a great morning. I'd gotten to learn more about her. But there were boundaries. She was here to do her job. I had enough problems to deal with. So the sooner the low hum that sparked in my veins when I was around her stopped, the fucking better.

"Cole. Hurry up." Charlotte slapped her hand against the music room door.

I sucked in a deep breath, and my heart swelled to the size of a beach ball. This having-a-kid thing was kinda cool. Walking backward toward Charlotte, I grinned and pointed at Ava. "I'll see you soon."

"You will."

Grinning, I turned and scooted down the hall. The moment I opened the heavy door, she rushed into the room and jumped onto the stool behind the drum kit. She grabbed a set of drumsticks out of the canister and tapped them against the snare.

I laughed as she hit and smacked everything she could reach. Future potential had been unleashed.

I ambled over to her, picked her up, and sat on the stool. I placed her on my lap and jiggled her into a comfortable position. Her little legs were too short to reach the pedals. "Want to play something together?"

"Okay." She swung the stick through the air, almost taking my eye out.

"Cool. First, this is how you hold the sticks. Palms out, facing down." I held my hand out to demonstrate. She copied. "It's all about balance. Place the stick between your index finger and your thumb, then wrap your hand around it. Like this." I wriggled her stick into position, then closed her fingers over it. "This is called a matched grip."

She held up the sticks. "Is this right?"

"Perfect." Not bad for her first lesson. "Now you tap this drum and I'll play the bass. Ready?"

"Yep."

"Let's go." I pumped the pedal in a steady four-on-the-floor beat. Charlotte struck the small tom-tom. Her beat was uneven and out of time. I chuckled and just let her play. The smile on her face and light in her eyes was worth it. "That's good. Keep going.

One. Two. Three. Four. One. Two. Three. Four." I picked up a stick and played the other side of the kit, showing off, hitting the drums at double the speed.

Glitter shimmered in her bright eyes. She wriggled on my lap, swinging and rocking her legs back and forth. *Yeah*, playing drums was super cool. I jerked my chin to the cymbal. "Hit the big shiny gold disk. Really hard."

She clutched the stick with all her might and slammed it against the cymbal. It tinkered softly and barely moved. But I was down for some healthy encouragement.

"Yeah. Do it again."

As Charlotte struck the cymbal a second time, I glanced up. Ava stood in the doorway, leaning against the doorjamb.

I hadn't heard her come in.

I was about to throw her a wink, but her watery eyes caught me off-guard. I grabbed Charlotte's hand and stilled her drumming. "Ava? Is everything okay?" How long had she been standing there? The whole time? Was I getting used to having her around?

Maybe.

She sniffled and nodded. "Yeah. Sorry." She thumbed toward the hallway. "I've just finished checking in. All's good. I'll head off and see you soon."

"Okay." I wouldn't mind if she stayed, but she'd made it clear she didn't want to. "Thanks."

She went to turn but stopped. "Cole? This is what having a kid is all about. Magical moments that create beautiful memories. Be the best father she could ever hope for."

With that, Ava took off.

I rubbed Charlotte's arm, then sat her higher up on my leg. She tapped away on the drums, awe sparkling in her eyes with every beat. Every time I looked at Charlotte my mind spun, my chest ached, and my heart cracked open a fraction more.

She was mine.

I'd do everything I could to give her a good life. A family. Anything she needed. I just needed to sort myself out in the process too. And that might prove to be impossible.

After playing on the drums for another twenty minutes, I made sandwiches for lunch. Peanut butter for Charlotte. Loaded chicken salad for me. We were just finishing up when Hannah came home.

She joined us then surprised me during her call to the social worker.

She didn't feed me to the sharks. Instead, Hannah told Arilla we were slowly adjusting and getting better every day. That Charlotte was well and loved her new home.

Fuck . . . I didn't deserve the tick, but I'd take it. I had to step up. Be better for my kid. Be there for my band. Take more onto my plate that was already overflowing.

Yep. I had to. I could.

Everything would be fine.

But when Ava returned at one o'clock sharp, the niggle in the back of my neck tightened. Rather than lingering by the front door, she came straight over to where I sat at the kitchen counter with urgency in her step. She handed me a photo of a black Mercedes parked down the street from my house.

"Bruno, on our surveillance team, captured this car this morning just before we left. We ran the plates, but they're fake."

"Fuck." A chill shot down my spine, erasing the good vibes I'd had from hanging out with Charlotte. Nausea flooded my gut as I scanned the picture. "Is this the same one that was at the park?"

"Yes, it is. "

"So we were followed?" I closed my eyes and swallowed the lump lodged in my throat.

"Looks like it." She folded her arms and leaned against the counter. "Bruno is certain a man was in this car. Not the woman we saw the other week."

"So it's someone new? *Shit.*" I didn't need this added stress. My pulse thudded in my temples. As I took in Hannah and Charlotte sitting on the sofa watching TV, my breath shuddered through my lungs. I'd never live with myself if something happened to them. I lowered my voice so only Ava could hear. "Was it just a photographer? A fan? Or someone we should be concerned about?"

"We don't know yet."

"I don't want anyone hanging outside my house, or some psycho hurting my kid, or Hannah . . . or me."

"Me either." Concern hooded her eyes, but her calm tone never faltered. "You know as well as I do the fans and the paparazzi get excited around tour time. They disappear when you're living a normal everyday life."

"But nothing is normal at present." As my shoulders sagged, I leaned against the counter. Exhaustion tapped at my bones, but I had to ignore it.

"Cole? We've got this." She gave my arm a gentle squeeze. I'd prefer her whole body wrapped around me, but the gesture was comforting. Grounding. I needed that so I didn't lose my mind. "We're here to make sure you, your family, and friends stay safe. There have been no issues raised at the other guys' houses. So as an added measure to keep a closer eye on this situation, would you object to having full-time security here at your house?" Her steel-like gaze didn't hint at any other option. "Just till tour kicks off—then I'm sure whoever these people are will stop coming around when they know you aren't home."

I drove my fingertips into the pressure points at the top of my nose, but nothing relieved the tension. "As in, have someone stand by my front door all day? Crash in the guesthouse?" Wasn't sure I'd get any sleep if Ava stayed in there.

"No, one of our team will be positioned outside your property, monitoring activity from the street. They'll be equipped with surveillance feeds. That way, you can still enjoy the privacy of your own home."

I puffed air through my nose and shook my head. "Not too much of my life is private."

"I know." She softened her tone. "It's just for a couple weeks until the tour."

Charlotte jumped on the sofa. Hannah laughed and tickled her tummy. I had to protect them at all costs.

"Fine. Get someone here." I handed the photo back to Ava. "Keep these fuckers away from my house."

"Done." She took the photo from me, folded it, and put it in her jacket pocket. "I'll make some calls at rehearsal."

"Thank you."

After a long afternoon and evening running through our set list several times, then having dinner at Flint's with my friends, I staggered through the door just after eleven o'clock, drained and utterly exhausted. I couldn't wait to crash.

It had been one crazy day—good, bad, fun, eye-opening, and daunting.

But just as I was about to dismiss Ava, an almighty, blood-chilling shriek came from upstairs.

Shit! Charlotte!

In the span of a second, I glanced at Ava. The fear in her eyes matched the ice spearing my heart and prickling my skin.

I didn't draw breath. I bolted up the stairs, taking two at a time.

I burst into her room.

"Charlotte? Oh my God. What's happened? Fuck . . . where are you?"

Chapter 15

COLE

Charlotte wasn't in her bed. I rushed over and flicked back the covers just to double-check. But then she screamed from the corner, sitting wedged in between the nightstand and the wall. She held Barney against her chest. A million tears streamed down her face.

"Char?" I rushed around to her and fell to my knees. "Hey. It's okay. I'm here."

Her hysterical cries tripled. She shook all over. Her big green eyes, full of fear, skipped to me, then Ava, then back again.

Fuck? What should I do? "Sweetie, come here?" I held out my arms, but she cringed and curled into the corner even more.

Did I just grab her? I didn't want to frighten her any more than she was. Where the fuck was Hannah? I didn't know how to deal with this.

Ava had charged into the room behind me. She'd checked the walk-in closet, the en suite, and the windows. "The room is secure, Cole. There's been no perimeter breach. No alerts have come through to my cell phone."

I nodded. This person hanging outside my house had unnerved me more than I wanted to admit, but I had to stay focused on Charlotte. I grabbed a tissue out of the box on the nightstand. "Can I dry those tears?" *And wipe that snot away.*

Her little chin trembled as she sobbed and cried and wailed.

"Cole?" Frustration sliced through Ava's tone. "Pick her up and cuddle her for God's sake."

Shit. Okay.

"Come here, baby girl. I got you." I drew her into my arms and cuddled her. She didn't put up a fight as she rested her head against my shoulder and continued to shudder and bawl. "Did you have a bad dream?"

I stood and paced the floor. As I rubbed and patted her back, I straightened the hemline of her blue pajamas T-shirt. *Now what do I do?* I'd seen movies. Other people with kids. This couldn't be that hard. I walked back and forth across the room. *Nope.* She still cried. I stopped and rocked side to side. That didn't work either.

I turned to Ava standing by the door. "What's wrong with her? Why won't she stop crying? What the fuck do I do?"

"Ride it out. She'll settle. Just give her lots of cuddles. Talk to her in a soothing voice. Maybe try singing." Ava scanned through her cell phone, then put it to her ear. "I'm just calling Tank. He's on duty outside tonight. I'll make sure he hasn't seen anything."

"Okay." I nodded and closed my eyes. She'd suggested I sing to Charlotte. I wasn't a good singer. I didn't know any kids' songs. "Twinkle Twinkle" was about it.

So be it. I'd try anything.

I sang the first verse. Softly. Slowly. *God.* I felt like an idiot. But Charlotte calmed down after the second time though the nursery rhyme.

I slumped my shoulders and mouthed '*thank you*' to Ava.

"It's okay." She softened her voice. "Tank said everything outside is fine. He's doing a walkaround just to be sure.."

"Good." I nodded as I stroked Charlotte's hair and combed her curls through my fingertips. "Hey, Char? Do you want to tell me what made you sad?" Not that I could do anything about it.

She sniffled against my hoodie. "I want my mommy. I want my daddy."

Fuck. My heart twanged and splintered. I did too. I didn't know how to cope with this shit.

"I know. But you have Ma and Pa who love you very much. You have me."

She clutched Barney underneath her arm and wiped her snotty nose across my clothes. *Ergh.*

The minute I stopped moving, Charlotte cried again.

Where was Hannah? How could she sleep through this noise?

I clenched my teeth and closed my eyes. Exhaustion twisted and twitched through every muscle in my body. My head throbbed. I needed a couple hours sleep before I hit rehearsal tomorrow. How could I survive the tour if this kept happening again and again?

Charlotte screamed and kicked.

"Fuck." Frustration got the better of me. "Please. Stop. Crying."

"Cole?" Ava snapped in a chilling but quiet, calm tone. "You can't talk to her like that."

"Please?" Desperation tore through every cell in my body. "Help me."

Doubt loomed in her eyes before she let out a breath, walked over, and took Charlotte from my arms. "Hey, sweetie. I've got you." She cradled Charlotte's head against her cheek. "It's okay to miss your mom. When you feel like this, you have to remember something really good about her. I've seen a picture of her. She was very pretty. She had a beautiful smile, just like yours. What did she do when you were upset? Did she read you books, or sing, or give you big hugs?"

"Hugs." Charlotte sniffled.

"Is it okay if I do that? Or would you like Cole to? He's got big strong arms, perfect for cuddles."

I raised an eyebrow. "You like my arms and my smile. Careful, Ava—I might begin to think you like me."

She ignored me and stayed focused on my kid. God, that did something strange to my heart. She held Charlotte close. Kept talking in soft tones. Rocked and swayed from side to side.

"Charlotte?" Ava whispered again. "You sure you don't want Cole?"

"No. You." Charlotte pouted as her teary eyes glanced at me

standing a foot away.

Ouch! Why did that sting?

Within a few minutes, Charlotte calmed down again.

I jutted my chin toward Ava. "You're good with her."

"You have to have nothing but love and patience with children."

Normally I was calm and controlled, but the long day had gotten to me.

After another couple of minutes, Charlotte grew sleepy. Ava placed her into bed and tucked her in. "Night, sweetie."

Charlotte's long eyelashes fluttered and brushed against her cheeks. She snuggled her teddy bear tight against her chest. *Damn.* Why did she have to be so cute?

Once she'd fully settled, I kissed Charlotte on the head, then snuck out of the room with Ava. We headed downstairs and Ava headed straight for the front door.

"Ava?"

She spun around. Her stunning brown eyes threatened to knock a brick out of the wall around my heart. She'd gone above and beyond her duty tonight. I'd be forever grateful. I stuffed my hands into the front pockets of my jeans, rounding my shoulders. "Do . . . do you want a drink or something? As a thank you for helping tonight."

"No thank you, Mr. Tanner."

I may have been tired, but my body still reacted to her voice. I didn't want her to leave. "I could use some tips on how to deal with moments like that with Charlotte better."

"I can't, Cole." *Boundaries, right?* "Ask Hannah. Talk to your parents. Buy a book or two."

That made me smile.

She softened her tone. "You of all people know what it's like to lose someone. Remember what that feels like? That's what Charlotte feels too. She lost her mom and dad. Talk to her. Comfort her. Be there for her. Most of all, love her. Treasure every moment because you never know when it may be your last."

That was my motto. I lived for the present . . . and fun. I'd avoided emotional ties and was adamant about doing so. But Ava threatened that stand. *Why?* I sidled over to her, holding her gaze as I took each step. My heartbeat drummed a touch too fast. "What if this is *our* last moment? Maybe you should stay." My gaze fell to her rosy lips and meandered back up to meet her eyes again. What would she taste like?

"Nice try, drummer boy," she sneered, but a shimmer of warmth flashed in the depths of her irises. "I'm flattered. But no."

With that, Ava walked off and left.

Ergh. I closed and locked the door behind her. I rested my head against the frosted glass and chuckled. She was impossible to work out. But I liked her more and more.

There was nothing wrong with that.

We could just be friends . . . *could we?*

I dragged my heavy feet upstairs, showered, and fell into bed just after one a.m..

After tossing and turning, I drifted off to sleep around two-thirty.

But jerky, jolting movement on my mattress ripped me from my slumber. I peeled my eyes open. Charlotte bounced beside me. At six fucking a.m..

"Cole, I'm hungry." She pounced on all fours beside me. "Can you make me breakfast?"

Half asleep, I mumbled, "Can't Ma do it?"

"I want you to."

I slumped against my pillow. I needed more sleep. My whole body felt like it'd been pummeled by a pack of stampeding elephants. "Go back to bed for an hour, then I will."

"No Mr. Sleepyhead." She tugged on the front of my T-shirt. "Get up."

"Alright. Alright." I rolled onto my back and blinked my eyes open. I wiped the tiredness from my face. "Are you always this demanding?"

Charlotte just grinned and nodded.

I tossed the covers off my waist and sat upright. She crawled across the bed and wound her tiny arms around my neck. "Piggyback ride."

Fuck. Too cute. But I was sure she'd be the death of me.

Chapter 16

AVA

Damn you, Cole Tanner.

I stood on guard, off to one side of Gabrielle's Boutique as the guys did their final fittings for the events they had on over the coming week. Having four men strip, prance around in their underwear, show off their ripped bodies, then re-dress and strut around in front of huge mirrors in designer suits wasn't a bad task for a Monday morning.

My other team members were on duty too, dispersed in or outside the shop. But I couldn't take my eyes off Cole.

One man should not look that good in a three-piece.

My palms sweat. My core clenched. My body overheated in my formal uniform. Ever since Thursday night, after helping him with Charlotte, the way Cole looked at me had messed with my mind. Conflicting emotions stirred through my system. Why couldn't he be the simple asshole I'd first met?

I'd never expected him to be such a contradiction. He portrayed confidence, worked hard, and cared about his family and friends. He never complained. But despite his incredible success and uncanny talent, underneath his shiny exterior was someone who suffered from major worry and self-doubt. He pushed himself to the limit to be fit for the tour. He played through their set list over and over to make it better when it had already been flawless. He was concerned he wasn't good enough to take care of Charlotte. If he just stopped and took a moment, he would see that he was amazing at those things. I understood drive, but his constant need to do more and be better was taking its toll. He'd lost weight and was frequently tired, but he wouldn't take a break.

After this fitting, the band had a rehearsal, a launch party tomorrow night, and a couple of days off to rest. I prayed Cole did that. I wouldn't be around to check. I had the next two days rostered off and time with Josh.

Kennedy would be covering Cole. I'd have a word with him before handover tomorrow to monitor Cole's activities. If Cole so much as went out to buy a bottle of milk rather than rest, I'd have to talk to Blake. I didn't want Cole to burn out before the tour started. But for now, I didn't mind keeping a close eye on him.

And I had to remember Cole was a smooth and sultry charmer.

He peeled off shirt number four and stripped down to his boxer briefs. Catching my gaze in the mirror, he raised an eyebrow. The sexy glint in those green eyes was dangerous.

Too much heat flushed my cheeks.

"You okay, Ava?" Beckett's voice chuckled low in my earpiece; our radios were on hands-free.

I kept my poker face in place as I glared at him standing across from me in front of the jewelry display cabinet. "You know I am."

"Did I miss something?" Sloane, on duty outside the front door with Wyatt, joined the conversation.

"Sloane, you didn't miss anything." I said, watching Cole slip on a new pair of suit pants. *Oh. Yes, he was.*

Wyatt glanced over his shoulder, peering through the glass door. "I'll trade places with you, Ava. I'm sure the scenery in there is better than out here."

"Sucks to be you." I clasped my hands in front me, trying to contain my smile. "But I stand corrected. You are missing out on a nice show."

My cell phone rang. *Shit!* Who was calling? Wells? Our surveillance team? Had they tracked down the person loitering around Cole's house?

The Mercedes had returned once over the weekend, but no one had gotten out of the car. No one had walked past Cole's house. I'd come across crazed fans before, but this was a whole new level of weird.

I grabbed my cell phone. The color drained from my face. Luther's name lit the screen. *Fuck!* Random calls from him were never good.

"Guys. I gotta take a call. Wyatt, let's swap." I headed for the door, switched my hands-free comms off, and answered my cell phone. "Hey Luther, I'm here. Hold one sec. I'm just stepping outside."

"Hurry up. I don't have all day."

Always such a pleasure. I made my way past Wyatt and Sloane at the door and walked into the small parking lot. I'd been to this boutique that was tucked in behind Rodeo Drive several times with other clients. Gabrielle, the owner, was a vision of classic Hollywood elegance and dressed many celebrities for events. She'd worked with The Flintlocks for years thanks to their friend and stylist, Kara Collins, who was based in New York.

I stopped beside Cole's car. "Okay, Luther. What's up?"

"I have to go to New York for the rest of the week and I have to take Josh with me. So you won't be able to have him tomorrow night."

"What?" The breath shot from my lungs. My heart tore in two. We'd already agreed on several date changes to suit both his travel arrangements and my tour with the band. This had been one of them. I'd always been flexible, but I was tied to a tight schedule for the next few months. Any alteration would impact my time with Josh. This was so Luther. He'd do anything to hurt me. *Asshole.* "No. It's my time with him."

"Zoe is coming with me." Luther's blunt voice sliced through the speaker. "So Josh has to as well."

"No." Desperation clawed my brain. "He can stay with me. He has school. Sport. I'd love to have him."

"No."

"Luther, don't do this." The pain in my chest crushed my ribs.

"It's an urgent trip. I'm sorry." There was not an ounce of compassion or sympathy in his cold tone. "I have a huge meeting to attend. It's all arranged. End of story."

My head dropped back. Tears pricked my eyes. "Please, let Josh stay with me."

"No. We're leaving tonight."

"Tonight? You're supposed to give me more notice than this." Pacing, I stabbed the air. "This is wrong, Luther, and you know it."

"This meeting was called an hour ago, Ava. I'm giving you as much notice as possible. I have the majority custody. What I say goes. Remember that."

"Fuck you." I clenched my fist, my jaw, every muscle. "Not for much longer."

"We'll see about that."

My blood boiled red hot. "Oh, we will. My lawyer will be hearing about this. You're breaking the rules of our agreement."

"You and your rules," he hissed. "Don't play dirty with me, Ava. You will lose."

"I don't have to play dirty." I said through clenched teeth. Acid-filled tears burned my cheek. I refused to let him get the upper hand. "The law is on my side, Luther. You're in the wrong. If you take Josh tomorrow, let me have him for a night when you get back. You're not allowed to keep him away from me."

Silence.

I pounded my fist against my forehead. My stomach twisted into knots. Listening to Luther's breath on my cell phone was not on my wish list.

"I'll think about it. I'll text you."

Luther hung up.

Fuuuuck! Fucking son-of-a-bitch. Motherfucking asshole. How had I ever loved that man?

Squatting near Cole's car, I wiped my hand down my face and took several deep breaths to regain my composure. My head ached. But as I looked up, Cole, dressed in his jeans and a hoodie, walked toward me, holding out a large takeaway cup with steam rising from the lip on the lid.

"Looks like you need this. Coffee?"

You have no idea how much. Pity I couldn't drink alcohol on duty, but this was the next best thing. *But shit . . .* I stood, sniffled, and wiped my cheeks dry on my suit jacket. "Thanks. But I'm fine."

"Ava. You're not. Is there anything I can do to help?"

I dug my fingernails into my palms to steady myself. "No."

"Get this into you." He raised the coffee cup again.

I held out my shaky hand and took the drink. "Thank you." As I took a sip, I did a quick scan of the busy car-lined street. Only two shoppers carrying their purchases headed along the sidewalk in the opposite direction. More security guards stood outside other high-end boutiques nearby. It was coming into awards season, so it was busy. But nothing raised concern.

Cole leaned against the back of his car. "Want to talk about it?"

I swayed on my feet, still overwhelmed by Luther's conversation. "Cole . . . I don't think I can or should or . . . I didn't mean to take a personal call while on duty."

"What the fuck? We're at a suit fitting—not in the middle of a crazy crowd. It's fine. We don't exactly have such thing as normal hours to work around."

Nodding, I stared at the cup lid. "I'm sorry. Luther's just being difficult again."

"What's happened?"

I took a long, slow mouthful of coffee, then savored the hot liquid sliding down my throat and hitting my belly. He's made it just the way I like it, strong and black. *Hmmm. He does notice.* Drawing in a slow breath, I cleared my head. There had to be some calm there somewhere. "Luther is traveling for work and has to take Josh with him. It means I miss my time with Josh tomorrow night."

"Shit. Can he do that? Do you get to swap days around?"

"Doubt it but I can always hope. Luther is rarely logical or reasonable." I raised a finger off my cup and pointed it at Cole. "You're lucky you never have to deal with a partner who doesn't agree with what you want, or puts hurdles in the way, or makes spontaneous, ridiculous changes."

"No." His deep voice lowered. "Becoming a single parent out of the blue isn't easy either."

"I know." I did feel for the guy. "Charlotte has upturned your life but be grateful you have her. She's so beautiful. You have the chance to be everything she needs. I would do anything to have more time with Josh. I live for every moment with him. When plans to see him change, it hurts."

"Hey. Come here." He hooked his arm around my shoulder and rubbed my arm. "I'm sorry. I know you miss him. I've never thought to ask, but is it difficult for you to be around Charlotte? I don't want you to be emotionally tortured or distressed."

He was torturing me right then with his scent, and touch, and compassion. I had to keep my wits about me. "No, not at all." I eased out of his hold. He shouldn't be hugging me. "I love being around her. She makes the days easier. Seeing you with her reminds me there are decent people in the world, trying to do the right thing."

"I'm trying, but I have a lot to learn. You're helping. You're always so calm around her. And gentle. And caring. So if you ever need a kid fix, Charlotte gives great cuddles if you ever need one to make it through the days and weeks until you see Josh."

Yours aren't bad either. "Thank you. Luther won't get away with shit forever. I'm over his games. But his time is nearly up. Karma is going to have a field day with him." I had to believe that. People who were spiteful would be served justice.

He chuckled, low and soft. "Remind me not to get on your bad side."

"No. Don't mess with a scorned woman."

"I'll remember that."

"So have you guys finished?"

"Yes. Lewis and Flint had to get jackets adjusted. They won't be long."

"Excellent. We're off to rehearsal then?" Movement caught my eye. Sloane waved from the top step. I pressed the talk button on my radio. "Sloane?"

"Heads up." His gruff voice came through my two-way. "Gold BMW across the street. Camera is on Cole."

"Thanks." I clicked my radio off.

Cole shrugged, seeming to dismiss any care. Resting his butt against his car again, he stuffed his hands into his hoodie pockets. "So now you don't have Josh, what are you doing tomorrow night?"

"Nothing." Nope, not a thing. Maybe I'd watch an action flick full of shooting guns and big bombs, picturing every round and explosion striking Luther. That had some merit.

"Why don't you come to Sutton's and Tia's launch party with us? It's the premiere of their TV show *Angels in LA*. We could hang out, drink expensive champagne, eat some great food, have some fun."

I coughed, choking on the last mouthful of coffee. My heart rate tripled. "I don't think so. I've seen you have *fun*. And I don't date clients."

"It's not a fucking date. It's a thank you for helping with Charlotte, and so you're not sitting at home alone, bored out of your brain."

I dangled the cup between my fingers and crossed my arms. "You just don't like being by yourself now that the other guys have partners."

"I don't need a chick on my arm." His confident tone never faltered. "I'm just being nice."

"Thank you. But no. We don't need to cross any lines."

The cutest smile curled his lips, but his voice remained cool and casual. "Lines won't be crossed. We'd just be going as friends. Like Maddy and Slip, only without any benefits." *Too suave ... and sexy.* "When was the last time you went to a hot party? One where you weren't on duty?"

"Geez ... um ..." As I scratched my eyebrow, I sifted through foggy, distant memories. "Not since my divorce." *God, I'm sad.*

"So this is perfect. For one night, wouldn't you like to enjoy a fancy outing rather than work at it?"

"I've been to a ton of events before with my ex. It's not new to me."

"But you haven't been to one with us." Too much mischief sparkled in his eyes. Too much temptation ate at my resolve.

"No. I can't. It goes against protocol."

"Fuck protocol. There are no rules prohibiting you from being a friend. You won't be on duty. We're not dating. I promise to keep my hands to myself unless, of course, you beg me not too."

"I'll never beg. Trust me." It didn't matter what the reality was—there'd be consequences. "If I'm seen with you, it will be all over the news tomorrow."

"The thing about me going out with so many chicks is it will be old news within a day or two."

There's a way to make a girl feel special. But that wasn't what this was about. "I can't walk a red carpet with you."

"Why not?" He jerked his chin back. "What's the worst the gossip will say? *'New scandal...Cole Tanner is dating his bodyguard.' 'Is Ava Matthews keeping an eye on her client, even from his bed?' 'Who wouldn't want to be a security guard if it involves banging one of The Flintlocks.'* I don't care if they put us beside Heidi Klum, Britney, and Kim Kardashian on the list of celebrities who have dated their bodyguard—we'll know the truth. It's just an invite. Fuck what people say. Stop being so uptight and live a little."

"Are you always this annoying and persistent?"

"Yes. It's a night out. It will be fun."

I sucked in a deep breath. I hadn't been to a party that didn't involve my work colleagues in months. A backyard grill for Sloane's birthday had been the extent of my raging outings. Thanks to my job, I'd lost touch with many of my girlfriends, and I missed clubbing and dancing. Life had undergone a drastic change since my divorce. I deserved a night out. *Shit.* I couldn't believe I was contemplating this. "I'd have to clear it with Wells."

"Call him." Cole waved toward my jacket pocket. "Right now. On speaker, because I don't want you making up excuses not to come."

There was no way out of this, was there? *Crap.* "Fine."

I handed Cole the empty cup and called Wells.

"Ava?" Wells answered on the second ring.

"Hey." I held my cell phone flat between Cole and me. "Luther's being a prick and taking Josh to New York, stuffing up my rostered time off."

"Shit. I'm sorry." The volume on Wells's voice dialed down. This wasn't the first time Luther had messed up my plans. "So, why are you calling? You want to work?"

"What the fuck? No," Cole jumped in. "No, she doesn't want to work."

"Ava? Is that Cole? What's going on?"

"Nothing." My palms grew clammy. I couldn't believe I was doing this. "Since I have tomorrow night off, Cole's asked me to the *Angels in LA* premiere party."

"Ava?" A million questions and a ton of concern ripped through Wells's tone.

"It's not a date. It's just a friendly invitation since Luther's screwing me over again."

"She needs a night out," Cole butted in. "It's one party. There'll be hundreds of people there. Tia, Sutton, and Maddy will be with us. It's a group outing. That's it."

"Wells, it's my night off." Grit set in my tone. "I don't need your permission to do things in my personal time. I haven't been anywhere in months. You know I love my job. I follow every rule and procedure." *And there is nothing going on between Cole and me.*

Maybe . . . Yes . . . No . . . Nope. Definitely not!

"Ava . . ." Wells's tone turned all fatherly. "If I didn't trust you, I wouldn't have assigned you to Cole. Thank you for checking in with me. But it's fine. You could do with a night out. So do me a favor?"

"What's that?" I winced.

"Have a good time."

Oh . . . "Um . . . I'll try." I scanned Cole up and down. My eyebrow flicked skyward of its own accord. "Hanging out with drunk, arrogant rock stars and their fabulous partners might be awful."

Wells laughed. "It will be better than mulling at home over Josh. If you need anything, let me know. Otherwise, I'll see you on Thursday."

"Okay. Bye." I ended the call and stared at my cell phone. My hand shook and shuddered. *Shit!* I was going to a party with Cole. I hadn't seen that coming. But it wasn't a date. I didn't need the lines to blur. "Guess I'm coming with you . . . on one more condition."

"What's that?"

"You rest on Wednesday." I jabbed my finger against his chest. "You sleep. Stay at home. Do nothing until rehearsal on Thursday."

He grabbed my hand, took a step toward me, pinning me to the spot with his gaze. "You gonna come over and make sure I do that?"

I yanked my hand free. Heat crept into my cheeks as I shook my head. "Careful, Cole Tanner. I might begin to think you like me."

"You're tolerable."

"So are you." *Oh, boy. Am I in trouble?* Maybe this wasn't a good idea.

"At least I'm not an asshole anymore." A lazy, cool smile slid across his lips. "Do you need a dress? Kinda know someone who can help out." He jerked his head toward the boutique.

"No." I tucked my cell phone away. "I have something."

"Nah. Come on. My treat."

"Cole. No."

He grabbed my hand and dragged me toward the door. But it swung open, and the band and my team walked out.

Flint looked from Cole, to me, to Cole's hand clasping mine. "What's going on?"

"Um . . . Ava's coming with us tomorrow night."

My team's eyes popped, and their mouths gaped.

'What the fuck?' Beckett mouthed silently.

Lewis slapped Slip in the arm. "You owe me a hundred bucks."

"Fuck," Slip grunted.

What was that about?

Flint chuckled and shook his head. "Cole, can I speak to you for a sec?" He waved Cole over toward his Ferrari. "What the hell is going on? Ava's your bodyguard."

"Av?" Beckett switched off his radio and edged in beside me. He caught my arm and drew me off in the opposite direction to Cole. *Damn it.* I couldn't hear what Flint and Cole were saying any more. Humor and concern swam though Beckett's eyes. "Can you please tell me what's happening here?"

I pulled my arm free of his hold and straightened my jacket. "I had this fight with Luther over Josh. He's taking him to New York. I was upset. Cole came out with coffee. As a don't-sit-at-home-and-sulk gesture, he invited me to the launch party."

"He asked you out?"

"It's not a date." Irritation swept through my voice. "It's with the band and the girls. Wells approved it."

"Do you have feelings for this guy? More than thinking he's just nice to look at?"

I glanced at Cole talking to Flint, all calm and composed. I may have been like that on the outside too, but my insides were backflipping and somersaulting. I liked the guy, maybe a bit too much, but there was no way those feelings could ever evolve. I didn't need another smooth-talking charmer to break my heart. "No. I don't." *Liar.*

"We're onsite tomorrow night. If he puts a foot out of line, you give us the signal, and we'll take the fucker down."

"Thanks, Becks." I loved that my friends looked out for me, but I was lethal. I could take care of myself.

"You know his reputation. Don't do anything stupid."

"I won't." *God.* That was the last thing I needed to do.

"Good."

I couldn't let my resolve falter. This was just a night out. Some fun.

Should be easy, right?

Chapter 17

AVA

God, this dress is short. I hadn't worn anything like this in years. My palms hadn't stopped sweating since I'd agreed to go to the *Angels in LA* launch party with Cole. In my hotel room, after having my hair and makeup done, I wriggled the sparkly dress into place, zipped it up, and hooked my boobs into position to show off my cleavage. I loved party dresses and high heels, but I hadn't had many reasons to wear them lately. If I wasn't in a uniform for work, I lived in yoga pants and T-shirts. The few dates I'd been on since my divorce weren't to any place fancy—just a local café or restaurant. Those outings didn't call for cocktail gowns and diamonds. I brushed my fingers over the jewels at my throat. This necklace probably cost more than my annual salary. Luckily it was only on loan.

Yesterday at the boutique, after the band had taken off, Cole had taken me inside to get a dress. While Gabrielle worked her magic on me, Cole sat on one of the velvet chairs and made a few phone calls, mainly to April to book me a room at the same hotel as the guys. I'd tried on four dresses. Cole didn't seem to care for any one more than the other, so I picked the one I liked—a red, long-sleeved, sequined minidress. I'd refused to let Cole pay for the outfit, but he'd insisted on doing so for the shoes and clutch, and renting the jewelry. So be it.

Our date, which wasn't a date, seemed to be turning into one more by the minute.

Stupid, right?

He'd probably ditch me the minute we walked into the venue and have his tongue down some chick's throat within the hour. But that reality didn't stop the butterflies from swirling in my stomach. Nor the way my heartbeat quickened when Cole stood too close or looked at me with his hypnotic green eyes.

We were somewhat friends. Going to a party. That was it.

I drained the remains of the glass of champagne I'd had from the minibar to take off the nervous edge. After touching up my bright red lipstick, I buckled on my black Valentino stilettos, grabbed my clutch, and walked out of the room feeling like a million dollars.

I headed up to Sutton and Flint's suite, where I was to meet everyone. As I stepped out of the elevator, Beckett and Kennedy stood outside the room, ready to escort us to the venue.

"Damn, girl." Beckett licked his fingertip, jabbed the air, and made a sizzling sound. "You look hot. Forgot you wore dresses."

"Don't get used to it," I sniggered, then smiled.

"You ready?" Kennedy asked. His warm smile would give Idris Elba a run for his money.

"Sure am." *Yep.* I needed a night out. I sucked in a deep breath and knocked on the suite's door.

Blake opened it, dipped his chin, and waved me in. "Evening, Ava."

As I walked into the living area of the suite, the band and the girls sat on the huge sofas having a drink. My entrance killed their conversation. Shock and surprise flitted through everyone's eyes. Was me being out of uniform that hard to comprehend? Cole jumped to his feet and dashed over to me.

"Wow." He scanned me up and down, and my skin tingled. "You look amazing."

"Um . . . thanks." I wiped my hands on the front skirt of my dress.

"I mean it." Seriousness deepened his tone. "I've never seen your hair out of a braid or bun."

"There's a first for everything." I smoothed my palm over the styled, wavy curls that reached my shoulder blades and touched the rhinestone clip that pinned one side back above my ear. The hairdo was nothing fancy.

"And damn . . . your legs are freaking hot."

"Okay . . . that's enough with the compliments." I slapped his arm with my clutch. Too much warmth touched my cheeks. "They're not necessary."

"They are when they're true."

"Remember, your charm won't work on me. But thank you." I took a small step forward and ran my hand down the silky lapel of his suit. "You don't look half bad yourself thanks to Dolce and Gabbana." I was glad he'd worn that suit. It was the nicest one he'd chosen.

"I scrub up okay when I have to." He grinned, wriggling his tie straight. *Show-off.* "Are you ready to go?"

"Yes."

Everyone stood, placed their glasses on the table and veered toward the door. Out of habit, I stepped back and let the band and their partners go first. But as Slip walked past holding Maddy's hand, he took a small step in my direction and lowered his voice. "It takes a lot to wow Cole. Own it, girl."

"Me?" Heat flushed my skin. *I'd wowed Cole Tanner?* I hadn't been out to impress him, but I couldn't deny Slip's comment gave my confidence a boost.

"You look incredible." Sutton glided by on Flint's arm.

"Thank you. So do you." Styled like a Hollywood screen siren, Sutton dazzled in an electric-blue satin gown.

"She's right." Cole placed his hand on the small of my back and guided me out of the room toward the elevators. His gaze fell to my cleavage and lingered. "You rock that dress."

My nipples hardened. God, why did I like him looking at me?

Lewis chuckled as he hooked his arm around Tia's shoulders. He glanced back and waved his finger back and forth between Cole and Tia. "I warn you, Ava. The Tanners are trouble. Trust me."

"Cole knows his place . . . *Trust* me." I jabbed my elbow into Cole's side, erasing the lusty smirk off his face.

He grunted and grinned as he straightened. "Ow. Thanks for that."

At the elevators, Tia caught my hand and swayed like a sailor at sea. "Damn, I like you. My brother needs someone to keep him in line."

Judging by the vapor of bourbon surrounding her and Lewis, they were well on the way to having a big night. She'd been out of her moonboot since Friday and loved that she had no pain in her ankle anymore. Celebrations were in order. "Tonight is about us girls, not the band. So let's have some fun."

I didn't know Tia, Sutton, and Maddy well, but I looked forward to a night with female company. I didn't see my friend Ramona often as we worked opposite shifts. "I'm off duty. I'm looking forward to letting my hair down."

Cole leaned into me and spoke low into my ear. The hint of alcohol lingered on his warm breath. "Hmmm. I like your hair down . . . a lot."

God. How much vodka had he drunk while I'd gotten ready? I elbowed him gently again. "I'd like you to behave."

"No chance." He swooped in to kiss me, his lips aiming for mine. Panic shot through my veins as I pulled out of the way.

He just chuckled. I blushed like a summer fire had ignited my cheeks.

Flint laughed and shook his head. "Are you two going to be at each other's throats all evening or fuck before the night is through?"

My breath hitched. Was Flint joking, or had he picked up on the simmering vibe between Cole and me? I couldn't afford to let my feelings for Cole develop any further. Lines had to remain in place. Drawing my shoulders back, I glared at Cole. "It certainly won't be the latter."

He raised a questioning eyebrow. "You sure about that?"

"Yes." *But damn.* He'd wanted to kiss me. It had no doubt just been a friendly gesture, but what would his lips feel like against mine? Why the hell had I leaned out of the way? *Oh yeah* . . . Beckett and Kennedy were watching my every move. *Not fun.*

We were whisked to the party in an extra-long stretch limousine. But at every traffic light we stopped at, Cole scanned my legs.

I mumbled to him under my breath, "If you keep doing that, we're going to have a problem."

He whispered, so only I could hear, "I was just picturing them wrapped around my face."

My thighs squeezed together. My core clenched. *Oh, boy.* He'd really drunk too much vodka. It was hard enough coming out with him; I didn't need his dirty talk to make it even more challenging. "I'm picturing my knee slamming into your balls."

Shards of sexy gold shimmered through his vivid green eyes. "I said picturing, not wanting. There is a difference."

"Well keep those thoughts to yourself, please."

"Fine. But I like making you smile and blush."

Was I blushing? *Yep.* God, he messed with my head. Was he just teasing or into me? It didn't matter—either way wasn't good.

As we exited the limo, a flurry of camera flashes hit us. Sloane and Wyatt joined Kennedy and Beckett, flanking us as we headed down the red carpet. Sutton and Flint led the way, followed by Tia and Lewis, then Slip and Maddy. Cole and I lingered at the rear.

He reached for my hand, but I sidestepped out of reach. "What are you doing?"

"We've got to walk the carpet."

"I'm not holding your hand."

His shoulders slumped. "What will be acceptable and look the most *friendly*? I'm either going to hold your hand, hook my arm around your waist, or link our elbows. What's it going to be?"

"None of those options appeal to me."

"Quick." He waved toward the guests coming in behind us. "We're holding up the line."

I glanced at his held out hand, his tall frame, then met his challenging eyes. The cheering crowd filled my ears. *Shit!* I could do this. "Fine. Take my hand." At least I could keep some distance between his body and mine and break his fingers if he tried to get too close.

"Thank you." He slid his hand around mine and entwined our fingers. Warmth and tingles meandered up my arm and shuddered through my chest. *Stupid nerves.* He squeezed my hand. "Are you okay?"

"Yes. I will be if you behave."

"No guarantees." He drew me in close, and we joined the others.

As Sutton and Tia caught up with their fellow castmates—Peyton and Mia—for photos, Maddy and I hung back with the guys. I didn't know where to look. I was so used to being on duty at these events, continually scanning the crowd for suspicious behavior, shady characters, and potential threats. Being on the carpet as a guest again was surreal.

We shuffled past the line of reporters and photographers, posing for random photos. My heart hammered in my chest with each one. What had I gotten myself into? Why was I there? *Oh!* That was right. I needed to take my mind off missing my son. But I wasn't sure spending more time with Cole was a sensible option.

Those eyes. That smile. His touch.

He was a total distraction. *Good . . . but not good.*

He trailed his fingertips across my bare lower back and rested his hand on my hip. "Ava, relax. You look incredible. Just smile. And have some fun."

"I'm usually watching your asses, not having mine on show."

"Your ass is hot. Show it off." He brushed his palm over the sequins of my skirt and drew me against his side. He smiled then moved his lips against my ear. "I do like this dress."

My heartbeat skipped too fast. I closed my eyes and swayed on my stilettos. Something in his tone chipped away at my sanity. Something in his calmness reassured me that everything would be okay. But no matter how much he affected me, I couldn't fall for his smooth talk. "If you keep touching me like that, you'll find yourself face down on this carpet. You know I'll do that."

Chuckling, he returned his hand to my waist. "We don't want

to steal the girls' spotlight."

"No, we don't." But I didn't step out of his hold. I liked him touching me. Maybe too much. Closing my eyes, I took a deep breath. I had to chill. Unwind. He'd been kind and thoughtful to invite me. I didn't want to come across as rude or ungrateful. It had been so long since someone had done something nice for me, I'd forgotten what it was like.

I didn't have to be tough on him all the time. Those defense mechanisms I had in place could slacken for one night. I wanted to enjoy the evening with everyone. He was tipsy; I could handle that. Maybe I could give him a taste of his own flirtatious medicine.

I half turned to him, leaned into his side, and injected a touch of sexiness into my voice. "But I'll rough you up when we get inside if you want me to. I'd like to see you down on your knees at my mercy."

"Yes." Laughing, he hooked his arm around me. "Finally, some sass. That's what I want to see. Let's have some shots and a shit load of fun."

I could only but try.

The second we entered the function room inside the hotel, I downed one champagne, followed by another.

As the night proceeded with speeches and laughter, more alcohol flowed. I didn't flinch when Cole put his arm across the back of my chair, or told dirty jokes, or brushed his arm or leg against mine.

He was being nice, funny, charming. *Shit.*

By the time dinner had finished and morphed into the after-party, everyone was buzzed. But when Slip returned from the bar with a bottle of vodka, a bottle of bourbon, and a stack of shot glasses, my head swayed. *Oh, boy* . . . I had to be careful, or things would get messy. By *things*, I meant me.

Fuck it.

I was there—I was damn well going to enjoy myself.

"Care for a shot?" Cole asked. "What will it be? Vodka or bourbon?"

"Um . . . vodka."

"Good choice. Let's get this party rolling."

We drank one shot. Then another. As we mingled with the guests, I talked to the girls and met the other ladies from the show and their celebrity friends. Aching in my high heels, I opted for a quick break and sat at our table with Tia. Her eyes swam with alcohol as she poured me another shot.

"So, what's with you and my brother?" she asked.

"Nothing. Why?"

"He hasn't taken his eyes off you all night."

"I don't think so." But yeah, I'd caught him staring on random occasions. "We're just work colleagues."

"Maybe. But I think he's into you."

Cole? Into me? "I doubt it. We have a love-hate relationship. I love keeping him in line, and he hates it."

Tia knocked back her shot, giggled, and nodded. "You remind me of his ex, Priah."

His old girlfriend? "How so?"

"You're feisty and don't fall for any of his bullshit. I like that. But you seem nice; Priah wasn't."

"You didn't like her?"

"Hell no." Tia had had way too much to drink, but I didn't mind her spilling about his past. "Cole was madly, insanely in love with her. She was smart. Gorgeous. Ambitious. But I'm convinced she was just with him because she didn't want anyone else to have him. I warned Cole, but he was too lovestruck. Her parents loathed him too. A musician wasn't good enough for their future-doctor of a daughter. I won't deny they loved each other, but her family always came first. She never told Cole about her arranged marriage. It broke him. He was an utter mess for months. He still hasn't gotten over being hurt."

Damn. His relationship sounded like mine. We'd been blind to see the truth, fallen for the lies, and had our hearts shattered. "Priah sounds like my ex. Luther was always jealous if I spoke to another guy. His parents didn't approve of me either. I was a commoner, not from the elite social circles they associated with."

"We came from nothing too."

"I know. I've done my homework."

"Cheers to that." Tia refreshed our drinks then chinked her glass against mine. We knocked back the liquor, then smacked the empty shots onto the table. She grabbed the bottle of bourbon and topped up her glass, then poured a vodka for me. "Is it weird, studying people for security assignments?"

"No." I opted for a glass of water. My head was spinning too fast. "We have to learn as much as possible about who our clients are and what they do each day in order to protect them."

"Then you know Cole's been through a lot." Concern rippled through her eyes. "He's a good person—just a bit messed up like the rest of us."

So true. But how much did she know? Tia seemed like a good sister—she loved Cole. Perhaps she could help me help him. "Have you talked to him lately? He's struggling at the moment. Not just with Charlotte."

"Yeah, I've noticed." I followed her gaze over to him. He was having selfies with some girls by the overcrowded dance floor. "I've tried talking to him, but he bottles everything up inside. I can't get through to him. Therapy has never worked for Cole. He's never been the same since Aidan died."

His high school boyfriend who committed suicide? "How so?"

She rested her elbow on the table and swayed toward me. "Would you believe Cole used to be super shy in school? He'd only come alive when he was behind the drums."

Unable to drag my eyes away from him, I shook my head. These days he lit up the room. "I cannot picture Cole ever being like that."

"Yep. He was." She straightened, took a deep breath, and stared into her bourbon. "Losing Aidan and being fucked over by Priah brought out this need in him to be fiercely protective of those he loved and this drive to live life to the fullest. He wants to enjoy every party, play every gig, and will go out of his way to make sure everyone is happy. He lives for the band. He has glued the guys back together more than once, especially after Phil died. But he's never gotten close to anyone since Priah."

"Are you sure about that?" I grabbed my shot and raised it toward Tia. "Have you seen the girls he brings home? He gets close ... a lot."

She giggled and play-punched my arm, spilling half my drink. I flicked the vodka from my fingertips, laughing along with her. She was wasted ... and funny ... and concerned for Cole too. "Yeah, but that's just sex. Some stress relief. It's not for intimacy or emotional connection. Or stable."

She was right about that. "He's heading for a burnout."

"I'm worried about that too. But . . ." A mischievous smile danced across her lips. "As his security, you'd better make sure he behaves so that doesn't happen."

"Not sure I have that much influence over him. He certainly has a way with women." I jerked my chin in his direction. He stood with Lewis and Slip, chatting with a group of eight girls that included his *friend* Min and a stunning young woman who had flawless dark skin, boobs to die for, and legs as long as the Nile River. She kept touching and knocking into his arm, and throwing Cole suggestive how-about-it glances.

A twinge tugged low in my gut and twanged through my chest. *Don't go there.* He could talk to whoever he wanted to.

But why did he keep looking at me?

"They're good guys." Tia patted and clutched my hand. "It's hard not to like them. When you take away the crap you hear about them in the media, you find they're hardworking and down-to-earth. That's what makes them so special. They're a bunch of great friends who grew up on the back streets of Pasadena. We've all defied our parents to follow our dreams. Every cent we've earned has come from our own sweat, blood, and tears. We really love and care about each other. We're family."

"Reality versus perception." I bobbed my head. Cole had shattered every one of the preconceived notions I'd had about him. The trouble with that was it created a whole new bucket of issues. I liked the guy. More than I should. *Shit.* "Tia, most people in the entertainment industry are dedicated, and passionate, and sacrifice a lot to follow their careers. So are those of us who work behind the scenes. We just don't have to put up with the limelight. And we don't make millions for it."

"I love that you aren't bedazzled by my brother's status or this celebrity crap."

"I've been around this industry for a long time, on both sides of the fence."

She wrinkled her nose. "I can't believe you were married to Luther Carrington."

"Neither can I," I grunted. "He's an asshole."

She laughed and fell against my arm. "I like you, Ava."

Cole waved and wiggled his finger at me to join him. I tucked my hair behind my ear and shook my head.

"Damn." Tia straightened and turned to me. A glassy haze shimmered across her stunning, green eyes. "You're into him, aren't you?"

Warmth rose in my cheeks. "Most days I want to kill him."

"But not today?"

I pursed my lips as Cole ignored the girls around him and burned me with his gaze. *He shouldn't look at me like that. Like I was the only one in the room.* "No. Not today."

"Go, have fun."

"I have to maintain professional boundaries."

"Boundaries can blur, warp, and change at any time. Trust me on that one." She blew Lewis a kiss. I didn't know much about those two other than he used to be gay but was now with Tia. Their blossoming relationship had been all over the Internet a couple of months ago. I just loved seeing them happy.

Cole ambled over to the table with a sexy swagger in his step and held out his hand. "Ava, would you like to dance?"

My pulse jumped a notch. "Um . . . Cole. No. I'm fine."

"I'm not taking no for an answer."

Somehow, I didn't think too many people ever said no to Cole Tanner. I was beginning to see why.

The music was loud. The beat, captivating. Cole, too alluring. I wouldn't win this battle. I held up my finger. "One dance."

"Let's just go with the flow." Cole took my hand and led me out onto the crowded dance floor.

He twirled me around and tugged me close against his chest. A shiver ran up my spine as his body heat enveloped me. I went to step back, but his hand on the small of my back pinned me in place.

My heart hammered too fast. "Cole, you're too close."

"Ava, it's just a dance." He spun me 'round, then he pushed me out, then pulled me back in. Laughing, we swayed and rocked from side to side.

More heat touched my cheeks. "Okay, you've got some moves."

"I'm just warming up."

"I thought you'd be all over some other girl by now. What happened to the one you were talking to before?"

"Raquel? She's um . . ."

"One of your casuals?"

"Used to be." His eyes shimmered when he smiled. "She's got a boyfriend now."

"I'm sure there are plenty of other women, including Min, here willing to take her place."

"Maybe. But I came to the party with you. I don't bring one girl to an event then take another home. Not my style."

"Oh . . ." He never ceased to surprise me.

The music changed to a slow song. Cole slid his hand around my waist and drew me flush against his chest. "So let's just dance, have some fun, and enjoy the evening."

"Cole . . ." I lowered my head, intoxicated by the scent of his divine earthy cologne.

"Ava." He cupped my cheek and tilted my head back so I met his gaze. I swear my knees wobbled and knocked together. "Just . . . dance."

"This is too much," I whispered. "We're too close."

"Ava. Stop. Dance with me."

Clouds fogged my mind. He looked too handsome in his dinner suit. It felt too good to be in his arms. *No . . . no, it doesn't.* I could do this. I stepped back and jabbed my finger against this chest. "No funny business. I don't want to have to hurt you."

"I know you can, so I promise."

"Okay, fine." I placed one hand on his shoulder, one hand on his waist, keeping a foot of distance between us. But within a few steps, he chuckled and tugged me against him.

"This is dancing. We're not fucking fourteen at a church ball."

I giggled. "No, you're right. I'm sorry."

"Better?"

"Give me a minute." In my stilettos, I wasn't much shorter than Cole. I took a deep breath and closed my eyes. With the sides of our heads almost aligned, we slowly swayed and shuffled around in a circle. As his body heat enveloped me, and his warm breath teased my hair, I melted against his chest. *Okay.* This was nice. Slow dancing. Breathing him in. Having his heartbeat against mine.

I slid my hands up his back and rested my chin on his shoulder. *Hmmm.* It had been too long since I'd danced with someone like this. I missed this.

He drew tiny circles on my bare back with his fingertips. I didn't flinch or fuss. But as we turned, I glanced toward the bar. Flint lifted his eyebrows. Slip chuckled and raised his drink. Lewis nodded and grinned.

Panic seized my throat. My heart lurched against my ribs. A sharp pain shot through my head. *Shit.*

I couldn't do this.

Shouldn't be doing this.

This was too much.

I pushed out of Cole's embrace, but he caught me by the arm.

"Hey? Are you okay?"

The intensity in his eyes made me forget how to breathe. How to swallow. And erased the world around me.

Oh . . . hell no.

I shook my head and stumbled a step backward. "Um. No. Excuse me. I need to use the restroom."

As quick as my two feet could carry me, I dashed towards the ladies' room. In the cubicle, I slammed the door shut and leaned back against the smooth surface. Closing my eyes, I sucked in deep breaths. *In . . . out . . . In . . . out.*

Cole had gotten under my skin, in my head, through my thoughts. This had to stop. My job was too important. I was too close to getting Josh back. I couldn't do anything to jeopardize that. I couldn't get involved with my client. If Luther found out, he'd somehow use it against me.

What was it about Cole that had me wanting to stab him with a blade in one moment, then burning for him the next?

Enough was enough.

I had to get out of there.

After doing my business and washing my hands, I headed out of the restroom. I made it halfway down the corridor when a hand caught my wrist and spun me around.

"Ava?" Worry swam through Cole's eyes. "Is everything alright?"

"Yes." I pressed my cool palm against my blazing brow. "I've just had enough. I'm going to head home."

"But it's early."

One a.m. wasn't early. "It's okay. You can stay. I'll be fine."

"No." Concern filtered through his voice. "I'll take you back to the hotel."

"Cole, I'm a big girl. I can catch an Uber."

"I'm coming with you. It's not up for any more discussion." He waved to Kennedy standing by the door and mouthed, "*Time to go.*"

"Ergh." I stormed toward our table. "You're so infuriating."

"I do my best." Cole said as he followed me.

After saying goodbye to the band and the girls, Cole and I slipped into a town car with Kennedy up front and headed toward the hotel.

But every minute that passed, every traffic light we stopped at, every corner we took, his glances became more frequent. The air between us hummed with a spark that shouldn't have been there. My palms wouldn't stop sweating. I could still feel his body next to mine from when we'd danced. I felt the fire in his gaze when he looked at me. This had gone too far.

When the driver pulled up at the hotel, I let myself out. Cole dismissed Kennedy and rushed to follow me. He matched my stride, step for step, as I stormed toward the elevator and up toward my room.

I needed to get away from Cole. I couldn't breathe. Or think. My whole body was overheating.

I swiped my card. It didn't work. I swiped it again. Nothing.

Fuck!

"Ava. Stop." He caught my hand. Took the card. Then opened the heavy door.

But before I could take a step inside, he spun toward me and blocked my path. He cupped the side of my cheek and crushed his body against mine, pinning my back against the open door. The heat in his eyes weakened my knees. "We have a problem, don't we?"

Oh shit.

Yes. Yes, we did.

Chapter 18

AVA

"Did I do something wrong?" Concern rippled through Cole's raspy tone as his breath teased my face.

"No." I closed my eyes and rested my head back against the door. My heart beat too fast.

"We were having a good time." He caught my hand, held it against his chest, and pressed his forehead against mine. "Weren't we?"

"That's the problem. *This* is a problem."

"Tell me about it. You infuriate me. Frustrate me. Order me around. I have tried to ignore you, hate you, but you just keep pulling me in. You drive me fucking crazy."

I slumped against the open door. I'd had too much to drink. Too much heat drew me to him. My voice came out in a pained whisper. "I hate you so much right now."

"Why?" He brushed the edge of his finger down my cheek, then swiped the tip across my chin.

"Because no matter how much I try to keep my distance . . . I can't."

"I hate you too." His lips hovered an inch from mine. "You scare me. I haven't felt anything for anyone in a long time. Every logical, sane reason says I should walk away, but I don't want to. I haven't wanted anyone as much as I want you right now."

I flattened my hand against his chest, stopping him from getting any closer. His heart beat as fast as mine. *Crap.* "You're with women all the time. You can have anyone. Why me?"

"Because you don't want anything in return . . . and . . . I like you."

My breath shuddered through my lungs. I didn't want to use him like one of his casual girls, or brag about him to my friends. I just couldn't turn off my attraction toward him. "I like you too, but this is wrong. I don't want things to get complicated."

"Too late for that. You should've picked the boring black dress at Gabrielle's yesterday, because in this one"—his hot gaze snaked over my outfit as he ran his hand down my arm—"I've struggled to keep my hands off you all night. I've been in agony every time I've been near you."

He'd noticed the dresses? "You're in agony? Do you know how good you look in that suit? Do you think tonight was easy for me?"

He brushed the tip of his nose along the edge of mine and smiled. "Then take it off me."

I swayed on my feet. *Too smooth, Cole.* "You've got all the lines and the moves, haven't you?"

"No games, Ava." Fire burned in the depths of his gaze. "I haven't been able to take my eyes off you all night."

Butterflies flipped in my stomach . . . or was it too much vodka? Maybe both. "I hate that I liked you looking at me."

A small smile played across his lips. "I hate how much I want to kiss you."

Oh, fuck. The heavy door tried to swing shut. *Shit.* I pushed back against it, slamming it against the wall. He chuckled, sending a wave of heat over my body in a hot rush. I drew my shoulders back, held his gaze . . . and whispered, "Where?"

"Here." He kissed the center of my forehead.

I closed my eyes. My heart stampeded against my ribs. *What has happened to my willpower?* 'Stop' formed in my mind, but something entirely different fell from my mouth. "Anywhere else?"

"Here." He pressed his lips against my cheek, buckling my knees.

"And?"

"Definitely here." He scooped my hair back off my shoulder and kissed the soft skin beneath my earlobe.

"That all?" I pressed my thighs together. *Oh God, I'm in trouble.*

Smoldering heat darkened his eyes. "I have a few other places in mind."

My whole body lit with fire. "I hate you."

"Hate me tomorrow." The want in his voice matched the burn blazing in my core.

"This is a bad idea. I can't risk losing my job."

"You won't lose your job. I promise."

"Cole . . ." I'd lost my freaking mind.

"Let me touch you." His breath brushed across my mouth. "Let me kiss you."

"Fuck . . ."

He slid his hand around my waist and edged closer. "I hate you for messing with my head. Making me want you. Making me hard. And making me want to throw you on the bed and make you come so hard they hear you in Manhattan."

Shit. Shit. Shit.

His lips hovered half an inch from mine. "Say yes."

I was a lost cause.

Resistance was useless.

"Yes."

I grabbed the front of his jacket and pulled him into my room. The heavy door fell shut behind us. In the soft darkness, he pinned me against the closet doors. His fierce gaze held me hostage.

"I don't know what it is about you, Ava, but you drive me wild."

I peeled his jacket from his arms, dropped it on the floor.

But then he cupped my face and kissed me.

The world stopped.

Humming rang in my ears.

My heartbeat hammered inside my head.

Oh, God!

He moaned against my mouth, turned his head to the other side, and deepened the kiss. Parting my lips, his tongue teased mine, tasting, taunting, and torturing me. Each kiss spun my head. Each touch scorched my skin. Each taste made me hungry for more.

He cradled the back of my head, drawing me closer, and enveloped me in his embrace. His hard-on dug into my abdomen, building my want for him even more. His loaded licks, sensual sucks, and naughty nips shot euphoric pulses through my entire body and pooled low and hot in my core. *Wow!* If I got nothing else out of tonight, being kissed by Cole Tanner would provide me with a lifetime of blissful dreams.

I yanked off his tie and unbuttoned his shirt. "Your charming smile finally worked."

This was crazy. So much was at stake. But something about this defied sense and sensibility. If seduction was an art, Cole was the grand master. He could paint me with brushes of his fingertips, swipes of his tongue and kneads of his hands. Each day he chipped away at my resolve. But I was too broken and damaged to be molded into something new. I wasn't delusional. I knew what he was like. He may have made a crack in the steel cage around my heart, but there was no way I'd let him in. Someone like him would destroy it in a millisecond. It had taken me too long to rebuild my life after Luther had shattered me. There was no way I could go through something like that again. Was it wrong to want to forget my problems for a while? *God.* I hoped not.

"My smile had nothing to do with it." Cole kissed his way up the side of my neck and nipped my earlobe. His fiery breath sent goose bumps shivering down my arm and jolted through my chest. "Everything about you has gotten to me, Ava. Your fucking sexy eyebrows. Your ass when you run. Your hot legs . . . and the way you are with my kid. You're the temptress here. Not me." He kissed me like every touch burned him, but with every raw moan, he craved more. He pushed me against the closet, slid his hand down my hip and fumbled with the bottom of my minidress. "Can I touch you?"

Between my legs ached in anticipation and with an agony I'd never felt before.

I wanted him to bury himself inside me but leave me alone. Stay but run away. This was ludicrous, pure madness, but I was addicted. I slid my trembling fingertips down his bare chest, over his rigid abs, and traced the shapely V near his hip. I ached to touch every inch of his body, feel him flush against me. The fire in my veins seared my skin. I slipped my hand around his naked waist, drew him forward, and crushed my lips against his. "Yes.

He groaned. The raspy rumble in his throat reverberated through me, throbbing in my core. If he didn't fucking touch me, I'd have to touch myself.

"Ava?" He slowly slipped his hand underneath my dress. As he placed his other hand against the closet door beside my head, he met my gaze with darkened eyes. Nothing but want and desire swirled in their depths. *For me.* Maybe this was just sex. I wasn't naïve. But it still felt incredible to be here with him. Slowly, softly, he brushed his hand across the front of my panties. "Is this okay?"

The breath rushed from my lungs. *Fuck.* They were already damp. "Uh-huh."

"Turned on, are we?"

"So are you," I murmured against his mouth. His erection digging into me had been impossible to ignore. "The thing is, what are you going to do about it?"

"This." He swept his tongue along the seam of my lips, then dipped his finger under the edge of my panties. He teased the front of my pussy, tickling and torturing me. Then he eased into my arousal, stroking me up and down. "Mmm." He drove into my opening. "Good to see you're not as cold on the inside as you are on the outside."

"I'll give you frostbite another day." Biting my lip to contain my grin, I closed my eyes. My head fell back against the door. My hips pulsed against his touch. I wanted more . . . of him. "Oh, wow. That's so good. Can I touch you?"

"You have my consent to do anything you want to. Okay?"

"Same." I fumbled with his belt, unzipped his pants, and lowered his trunks. *Holy. Fuck!* Air shot from my lungs. My insides clenched, skipped, and happy danced. I wrapped my palm around his long, thick cock and rubbed it up and down. "You better have more endurance using this than you do when running."

"I guarantee it." He chuckled, raspy and hot, then . . . he kissed me. Every time, he stole my breath.

He repositioned his hand, dipping it into the top of my panties. In masterful strokes, he slid through my wetness, rubbing and working my clit. I raised my leg, widened my knees, and curled my ankle around his calf. Two fingers entered me; his thumb tortured my clit. *Oh, yeah.*

His breaths grew shorter and heavier than before. "Fuck, you feel good."

My knees weakened. As I circled my thumb over the tip of his cock and stroked him up and down, he thrust against my touch. He rubbed me harder, curling and pulsing his fingers inside of me. Fast. Slow. Deep. *Oh yeah.* I rocked against his onslaught. Our kisses turned into nothing but fiery breaths and hot pants. Like when we'd first exercised to outdo each other, our hands were desperate to see who could make the other one come first.

This time, he was winning.

As he pressed harder against my clit, I dug my fingers into his shoulders. "There."

"Hmmm." He rubbed and circled me. His fingers made me forget my own name . . . and where I was . . . and who I was. All the frustrations from the past few weeks of Cole testing me, pushing me, annoying me, and being so nice and kind and caring built higher, tightened more, coiled through me . . . then snapped. He took me over the edge. Fire shot through my veins, snaked up my spine, and shivered across my skin. Electric shocks jolted my core and shuddered through my entire body. I clutched the back of his short hair. "Oh, fuck. I needed that."

My knees buckled, but he caught me. He smiled against my lips. "We're not even close to done."

"Prove it, drummer boy."

Taking my hand, he drew me toward the bed. As he kissed my shoulder, he undid the low zip on my dress, eased the sleeves off my shoulders, and let it fall to the floor. It pooled in a pile of silky beads and sequins on the carpet. His pants, trunks, and shirt, and my lingerie quickly joined it.

He kissed me, then licked his lips. "Mmm . . . stay."

Standing naked in the middle of my hotel room, I swayed on my feet. Cole dashed over to the door, swiped his jacket off the carpet, and pulled out his card wallet. He ripped out a condom. "You still sure about this?"

I stole a glance at his huge erection. *Am I?* "Yeah. I am. You?"

He came over, slid one arm around my waist, and cupped my cheek with his other hand. "I hate how much I want you."

I curled my arms around his shoulders. "I hate that I want you too."

As we crawled onto the bed, his electric eyes bored into me. Something about them threatened to take a blowtorch to the lock on my heart . . . but no. I wasn't going to lose my head or heart to Cole. This was just sex. Nothing more. We both needed to get this out of our system. Move on.

Kissing me, he pushed me down onto the mattress. Playful touches, small smiles, and silly laughs mingled with our heated gazes and hot kisses. Fingertips tickled and traced arms and hips. Hands massaged and caressed skin, hair, and faces. Lips tasted and teased.

Cupping my breast, he massaged it gently, then swiped his thumb across my peaked nipple. Dipping his head, he took it into his mouth. *Oh, wow.* I drove my fingers through his hair and cradled his head, savoring the tingles his licks sent through my system. Finally, I'd found a way to stop him talking. But wow, his attentive detail and ability to make every cell in my body hum was uncanny. That mouth of his deserved an Academy Award—it was pure talent. But enough was enough. Tickling his ribs, I shoved him backward. I flung my leg over him, straddling his waist. Clutching his hands, I pinned them beside his head. "Are we going to fool around all night or get down to business?"

"Both." He swept my loose hair off my face and tucked it behind my ear.

"We can't. You need to get some rest, remember?"

"There is no chance of that happening while I'm in your bed." He drew me forward and kissed me until I didn't know which way was up or down. He tormented my sanity with his magnetic gaze and smooth talk.

But after flipping me back down onto the bed and making me come with his tongue, something in the air changed. My heart beat against his in a steady rhythm. Our kisses weren't so rushed. My fingers dug into his flesh, wanting to hold him closer, tighter. Our frenzied, fun, and frantic pants morphed into slow and sensual intoxicating breaths. He slipped the condom on, drew my leg over his hip, and entered me—first the tip, then he worked his way in deeper and deeper. *Holy geez.* In a hot haze, we moved as one. He thrust; I rocked. My fingertips blazed as I circled them over his back and arms, stroked and clutched his hair, and caressed his face.

But the need for release burned like a wildfire inside me.

Rolling him onto his back, I straddled him again. I took him in deep and rode him hard. His eyes fluttered shut as I lost myself in a blissful beat. His moans urged me on. My core clenched around his throbbing cock, driving him in deeper to hit me in that sweet spot. *So. Damn. Good.*

His jaw locked. "You keep doing that, I'm gonna blow."

"Me too."

"Fuck," he hissed through his teeth.

The veins on his neck strained.

He dug his fingers into my thighs as he thrust into me harder.

"Ava." His whole body tensed, jerked, and quaked. As he orgasmed, a huge grin inched across his face. Panting, his chest heaved with each jagged breath. "Fuck, that's good."

"Don't move. I'm close. There!" With no holding back, I rubbed and rocked against him. I clutched onto the bedding. Concentrated on grinding and pulsing and taking his hardness into me. Tension coiled, spiraled, and built inside my depths . . . *Yes. Oh . . . yes.* My orgasm shot through me. Shivers danced across my skin, skipped up my spine, and shot over my scalp.

Leaning forward, I kissed his gorgeous lips. "Wow. That was

hot." I hadn't had sex this good in a long time. In fact . . . ever. What the hell had come over me? Oh, that was right. *Cole Fucking Tanner.*

As I collapsed beside him, he combed his fingers through my hair and rubbed the back of my head. He smiled against my lips. "You are full of surprises. I'm not sure that's a good or bad thing?"

"Hopefully good."

"I have two more condoms, and it's not morning yet."

Delectable pulses still throbbed between my legs. I hadn't recovered from round one. "Isn't that enough?"

"That fuck was for looking so hot in your dress. Now I'm gonna fuck you because seeing you naked is a whole new level of craziness I need to get out of my system. That okay?"

I didn't have any other plans on my agenda. But he did. "You need to rest."

Mischief coursed through his eyes. "Let's go take a shower and see what happens."

I trailed my fingers down his chest and headed toward his cock. "Oh, I think we both know what's gonna happen if we do that."

"I'm glad we're on the same page."

Yes. For now.

But after tonight . . . after this . . . how was I going to hate him in the morning?

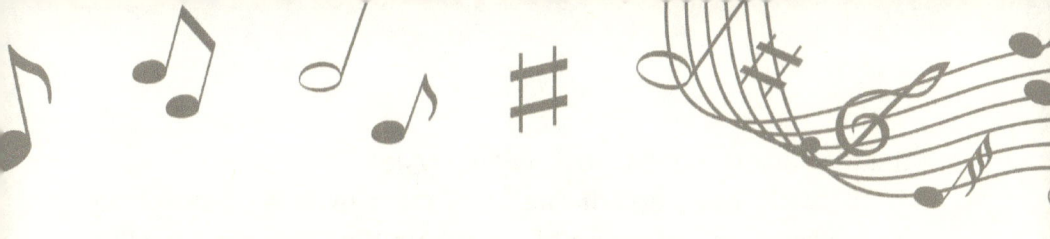

Chapter 19

COLE

I woke, squinting against the soft morning light that filtered into the hotel room around the far edge of the curtain. My head ached, fuzzy from too much drinking. But as my vision cleared, my breath hitched. Ava slept beside me. Her face loomed inches from mine. *Fuck!* Our arms and legs were tangled together. The crisp, white hotel sheet was a twisted, knotted mass draped over our waists. Last night flashed before my eyes. The party. Dancing. Rushing back here. Fucking her senseless.

The whole room smelled of sex . . . and Ava. *Shit!* How many times did I make her come? By the door, on the bed, during sex, and in the shower . . . *Damn.* That had been a good night.

But the dull ache in my head turned into a pounding hammer. Nausea loomed low in my gut. How could I have been so reckless? I covered my eyes with my arm. I'd done some stupid things in my time but sleeping with my bodyguard was a new level of crazy even for me. This wasn't good. Another huge mistake. But why did she make me feel things I didn't want to feel? That pull, that draw, that burn to be with her had to stop. The last time I'd fallen for someone, my heart had been obliterated. That was not a path I wanted to venture down again.

That wasn't what this was, was it?

My blood pressure crept higher and higher. My temples

thudded and throbbed. *No . . . definitely not.*

I took a deep breath and let it out slowly. As I swept my gaze over Ava's sexy mass of wavy hair, the three dark freckles that formed a perfect triangle on her cheek, and the swollen lips I'd kissed until I could barely breathe, the tightness in my chest dissipated. What was it about her that made me want more? I wanted more . . . but couldn't have it. Not ever. I had nothing to offer her. Nothing more than a hot night between the sheets. My life was music and travel, women and parties. Her life was Josh. It was ludicrous to contemplate this going beyond one night. I'd only end up hurting and disappointing her. Fucking up like always.

Ava deserved to be with someone better than me.

The sooner I killed my feelings for her, the better. I had the tour and Charlotte to focus on . . . not Ava.

She wriggled and stretched beside me, giving me a damn good eyeful of her gorgeous naked tits. Her lazy, sleepy smile nearly had me coming undone.

But then she opened her eyes. Wild panic flashed and flared in their brown depths.

"Oh, shit." She sat upright and drew the sheet over her chest. "You've got to get out of here. Now."

There's a blow to the ball sack. Ignoring the low twang in my chest, I summoned a playful smile. I wasn't kicked out of bed very often. I agreed with her, I did have to go, but I wasn't an asshole. Rolling onto my side, I propped my head on one hand and draped my other one over her hip. "Good morning to you too."

"Cole." She flicked the sheet off and leaped out of bed. She picked my clothes off the floor and threw them at me, hitting me in the face. "You have to go. Before someone realizes you're not in your room."

"Ava." I piled my clothes into a heap beside me. "Hotel security are covering us until we leave—not your team. We're fine."

"It doesn't matter." She rushed over to her bag, yanked out a bra and panties, and slipped them on. "This isn't good."

I rubbed my brow. Her stress levels didn't help lower mine. "No, it's not ideal. But we need to talk—"

"Cole, I don't want to talk." She ripped on a T-shirt. "Last night shouldn't have happened."

"Maybe not. But it did." I found my trunks, jumped off the bed, and pulled them on. "We had a fuck-load of fun in the process."

"Fun?" The anguish in her tone shuddered through my bones. "You're my client. Getting involved blurs the lines. I need to stay focused on protecting you, not getting emotionally involved. Fuuuuck!" She paced in front of the TV cabinet. "What have I done? I needed a perfect record and reference from Wells for the courts. Without one, I could lose Josh or not get more time with him. Oh, no. No. No. Oh, shit." The fear quaking in her voice stabbed every muscle in my chest.

"Ava." I stepped over to her and caught her upper arms. She wouldn't lose her son because of me. "I won't let that happen. I'll provide you with whatever reference or high recommendation you need. Last night had nothing to do with your job. We got carried away in the heat of the moment. We let off some steam. We got whatever has been brewing between us out of our systems. It's okay."

"How can you be so calm?" She closed her eyes and swayed on her feet. "We fucked up."

"I'm not calm. Trust me." I may have been on the outside, but my pulse was shooting through my veins, rapid-fire. "But we need to work out how to handle this and set our story straight. I don't want you to lose your job. I don't want things between us to change. I don't want you to regret last night. Because I had a fucking great time. You were amazing."

She met my gaze. The storm of panic that had been brewing there transformed into clouds of doubt. "Really?"

"Yeah. Really." I never lied about great sex.

Her shoulders slumped. She twisted out of my hold and sank onto the end of the bed. "Shit." Her fingers trembled as she ruffled them through her hair. "We got carried away, didn't we?"

"We certainly did." I sank beside her. I hooked my arm around her back and gave it a rub. "It wasn't my intention or part of a plan. Please believe me." I'd honestly just wanted her to come to the party and have a fun night. But when I'd danced with her, something in the air between us had shifted. I'd upset her. I'd wanted to make sure she got back to the hotel safely, but that was when things had spiraled in a completely different direction.

"It wasn't mine either." She pursed her lips, then blushed. "I don't think I've ever had four orgasms in a week before let alone in one night."

"You've been missing out." I chuckled, tugging her against my side.

"Clearly." She play-punched my arm. "But don't get a big head over it."

"I won't." *Maybe just a little.*

She winced and rubbed the deep grooves in her brow. "But when Wells finds out, this isn't going to go down well. I could get pulled from this gig or fired. Fuck!"

My head raced, searching for a reasonable story. Everything from *I got wasted and passed out* to *I tried to hook up with her but she knocked me unconscious* to *I spent the night throwing up in her bathroom* flitted through my mind. Funny thing was, they were all believable. I just didn't want our night together to cause any problems. "Hey?" I rubbed her back again. "Why does he have to find out? No one knows I'm here. Kennedy left us last night out the front of the hotel. Does your team access hotel footage? Will they see I didn't go to my floor and stay in my room?"

"No." She shook her head. "We only do that if there is an incident."

"Has there been an incident?"

"No." She fidgeted with her hands in her lap and stared toward the door. "But what if you run into someone when you walk out the door and return to your floor?"

I shrugged my shoulder. I'd left plenty of hotel rooms that hadn't been mine before. "I'll just say I picked up some chick in the hotel bar and stayed in her room."

She faced me, raising both eyebrows, then softened her voice. "You'd do that to cover my ass?"

"It's a damn fine ass, so yes." I covered her hands with mine and held them against her bare thigh. Thighs I'd explored every inch of last night, and I'd enjoyed every moment spent doing so. "I'll take this to my grave if you want. I'm good at keeping secrets." Until they blew up in my face, like sleeping with Shelby had. But no. I didn't want Ava to get into trouble. We'd keep this between us.

She lowered her chin. "I don't want to be dishonest with my team, but I can't risk this somehow getting back to Wells . . . or to Luther. He'd find a way to use it against me to keep Josh."

"I won't let that happen." I swirled my thumb against her soft flesh in slow circles. "I don't want to lose Charlotte either. I've got Hannah watching my every move too, reporting to the social worker. Neither of us needs this to go beyond that door. I'm not sorry for the incredible night we had. I certainly won't forget it in a hurry. But for now, we have to act like nothing happened."

"How can I do that?" She turned toward me and clutched my hands against her chest. She searched my face—for what, I had no fucking idea. Her voice jumped, taking on an anguished, desperate tone. "You want me to lie? I can't do that. I'm falling in love with you. Don't you feel the same way? Don't you want me to be your girlfriend? Be with me forever?"

"Shit." Hot nausea swept over me. Where the fuck had this Ava come from? I closed my eyes, shook my head, and lowered my chin. My heartbeat pummeled my ribs. Painful jolts stabbed behind my eyes. I didn't want this. "Ava . . . you know who I am. I like you, but . . ."

"Cole." She shoved me hard on the shoulder and burst out laughing. "I'm fucking with you. I'm not in love with you. I'm not stupid. We had one night of crazy, hot sex. But it can't happen again. We have to be sensible and responsible. For our kids' sake, if nothing else."

"Yes, but fuck me . . ." A wave of relief shot through my bloodstream. I swiped my hand down my cheek, then rubbed the center of my chest. My heart rate still hadn't returned to normal. "You scared the shit out of me. Don't do that. You get too much satisfaction out of torturing me, don't you?"

"I can't deny that." Her eyes sparkled as the outer edge of her eyebrow flicked upward.

Hmmm. I liked that. "You're mean."

"I'm sorry." As she giggled, the most gorgeous smile lit her face. "But your reaction was priceless."

I slid my hand up the inside of her leg and buried my face into the small of her neck. "I should throw you down on this bed, have my way with you again, and make you pay. I'd torture you in a completely different way."

She placed her palms on my chest and pushed me back. She pursed her lips, unable to hide the heat rising in her cheeks. "Um . . . no. We can't. From now on, it's best if I don't go to any more parties with you. Don't drink around you. And keep everything between us professional and work-related."

"Yeah." I brushed my thumb down the side of cheek. I had to agree with her. We'd had an amazing night, but it was time to put it behind us. It didn't change the fact I liked looking at her, being with her, and taunting her though. "You can go back to kicking my ass during our runs, getting me to places on time, and pulling me into line when necessary."

"Deal." She placed her hand over my face and pushed me away. "Now get dressed and get out of here."

As I stood, her cell phone rang.

She grabbed it off the cabinet beside the television. The color drained from her face as she answered it, putting her cell phone to her ear. "Luther?"

"Ava." Luther's voice reverberated from Ava's phone. The volume was so loud, I could hear Luther clearly. I didn't mean to eavesdrop, but it was impossible not to listen. "My meeting in New York was successful. I didn't have to stay for as long as planned. I've just landed in LA. You can have Josh for the night. That way I can head out to Palm Springs and play golf."

"You're back?" Her face lit up, and she stood two inches taller. "Of course you can bring Josh over. I'd love to have him . . . and tomorrow night too if you want to stay out there longer." Hope filled her voice, but she winced as if knowing the answer to her request before he'd spoken a word.

"No. It's tonight or nothing." His surly tone dripped with acid. "I'll see you in forty-five minutes."

He hung up.

For a brief second, hurt washed across her eyes, no doubt at Luther's blunt tone, changes, and not being able to score more time with her son. But then she sucked in a deep breath and the sun rose in her big smile. "I get to see Josh today. Yay!"

Would I ever look forward to seeing Charlotte? Hannah had taken her to San Fran on Monday to see Paul. They'd get home later tonight. Did I miss my kid waking me early? Leaving her toys all over the floor? Her big smile, cuddles, and laughter? Yeah . . . I kinda did.

"That's awesome." I pulled on my suit pants and zipped them up. "Do we have time for me to go change and then meet you downstairs for a quick breakfast?"

As I slipped on my button-down shirt, she raked her gaze over my bare chest. The low simmer in her eyes warmed my blood a few degrees too much.

"Rain check." She stepped over to her bag and grabbed a pair of jeans. "I need to get home."

"I'll take you. But we at least need coffee first. I'm dying here without it." My hangover wasn't too bad, but I needed caffeine.

"You don't have do that. I'll catch a taxi or Uber."

"No, it's fine." I sat on the bed and put on my shoes and socks. "As my date-that-wasn't-a-date, I'd like to take you home. I'll call Kennedy. He's gotta pick me up anyway. He can drop you off too."

"But it's twenty minutes out of your way."

"In this town, that's nothing." I swiped my jacket off the floor and smacked her arm with it. "Stop arguing. I'm happy to take you home. Consider it a thank you for coming to the party and for a mind-blowing night of hot sex. "

"Fine. One sec." She dashed past me into the bathroom. She returned with the diamond necklace, laid it in its velvet box, and handed it to me. "Can you return this to Gabrielle for me?"

"Sure. I'll get the hotel concierge to deliver it back to her." I took the box. "It looked good on you."

She tucked her hands into her jeans pockets and rounded her shoulders. "Like Cinderella, I'm back to plain Jane me."

"You're not plain, Ava. Far from it." I stepped toward her, brushed my thumb across her mouth, then kissed her soft lips. Just a gentle touch. My balls ached for more action . . . but no. We were done. "Thank you for a great night that didn't happen. I'll meet you in the lobby."

"Uh-huh. Yep. In five minutes?"

Had my kiss flustered her? Maybe a fraction. *Cool.* "Make it ten. Don't be late."

"I'm never late. But you always are."

"I'll be there. If not, you can ditch me."

"If you're a second late, I will."

"I like a challenge. I'll see you soon, Ava."

I headed out the door. The hallway was clear. I rushed to the elevator and pressed the call button.

God. What a night. That had been fucking wild. But now I had to forget about it and put it behind me.

I wasn't sure how I'd do that. But I had to.

I didn't want to cause any problems. For Ava. For her job. For our kids. I had enough to deal with—I didn't need to add any more items onto my long list of never-ending worries.

How bad would the fallout be if someone found out about us?

Shit. Don't go there.

I never wanted to find out.

Chapter 20

AVA

I grabbed two takeaway coffees from the café in the lobby and stood by a huge flower arrangement, waiting for Cole. I stayed clear of the bustle of people checking in and out at the reception counter, gathering in small groups to chatter, and dashing outside to catch their rides. Kennedy stood waiting by our Suburban, blocking half the driveway. With an air of over-importance in his stiff stature, dressed in full uniform and with comms and black Ray-Bans on, no one dared to question him.

My hungover, over-sexed body was grateful he was on duty this morning, not me. The late night, the scent of Cole lingering on my skin, and the remains of a dull headache had left me weary and woozy. But it was nothing two Advil and a strong black coffee wouldn't cure. Seeing Josh would erase the ache too.

I glanced at my watch. Cole had two minutes until I was out of there.

But as I looked up, one of the elevators pinged and opened. Cole stepped out. As he ambled across the foyer with his dark shades on, cell phone to his ear, and overnight bag and suit draped over his shoulder, all eyes turned in his direction. Butterflies fluttered in my belly. I'd seen what was under those ripped jeans and that gray hoodie. Touched every fine inch of his naked body. Those visions wouldn't leave my head in a hurry.

He ended the call and had a quick word with the concierge, handing over the box with the necklace I'd worn in it.

I picked up my overnight bag, joined him, and handed him his coffee. "You're on time. I'm impressed. Here. This will help clear the head."

"No hangover here." He took the cup and threw me a devilish grin. "I burned all the alcohol out of my system last night."

"I don't know what you're talking about." I played coy, but between my legs clenched, recalling every hot, orgasmic moment. So did my tingling nipples. And my quivering fingers. My time with him played on repeat through my mind. Now, somehow, I had to hit stop. *Soon . . . maybe tomorrow . . . when I'm back at work.*

He chuckled and took a sip of coffee. A soft moan murmured in his throat as he licked his lips. "Mmm. That's good. But not as good as last night. I had the most incredible dream." He leaned in and whispered in my ear. "It was very vivid and very hot."

"Lucky you." *God.* My cheeks were ablaze. We had to get out of there.

He straightened and a playful smile inched across his mouth. "Best dream I've had in a long time."

"Is that so?" I teased. "I had a shocking night. I didn't get much sleep. And I ache all over."

"I'd be happy to give you a massage."

My muscles screamed *yes* at his suggestive, how-about-it tone, but no . . . we had to put last night behind us.

"No, thanks. I'm good." Spinning around, I walked backward toward the door. "We have to go."

We headed outside. From across the road, at least twenty paparazzi stood posed with their lenses directed at the hotel, no doubt desperate to catch a picture of the aftermath of a big party. The Flintlocks and the cast of *Angels in LA* weren't the only celebrities who had stayed there last night. But the gold BMW parked in front of them caught my eye. A telescopic lens was aimed straight at us. Was it the same one that had been outside Gabrielle's Boutique? I didn't know how the guys put up with being followed to feed Internet gossip. But if the photographers were after a shot of Cole looking his worst, they'd be disappointed. The guy could be a fucking supermodel. But a shot of him to create gossip about his latest hookup? . . . That was a whole different dilemma. My stomach swayed. *Ergh!* Why had I agreed to go out with him again? *Oh yeah* . . . to have a night of fun. A smile curled across my lips. I'd had that along with a few unexpected bonuses.

I could handle a couple of days of gossip. I'd known what I'd be in for when I'd agreed to go with him. Everything would be fine.

Cole waved at the cameras and smiled.

Crazy man.

Kennedy nodded and opened the door. "Good morning, Mr. Tanner." As Cole climbed into the car, Kennedy pulled me aside. "Hey? You didn't look happy when I dropped you off last night. Is everything okay?"

"Yeah." I patted his arm. "Cole and I just had a misunderstanding. We talked it out. Everything's good." That wasn't entirely a lie. Cole had thought he'd done something wrong and upset me, and talking things out involved a lot of mind-blowing sex. But yeah . . . we were cool.

"I'm surprised all his limbs are still attached."

"So am I. He might have a few scratches and bruises though." That was highly possible. Last night had been wild and wicked. "Are you sure you want to give me a lift home?"

Kennedy dipped the rim of his baseball cap. "Mr. Tanner insisted on it."

I sighed and grabbed my cell phone out of my purse. "Okay. But first I want to get some photos of the gold BMW across the road. I'm sure it's the same one that was at the guy's fitting on Monday. Stand there and smile."

Kennedy sneered as I took a few steps back and took photos over his shoulder of the car.

Once I'd finished, he waved me into the back seat. "We'll drive by and record the car on the dash cam too."

"Excellent. Let's go." I slid onto the seat beside Cole. Kennedy jumped in the front next to Eric, our driver, and we took off toward my house.

Cole tilted his head toward me. "Everything okay?"

"Yeah. He was just checking up on me." I didn't need to raise concerns about the suspicious car. I was sure it was just one of the paparazzi pack.

"Big brother keeping an eye on you?"

"Always."

He scanned a message that popped up on his cell phone but didn't reply, turning his phone face down against his leg. "I talked to Flint before. I'm going to hang out with the guys later this afternoon at his place. Sutton wants to make us a few homecooked meals before the tour."

I jabbed my finger into his thigh. "You're supposed to be resting. Sleeping. Not going out."

"Dinner with friends isn't going out."

"Yeah. It is."

"Charlotte and Hannah don't get home from San Fran until ten-ish. I promise I'll be home for them and in bed by midnight, maybe one at the latest."

"Cole." I pointed at him. "By eleven." I didn't want to mother him, but the guy needed a good ass-whipping.

Mischief danced through his eyes. "You gonna come over and make me?"

"No. I'm off duty and will be with Josh. Kennedy or Tank can tuck you in if needed."

"I don't do no tucking," Kennedy hollered from the front. "I'll get your drunk ass home and into your house, Mr. Tanner. But that's it."

Cole chuckled, jutting his chin toward Kennedy. "No tucking required, thanks, Kennedy. Nor from Ava. She'd probably smother me with a pillow or strangle me with the sheets."

Wasn't sure if they were things I wanted to do to Cole in his bedroom, but I played along. "Don't give me any ideas."

Ten minutes later, we pulled into my street and drew to a halt on the curbside. Kennedy jumped out and opened the car door for me.

I grabbed my belongings and turned to Cole. An awkward tie

of invisible air warped between us. I wanted to lean over and kiss him goodbye but couldn't. "Thanks for an . . . interesting night." That was one way of putting it. "I had fun. I'll see you tomorrow."

I slid out of the car, but Cole followed me. "I'll walk you to the door."

"You don't have to do that."

"I know. But I am." He eyed Dad's small, white stucco house with its brown wooden fence line, rickety gate, and broken concrete pathway. "Cute place."

"It's old and crappy, but it's home." I headed for the gate. "I grew up here. My intention was to only stay here for a couple of months after my divorce, but then Mom got sick. Luther turned into a nightmare. I started my new job and haven't had time to find somewhere to live."

"Ava, you don't have to make excuses or justify why you live with your dad. You've got to do what's right for you. I couldn't wait to get out of home, but I didn't always live in a multimillion-dollar mansion." He lifted the wooden latch on the gate, held it open as we entered, leaving it ajar behind us. "I grew up in a house similar to this in the backstreets of Pasadena, only our place was two stories. My parents totally gutted and renovated it after I moved out."

"Are they still there?"

"Officially yes, but they hardly spend time there anymore. Mom works for a big pharmaceutical company and spends most of her time in Paris. Dad goes with her, consulting on engineering projects whenever he feels like it."

"Living the dream." We ambled along the short pathway and climbed the three front steps.

"More like good riddance."

"You don't get along?" I dropped my overnight bag in front of the door and dug for my house keys in the bottom of my purse.

"No." He leaned against the porch pole and crossed his ankles. "Tia and I didn't turn out like they'd planned. They wanted Noble Prize winners and corporate geniuses who changed the world, not rock stars and actress-cum-sound-engineers."

"But you're so successful. You touch people's lives with music and entertainment. You're one of the few who've made it. Aren't they proud of what you've achieved?"

He shrugged one shoulder. "I assume they are, but I wouldn't know it. I barely remember a meal with them that didn't involve heated arguments over us wasting our intelligence and not doing something more constructive with our lives." He lowered his chin and stuffed his hands into his pockets. "Would you believe I graduated in the top five kids in my class at high school? Tia did the same."

"Wow." I didn't know that. I pushed the door open, tossed my bag inside, and turned back 'round to face him. I leaned against the doorjamb. "So you're good-looking, talented, and smart?"

"Nah." He pulled a leaf off the nearby shrub and fidgeted with it. "I'm just a guy who loves playing the drums, hangs out with my friends all day, and gets to travel the world doing those things."

"That's pretty incredible." *Wouldn't we all love to do that?* "But it must have been hard in the beginning without encouragement and support from your parents."

"Music was good for the brain but not a career."

"You wanna sit for five?" I pointed toward the steps. Luther wouldn't be far off. Talking to Cole would help pass the time until Josh arrived. And Cole intrigued me. He rarely opened up. So much went on inside that head of his, I was more than happy to listen . . . and get to know my client better. Kennedy and Eric wouldn't mind waiting a few more minutes. "I'd ask you inside for another coffee, but Dad will probably be asleep after coming off night shift."

"Ava, I don't want to come inside." A small smile played across his lips. "I just wanted to be a gentleman and walk you to the door."

"Oh . . . okay. Good." I was glad we'd cleared that up.

"Have you always got along with your dad?"

"Yes." We took a seat on the top step. "My family is really close. Mom and Dad always encouraged me and my sister to follow our dreams. Celina always wanted to be a nurse for as long as I can remember. I wanted to be a cop. They were stoked when I joined the force. Luther wasn't. When the shit hit the fan after my divorce, they said I could stay here until I sort myself out. I'm still working on that bit. But it's been good living here with Dad since Mom died. We've helped each other through the rough times."

Cole rested his elbows on his bent knees. "You're lucky to have a family like that. My band is my family. We've had our ups and downs but survived. Some days I don't know how."

"But you seem to get on so well." I stretched out my legs and crossed my feet.

"We do. They're my life. But there've been several times we've come close to calling it quits. Most of those times were over some girl." His eyebrows pinched together as he half-smirked. "We have this thing called the dibs rule. You're not allowed to touch each other's girlfriends, their friends, or anyone's exes. It came about after Phil and Flint got into a fight over Shelby in high school. Flint was so in love with her. So was Phil. So was everyone. She was popular. Pretty. Smart. It was impossible not to like her."

"You included?" I nudged my shoulder against his.

He lowered his chin and shook his head. "Just as a friend."

"So how did you end up sleeping with her?"

He took a deep breath and stared toward the open gate. "I wasn't in a good place at the time." Cole relayed the night of the drunken drug-fueled Christmas party, how broken he'd been after Priah left, how the grief and guilt had crippled him after Aidan's suicide and how consoling Shelby, who'd been upset over Flint, had gone too far. The agony and anguish in his voice speared my heart. "Flint is like a brother to me. I never wanted to hurt him. I never wanted to lie to him. But I was unsure Shelby really happened until Tia told me a few months ago she'd seen us fucking at that party. I wanted to keep it buried, but then . . . I got a letter about Charlotte."

"Love fucks us up, doesn't it?" But what hit me the most was that even after therapy, Cole still struggled with the things that had happened. Maybe he needed more professional guidance. Maybe, in some way, listening to him would help.

He scratched his sexy stubble. "It certainly does. Priah messed me up good. She was amazing. I thought she loved me as much as I loved her and wanted to be with me forever, but it was all a lie. I nearly quit the band for her. Thank fuck I didn't. Tia warned me about her using me—I didn't listen." He seemed to flick away his pained memories and pasted on a cool, casual smile. "I don't want to ever be blindsided like that again."

"Nobody would." What would it be like to have someone like Cole treasure you, love you, and want to give up everything to be with you? Have him love you so much you ruined him for anyone else? "I don't think I've ever been that in love before. Luther and I did love each other to some degree but it slowly corroded as his career took off, then it turned into nothing but a toxic infestation."

"We all make mistakes." He picked up a pebble of concrete from the edge of the cracked step and rolled it between his palms. "Mine hurt my friends. Killed people I loved. Messed with my head."

I slapped his leg. "You didn't kill anyone."

He lowered his chin. "I'm not so sure about that."

"Cole?" Something about his comment troubled me. "What are you talking about?"

"Nothing. It's nothing." He straightened, chuckled, and tossed the pebble into the shrub. "I'm just messing around."

I wasn't so sure about that. I turned toward him. "Are you okay? I worry about you. You overexercise, you don't get enough rest, and you push yourself to do everything, every day. If you need help, ask. If you want to talk, I'm here. But please take care of yourself, or you won't survive the tour."

"Careful, Ava." The corner of his lip curled into a small smile, and his voice held a sexy lilt. He clutched my knee and gave it a gentle shake. "I might begin to think you like me."

Heat crept into my cheeks as I picked up his hand and placed it on his leg. "We established we liked each other last night, but we're nothing more than friends."

"I *like* you for that reason. But trust me." He placed his hand over his heart. "I'm good. Yes, I'm stressed over juggling a few too many balls—the tour, promo, appearances, interviews . . . and

Charlotte—but it's nothing I can't handle."

I prayed that he was right. But I'd be keeping a close eye on him anyway. "She's a beautiful kid."

"She's more like a destructive hurricane destroying my house." He rubbed the back of his neck, then softened his tone. "But she is fucking cute."

"All kids are. You're lucky you can hire help and have incredible people around you who love and support you. You can do what you love and have a family—remember that. You're not *your* parents. Be the father you never had. Find balance and time for her. It's not hard to do. She's worth it."

"I hope so." He smoothed his hands down his jeans. "Would I be crossing the line if I asked you to join me for a playdate? You and Josh? Tomorrow morning? So I could get some more parenting tips?"

I'd have loved for our kids to play together. They'd have fun. But I pressed my lips together and shook my head. "I can't do that, Cole. Josh has school. I have a staff meeting before I take you to rehearsal." An ache rippled through my chest, but I took a steady breath and pushed it aside. "Tomorrow, it's back to business. I'm your bodyguard—that's it."

"It's fine." He chuckled and patted my thigh. "Just thought I'd ask . . . and I forgot about school." He glanced at his watch. "I'd better go. I've kept Kennedy waiting long enough. You enjoy your time with Josh. I'll see you tomorrow. At eleven?"

I nodded. "Yes."

Just as he stood, a black town car pulled up to the curb. The back door flung open, and Josh shot out. He ran into the yard. I rushed to him and sank onto my knees on the grass. He flung his arms around my neck and squeezed me tight. "Mommy. I missed you so much."

My heart ached. I closed my eyes and breathed him in. God, I'd missed my boy. "I missed you too. Every day."

"Ava." Cole strolled halfway down the path and stopped. "Thanks for a great night. Catch you tomorrow."

Josh tilted his head back and stared up at Cole. "Who are you?"

I rubbed Josh's tummy. "This is Cole. He's a friend and a client of mine." I rose and dusted off my knees. "Cole, I'd like you to meet Josh."

Cole bent forward, lowering to Josh's height, and shook his hand. "Hi, Josh. It's nice to meet you. You have a great time with your mom, okay?"

"I will." He jumped and clutched my arm. "We're going to play games and cook and watch TV."

"Yes, we are."

"Yay!" Josh dashed up the steps as I walked Cole out to the car.

But as we stepped onto the sidewalk, Luther stood waiting, leaning against his ride which was parked behind Kennedy. My pulse spiked. *Shit.*

"Hi. Everything okay?" I asked Luther.

"Who's your friend?" Jealousy iced Luther's tone and prickled my skin.

I jerked my thumb toward Cole. I didn't want Luther to get any ideas. "This is my client, Cole Tanner. Cole, this is Luther."

Luther stepped forward, eyeing Cole up and down. "Tanner? As in The Flintlocks drummer?"

"The one and only." They shook hands but I didn't miss the sizing up and puffed out chests. Cole was inches taller than Luther. There was no competition—not in height, nor the size of the package contained within their jeans. Cole won, hands down.

"Who's *your* friend, Luther?" I waved toward the back seat of the car. All I could see was a long set of bare legs and pink platform metallic stilettos . . . those didn't belong to Zoe.

"A client." Luther straightened his sunglasses on his nose. "We have a lunch date."

"Damn. I wish my lunch dates had legs like that." Cole leaned sideways, presumably to get a better look of the lady waiting in the car.

"I'm sure you've had many." Smugness slithered through Luther's voice. He raised a questioning eyebrow as he tucked his hands in his suit pant pockets. "What are you doing here, Mr. Tanner?"

I jumped in. "Not that it's any of your business but we had a function last night on the boulevard. For security purposes, we had the band stay at a nearby hotel. Cole dropped me home. My guys are waiting for him." I flicked my finger toward Kennedy, standing patiently by the Suburban. Eric sat patiently in the driver's seat.

Luther's beady eyes narrowed. "I thought you had the night off."

"I thought I was supposed to have Josh," I sneered. He didn't need to know I'd gone to the launch party as Cole's plus-one.

"Ava helped us out. She kept us boys in line." Cole turned and walked backward toward Kennedy. I let out a breath, thankful for the distance and that he was quick to play along. "I'm gonna go. I'll see you tomorrow. Enjoy your time with Josh."

"I will. Thank you."

He jumped in the car with Kennedy, and they sped off. I waved as they drove down the street. But a new emptiness loomed in the center of my chest. What was I going to do about Cole? He kept dissolving my resolve, and I couldn't let that happen. I didn't think I missed having a steady relationship. I'd been so focused on sorting out my life and getting Josh back, I hadn't had time to think about anything else. The dates I'd had were hookups. Maybe when I started my new role after the tour, and I had more custody of Josh, I might find a crazy minute to venture down the relationship road again. It would be nice to find someone who treated me right, had common interests with me, and loved Josh as much as I did. Wasn't sure if someone like that existed. Maybe I was too resentful and bitter to even look.

Luther jutted his chin toward me. "You sleeping with him?"

"What? No." I scrunched up my nose but sweat broke out on the back of my neck. *Once didn't count, right?* "We had a work function."

"You were never good at lying."

"All you ever did *was* lie. Nor have you been civil since we separated."

"Things may have been different if you hadn't taken me to the cleaners in the divorce."

Jerk. "My lawyer got me what was rightfully mine. I'd give every cent back if you'd let me have full custody of Josh."

"That's not going to happen."

"I *will* get more custody at our next hearing." I stared at him, not breaking eye contact. Not giving him any sign of the fear and heartache thudding in my chest.

His lip twisted and twitched. "Not if I have anything to do with it."

"The courts will decide—not you."

"We'll see about that." The smug smirk on his face bordered on evil as he stepped toward the car door. Luther despised me, but lately he'd been even more unreasonable and erratic than usual. What game was he playing? Hadn't we hurt each other enough to move on? I'd prefer full custody, but Luther was Josh's father. I couldn't deny him the right to see his son. I'd never speak ill of him in front of Josh. But I didn't have to. Josh was learning Luther was a prick all by himself.

Ergh!

Luther could wait.

I had an amazing afternoon and night with my son ahead, and I wasn't going to waste one second of it. I jerked my chin toward the car. "Don't keep your client waiting any longer."

"No. I won't." Luther put one foot into the car and turned to me. "Josh is all yours. Zoe will pick him up from school tomorrow afternoon. Then you've got him the weekend before the tour starts. Correct?"

"Yes." I'd submitted my entire tour schedule to him via our lawyers to lock in the dates I'd fly back and see Josh. But knowing Luther, my consideration and careful planning wouldn't mean a thing to him.

"Fine. Have fun with Mr. Tanner too." A slimy grin inched across his lips as he slithered onto the back seat. He slammed his door shut and the driver sped off.

Good riddance.

And . . . oh yeah . . . I'd had incredible fun with Mr. Tanner. Now . . . he was just a client.

Yep. Absolutely.

Just. My. Client.

Josh raced out of the yard, poked his tongue at the car driving away, then blew raspberries.

I wrapped my arms around Josh and drew him back against my stomach. "Josh. Don't do that. Be nice."

"I hate him. He's so mean."

My heart ached and cracked. It broke my soul that Josh didn't like living with Luther, and there was nothing I could do about it. Not for three and a half more months anyway. I wanted my son to be happy, and it was all my fault he wasn't. I'd let him down— something I'd never do again.

"I want to stay here with you and Poppy, Mommy. Please?"

"I want that too." I kissed the top of his head. "More than anything. We just have to wait a little longer."

"All Daddy does is talk on the phone, have girls over for parties, yell at me to stay out of the way, and go to work. He never plays with me, never takes me to school or soccer."

I didn't miss the long hours Luther worked or the client parties—not one little bit. But him not spending time with Josh wasn't acceptable. "Doesn't Zoe do all those things with you?"

"Yeah, she does. Zoe's nice. But she can't cook like you can, Mommy. Can we make lasagna tonight?"

"I'd love that. But how about we make loaded hot dogs for lunch first." I needed some greasy food after drinking last night.

"Oh, yay. I love hot dogs."

But as we headed toward the gate, a shiver ran up my spine. I glanced down the short street. Three cars were parked on the curbside. Two were my neighbors', but a third blue one on the other side wasn't one I recognized. The Leighs could just have a visitor. But my pulse quickened. My skin crawled. Was someone watching me?

Why? . . . No. That's silly.

It was just the aftermath of being in Luther's presence. I shrugged the feeling aside and wandered into the garden, locked the gate, and skipped into the house with Josh.

"Poppy." Josh rushed over and hugged Dad, sitting in his robe at the kitchen table.

"Oh, my dear boy, Josh. Have you grown another inch since I saw you two weeks ago?"

"No. I'm still the same."

As I walked past Dad, I kissed the top of his graying hair. "I thought you'd be asleep."

"I heard noises on the front porch." He winked at me and rose, heading into the kitchen. "Josh, why don't you get a juice from the fridge, and I'll make a pot of coffee. Your mom looks like she needs one."

"Oh, yes please." I dragged my weary feet to the small dining table and took a seat.

"So? . . . How was last night?" Dad grabbed the coffee from the pantry and put on a brew.

"Next question." I rubbed my tired eyes.

"I saw who dropped you home."

"So?"

"Ava?"

"It's fine, Dad. I know what I'm doing."

"You haven't been yourself since you started working for this drummer. You went out with him last night. You can't risk getting involved."

I flopped my hands on the table. "I'm not."

"You are, and you know it."

"No. I'm *not*." I held up palms. "We got whatever was in our systems out last night. It won't happen again."

"Again?" His eyebrows shot upward as he grabbed two fresh cups off the shelf. "So *it* happened?" An oh-do-tell smile curled one corner of his mouth.

"Dad." I blushed.

"Ava?"

"I won't risk my job or Josh—you know that."

"Sometimes your head and heart don't play on the same team."

"Luther killed my heart, so I'm only using my head. Cole is my client. He's nothing more than that."

"Okay then."

"There is nothing more to discuss."

"If you say so."

"Good." Oh, Dad didn't believe me, but he had to. *I* had to. I shot to my feet, stormed into the kitchen, and yanked the fridge open. It was full of food but I couldn't remember what I'd said I'd make for lunch. Images of Cole in his suit, dancing, smiling, drinking, and taking me to bed filled my head. I could still feel his hands on my body, his lips on my skin, his breath on my face. I could still smell his heavenly cologne. *Shit.*

He was in my head.

He'd been in my bed.

Between my legs ached to be touched again.

No. No. Not by him.

We'd had some fun, but we were done.

The walls around my heart were impenetrable. Luther had made sure of that.

The sooner this three-month tour gig ended the better.

Three months and counting.

I could put up with Cole Tanner for that long.

Bring on the tour.

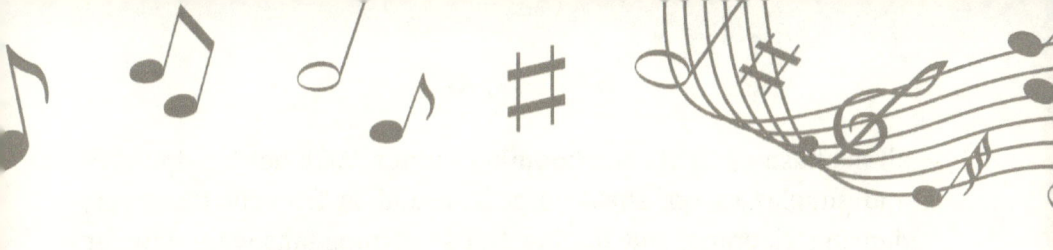

Chapter 21

COLE

Cradling Charlotte against my chest, her head tucked into the side of my neck, I stepped out of the van at our hotel in Inglewood. Hannah and Ava followed. From behind the barricades on the sidewalk, the shouts, cheers, and screams from the fans pummeled my ears and hummed through my veins. Paparazzi camera flashes flickered in my eyes. The guys and I had never had so many people gather outside our hotel to see us before. And this was just the beginning of the tour. The crowds would only get bigger and better. *This shit rocks!*

But Charlotte didn't share my high. She whimpered and hid her face, curling into my T-shirt. Her little body trembled in my arms.

"Hey?" I rubbed the back of her head. "It's okay. They won't hurt you."

Ava flanked us as we aimed for the hotel lobby. Slip and Lewis were ahead of us. Flint came in behind me.

"It's loud." Charlotte covered her ears with Barney and her eyes with her hand. "The lights hurt."

That's a first. She loved music and lights.

Over the past several days, Hannah had brought Charlotte to see our final rehearsals and she would come to some of our live shows. Every time we'd played, Charlotte had been mesmerized by all the flashing lights and booming sounds. With her headphones and sunglasses on, she'd zipped around in front of the stage, dancing, clapping, and singing. But screaming fans were new for her and clearly a different issue.

Hopefully within a few days she'd get used to them. If she didn't, I'd have to arrange for Hannah and her to arrive at our hotels separately.

"Here." I pulled off my sunglasses and put them on Charlotte's face. "That better?"

"Yeah."

"Do you want your headphones too? They're in your backpack." I'd bought them for her to wear at our shows to protect her eardrums. She didn't need industrial deafness like I'd probably end up with.

When Charlotte had first come to stay with me, I'd been unable to comprehend fitting her into my life and I hadn't wanted to change; now I was doing everything I could to ensure she was taken care of. Every day she wound a new thread around my heart. But fears of losing her played on my mind. Ava's battles with Luther over Josh didn't help. She'd done everything in her power to gain more custody. Luther kept ripping her chances to shreds. Would the courts do the same at my pending court assessment? I was no fucking angel; I never would be. Hannah had raised concerns about my workload again. But I'd made changes. I'd spent time with Charlotte. I'd gone to every function and pre-tour promotion and rehearsal but . . . I hadn't brought any girls home. There'd been no one since Ava.

Since our night together almost two weeks ago, we'd acted like nothing had happened when we were around everyone else. No one suspected a thing. Only when we were completely alone, the random flirty comment slipped out, and the dirty suggestive digs we cracked at each other made us laugh. But that was it. There were no playful touches, was no time spent together outside of work, and was no hint of a repeat. We'd gotten each other out of our system.

Well . . . *she* had.

I hadn't.

I hadn't been able to stop thinking about her.

It drove me fucking crazy.

My dick ached every night, wanting her. Visions of my face between her thighs, her mouth around my cock, me being buried inside her, and coming so fucking hard I'd seen stars before my eyes. Who knew she'd be so good in bed?

Crap.

This had to stop.

I was single. On tour. I wanted to enjoy different women at every chance I got.

But right then, I had other things to focus on. This was the first night of the tour. I was going to treasure every second. Meeting the fans was my priority. The guys had headed straight over to sign autographs and have photos. I didn't want to miss out.

"Char?" I rubbed her back again. "Did you hear me? Headphones or not?"

"No. Just Barney." She cuddled the bear against her chest.

"Let's get you inside." I strode into the hotel through the sliding glass doors. Half our entourage and crew filled the lobby, dragging suitcases and carrying bags. Everyone was checking in for the next three nights. I gave Charlotte a big hug. "Okay, sweetie. You need to stay with Hannah. I have to go meet the fans."

"No. I want to stay with you." She tugged on my T-shirt.

I kissed the top of her head. "I have to work. Hannah will look after you."

Hannah peeled Charlotte from my arms and sat her on her hip. But Charlotte reached for me. Tears welled in her eyes. "No. Cole."

Fuck. Why did that stab my heart and pummel me with guilt? I didn't need that on top of all the pressure and excitement surrounding the long days ahead. We'd be performing show after show for the next nine months.

Hannah placed Charlotte on the floor and held her hand. "We'll go with Cole this afternoon to sound check and watch the show tonight. How's that sound?"

"Will it be loud?" Charlotte sniffled.

I bobbed down in front of her and wiped a tear off her cheek. "Super loud. With lots of music and bright lights and dancing."

Glitter twinkled in her eyes and a mischievous smile skipped across her lips, then she pouted and sulked, tugging on the front of her dress. "Okay."

Oh, she was such a performer. Definitely had Tanner genes.

Hannah sighed. "I'm not looking forward to that part. I'll need earplugs too."

"The crew have some if needed. But you'll be fine." *Hopefully.* Our shows were fucking loud. No point in denying it. "You can hang out in our dressing room backstage if you need a break." Turning to Charlotte, I brushed my fingertip down the bridge of her nose and tapped the tip. "You be good for Hannah, and I'll see you soon."

Charlotte flung her arms around my neck and gave me a big hug. "Bye, Cole."

Warmth sank into my chest as I savored the smell of her bubblegum-scented hair. This kid had some wicked power over me. I had no control over it. It kept chipping away at the barricade around my heart. I hadn't thought I'd love somebody ever again. But this was a different connection. One that was unavoidable. Unexplainable. Unconditional.

"Cole?" Ava waved me toward the door. "You're needed outside for photos."

"On my way." I stood and ruffled Charlotte's hair. "Bye, sweetie."

Ava ushered me outside, then I rushed over to join the guys. I took a deep breath and absorbed the energy radiating off the screaming fans and let the noise sink into my soul. Cameras flashed. Hands reached toward us.

April thrust a Sharpie at me. "You've got fifteen minutes, then we have an interview inside."

"Got it." I took the pen and headed along the line, signing photos, T-shirts, and posters. My heart raced, and a wild buzz surged through my veins. Unable to stop smiling, I leaned in for selfies with the guys and girls who were overexcited to meet us. Our previous tours had been incredible, but this was beyond wicked. Absolutely amazing. Fucking insane. We'd worked so damn hard to get here. Our dreams had become reality.

"You good, man?" Lewis slapped me on the shoulder.

"Yep. Everything is under control." We were hours away from our first show. Most of our concerts across the globe were sold out. We'd rehearsed. We had an incredible road crew. We'd put on a spectacular performance every night. "I can't believe we're finally here."

"This is fucking awesome." Flint waved at the crowd. His smile was as big as Bel Air.

"It's only going to get crazier everywhere we go." Slip hooked his arm around my back and leaned in, smiling for the cameras.

The hype didn't die as we were ushered inside the hotel, up to the private lounge, and straight into an interview with *Access Hollywood.*

But halfway through being questioned by Suzanne, the journalist, April stepped forward, waving her palm at us and thrust my cell phone at me. "Sorry to interrupt. We need to stop for a few minutes . . . "It's Harper."

Fuck! Finally! "Excuse me." My hands shook as I grabbed my phone, put it to my ear, and rushed to the far end of the large room. "Harper. About fucking time. I've been trying to contact you for weeks." I'd called, sent text messages and emailed her, but had no reply.

"Sorry about that. I've been away teaching at a local village, and we got hit with early snow. Travel was impossible. Cell phone reception was nonexistent . The satellite phone was glitchy, and access to the Internet was down."

"Are you okay?" It'd be close to midnight in Kathmandu.

"Always." Her cheery voice never faltered. "It wasn't my first time being snowbound for a few weeks."

"You can have that shit." I loved the mountains, but I'd stick to my snowboarding and five-star lodgings. The wild wilderness wasn't for me. But as I spun to face the window, dizziness swam through my head. I staggered sideways. *Shit!* I placed my hand on the window sill and took a few deep breaths. I swiped my hand across my face. Blinked a few times. I'd passed my medical. My blood pressure had been a bit low and I'd been told to take it easy. Rest. Relax. But there was no chance of that happening now we were on tour. *Yep. I'm fine.*

My head spun again.

Crap. I took a seat on the nearby wingback chair. "Harps, I'm in the middle of an interview—I can't talk long. There's so much happening. It's opening night."

"How exciting. I'm glad I caught you."

"So did you read my emails? About Charlotte?"

Ava appeared and handed me a glass of water. '*Are you okay?*' she mouthed.

Shit! She'd seen me stumble. I had a dull headache, but it wasn't anything major, so I nodded, took the water, and had a sip.

"Yes, I read your novel-length emails," Harper groaned, never sugarcoating anything. "Finding out you had a kid would've shocked the shit out of you. Your offer is amazing. But I'm not sure it's me. I'm a teacher, not a nanny. Why do you want me to work for you?"

"Because you're the best." I eased forward on my seat and placed the glass of water on the coffee table. "You're amazing with kids and I need someone I can trust and rely on."

"And you want someone you won't end up fucking." Smugness skipped through her tone. She knew me too well.

"True. I'm not saying it would happen, but it could. I love being single too much and want to avoid any complicated situations. But most of all, I want you because you're family."

"Our family is fucked up, Cole." Her parents were as bad as mine, if not worse. Harper wanted to work with children—not run a property development empire like her parents.

"Okay. Fair point." I slid back into the chair. The guys lazed on the sofa chatting while April, Blake, and Falcon kept Suzanne talking. I couldn't keep them waiting much longer. "But we've always got along."

"LA is a shit hole. Why should I come back?"

"You love kids and love to travel. No two days are the same.

You live for those things. I have a huge house and hot showers that *always* work." She'd vented on social media when the water heating had failed where she stayed.

"That's a bonus."

"You love us but you're not into flashy parties, or the celebrity spotlight, or the music scene. I want someone who wants to help take care of my kid and doesn't want anything else from me. I want someone who doesn't want to fuck me or use me to climb some popularity list, or get into some swanky event." I loved my job, women, and going out, but I didn't need my nanny to want to be with me more than my daughter. "Charlotte needs stability. I need to protect her from some elements of my life."

As I scanned Ava standing by the door, a dull tug tweaked deep inside my chest. She hadn't wanted anything from me. She hadn't been out to sleep with me. She loved her family and certainly wasn't after celebrity status. Why did that drive me crazy? Why did I like those things about her? Ava was no nanny. She had her career, but something else kept playing on repeat in the back of my mind. Was I tired of casual hookups and did I want something more meaningful? . . . *Nah . . . maybe . . . No. Just no!*

"Why don't you hire a male nanny?" Curiosity simmered though Harper's tone.

I grunted. "I'm not sure that'd make any difference." It wouldn't. I liked my women. I hadn't been with a man since Aidan in high school. But I didn't want to rule anything out. I just wanted to avoid any temptation in my home.

"Cole, I have a great life here. I love teaching. I have incredible friends."

Shit. I clenched my fist, distracting me from the disappointment mounting in my veins. Why was nothing easy? Who would I hire if Harper said no? What could I do to sway her toward coming home? *Maybe nothing.* "I'd never want you to give up something you loved." Not ever. I was all for fun and following your dreams. That was my motto.

"It's not that . . ."

"So what is it then?" What *was* stopping her from jumping on a plane?

"I don't want to be on the same continent as my parents."

The truth slammed into me like a torpedo hitting its target. She'd been cut off by her family, cast aside for following her career. That was when she'd come to stay with Tia and me during my senior year.

"Hey. I don't blame you. But they're in Delaware. There's no chance of them popping in for a visit. I have security. No unwanted guests can get through my gates." *Hopefully*. "Harps, you've been away a long time. I missed Tia when she was in Chicago filming her TV show. I miss you too."

"I never took you for a family man."

"Always have been." Mine came in the form of my friends and my sister. "The band is family. So is Charlotte." *Fuck*. I never thought I'd hear myself say that. But she was. So was Harper. She was one of us. "You belong with us too."

"It's such a big decision, Cole."

She hadn't said no, so she must be contemplating the idea. Numbers ticked through my head and the offer I'd sent her.

"Do you want more money?"

"Money doesn't interest me."

Then my stomach cinched. *Crap*. "You're not still hung up on Slip, are you?" Their brief relationship had never been smooth.

"Oh, God no. Not at all." The horror in her tone made me laugh. So that wasn't it.

I glanced toward the guys sitting on the sofa, getting restless waiting for me.

Slip held up his hands and pointed to his watch. '*Hurry up*,' he mouthed.

I held up one finger and nodded.

The dull ache in my head morphed into a throb. I'd kill for an Advil or two. "Harps, what can I offer you to come home? Name it."

"You want me to leave Nepal, my job, and my friends, to be your nanny? Live with you? And pay me a shit load to do it?"

"Yes, but we'd have fun too. We'd hang out. Chill by the pool. Go to the beach." I couldn't remember the last time I'd done those things. *Damn.* Maybe the people around me were right—I needed to take some time out. The problem was that would have to wait until after the tour.

"There's too much uncertainty about you keeping her."

Nausea flooded the pit of my stomach, but my determination kicked in. "I'll only lose her if I fuck up. I'm not going to do that. If you don't come, I'll have to go through the shitty process of finding someone to be her nanny. I just wanted you more than anyone else. You have the best heart and love kids. It won't always be easy, this life isn't for everyone, but I promise I'll take care of you too."

"It's not a yes . . . but if I did it I couldn't start until the end of February."

I sat straight. Hope sparked in my chest. "That's perfect. Hannah's with us for the first leg of tour. You'd miss the US."

"That's the point. Give me two weeks to think about it."

"Why that long?"

"I only got back yesterday. I need more time to process everything. Okay?"

"Fine. Call me. Any time."

"I will. Good luck with the show."

"Thanks."

Harper ended the call. I buried my head into my hands. That hadn't exactly gone to plan. I still had no answer. I needed a fucking nanny. I needed certainty.

As I stood, I swayed again. *Fuck.* I didn't need this.

Ava rushed over. "Cole, I'm getting the doctor."

"No. I'm fine. It's just pre-show nerves kicking in." I was sure that was it. It had been a long time since breakfast. "I need food. I'll finish this interview, then eat."

"And drink." She picked up my water and handed it to me. "If this happens again, I won't hesitate. Got it?"

"Yep. Thanks. Got it."

I rejoined the guys and finished our interview. Over lunch I told them about Harper's pending decision, but within minutes, the high of opening night took over. After checking into our rooms, we were driven to the venue for sound check.

During the drive, I tried to rest, but my mind wouldn't stop racing. *Charlotte. Ava. Harper. The show.* I had to hold our performance together. Not miss a beat.

I ran through the first song in my head, counting the rhythm. *One. Two. Three-four.* My heart thudded as I transitioned into the second track. *One. And a two. And a three. And a four. Pause, two, three, four. Play.* I tapped my fingers against my thigh, our medley of hits playing through my mind. I fast-forwarded through the rest of our set list, my solo, then the encore pummeled my brain.

I couldn't fuck up.

The guys played off the pace I set.

They depended on me.

I knew the set list backward. Every song. Every beat. Every element. So why did I want to throw up? I lived to play. I'd hadn't been like this during our last two tours.

"Cole?" Slip shook my arm, pulling me out of my thoughts.

"What?"

"You with us?" Excitement charged through his tone.

"Fuck yeah." Of course I was.

At the venue, fans were already lined up at the entrance. *So cool!* We waved to them as we drove through the parking lot and headed straight inside to run through sound check. It went off without a hitch.

Stopping to take in the moment, the guys and I stood in a row with our arms hooked around each other's backs in the center of the stage. The empty-seated auditorium stretched before us. Crew scuttled across the floor, securing cables, adjusting lights, and wheeling equipment trunks out of sight.

"This is it." Flint clutched onto a handful of my hoodie and gave me a gentle shake. The energy radiating off him was as electric as a disco beat. "We're here. Ready to take on the world."

"Never want to be anywhere else." I swung my arm around his neck and ruffled his hair.

"Opening night at The Forum." Slip clapped and pumped his fist. "We're gonna rock the shit out of this joint."

"This is beyond my wildest dreams." Lewis placed his hand

over his heart. "We're gonna kick some major ass."

"Oh, we will for sure." Flint slapped Lewis on the back. "It's time to get ready for the meet and greet. It all starts now, boys. We're on the ride. Enjoy it."

"Woohoo!" I hollered as we headed to our huge dressing room. It was decked out in black drapes, with three leather sofas clustered around a coffee table and small glass tables with silver lamps and some fake plants. Racks of our clothing lined one side of the area, mirrors and makeup stations the other. It looked more like a bachelor pad than anything else. But it was our space to relax and rest in before the shows. Not that we'd get much time to do that.

We showered, changed, and had a huge group photo in front of the stage with our road and production crew. After that, we ate and had a drink with our support act before hitting the meet and greet. The nerves in my belly somersaulted with each passing minute.

None of us could sit still as the show drew near. Blake, April, and Falcon wished us luck and headed out to mingle with executives, sponsors, and special guests in the VIP section. Everhide had flown out to see us. After a few words of encouragement and a quick shot of vodka, they headed off to join Blake. Keeping an eye on the clock on the table, I sat on the sofa, tapping out the opening song on my thighs with my sticks. My head was clear. There were no signs of dizziness. I'd just needed food and water. Nothing was going to stop me from playing opening night.

The guys fussed and fidgeted in their chairs as Penny, our makeup artist, styled their hair, and Cassidy, our wardrobe assistant, fixed the transmitter holder on Slip's belt. As we ran through warmup vocals, the girls arrived. Sutton and Maddy rushed into the room and hugged everyone. Every hair on my body tingled as the electric vibe jumped to the next level and time to kickoff ticked down.

The door swung open again. Blake peered into the room. "Five minutes everyone." He pointed at me. "Cole? Someone is here to see you."

"Who?" I wasn't expecting anybody.

Charlotte ran through the doorway, and my heart swelled to the size of a beach ball. She rushed over to me with her headphones hooked around her arm. I bent down and she flung her arms around my neck.

Why had this become the highlight in my day?

"I'm gonna watch you from the front with Ma. Will you wave to me?"

"I sure will." From my riser at the back of the stage and with stage lights flashing in my eyes, I wouldn't be able to see the audience, but I'd make sure the guys told me where she was.

Hannah stuck her head into the room. "Charlotte, come on. We have to go find our seats." She twinkled her fingers at us. "Good luck. Have a great show."

"Bye." Charlotte waved and skipped over to Hannah.

"She's so fucking adorable." Lewis put his boot up on the sofa and double-knotted the laces. "Makes my balls ache. I can't wait to have kids."

I grabbed my in-ear monitors out of the box on the accessories table, threaded the cords through my shirt, and hung the buds around my neck. "Please tell me you haven't knocked up my sister."

He slapped me on the shoulder. "Not yet. But if things go well, I will after the tour."

I chuckled. He and Tia just clicked. They'd become inseparable. I'd never seen my sister so happy. I couldn't ask for more than that. But children? Already? "I don't know why people would willingly want kids." *They're way too much work. Way too much stress.*

"Usually it's for love." Lewis grabbed his transmitter and stuffed it into the holder on the back of his belt.

"Oh yeah . . . that." *That* hadn't been my case. But regardless of how Charlotte had come into my life and the changes I'd had to make, she was amazing. For the past couple of weeks, the guilt of being with Shelby didn't haunt me as often as my other mistakes did. I'd take that as a win.

Ava walked through the door. "Time."

I threw her a wink. She just glared at me, her expression

neutral as always. My laugh rolled deep inside my chest. I saw her morning, noon, and night. But for some unexplainable reason, every time she walked in the room, my heart beat to a quicker tempo. I didn't want it to. I had to focus on the tour. The guys. The show.

I closed my eyes and sucked in a deep breath.

This was it.

Opening night.

Here we go.

Flint jumped up and down in the middle of our dressing room and stretched his neck from side to side. Nervous energy, excitement and focus shimmered in his eyes. We each had our part to play, but he was our front man. The star. Our leader and my best friend. I loved him like a brother and would do anything for him. I'd do the same for any of these guys.

"This is going to be a fucking awesome night." He drew us into a huddle, hugged us tight, then hollered, "I love you guys. Let's rock."

Twirling my drumsticks around my fingers, I followed the guys to the back of the stage to join our crew. In the dim lighting, we formed a circle and held hands. As I clutched onto Tia, Flint gave the group a quick pep talk, hoping everyone would have fun and enjoy the show. We wouldn't be able to do this without them.

"Go The Flintlocks!" We cheered and high-fived the crew as they scurried off via torchlight to their positions. We made our way toward the stage. I was about to bound up the metal steps after the guys when Ava caught me on the arm.

"Hey." Her eyes glistened in the soft beam of light coming from her torch "I just want to wish you luck. Have a great time out there."

"Always. But thanks." I glanced at my forearm where she still touched me. Within a second, she pulled away. "Hmm. Careful, Ava. I might think you want another round with me."

"No. I'm still recovering from the first." She blushed. I liked that.

"I'll see you after the show."

"Knock 'em dead."

"We will."

I raced up the stairs. Adrenaline coursed through my veins as I gave the guys one last hug before we rushed to our places. Joel, our stagehand, helped Flint with his guitar. I took a seat behind my drums. In the darkness, the cymbals and chrome edges on my snares and tom-toms shimmered and glistened as they caught the small beam of light from the floor. They begged me to play. *Oh, I will.*

From the other side of the curtain, the crowd chanted and clapped for the concert to begin.

My heart thundered against my ribs.

I checked and wriggled on my stool, then balanced my sticks in my hands. My canister of spare sticks was in reach. So were my water and towel. The guys and I gave Jackson, who was standing on the side of the stage, the thumbs up. We were set. He gave us the green light. *Showtime! One. Two. Three.*

The stage curtain fell away. The crowd erupted with deafening cheers and whistles. With a huge grin on my face, I stuffed my ear monitors into place. The projection screens behind me flickered to life with graphics and videos.

I tightened the grip on my sticks. I closed my eyes, counted to three, then struck the first beat of our song. The reverberations from the cymbals charged up my arms and struck the center of my chest. *So freaking good.* The muffled screams from the audience teased my ears. Then, it was on. I pummeled the drums, pumped the pedals, pounded the snare, the toms and cymbals. Hit after hit. Strike after strike.

Fuck yes!

Flint took to the mic, opening the show with the hyped-up party song off our latest album.

> *I've been living in a dream, watching the hours go by*
> *Now tonight is here, I can't believe you're by my side*
> *You're standing here with me in your red party dress*
> *I've got new jeans on, trying to look my very best*

I kiss your sweet lips, everything feels so right
Oh yeah . . . I'm gonna take you out tonight

We'll jump in my car, and drive beneath the moonlit sky
Hit some club and dance all night
We'll sing along to songs and get on down
The crowd will be wild, jumping all around
I'll hold you close, and we'll get lost in the beat
But in the disco lights you'll be all I see

Oh, baby I don't ever want to let you go
Yeah, I want you next to me . . .

Every thud coursed through my veins. By the fourth song, sweat licked my skin. My muscles strained and burned. But I never missed a beat. The sea of fans, yelling and screaming, was nothing but a distant sound in my ears as I focused on every track. Every transition. Every element I had to deliver.

Following our melody of hits, the auditorium lights brightened. Flint raised his arms high and pointed at the crowd.

"Good evening, LA. Glad y'all could make it . . ."

I scanned the VIP section, searching for our family and friends. There, in the front row, Charlotte stood on her chair between Sutton and Hannah, with her headphones covering her ears. A big grin slid across my face and warmth rippled through my chest. I waved at her. Her little eyes widened. She clapped and waved back. *Fuck.* That stole my heart.

After Flint had flirted and chatted with the crowd, hyped them up and commented on some banners, he dialed down his voice and injected a ton of sultry charm into it. "Alright, folks . . . Does anyone object if we slow things down a little? Set a little mood lighting?" The auditorium lights dimmed, and a blue wash flooded the stage. Flint clutched his mic. "I want y'all to take out your cell phones, turn the light on, and wave them in the air, like this." He swung his arm from side to side above his head. Flickering to life, a sea of lights filled the venue as the fans switched their phones on. "Yes. That's fucking awesome."

The cheering shook through the walls and prickled my skin. *So cool.*

Flint pointed across the crowd. "This one is for all the lovers out there. To those of you who are in love. Looking for love. To my love." He blew a kiss toward Sutton. "But to those of you who are afraid of love . . ." *Shit.* Flint had gone off script. He glanced over his shoulder at me, jutted his chin in my direction, then spun to face the audience again. *What was that about?* " . . . Stop being a fool. Love isn't always easy. It can mess you up, big time. But when you find someone special, make it work—don't let them go. We all deserve to be happy. There's no better feeling than being in love. Trust me." He grabbed his mic, lowered his voice, and swooned sexily at the audience. "So who here is down for being *hopelessly in love?*"

The crowd whistled and hollered as they waved their cell phones in the air. On cue, I pressed down on the pedals and tapped my drums, churning out the slow steady beat of our song "Hopelessly in Love." Ava stood on the side of the stage with her hands folded in front of her. Her eyes were on me.

My skin tingled. My stomach cinched.

Flint was wrong.

I wasn't being a fool. I wasn't in love. Wasn't looking for love. Didn't want to be in love ever again. *Did I? No . . . nope . . . no way.* Well . . . maybe one day in the very, very distant future, but not today.

Slip churned out the haunting electric riff on his guitar. Lewis blended in with his bass. Flint seduced the crowd with his soulful raspy voice:

> *You came to me in the dark of night*
> *Like a summer's breeze, you felt so right*
> *Your eyes, so bright, like a star-filled sky*
> *Your touch, so warm, made me feel so high*
> *I wasn't looking for this, thought I was out of my mind*
> *I'd been hurt before, thought I was lost in time*

But you asked me to dance and took my hand
Never thought my heart would beat like this again

I wasn't looking for a lover, I was set in my ways
Now I'm watching the clock, counting down the days
Until I see you
With me
Dancing beneath the stars
Just you
And me
As one
Holding you in my arms
So hopelessly in love
Giving you all my heart
For now and forever, oh yeah
I don't want this high to ever end

My hands were a blur as I galloped across the drums, then pummeled the tom-toms with slow, hard strikes. But with every crash of the cymbals, I couldn't drag my eyes off Ava. *Shit.* The song Flint had written about Sutton hit me in the chest and meddled with my mind.

Fuck. I *was* a fool. A fool for liking someone I shouldn't.

She'd be gone in three months. I'd never see her again.

I couldn't fall for her. Couldn't let anyone get close. Couldn't face more heartbreak.

I had to forget about her. Move on.

Right now.

Focus.

This was living.

Music. Playing. My band. The tour.

I had everything I'd ever wanted. I was living the dream.

So why the fuck did my chest ache so goddamn much?

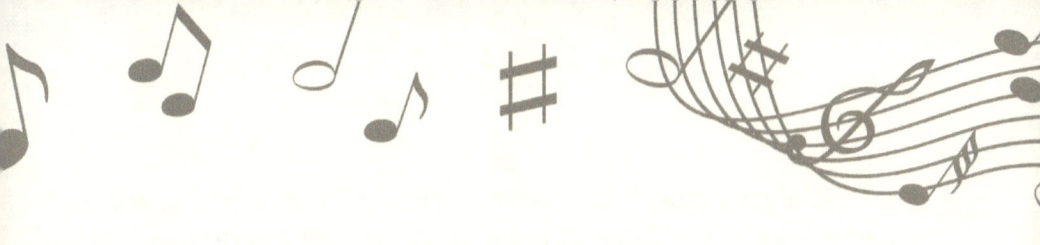

Chapter 22

COLE

Three weeks into the tour and the knots in the back of my neck wouldn't release. Deep-tissue massages after our shows hadn't helped. The high from hanging out with the guys, traveling, meeting more fans, and performing fed my soul. It kept me wanting to give more and more. Despite our hectic schedule and my lack of sleep, I wouldn't miss a beat. I lived to tour.

But some days were tough. Exhausting.

At the end of each show, the guys and I would wind down over a few drinks, tell stories, and crack jokes about our concerts. But my mind was often elsewhere—on Charlotte . . . on Ava . . . They were traveling in the other buses in our convoy or asleep in different hotel rooms. Flint had never said anything to me after having a dig at me onstage about being a fool. I was convinced he suspected something was going on between Ava and me, but there wasn't.

I'd tried to avoid Ava since our night together, but that was impossible. Something about her kept drawing me in. Something about *me* kept pushing her away. That was a good thing. There was nothing foolish about being sensible.

After our show in Salt Lake City, we had an overnight drive to Denver. As the bus hit the highway, I sat at the table with the guys and sipped a beer. The high from performing still hovered in the air.

"Tonight's crowd was freaking epic." Flint grabbed us fresh beers from the fridge and flopped on the seat beside me. "The signs and banners people make are so cool. It still blows my mind when people sing along to our songs. That's so dope." He took a sip of beer and swallowed it down. "We're only three weeks in. I still can't wait to hit the stage every night. But I'm not gonna lie to you. I'm so looking forward to a couple days off after our Denver shows."

I elbowed him in the arm. "You're only excited about going home and fucking Sutton."

"Flint, you're pussy whipped." Slip cracked the top off his beer and flung the lid at Flint, hitting him in the shoulder.

"Yep." Laughing, Flint caught the lid and pegged it back at Slip's chest. "I'm happy to admit it. I could say the same thing about you and Mads."

"Yep. Here's to that." A sparkle shimmered in his eyes as Slip chinked his beer against Flint's bottle. "If I could get Mads to agree we're more than casual everything would be great. I'm working on that. The minute we finish in Denver, I'm outta there. Vancouver, here I come."

"You'll be *coming* all weekend." Chuckling, I lazed back on the seat. I hadn't seen Slip smitten with anyone since Courtney. I prayed they worked things out. *But crap.* When was the last time I'd had sex? With Ava? Five weeks ago. *Shit.* What was wrong with me?

"That's the plan." Slip nodded then took a mouthful of beer. But then he winced, stretched out his legs and rubbed his right hip.

I waggled my finger toward his waist. "Is that surfing injury causing you grief again?"

"Yeah." He massaged his side. "It's hurting like a bitch. So is my knee. I jumped around too much on stage tonight. I'll take a painkiller before bed. It'll be fine if I take it easy for a few days."

Slip? Take it easy? Never. We were too alike.

"You won't be getting any rest when your with Mads." Lewis

chuckled as he stood and grabbed a bag of potato chips from the cupboard. He ripped them open, tipped them into a bowl, and returned to the table. "I'm stoked I don't have to go anywhere or do promo for a couple days once we get to Santa Fe. I'm looking forward to having Tia in my bed and if we can be bothered to leave the hotel, we might do some sightseeing."

Tia often joined us on our bus, but she loved traveling with the crew as well. She'd insisted on not having special treatment just because she was my sister and dating Lewis. He seemed fine with it, most of the time. It gave us guys a chance to chill, spin shit, and just be ourselves. *But damn.* If I had a girl, I'd want her next to me every night.

I'd hated being away from Priah during our last tour. I'd kept counting down the days until we had a break so I could rush home to see her. So much for all that effort—she'd fucking dumped me two days after the tour had finished.

"What about you, Cole?" Flint play-punched me in the arm. "You gonna break a few hearts while we're away?"

"Me?" Grinning, I swiped my fingertips over my stubble.

I'd loved our after-show parties and hanging out with the VIP guests and ticketholders. But every time a girl had flirted with me, had gotten that sexy how-about-it glint in her eyes, I hadn't been interested. Ava's gaze often burned into me. It wasn't one of jealousy—it was more of a been-there-done-that smugness. I'd never met someone like her. Most women I'd been with wanted to get my number and hook up again. But nope, not Ava. I didn't think I had a big ego, or oversold myself, but Ava's ability to put our one-night stand behind her and move on tangled my insides. I hadn't wanted to be with anyone since her. Every time I smelled her floral perfume, or she guided me through a sea of fans, or said good night at the end of the day made me crave her more.

That wasn't healthy.

I needed to get her out of my system.

I picked out a chip from the bowl and munched on it. "I'm sure I'll cause some havoc in Santa Fe, but our break might involve more time with Charlotte than hooking up with some sexy chicks."

When we stopped at hotels, she and Hannah shared a two-bedroom suite with me or stayed in an adjoining room. Charlotte hadn't caught on to my need for rest during the tour. She rushed into my bed every morning. Her smile made it impossible to be mad. "My partying may involve a playground or two rather than bars and clubs."

Flint leaned forward and rested his elbows on the table. "I appreciate you need to spend time with your kid, but you haven't been yourself this tour. What's up?"

"I'm fine."

"You're not." Flint groaned and shook his head. "And I wish you'd stop saying you are. You're not sleeping. You're not fucking women. Your mind is often elsewhere."

He wasn't wrong. I slumped in the seat, but the knot in the base of my neck twisted tighter. I hated he worried. I didn't want that. Thoughts of our tour schedule and Ava continually bombarded me, but my biggest concern was for my daughter. "It's Charlotte. I like having her around, but I'm not sure if this life is ideal for a kid, or if I'm doing the right thing, or if I'm a good father for her."

"Why would you think those things?" Slip jerked his chin back. "Charlotte doesn't seem stressed. And you've changed. You've toned down the drinking and fucking, haven't you? You spend time with her. You care about her. What else is a dad supposed to do?"

I glanced out the front window and stared at the bus traveling in front of us. The red taillights glowed in the dark. "I worry it's not enough. I feel guilty about everything I do." I was over feeling like shit, dealing with so many things. My kid. My band. Ava. Hadn't I made enough changes already? "I want to be here with you guys, but then . . . I want to be with Charlotte too. What's with that?"

"I'd say that's natural." Lewis raised his beer toward me. "She's your daughter—of course you want to be with her."

I puffed air through my nose and shook my head. "My problem is I now suffer from too much fucking FOMO. I want to be everywhere, do everything, and I can't. There is no balance."

"Oh, we know you suffer from FOMO." Flint's eyes glinted in the soft lighting. "You're a socializing addict. But when we're on the road like this, why don't you alternate nights between us and Charlotte and Hannah? Or occasionally bring Charlotte on our bus. There's a spare bunk."

"You'd be okay with that?" We did get rowdy on occasion, staying up for hours, drinking, singing, playing music, and talking. But that wasn't every night on the road. Charlotte had fallen asleep through the second concert Hannah had brought her too, I didn't think the noise we'd make on the bus would keep her awake.

"Absolutely." Slip dipped his chin. "She's a Flintlock."

"So . . ." Lewis kicked my foot. "Is it just Charlotte you're worried about or is there something else? Or someone else? Maybe a certain bodyguard?"

My heart stumbled against my ribs. *He'd noticed?* "What the fuck do you mean by that?"

"Come on, bud." Chuckling, Lewis puffed air through his nose. "Take it from someone who hid being into your sister for months—I can tell something is going on with you and Ava. There's this spark between the two of you whenever you're together. You've fucked her, haven't you?"

"What?" I rubbed at the thud throbbing in my brow. Hadn't we been discreet? "What makes you think that?"

Flint counted on his fingers. "You invited her to a party. You always get her coffee. You're not sleeping around. You can't take your eyes off her. You try to ignore her but fail dismally. Shall I go on?"

"Is she why you're not screwing some girl at every stop?" Slip asked.

The pit of my stomach lurched. *Was she the reason?* "Ava infuriates me. She gets under my skin, doesn't take my shit, plays by the rules, and all I want to do is—"

"Damn . . . you have slept with her." Slip tossed his head back and laughed.

My mistakes had caused too many problems in the past, and I wasn't going to do that again. I wouldn't lie to them. "Fine. Just one time. After Sutton and Tia's launch party. It hasn't and won't happen again. She could lose her job, so you can't say anything."

Flint chuckled over the rim of his beer. "You're so into her."

"She's not my type." No, she wasn't the typical woman I was attracted to. She was no supermodel or groupie. Ava would eat those women for breakfast and use their bones as toothpicks. But her love of exercise and the outdoors, her devotion to her family and need to protect people hit home for me. Maybe we had too much in common. I just didn't want or need someone like that in my life right then, or ever . . . *right?*

Lewis's laughed, low and deep. "Don't talk to me about types. I was gay before I met your sister. Tia was not *my* type. But fuck . . . since being with her, I'm the happiest I've been in a long time."

"I'm stoked for you. But there's nothing going on between Ava and me. I'm not going to fuck up her life or her job just because we slept together." I'd hurt and screwed up enough people's lives over the years—I didn't want to add any more to the list. I wanted to make the right choices, make good decisions, and be a better person for my kid. I had a long way to go. Ava didn't need to be dragged into my mess. This being responsible thing sucked.

"You haven't fucked up her life." Flint placed his beer on the table. "We've got your back always. We won't say anything." Then a suggestive smile slid across his lips. "She's nice though . . . just saying."

"Yeah, it'd be better if you didn't say anything." I finished the last mouthfuls of my beer. "I've got too much other shit to worry about. Charlotte. Finding a nanny if Harper says no. And keeping you guys in line. We've only just begun the tour and have months ahead of us."

"Fuck yeah." Slip pumped his fist. "Bring on Denver."

"It'll be wicked." I eased off the seat and tossed my empty bottle into the trash can. "But I'm done for the night. I'm gonna hit the sack. See you in the morning."

Just after two a.m., I crawled into my bunk, put my earbuds in, and listened to some classic rock. But I couldn't sleep. I trusted the guys wouldn't say anything to anyone about me being with Ava. I had no reason to doubt them. But I hadn't had the best of luck with my secrets remaining hidden. Nor at being able to relax.

I closed my eyes and took long, slow, deep breaths, but a gazillion other thoughts bombarded my mind—who'd followed me and staked out my home? Did they want to hurt me? Why the fuck hadn't Harper replied to my emails or calls? Then my thoughts diverted to our next shows, interview schedules, and promo agenda, to Christmas gifts and lunch that had to be organized, then to Charlotte, Hannah . . . and Ava.

I didn't want to cause Ava any issues.

I hoped everything would be okay.

But the dread in my stomach wouldn't disappear.

The following morning, after we'd checked into our hotel in Denver, Ava flew to LA to see Josh. It was ridiculous to consider missing her for two days. Surely it was just that Kennedy wasn't as much fun to tease and torment as she was.

After an afternoon of interviews, photoshoots, and dinner, everyone had an early night before our two Denver shows. But there was no such thing as time out with a three-year-old. Hannah had taken Charlotte to the zoo today. As I tried to read her a bedtime story, she jumped around my bed with Barney, impersonating every animal she'd seen, roaring, stomping, and screeching.

Laughing, I grabbed my cell phone and took her picture. Her big smile and bright eyes lessened my worries for a few brief minutes.

Skipping across the mattress, she flapped her arms like a bird. "Can I sleep with you tonight?"

My lungs filled to capacity. Warmth wrapped around my heart. Charlotte had never wanted to do that before. "Really? You want to stay with me?"

"Yes." She gave me a big nod, then jumped higher and higher. "Can we be monkeys now?"

I was all animaled out. I patted the bed beside me. "No. It's story time."

"Tigers?" She made her hands into claws. "Roarrrr!"

"No. It's bedtime."

"Five more minutes, please?"

How could I say no? Discipline was not my strong point. "Fine." I waggled my finger at her. "Five minutes. Then sleep."

"Yay."

Was Josh like this with Ava?

As Charlotte plonked onto all fours and crawled around my king-sized bed, roaring, I sent Ava a text and the picture of Charlotte I'd just taken.

> ME: SO MUCH FOR REST. THIS IS BEDTIME.

Seconds later, Ava sent an image of her and Josh, cuddled together on the sofa, eating popcorn, with the message:

> AVA: THIS IS FAMILY TIME. ENJOY IT.

I stared at the photo of Ava dressed in blue-striped flannel pajamas. Her hair hung loose around her shoulders, and the light from the TV shimmered in her gorgeous eyes. My breath snagged in my chest. Was I falling for her when I didn't want to? *Nope* . . . I couldn't. *Don't be ridiculous.* I sent one final text.

> ME: NIGHT

She replied:

> AVA: XO

I tossed my cell phone aside and read Charlotte a book. She fell asleep before I made it halfway through the story. But I lay awake for hours before falling asleep somewhere around two.

Charlotte woke me at five-thirty.

Ergh!

Our shows in Denver were phenomenal. The crowds were mind-blowing. I poured my heart and soul into playing, giving the fans an incredible performance. The moment we came off stage, Flint and Slip took off for three days to see Sutton and Maddy. The rest of us traveled to Santa Fe where Ava rejoined us.

With two free days, I took Charlotte to the Children's Museum and a park, and I had dinner with Lewis and Tia. I worked with

April to plan Christmas for the band and crew members who weren't traveling home. But there was one person I wanted to do something special for. I wanted to show my appreciation to someone who had helped me out with Charlotte the most. Someone more than Ava. That was Hannah.

"You want me to what?" April snapped at me over a morning coffee.

"Please. It's one tiny request."

"Tiny? Cole, are you crazy? It's the holidays. Everyone is traveling. I'm too busy to organize this."

"April." I splayed my hand over my heart. "I know it's a lot to ask, but you can do this. I know you can. Please?"

She mumbled and muttered and rubbed her smooth brow. She stared at her cell phone and cursed. "Fuck. Fine." She pointed a finger at me. "My fucking bonus better be beyond my expectations this year."

"It always is." I leaped from the dining chair and darted around the table. I gave her a hug and kissed the top of her head. "Thank you."

"Good thing I love you guys." She rested her head against my side.

"We love you too," I patted and rubbed her shoulder. April was a machine. One that was overworked. We were getting to the point where she'd need help. I tried not to add too much to her list, but this was important to me.

At the end of each long day, I crawled into bed. But yet again, I'd fall asleep for two or three hours, then wake. My mind spiraled over everything—the tour, our schedule, Charlotte, Ava, my weird stalkers back home . . . even new songs and beats drummed in my head.

Fuck, I needed to sleep. More rest.

But it never came.

My body and head ached, but that wouldn't stop me.

After our concert in Santa Fe, the tour headed to Oklahoma City, Austin, then to New Orleans. We'd be based there for four days for Christmas and a show.

Most of the tour's crew flew home to see family and friends. Sutton and Maddy had traveled across the country to spend time with us.

As we checked into our hotel late in the afternoon on the twenty-third, I stretched my body from side to side, grateful to be off the bus. Following a late dinner, I crashed in my room. But two hours later, I was wide awake. I tossed and turned, unable to sleep.

Fuck.

At four a.m. I'd had enough.

At home, to distract my mind, bury my guilt, or alleviate my stress, I used to play my drums, have sex, or run. With no drums or girls on hand, running was my only option.

Charlotte was asleep in the adjacent room with Hannah. They were fine.

I crawled out of bed, dressed in some exercise clothes, grabbed my gym bag, and headed down to the hotel gym.

I needed to deal with my shit. I needed to run.

I'd only be an hour, tops.

Chapter 23

COLE

I hit the treadmill.

At pace, I ran. I had the hotel gym all to myself. But my brain was far from quiet.

As I pumped my fists, my legs burned. I ran for miles. With my earbuds in, I turned up the music on my cell phone to silence my thoughts. But it didn't help. I wanted to stop worrying about everything and dwelling on every what-if scenario. I wanted to slow down and enjoy the tour, but everything kept hammering my head harder and faster. Harder and faster.

Aaaarrrghhh!

I hit the stop button on the treadmill.

Dizziness swayed through my head. I grabbed the safety rail to steady myself. I blinked, took a deep breath, but my vision tunneled.

Panic seized my lungs.

What was wrong?

I'd only been running for twenty minutes, not an hour.

I grabbed my towel, wiped the sweat off my face, and sat on the edge of the treadmill. Glancing at my smartwatch, I checked my heartrate.

Fuck! It was way too fast.

The door to the gym shot open and Ava rushed in . . . in her tracksuit and running shoes. Fire blazed in her eyes as she stormed toward me.

I yanked out my earbuds. "What's up?"

"What do you think you're doing?" She flicked her hand at me. "You can't leave your room without telling someone."

I closed my eyes, unable to focus. "How did you know I was here?"

"Hotel security saw you on the monitors. They contacted me as your bodyguard."

"I needed a run." I pressed my thumb and index finger against my closed eyelids and took a big, slow breath. *Hmm. That's better. No spinning.*

"At this hour?" she fired at me.

"Yes."

"You should've called me."

"You're not on duty until seven." I stood, grabbed my gym bag from beside the treadmill, and veered around the exercise equipment, aiming for the showers.

But I caught the scent of her alluring perfume and my knees weakened. Not from my dizziness, but from her.

"Cole. Stop." She caught my arm and drew me to a halt. "You do not do this. You do not put your safety at risk."

"What risk?" I waved around the gym. There was no one here but us. "I'm in a fucking hotel."

"There are fans camped out on the sidewalk." She stabbed her finger toward the door. "Some could be staying in this hotel. Some could be dangerous. Those people who we couldn't identify outside your home in LA could be following you."

I got up in her face. "Did I go outside? No. Security clearly saw me, so where's the fucking issue?"

"Please, follow the rules." Anguish embedded into her tone as her volume plummeted. "For your safety."

I clenched and released my hands. "Rules? I'm over rules." Was that it? I missed causing havoc with the guys. They were all tied down with partners. We used to party hard until dawn. Have wild times. Drink ourselves stupid. We still did, but with me being the only one single, our nights weren't as crazy as they'd been when Phil had been around. Even I'd toned down my behavior because I had a fucking kid.

I was over it. Over everything being different. I wanted my friends. My fun. My wicked nights out. My freedom. But then I met Ava's gaze and my heart strummed to a different beat. The air between us sparked. I wasn't sure if it was frustration, anger, desire, lust, or a combination of everything . . . but it was dangerous and hot. *Not good.*

Her chest heaved. "You need to go back to your room."

I leaned toward her, just an inch. "Make me."

She lifted her chin, challenging me. "You really want to go down that road?"

"You wouldn't dare." I stormed into the men's locker room. Of course, she followed.

"Cole?" She grabbed my shoulder and spun me 'round. My head struggled to keep up. "I get that you have a lot going on. That tour is demanding. You've got Charlotte to worry about. But why are you awake at this hour? What is going on? Talk to me."

I tossed my bag onto the bench in the middle of the row of lockers. "Ava, we're not supposed to get personal." That was a pathetic excuse considering we talked all the time.

She grimaced. Concern darkened her eyes. "So . . . is this about us?"

I took one step toward her, leaving a foot of distance between our bodies. "I've done everything you asked so no one finds out what happened between us. But the guys know. They won't say anything. I promise. I've tried to forget what happened—"

"And have you done that?"

"No."

Her voice softened. "Why not?"

God. She was beautiful and frustrating. "There are a million reasons why I should stay away from you, everything from you're my bodyguard to our different paths to our messed up lives, but one reason why I can't."

"What is that?"

"I didn't get you out of my system."

She closed her eyes. "I hate you right now."

Pain shot through my chest. "Why?"

She met my gaze and whispered. "I haven't gotten you out of mine either."

I took a step forward, cupped the back of her head, and drew her lips to mine. Spinning her, I pinned her against the wall of lockers. Showering her with kisses, I nipped her lips, her neck and face.

"Shit, Cole." She dug her fingernails into my biceps. "We can't do this."

"You're not on duty. So fuck any other rules." I yanked off my T-shirt and tossed it on my bag. "You down with that?"

She raked her gaze over my chest, my hard-on straining in the confines of my shorts. My lips begged to kiss her again.

"Yeah." She unzipped her tracksuit jacket, stripped it off and shed her T-shirt.

No bra. So freaking hot. We ripped off the rest of our clothes. I grabbed a condom from my bag, tore open the packet with my teeth, then sheathed my cock. We fell into one of the shower cubicles. I flicked on the taps. Hot water shot over our bodies. Caressing her face, I guided her backward until she connected with the tiles. "Fuck, you make me hard."

"You make it hard to say no."

"Then don't."

"I'm not." She clutched my hair and pulled my lips to hers. Our tongues lashed together, tasting and taunting each other. Each lick fueling the fire between us. "Just fuck me. Please?"

A guttural groan erupted in the depths of my throat. "Gladly."

She hooked her arms around my neck and curled one leg around mine. As I snaked my hand around her thigh, I dipped my knees and thrust into her, hard and deep. Shivers charged up my spine. Fuck, that felt good. Her warmth. Her tightness. Her touch. Everything about her ignited my blood. But there was nothing sensual about this. Nothing gentle. I needed a fuck. So did she.

I eased back a fraction, then drove into her again. And again.

"Oh wow." Her eyes fluttered closed, and she clawed at my hair. "Please don't stop."

She didn't have to ask twice. I withdrew a fraction, then pushed into her hot depths.

"Fuck, you feel good." I licked the droplets off her neck, teased my breath against her skin, then found her lips. The taste of her tongue heated my blood. Each touch sent shudders meandering through my veins and tapped on my guarded heart. I hadn't wanted anyone like this in years. It fucking scared me, but I couldn't stop.

She rocked against my thrusts. Her fingers quivered and dug into my flesh. My dick ached for more, more of her. But I had to keep my wits about me. This was just sex. Some stress relief. Some nasty, wicked fun. This . . . was just what we needed.

I embedded my fingers into her wet hair and cradled her head just so I could crush my lips harder against hers. The fire in our breaths sizzled the air. Her hand found my ass. She pulled me forward and rode my cock faster. My knees weakened. I loved her pace, her control. Moaning into her mouth, I slid my hand down her chest and cupped her boob, taking the firm weight in my hand. Her skin was so smooth. So silky and soft. Her perfect tits were bigger than the tits of most girls I'd been with. Grinning against her mouth, I couldn't deny I liked them. I circled my thumb over her hard nipple, massaged it, tweaked it.

"Oh." Ava's head fell back against the tiles. Her pussy tightened around my cock. *Holy shit.* I was going to come quickly if she kept doing that. "Mmm. A little harder."

Fuck . . . so be it. I rolled her bud between my fingertips and drove into her deeper. She clenched around me again.

"You're gonna break my cock, but don't stop." I thrust into her, pinning her against the wall.

"Okay, I won't," she moaned, arching her chest into my touch. *So hot.* She pulsed her hips in time with mine. "I'm close. Real close."

Sliding in and out of her rubbed me in all the right places. It made me harder and burn hotter. But I didn't want to blow before she did.

I ran my hand down her side, across her hip and edged it between us. Working my way lower, I eased my fingers into her slit and stroked her clit. As I pressed, and circled, and teased her, she bit her lip, dug her fingers into my shoulders, and crushed my body to hers.

But then our gazes locked.

Time seemed to stop.

My heart hammered against my ribs.

Our breaths entwined, panting in sync.

The burn in my system begged for release.

"Cole." Her lips parted as she threaded her fingers into my dripping hair and clutched it. "I'm gonna come."

"Race you." Smiling against her mouth, I buried myself into her pussy, pounding away my frustrations, my stresses and my want for her. My head spun from too much heat. Closing my eyes, I snaked my hand around her raised leg and drove deep inside her. So hot. So tight. So good. "Oh yeah." *There.*

With a hot rush, my release fired into the condom. My cock pulsed and throbbed, hard and fast. Each convulsion coursing through my body charged every cell with an electric spark. I couldn't get enough of the taste of Ava's lips, her tongue, her skin. Couldn't get enough of her touch, her scent, her pussy. Over our fiery kisses, she moaned against my mouth. As she orgasmed, her gorgeous body quaked and shivered with mine. Wrapping her arms around my shoulders, she held me closer.

Panting to catch my breath, I pressed my forehead against hers. My cock thudded inside her. *So freaking good.*

"Shit," she whispered, clutching onto my arms. "I need to get you back to your room."

"In a sec." I swayed on my feet as I swiped my thumb over her swollen lips. "Are you okay?" *Am I?*

"Yes." Worry flitted across her eyes, but it disappeared within a blink. "We have to go."

As I eased out of her, a dull ache hammered in the back of my skull. She kissed my lips and slipped out of the shower. She grabbed one of the hotel towels off the fresh pile on the counter and hurried to dress.

I took my sweet time, peeling off the condom, rinsing under the spray of water, hopping out of the shower, and discarding the rubber into the trash can.

"Move it, Cole. Please." Urgency skipped through her voice as she yanked on her tracksuit and swept her hair back into a bun with the band she'd had on her wrist.

My ribs constricted tighter and tighter. I'd always acted before I thought things through. The consequences always came back to haunt me with a vengeance.

The ramifications of this terrified me.

I didn't want her to get into trouble.

Fuck.

I tugged on a fresh pair of boxer briefs. But as I straightened, my head spun. Stars sparkled before my eyes, blurring my vision. My heart rate tripled, thundering against my ribs.

I staggered and caught Ava's arm.

"Ava? Something's not right." The blood drained from my face. Nausea flooded my gut. "Oh, shit. I don't feel so good."

I stumbled. Swayed. The world spun. My knees buckled.

With a thud, I hit the floor.

Everything went black.

Chapter 24

AVA

"Cole?" My heart jolted as I fell to my knees beside him, sprawled out on the locker room floor. I rolled him onto his side, checked his breathing and his pulse. *Fuck.* His heartbeat was way too fast. He'd fainted but was still unconscious. "Cole?"

As I placed my hand on his brow, his clammy skin burned my palm. I hooked his feet up on his bag to elevate them, then rushed to the cupboard, grabbed a fresh towel, wet it with cold water, and wiped his forehead to cool him down.

"Come on, Cole." I tapped his face and gave him a gentle shake. "Wake up."

I knew first aid, but nothing I tried worked. I'd been trained to stay calm and controlled, but fuck that. My hands trembled as I grabbed my cell phone out of my track pants to call Jade, the tour medic. I was about to hit the dial button when Cole moaned.

"Cole?" I tossed my phone aside. My breath shuddered though my chest as I swept his damp hair off his brow. "You're okay. You fainted. Just stay down. Everything will be fine." *Hopefully.* I'd seen him struggle over the past few weeks. I should've said something sooner. Got him help sooner. I'd tried to not get involved, but I cared about him too much.

He blinked his eyes. Their focus and clarity slowly returned as did the color to his cheeks. "Shit, huh?"

"You scared the crap out of me. Don't do that again."

"Sorry." He rolled onto his back and rubbed his eyes.

I grabbed his water bottle and gave him a sip. "Well, that's a first." I smirked. "I've never had someone faint on me after sex before. Was I that good?"

He smiled and chuckled softly. "First for me too. And yeah, it was good." But then he grimaced and wriggled his jaw. "But my cheek hurts."

"You hit the floor, hard. I'm gonna call Jade to come and check on you."

"No. I'll be fine."

Concern lodged in my chest. I couldn't stand back and not say anything anymore. "You're not." I clutched his hand and gave it a tight squeeze. "You're not sleeping. You've had dizzy spells before, and don't pretend you haven't because I watch you. You're pushing yourself too hard. You're *not* fine. And it's okay to admit that. I've been through this too. I can see the signs. You need help and rest. I'm worried about you. So I'm calling Jade or the paramedics. Which one will it be?"

He closed his eyes again, still looking pale. He took a deep breath and nodded. "Okay. Make it Jade. But help me back to my room first. I don't want to cause you any problems."

Guilt twisted in my gut. Panic constricted my veins. I'd crossed too many lines. But his health was my only immediate concern.

"Careful, Mr. Tanner. I might think you care about me." I hooked my hand underneath his shoulder. "Let's get you sitting upright for a minute or two and see how you go."

He eased onto his butt and placed his head between his knees. "Whoa. That's not good. I'm still dizzy."

"Take your time." I rubbed his back and called Jade. I told her he'd fainted, and she said she was on her way.

"Ava?" he whispered. "I do care. It's just . . ."

"Just nothing." It wasn't nothing. It was impossible to deny we had a connection. One that we kept fighting, but it kept pulling us back together.

"It's not nothing." Worry swirled through Cole's eyes. So many unanswered questions and unresolved feelings swirled between us. Was this something? *Yes.* But it was something that couldn't evolve. I need a clean record for Josh. We'd never cross paths or have aligned schedules after the tour. He knew that. I knew that. End of story. "Ava, if I have to be honest, so do you. We need to talk about what happened. About us."

My chest constricted, hard and tight. The wall protecting my heart wavered. "We'll talk later." But there was nothing to talk about. There was no us. I wasn't going to be one of his casual hookups or regulars. It was too risky when Josh was at stake. We both didn't want a relationship. I had to be sensible about this. Just because we liked each other didn't mean we should be together. "Let's get you dressed before Jade gets here."

"Ava. Stop." He leaned back against the melamine lockers. "This, you and I, is so hard to process. I had a plan for this tour, to live it up and be with women across the globe, but you're constantly in my head."

I am? Shit. I grabbed his gym bag for his clothes and sat on the floor next to him. I took a deep breath and let it out slowly. This was a total lava pool of mess. A mess that had to stop. "Cole, neither one of us expected this or wants this." The ache in my chest burned. I liked him too much, but the tie between us had to be severed. "I don't want this to be anything. I have spent too long getting my life back on track after my divorce. I need to do my job. Do everything for my son. I'm not going to fuck that up. We can't and don't want to become involved."

"It's fucked up, but we are." He pulled on his T-shirt, then leaned back against the lockers again. His shoulders slumped. "Trust me, a relationship is the last thing I want. But I'm putting it out there—we could have fun for the next couple months before we go our separate ways."

My body still hummed from orgasming. Fucking Cole on a regular basis would be mind-blowing, hot, but just not sane. My heart wanted to shake me, slap me, and say *'go for it,'* but my head overruled it. "Nice try, drummer boy. I can't do that. We don't want these feelings to develop further. We'll only end up hurting each other. I can't go through that again. "

He lowered his chin. "Neither can I."

I swiveled to sit beside him and rested my head back against the lockers. "We can't repeat this. I'm going to swap with Beckett when he gets back after Christmas. I can't cover you anymore."

"I don't want you to do that. For Charlotte's sake. She trusts you. I trust you."

"Cole, I'm sorry." *Stay strong.* "I can't jeopardize my team. My job. Your safety or the band's."

"I'm sorry. But I'm not sorry I like you."

"Same." I patted his bare leg. Legs I'd wrapped mine around, clawed my nails into, kissed, and touched. *Nope, no more daydreaming.* "You'd better get your shorts on before Jade gets here."

Just as he finished dressing and took a seat on the bench, Jade rushed in with her medical bag. Her short black hair spiked in different directions like she'd been zapped by a power socket. Dressed in a hoodie over her pajamas and UGG boots, she'd gotten here quicker than the Flash. I'd hated having to wake her.

"Cole?" Jade placed her bag on the bench and opened it. "Ava said you fainted. Have you been getting headaches? Dizzy spells? Feeling nauseous?" She checked his throat, ears, eyes, and temperature.

"Yeah." Cole nodded; his leg never stopped jiggling. "Occasionally."

"For how long?" As Jade took Cole's blood pressure, the grooves in her brow deepened.

"It started about two months before the tour."

"Are you overly anxious? Stressed? Worried?"

"Right now I'm not." His eyes glinted as he glanced at me.

Sex might have helped a fraction, but that was a temporary fix. He took too much onboard, never stopped, and never asked for help. But it was time he did.

My concern for him got the better of me. "Cole?" I cut in. "Tell Jade the truth, or I will. Be honest. Please."

The glint in his gaze disappeared only to be replaced by dark clouds. His eyebrows pinched together. He fidgeted with the neckline of his T-shirt, then rubbed the back of his neck and tapped his foot. He sucked in a deep breath and nodded. "I worry about everything, all the fucking time. My mind never stops racing."

After a few more checks, Jade put her stethoscope back in her bag. "Cole, your blood pressure is low. You're dehydrated and fatigued. Let's get you back to your room. I'm going to give you an IV of fluids and you're on strict orders to rest. That means no going out partying. No exercise. No late nights. No alcohol. Nothing. You stay in your room. Read a book. Watch TV. Sleep."

"But—"

"No buts. You have two days off, so you have no excuse. If you don't, you won't make it through the next show or to the end of the tour. I'll get Ava to make sure you don't leave your room." She threw me a sideways glance. "Can you do that?"

"Um . . . yes. I'll sort out something." Hotel security could alert me if he left his room. *Easy.*

"Good." She sighed and sympathy softened her tone. "I can't believe you had to work out with him at this hour."

Oh, we'd had a steamy workout. But there would be no more working up a sweat with Cole. I smoothed my hand over my wet hair. "The joys of being security detail."

"Lucky you were here, found him, and called me."

"I would prefer to be asleep." That was the truth.

She zipped up her bag. "Cole, are you sleeping?"

"No. Not well." He pulled on his socks and shoes.

"Okay, I'm going to give you some medication to help. You need to take care of yourself. We're only six weeks into the tour and have a long road ahead."

"But I have Charlotte. I can't be drugged to the eyeballs."

Jade dug in her bag, pulled out a packet of tablets, and tore off two pills from the blister pack. "Take these when you get back to the room. Hannah can take care of Charlotte today. You need to rest. No exceptions."

As Cole tucked the pills in his pocket, his hands shook. "I . . . I don't like doing nothing. I need to exercise. Get fresh air. Go out.

Drum."

Jade placed her hand on Cole's shoulder. "Cole. Just breathe. You're going to be okay. I'm going to get some meds to help that anxiety too. We'll talk about other options later. Some therapy, meditation, yoga, and other techniques might be viable solutions to help you relax."

"No. I don't need those things."

"Yes, you do," Jade snapped. "You're not superman. Your schedule is demanding. It is my job to make sure you're healthy, physically and mentally, to make it through the tour. You may have passed your medical weeks ago, but this is serious. You're on my radar now; I'll make sure you get better. I'll go grab an IV bag from my supplies, some meds, and meet you in your room."

"You're as bad as Ava, bossing me around." He winked at me.

"Looks like you need it." Jade closed her bag.

I picked up the wet towels and tossed them into the laundry hamper. "Us women have to keep you in line, Cole. You wouldn't survive without us."

"Or survive with you." He grinned as he packed his gym bag and zipped it up.

I held out my hand to Cole. "Are you right to walk if I help you? Or do I need to carry you?"

He gave me a you-wouldn't-dare glare, but yes, I could and would carry him if I had to.

"I'll walk, thanks."

I hauled him to his feet, but he swayed and staggered as he picked up his bag.

"Let me help you." I hooked his arm around my shoulders and headed for the door. Jade followed.

In his suite, I helped him into his room and onto the bed. As our eyes locked, I rubbed his arm. He covered my hand with his. Too much passed between us. Too much care and concern. Too much warmth. I tugged my hand free. "Can I get you anything?"

"Maybe some water."

As I fetched him a bottle from the fridge, Jade knocked on the door. I let her in, and she hooked Cole up to an IV.

"I've set this to release slowly as you sleep. You'll feel better in a couple hours. I'll check on you later in the morning around nine. You do not leave this room. Okay?"

"Yes, doc."

I nodded at Cole. "I'll see you later, Mr. Tanner. Get some rest."

Heat flared in his eyes. "I will. Thank you. For everything."

I left Cole's suite with Jade.

She pressed the elevator call button and turned to me. "Make sure Cole stays in today. You lock him up, restrain him, do what you have to do to keep him from going out."

"It's Cole. That's easier said than done."

"His low blood pressure is a concern. We don't need him passing out on stage."

"No. I'll update my team, and we'll keep our eyes on him and kick his ass if he puts a foot wrong."

"Good. He needs to relax. Maybe try yoga and meditation rather than running for the next couple of weeks while I monitor him."

"Will do." I nodded. "But now, I'm going to try and get some more sleep."

"Me too. See you later."

As I stepped out of the elevator onto my floor and headed toward my room, my own head spun. Cole was worse than I'd expected. I'd been through everything he was experiencing when Mom died—the demanding job, worrying about your child, stresses, grief and life changes. He had additional pressures of dealing with the fans, the media, performing every night, and strangers lurking outside his home.

I should've raised concerns about his health sooner. I'd tried not to get involved. But now I was.

I cared about him.

Shit.

Beckett would hate doing yoga or meditating with Cole.

Could I bury my feelings and stay covering Cole? *Probably not.* But maybe I could just do yoga with him in the mornings. Teach him to meditate. Then Beckett could cover Cole for the rest of the day. Slip was a late riser, so that might work.

No . . . it had to.

Was I prepared to risk my heart and my job for Cole? Risk Josh?

Fuck no.

But I had to do something. As long as I was never alone with Cole, and I kept my distance at all other times, everything would be fine.

Cole's friends would help him though this, and so could I.

It was only for two more months.

Surely Cole and I could keep our hands off each other for that period of time.

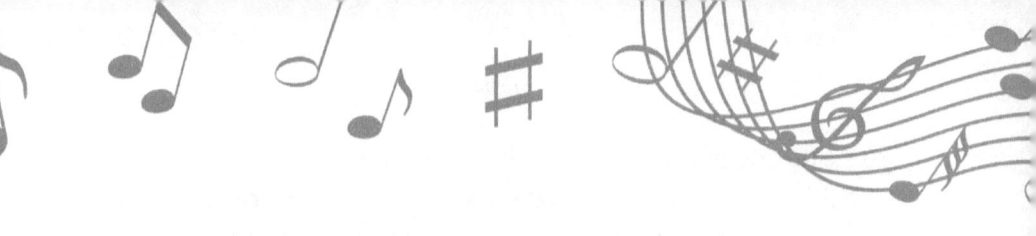

Chapter 25

COLE

Calling the guys to meet me in my room and admitting I wasn't well wouldn't be easy. I was the consistent one, the one who showed up, the one who kept everyone together. I'd never expected to be the one to fall apart. I'd been fucking stupid. I'd pushed myself too hard for too long. But fainting had been my wake-up call.

I had to get better for Charlotte. She needed me. I couldn't think about myself. And definitely shouldn't be thinking about Ava.

But I did.

I'd gotten two hours sleep after Jade and Ava left before Charlotte rushed into my room to wake me. So much for resting. When Hannah had peered through my open bedroom door and gaped at my IV, I'd told her what happened. She seemed glad I'd been ordered to slow down. Charlotte rushed from the room and returned with her doctors play set. As she crawled around me on the bed, she took my temperature, wrapped a bandage around my head, and stuck a Band-Aid on my hand. Her smile did make me feel better.

Just after nine, Jade gave me a second IV bag to tackle my dehydration. At ten, the door buzzed, and Hannah let the guys into my suite.

Flint's face blanched the moment he saw the IV, and he rushed to sit beside me on the bed. "Fuck. What happened?"

Slip pulled up a chair. Lewis sat on the end of the mattress.

"I fainted." I shrugged like it was no big deal. "In the gym. Ava was with me. She called Jade."

"Why the IV?" Slip eyed the bag hanging off the metal pole.

"My blood pressure's low. I'm dehydrated and haven't been handing stress well."

"Why didn't you say anything? Can we help?" Lewis asked.

"I don't think so." As I filled the guys in on the long list of issues I'd been dealing with, from my pending review with Charlotte to my security concerns at home and my dizzy spells, their faces grayed. Every word burned my lungs but at the same time, a weight lifted off my shoulders. It felt good to spill what I'd been struggling with. I had always strived to be strong. To be the best. Do more. Be better. Be everything to everyone. I could thank my parents for that mental fuck-up. But no more. This scare had shaken me to the core. I'd never make my parents happy, so fuck 'em. These guys and Charlotte were all that mattered.

Flint swiped his hand over his unshaven jaw. "Fuck. I knew you had shit going on. Why didn't you talk to us?"

Oh, there was more messing with my mind, but I'd told them enough for one day. "I didn't want you to worry. You've got enough going on with the tour."

"No." He clutched my hand. "We're in this together. All four of us."

I fidgeted with the sheet draped over my waist. "I'm sorry. I thought I was okay."

"Don't be sorry." Slip shook his head. "We're always here for you. Health comes first."

It had been a little more than five hours since I'd fainted in the gym, and I was already itching to get outside and do something. It was the day before Christmas. I wanted to check out the city, take Charlotte to see Santa and the lights, and go drinking with everyone. "I'd love to go to a bar and get shitfaced and have a good time. But I can't. I have to rest and have this stupid thing in my arm." I shook my wrist, hating the IV digging into and pulling at my skin.

"Fuck." Slip slapped and rubbed his thigh. "We have a huge night planned on the town too."

I pointed at him. "Do not feed my FOMO." I could do with ten shots of vodka right then.

Lewis chuckled and scratched his stubble. "Damn, I had Jell-O shots lined up for you to do off girls' bellies too."

Fuck. I loved doing that. But then I smirked. "From their cleavage is better." Nothing like a face full of tit while downing vodka shots.

"Are you sure you're sick?" Flint laughed.

"I fainted. I'm not dying."

Flint leaned back on his hands; worry clouded his ice-blue eyes. "Are you gonna be right by the next show?"

"Yes." I set assurance in my tone. I would not miss playing. I'd find a way to drum even if I broke my fucking arms and legs. But my head spun and the reality of what happened kicked in again. I closed my eyes and lowered my tone. "It fucking kills me, but I have to ease up on the drinking and the partying to all hours. Jade's putting me on some meds too . . . for anxiety and to help me sleep."

"Anything to help you get better." Sadness swallowed Flint's eyes. "It sounds like a much more sensible solution than the self-medicating I did on vodka when Phil died."

My heart sliced my ribs. I'm part of the reason he's dead. The guilt still weighed heavily on my bones. "None of us want to go down that road again." Maybe it was a good thing I'd fainted around Ava. I didn't want the guys to give me an ultimatum to get my shit together like we'd had to do for Flint.

"No, we don't." Slip play-punched me in the arm. "At least, Ava will enjoy the break."

"Um . . . she won't be getting one. Ava's covering you after Christmas, Slip. Beckett will be with me."

"Why?" He raised a questioning eyebrow. "Did you fuck her again?"

My head fell back and hit the headboard. "Yeah."

"Told you you're into her." Flint chuckled.

Damn, she did my head in. Thinking about her made the emptiness in my chest ache even more. "Why her? We can't and don't want to be together. How fucked up is that?"

We had other responsibilities. Other commitments and priorities.

Being sensible sucked.

"Sometimes what you don't want turns out to be what you want." Slip grinned as he leaned back on the chair.

"You talking about Maddy?" Lewis lay sideways on the bed, propping his head on his hand.

"Yeah." Slip bobbed his head. "Thanks to you, Lewis, you fucker. I'm stoked. But I'm just not sure Mads is though."

"If it's meant to be, it'll work out." Lewis threw him a sly smile, then turned to me. "Sometimes you just have to say fuck it, take the leap, and find out if you're meant to be together."

"I'm not leaping into anything." Irritation twisted my veins. "Ava's more like an itch that won't go away. She's always in my face. Ordering me around. This tension builds between us, then we snap, fuck, and now have to move on. That's not healthy. That's not normal."

Flint jabbed his finger into my thigh. "I like her because she says no to you."

"Maybe she's exactly what you need." Slip added.

"No. She's not." I shook my head, and my stomach sank. "Why get involved with someone who's only going to leave?" Just like Priah did. "And I don't want to jeopardize her custody case. I don't need any more complications. We're on tour. I want to have fun. Have a ton of sex with different women. Party hard. Live life to the fullest."

"While resting with an IV in your arm." Lewis waggled his finger toward my drip.

I grabbed a pillow and pegged it at him. "Fuck you."

As we laughed, Charlotte skipped into the room dressed in a Christmas dress and red tights. She crawled onto the bed and plonked down beside me. She curled against my arm. "Can we go see Santa now?"

I hooked my arm around her. "After lunch when I get this medicine out of my arm." A couple hours out of bed wouldn't kill me.

"Does it hurt?" She leaned across me and touched the edge of the waterproof gauze covering the needle above my wrist.

"No. It's making me better." I kissed the top of her head.

Lewis wriggled Charlotte's foot. "This little lady has definitely stolen your heart."

"Yeah. She certainly has." Something good had come out of fainting. I'd have more time with Charlotte.

After the guys left and Jade had returned to remove my IV, Ava and Riley—another security team member—escorted Hannah, Charlotte, and me to see Santa. Jade wasn't happy I was going out, but I'd promised not to be out long. Avoiding the crowds as much as possible, we headed to Lafreniere Park. With a beanie, jacket, and sunglasses on, I tried to remain inconspicuous. But it didn't work. Luckily I wasn't too overwhelmed by overzealous people. Being recognized and stopped by excited fans, asked for photos and selfies, and the random request for an autograph still blew my mind.

Fuck, I loved my job.

As Charlotte sat on Santa's knee and rattled off a gazillion toys and books she wanted, Hannah touched my arm. The trembles in her hands seemed worse today.

"Are you feeling better, Cole?"

"Yeah, thanks." I was. The IV had helped. So had another hour of sleep before lunch. "You?"

"I'm well." Hannah always had a friendly smile and light in her eyes. She was the best grandmother Charlotte could ever have had. "While you were resting before lunch, Arilla from children's services called. To help put your mind at ease, I gave you a five-star report. I'm proud of you, Cole. You've made changes, and you're spending time with Charlotte. You've just got to work on you now. Promise me you will. For Charlotte."

"Wow." Humbleness swelled in my chest. "Thank you for the

report. And yeah, I promise. I'll take better care of myself."

"Good. I don't want to have to ask Ava to kick your butt into line again."

I stuffed my hands into my coat pockets and smiled. "No. Me either."

Ava stood off to the side of the crowd, on duty like she always was. The butterflies in my stomach threatened to take flight as I daydreamed about stripping off her uniform when we got back to the hotel, but something about her was off. My skin prickled. I followed her line of sight. She'd zoned in on a middle-aged man standing on the other side of Santa's fenced-off area. He had a high-end camera, pointed in our direction. Was it just the paparazzi? Some sick fuck taking pictures of kids? He didn't look concerned about any of the children. *Oh shit* . . . Was that the guy who'd been outside my house?

Ava spoke into her headset. A chill ran down my spine as Riley nodded and edged toward him.

But the moment Riley got within a few feet of the man, the photographer lowered his camera and disappeared into the crowd. *Fuck.*

So much for lowering my stress levels.

Hannah fidgeted with her scarf. "Cole, it was hard not to overhear some of your conversation with your friends this morning in our small suite. I'm sorry that you and Ava can't work things out, but I understand where she's coming from. Her family comes first. And for you, so does yours."

Ava nodded at me, easing my concerns a fraction. "Hannah, some things aren't meant to be."

"No, but some are." Hannah smiled at Charlotte, still chatting to Santa. "I miss Shelby every day. There's a hole in my chest that hurts all the time. But a higher power had other plans. You were meant to be Charlotte's father, not Keith. You have a good heart, Cole. You're a brilliant musician. Enjoy your music. Your fun and parties and friends. But treasure time with Charlotte. Work on that balance. You'll get there. I know you will."

"Thanks." I wrapped my arm around her shoulder and gave

her a hug. "You might like me even more because I've got you something special for Christmas." I'd had enough of the crowds; my anxiety wasn't under control yet.

"Oh, I like surprises." She tightened her scarf. It wasn't cold though.

"It's back at the hotel. Shall we go?" I tilted my head toward the parking lot.

"Yes."

After I took more photos of Charlotte with Santa and I managed to coax her off his knee, we zoomed back to the hotel.

As we walked into the lobby, Hannah cried. "Paul!" She rushed across the lobby to where he sat in his wheelchair by the sofas, having a cup of tea.

Charlotte slid out of my arms and rushed over to him. "Poppy." She flung her arms around his neck and hugged him tight.

"You did this?" Ava's eyes glassed over with tears.

"Yeah . . . well, with the help of April. I asked her to get Paul here; she made it happen." I nudged my arm against Ava's elbow. "I like making people happy."

"And what makes you happy?"

"That." I waved at Paul, Hannah, and Charlotte hugging and kissing each other. Music was in my soul, and I lived to drum, but making people smile was up there. *Fuck.* With all the tour and stress, I'd forgotten to focus on the simple things. I had to do that more often.

Leaving Riley to keep an eye on Hannah and Charlotte while Paul finished his tea, Ava and I headed up to my room.

As we headed along the hallway to my suite, my cell phone pinged. I grabbed it out of my jacket. An email from Harper lit the screen.

My hands shook as I swiped the screen to read the message.

Hey Cole, I accept your job offer.
I'm taking twelve months leave.
If being your nanny doesn't work out, I can come back to Nepal.
I'm looking forward to more travel.

I can't wait to meet Charlotte and see everyone.
Merry Christmas,
Love Harps

"Arrrrgh!" I screamed. I grabbed Ava, kissed her sweet lips, then picked her up and swung her 'round. "Yes."

"Cole, put me down." She slapped my shoulder.

I placed her on her feet, my heart still stampeding. "Harper's coming." Excitement elevated my voice as it echoed through the hallway. "She's going to be Charlotte's nanny. This is the fucking best Christmas present."

"That's awesome." Ava cleared her throat, straightened her jacket, then smoothed her hand over her pulled-back hair. A hint of redness colored her cheeks. I loved it when she blushed. I loved stealing a kiss.

"This is brilliant. One less thing to worry about." I stared at my cell phone and re-read the message, just to make sure I hadn't made a mistake. *Nope.* Harper was coming. *Yes!*

"Good." Ava squeezed my arm. "Now you need to get some rest and can relax even more."

"Yeah. That would be good."

It would.

Finally something had gone right.

But the knot in my stomach didn't ease. That worried me. From my experience, that usually meant something was about to go wrong.

Chapter 26

AVA

Ahead of schedule, just after nine a.m., our tour buses pulled up on the street, one hundred yards from the hotel in Atlanta. Four coaches with *The Flintlocks* logo plastered over the sides were far from inconspicuous. The other five buses with the road crew had gone straight to the venue to set up the stage for tonight's show. The sea of fans waiting to see the guys wasn't too overwhelming, but they were scattered along the street, not blocked by barricades or guarded by hotel security.

Wells had called ahead. Nothing made him more irritated than places not being ready for our arrival. He was a meticulous planner. I'd learned from the best. He was on the phone to the hotel's team, ranting orders within seconds.

I savored the few calm moments on the bus before we disembarked.

Atlanta was my last stop before I'd fly home to see Josh for the New Year's weekend. I couldn't wait. But I'd had a rough night on the bus and had barely slept.

Cole had occupied too many of my thoughts.

We'd barely spent a moment apart over the past few days. I'd been on duty with Wyatt, Sloane, and Riley while the band had enjoyed Christmas. They truly were a family. Their laughter was infectious. Their love, contagious. Cole's smile, too mesmerizing.

When I'd turned up to his room to take him to lunch, he'd worn a gaudy festive knitted sweater covered in llamas wearing Santa Claus hats and sunglasses. Stupid butterflies had fluttered in the pit of my stomach. *Damn* . . . he made ugly look hot. He'd surprised me by getting me a Christmas present—a travel coffee mug that said *'Boss Bitch—Fuck Off Until I Finish My Coffee.'* He knew me too well. But he hadn't been surprised I'd turned up bearing gifts. I'd bought a pamper pack for Hannah, a piano dance mat and coloring books for Charlotte, and a sleeping eye mask for Cole with *'Fuck Off—I Need My Beauty Sleep'* printed across the front. His present was now essential considering he needed to rest.

My soul had ached at not spending Christmas with my family or opening presents with Josh. But this year was Luther's turn with him . . . and hopefully, it would be his last.

Beckett swiveled on the bus seat to face me. "You ready?"

"Always." I shook my thoughts aside and hooked my earpiece into place. "Are you going to be okay with Cole?"

"You know I will. But are you alright? After you two . . . you know . . ." He smirked. "He's not the type of guy I thought you'd fall for."

"What?" I jerked my chin back. "I haven't fallen for him."

"Hello. Ava." He tapped his knuckles against my forehead. "Your attempt at yoga with him yesterday ended up being an hour of girly giggles, sexy glances, and flirty touches. No one needs that much manhandling into a triangle pose. I saw it all go down from the treadmill. Don't deny it."

"I deny everything." I pursed my lips, trying not to smile. But the fire in my cheeks was no doubt a dead giveaway. "He's just not what I expected."

"What?" Sarcasm laced his voice. "He's not an arrogant, narcissistic, son-of-a-bitch like your ex?"

I giggled. "No . . . he's not."

He rested his arm on the back of the seat. "Technically he's not *your* client anymore—he's mine. You can date whoever you want."

"Ah, no. I can't compromise the team." I checked my holster, belt, and radio. "If I ever date again, it won't be Cole Tanner."

"Ava?" He caught my hand and held it against my leg. "Your whole energy changes when he's in the room. Are you sure there's nothing between you two that's worth pursuing?"

"Becks, stop." I pulled my hand free. "It's something . . . it just can't be anything. So drop it."

A sly grin curled the corner of his mouth. "I'd staple his balls to his asshole if he hurt you."

"You won't have to do that. He's out of my system. We're moving on." I put on my cap and wriggled it into place. "I'm happy covering Slip. He's easy compared to Cole."

"You think?" Beckett shook his head. "He's a crazy motherfucker when he's on the booze, he's popping painkillers like party pills when the guys aren't around, and when he's with Maddy, they flirt, fight, then fuck like rabbits."

"That I can handle." I clipped my radio onto my jacket. And I'd definitely keep an eye on the tablets he was taking. If it was cause for concern, I'd talk to Blake . . . and Cole. Another band member who had issues . . . Go figure! "But do me a favor. Make sure Cole rests. Drag him home from their after-parties if you have to . . . and take care of Charlotte."

"I will. Promise." He patted and rubbed my knee. "Let's get these fuckers into the hotel and get some rest before sound check."

"Deal." I nodded.

"Okay team," Wells hollered from the front of the bus. "We're ready to go."

Our team of twelve was quick to act, stepping out of the bus. Ramona, Kennedy, and a few others formed a line of defense, herding the onlookers to the inner edge of the sidewalk to clear a path for the guys to enter the hotel.

Once we were in position, Wells slapped his palm on the band's bus door. It opened with a *whoosh*. In formation with Beckett, Wyatt, Sloane, and Wells, we created a protective circle for the band. Flint stepped out of the bus first with a sexy swagger in his stride, his rock star smile dazzling in the winter sunshine, and waved to the fans. The elevated screams and cries from the crowd electrified the air. Slip skipped out of the bus, followed by

Lewis and Cole. They all looked too fucking good for this hour of the day.

"Morning." Cole nodded in my direction as he straightened his leather jacket. "Sleep well?"

"No." I shielded him from the crowd. "I'm looking forward to a night in a bed." Tiny bunks on a bus where I slept with eleven other members of our security team, with two of them snoring profusely, wasn't ideal. But we'd stayed up late, having fun, playing cards, telling stories, and teasing each other after the show. Then when we'd crashed, I hadn't been able to sleep. *Shit!* I'd turned into Cole.

He leaned in to me and lowered his voice. "I'd like you in my bed."

Heat rippled through my veins. But I sucked in a deep breath and glared at him. "You passed out in the shower; you wouldn't handle me in your bed."

"I survived the first time we were together. I'd be willing to give it another go."

Between my legs throbbed. My pulse quickened. *Oh no. Focus.* I sneered at him. "Keep dreaming. Now move your ass and get into the hotel . . . Mr. Tanner."

Cole growled, low and sexy. "I love it when you call me that." His eyes flashed with too much sexiness as he stopped for photos with fans.

"I'd love you to behave." I mumbled as I waited for him.

He leaned toward me. "You make it difficult, Ms. Matthews."

Ergh! I didn't need my challenging relationship with Cole to get even more complicated. Beckett was supposed to be covering Cole—not me. I clutched Cole's shoulder and nudged him forward. "Move."

As we headed down the street, the crowd got pushy, closing in around the guys. Cell phones and banners waved before us. My team tightened our circle surrounding the band, shielding them from the onslaught of fans.

"Move back." Wyatt held out his arm, holding some teenage girl at bay.

Cameras flashed. Screams and hollers grew louder. Hands and arms reached around us to touch the guys. Some college-aged chick grabbed my shoulder and tried to yank me out of the way to get to Cole. She had no chance. I flung my arm up and used my shoulder to break her hold. With a gentle shove, I eased her back into the crowd where Beckett stepped in to block any further advances.

Once the band was inside the hotel, a huge grin lit Slip's face as he hooked his arms around my shoulders. He waggled his finger between Beckett and me. "So this bodyguard swap thing didn't happen."

I stepped out of his hold and lifted my chin. "We just responded to the crowd and the situation." I'd been doing my job. Quick thinking and action were necessary. No one had been hurt. That was the key.

Slip shook his head, chuckled. "Well . . . any time you want to *swap* is fine by me." He ruffled Cole's hair. "Right, Cole?"

Cole threw Slip a mischievous grin. "I'd be happy, too, but Ava's rules. So don't fuck with them."

Slip held up his hands. "Okay. Just saying . . ."

Too much humor shimmered in Beckett's eyes too.

Ergh! I needed a break. The sooner the weekend came, the better.

Everyone gathered at the side of the foyer while April and Blake checked the group in at reception, then handed out the room keys. We'd have a few hours of rest before we'd head to sound check at three this afternoon.

After we'd escorted the guys to their suites, Ramona and I fell into our room and collapsed onto our twin beds.

"Oh my God. This bed is heaven," Ramona moaned. "I'm never getting up. I swear."

Fluffy quilts. Big pillows. A big bed all to myself. *Bliss.* "I'm with you. I'm seriously gonna catch a couple hours' sleep before we have to take the guys to the venue."

"Me too." Ramona covered her eyes with her arm.

I eased off my jacket, holster, belt, and radio, and dumped

them on the desk. After setting my alarm, I tossed my cell phone on the nightstand, kicked off my boots, and sank my head into the pillows. As I closed my eyes, wooziness swayed through my head, like I was still traveling on the bus. The hum of the wheels continued to buzz in my ears. But oh, this was a gazillion times more comfortable.

Slowly, sleep pulled me under.

But my vibrating cell phone startled me awake. I grabbed it, not wanting to wake Ramona. *Shit.* I'd had forty-five minutes rest. That was better than none. The caller ID blazed with *Wilson*, my lawyer's name. My stomach cinched and swayed. When Wilson called, I never knew whether to be hopeful or terrified . . . usually the latter if it involved my ex.

I swiped the screen. "Hey," I whispered and dashed into the en suite, shutting the door behind me. "How are you?"

"Hi, Ava. I'm good. How's the tour?"

"Long and tiring. And it's only week six."

"You're not going to like this." His nasal voice vibrated through the speaker. "Luther's lawyers have sent a formal request to postpone the date of your hearing for two weeks, pushing it into the first week of March. He has to travel overseas for awards season."

"What?" Fire burned through my veins. He'd have to take Josh with him. I'd miss my days with my son. "Change our court date? Oh, hell no. And that's a hard no, Wilson." Ice set in my heart. Our hearing was set for February twentieth, a few days after the US leg of the tour ended. There was no way I'd push it back. "I'm not going one day longer without getting more custody of Josh."

"It's only two weeks."

"That's a lifetime. He's just trying to delay the inevitable. Our date is set. If he doesn't show, tough shit. The judge will rule in my favor, and he knows that. I'll get Josh." I was over bending to Luther's requests and being terrified of his bullying tactics and threats to keep Josh away from me. I wasn't afraid anymore. During this assignment, being with the band, my team . . . and Cole . . . I'd learned how strong I was. How determined I was. Luther had nothing to hold over me anymore. "Do your job, Wilson. This request is denied."

"Ava, Luther's offered to be flexible and give you more time on your dates with Josh beforehand."

Luther? Flexible? That was a first. "Are you shitting me?" What was I paying this lawyer for? Incompetence? "That's useless and impossible. I'm on my last assignment. I can't change my roster. Wilson, this is a big no. Luther's playing games. He's not going to win. If he travels and takes Josh out of the country without my consent, he's fucked. So let him go. That will be in my favor." But not seeing Josh would kill me.

Wilson sighed as if he was over my custody battles. I certainly was. "Fine. I'll deny the request and ensure the date is kept."

"You do that." Tears pricked my eyes as I paced the width of the small bathroom. "Luther's got away with too much for too long. He's not going to do that anymore."

"No. He's not." Wilson's tone was as flat as a deflated tire. "I'm on it."

"Good." But nausea flooded my gut. Had my lawyer lost interest in my case? I wanted someone who'd fight for me. Do whatever necessary to help me gain more custody of Josh. *Fuck.* I didn't have time to find a new lawyer. I hated this process. I just wanted my son.

I ended the call and wiped the tears from my eyes. *God*, I hated lawyers. I hated Luther even more.

There was a soft knock on the door. *Who the hell is that?*

I sniffled and headed out to check. I peered through the peephole. *Damn it. Cole . . . and Charlotte.*

I swiped the last tears from my eyes and heaved open the door. "Hey? What's up?"

Cole's smile morphed from bright to a worry-filled frown. "Ava? What's happened?"

"Nothing. I'm fine." *I wasn't.* But seeing Cole in his leather jacket made me feel a bit better. "Beckett's in room seven-oh-two. We don't have to head to the venue until three." It was just after eleven.

"Charlotte wants pancakes and ice cream. There's a café across the road. Beckett insisted on you being his backup. He's waiting downstairs for us. I said I'd stop by your room and get you." Concern darkened his eyes. "Can you join us . . . or . . . you want me to get someone else?"

Damn you, Becks. I was convinced he was trying to get Cole and I together. Well, he was wasting his time. That wasn't going to happen. But I'd do my job. "No. It's fine. The fresh air might do me good. Just let me grab my gear."

"Cool. We'll wait for you out here."

"I'll be one sec." I let the door close and scurried to put my boots on, grabbed my two-way, belt, holster, and jacket.

"Where are you going?" Ramona didn't open her eyes.

"Cole wants to go out with Charlotte. Becks wants backup. Duty calls."

"Have fun. Don't do anything I wouldn't do."

I laughed softly. She was fucking the boss. I'd fucked my client. Were we much different? *Nope.*

Given the crowd of fans we'd encountered on our arrival, Beckett calling for additional security was the right thing to do. Slip was sleeping and would text me if he needed to go out. As I stuffed my earpiece into my ear, I walked out into the hallway full of laughter and shrieks. Cole and Charlotte raced up and down the long corridor. Charlotte crashed into my legs, giggling, and cuddled me. "Cole's slow."

Cole sighed and jammed his hands on his hips. "Charlotte, you are just too fast. You're superwoman. See?" He picked her up, held her flat in his arms, and spun her around like she was flying.

Charlotte squealed and laughed.

My heart ached from missing Josh, but butterflies skipped in my stomach as Cole played with Charlotte. He was so good to her. It helped that he was just a big kid who loved to have fun too.

"Ava? Are you coming?" Beckett's voice came across my two-way.

I pressed the button to talk. "On our way. Heading down in the elevator now."

"Thanks for this." Cole zoomed past me with Charlotte. "So much for rest time."

"Time to sleep when we're dead."

"So true. Let's go."

Beckett met us in the foyer. More hotel security personnel were on duty now the band was in the building. Two policemen stood outside. It was good to know they were there if needed.

Cole pulled out a cap from the back pocket of his jeans and jammed it on his head, then grabbed his dark sunglasses out of his black leather jacket and slipped them on. "Ready."

Charlotte set a pair of pink glittery sunglasses on her face and struck a pose. "Me too."

Like father, like daughter.

I had a quick chat to hotel security and the two cops out the front to let them know where we were going. Beckett and I scooted across the road with Cole and Charlotte and entered the café. I guided them to a clear booth at the rear of the store, taking mental notes as I went. Twelve tables. Three spares. Three waitstaff. Fire exit, rear left. Restrooms were past the small kitchen. A few patrons' faces lit up as they recognized Cole, but no one made a move. Most looked like mature folk having lunch and coffee, not screaming teenage fans. But the lady in the corner with long blonde hair tucked underneath her beanie made me double take.

As Cole took a seat with Charlotte, I caught Beckett on the arm and lowered my voice so only he could hear. "Front, right corner. She look familiar? Remember the footage from Cole's place?"

"Yeah." He scanned the café, not taking any more time looking at one person than the next. "Different hair color. Rounder face. It's not her. But best we keep an eye on things. You stay here with Cole. I'll stand at the front."

"No. I will. Cole's your cover—not mine."

"I know. But you'll enjoy the view from here more than I will." He winked, patted my arm, and made his way to stand by the front door.

Damn you, Becks.

"Ava, do you like ice cream?" Charlotte stood on the padded

seat beside Cole. His arm was wrapped around her legs, holding her steady.

"Yes." I summoned a gentle smile and softened my tone. "I love ice cream. What's your favorite flavor?"

"I like rainbow."

"Good choice. You enjoy your treat with Cole." I tilted my head toward the back wall. "I'll wait over there for you."

"Why not sit with us?" She pointed at the seat across from her. *Gotta love her sweet innocence.*

"Um." Cole winced and rubbed her little legs. "Ava's working."

"But you're not playing moosic 'til tonight."

"Yes. But she has to watch over us."

"But she can do that from here."

Cole chuckled. "True." He shrugged and raised a how-about-it eyebrow. "Ava, would you like to join us?"

I scanned the other tables, the suspicious woman in the corner, and then the booth seat opposite Cole. It would be the best position to keep an eye on the café from. I radioed Beckett to let him know and he nodded.

"Okay." I slid into the booth. "This is only because I can watch everyone from here."

"Yay." Charlotte clapped.

A young waitress with a white frilly apron on came over to our table. She wiped her hands on her skirt. "Hi. I'm Ella. I'm such a huge fan." Her voice shook in her fluster. "What can I get you?"

"Hi Ella. I'm Cole. How you doing?"

"I'm good. Really good." She giggled.

She took Cole's order of a pancake stack loaded with fruit, ice cream, and maple syrup for him to share with Charlotte, and coffees for me and Beckett.

"Would you mind signing this for me?" The waitress held out her pen and order pad for him to autograph.

"Sure." Cole grinned as he signed the page.

Not once had I seen him get annoyed with fans or frustrated when they invaded his personal space or private time. Luther used to hate it when people recognized him and interrupted our dinners or outings to get a photo with him. Cole never did. *God*, he infuriated me and impressed me. Why couldn't he be a cocky, arrogant asshole instead of this nice, caring man who treated everyone around him with respect? It made it so hard not to like him.

While we waited for our food, Charlotte scooted over to the kids' play area in the opposite corner to play with the box of toys.

Cole fidgeted with a napkin as he rested his hands on the table. "So, are you heading home tomorrow morning?"

"Yeah. I can't wait to see Josh."

"I bet." He smoothed the napkin flat on the table. "You can tell me to mind my own business, but you were upset before. Is everything okay?"

"I hope so. Luther wanted to delay our custody hearing and take Josh out of the country on one of my scheduled weekends because he has to travel for work. I said no."

"Good for you."

"I'm tired of his games. I want the court hearing over." Tears burned the backs of my eyes. *Shit.* Pull it together. I was working. "I don't want his fingers around my throat anymore."

"I hope you don't mean that literally."

"No." I blinked my tears away. "I just want more time with Josh to settle into my new job and get on with my life."

"You're going to miss this though, aren't you? Being in the field?"

"Yeah, I will." I nodded. "I love my team. Every day is different. We meet so many interesting people and have a lot of fun behind the scenes."

"So do we." His gorgeous green eyes glinted in the soft light.

"So I've seen." I tried not to smile.

"Hey?" He reached across the table and rubbed my hand. "Is there anything I can do to help you?"

"Do you know how to take down a narcissistic prick?"

"I wish I did." He rubbed his thumb across the back of my hand. Warmth meandered up my arm. "But if you need anything for your hearing, a testimonial or character reference, I'll give you one."

"Thanks." I pulled my hand free and wiped my palms on my work pants. The line between friends and work couldn't be crossed while on duty. *Focus.*

Beckett tilted his head toward two customers. They took out their cell phones and took pictures of Cole, then giggled as they no doubt posted them online. So did the guy and girl over by the far wall. But that didn't raise the hairs on my arm or warrant any concern. Beckett didn't move another inch. All was okay . . . for now.

"I'm sorry Luther's giving you a hard time." Cole slumped his shoulders. "Kids certainly mess up your life."

"Kids don't mess it up. They change it." Then I smirked and injected sarcasm into my tone. "Relationships with exes are completely different stories."

He glanced at Charlotte building a tower with some wooden blocks. "I never had a relationship with Shelby, other than being friends. I understand why she never told me about Charlotte. I don't want to share her with anyone. That makes me constantly worry about my final court assessment. I'm afraid the social worker will rule me unfit and take her away." Worry darkened his eyes. "Losing Charlotte would kill me. She's weaved her way into my soul with every smile, snotty nose, and tight hug. I finally understand that unexplainable, unconditional care, and protectiveness people have for their kids. I'd do anything for her."

A tear slipped down my cheek.

"What?" His brows pinched together.

I swiped my damp cheek. "You continually surprise me. If you're not careful, Mr. Tanner, I might actually begin to like you."

He nudged my leg under the table with his knee. "I know you like me."

"Yeah, I do. "

As Charlotte grabbed a toy car and raced it across the floor, sadness glossed over his eyes. "She still doesn't call me Dad."

My heart sank into my stomach. "She will when she's ready. It's like you call her kid more than your daughter. You're both still adjusting. Bonding. Learning to love and trust each other."

As Ella arrived with our food, my gaze drifted past Cole's ear. Two women in business suits rose from their chairs and headed to the counter to pay. Yes, it was cell phones they grabbed out of their purses. Nothing more threatening.

Charlotte raced across the floor to join us. "Yay. Ice cream."

Cole lifted her over his legs and placed her on the seat beside him. She grabbed the big spoon and dug into her dessert.

Another male customer finished his lunch, paid for his items, and left.

"Do you ever fucking relax on the job?" Cole stuffed a fork full of pancakes into his mouth.

"No. Not when I'm on duty, Mr. Tanner."

He chuckled.

"What?" I took a sip of coffee and licked my lips.

Cole leaned forward. Charlotte remained focused on mushing, stirring and eating her ice cream as Cole lowered his voice. "Every time you call me Mr. Tanner, it fucking turns me on."

My breath skipped through my chest. Just looking at him made my body temperature rise. "Cole . . ." Too much want and emptiness hovered through my whisper. "We agreed not to . . ."

"I know. But you, in that uniform, bossing me around gives me a permanent semi."

Heat flared in my cheeks. I pressed my thighs together to ward off the throb and need for action that pulsed deep inside me. "You shouldn't wear that leather jacket. Makes us even." Yep, leather jackets were my new weakness . . . on Cole anyway.

"Shouldn't we do something about it?" He licked cream off the tip of his finger.

Oh, boy. "No, we shouldn't." But damn, he made it difficult not to.

"Ava?" Beckett's voice hummed in my ear piece. "You watching the woman in the corner? She hasn't stopped fidgeting, playing with something in her tote or looking your way. I'm not liking her vibe." I'd felt the same way when we'd walked in. *Shit.* I'd been distracted by Cole. That wasn't good.

The woman held up her cell phone and the camera flashed in our direction. She didn't stop pointing it at us as she ran her hand over her head and stared out the window. The hairs on the back of my neck stood on end.

I clicked my radio to talk to Beckett. "Me either. Let's move." I downed my coffee and wiped my mouth on a napkin. "Cole, we have to go."

"But I haven't finished."

He'd demolished half his food. That would have to do. "A few people here have taken photos of you. They've all had that OMG-it's-Cole look in their eyes. But the woman in the corner is holding up her cell, pretending to use it to do her hair or something, but I'm convinced she's filming you and taking photos."

"What's wrong with that? I get photographed all the time."

"She's not looking at us as she does it. I've got a bad feeling about her. So has Becks."

"A feeling?" Worry flitted across his eyes.

"Yes. Plus there's a crowd growing outside. We need to get back to the hotel."

"Okay." He wiped his mouth on a napkin and tossed it on the plate. "I'll pay then we'll go."

I nodded as he stood and headed to the counter. I buzzed Beckett. "We're moving. The blonde is unnerving me too. That's not fandom we're dealing with."

"No, it's not. I'm ready when you are." Beckett edged closer to the door.

I grabbed a napkin and wiped Charlotte's hands and mouth clean from sticky ice cream. She'd finished the whole bowl in record time. Cole returned to pick her up and placed her onto his hip. "Time to go, munchkin."

"Walk to the right." I shielded him from the patrons as we headed out the door. Out of the corner of my eye, the blonde filmed every step we took. Again, she wasn't doing it in some fan-type way.

"Becks, did you get a photo of her while we were in there?" I asked as we crossed the road.

"Sure did." He waved at a taxi to stop as we dashed across the hotel's driveway. "It's not the same woman from LA."

"You think someone new is following me?" Cole cradled Charlotte's head against his shoulder. "Fuck, how many psycho fans do I have?"

"Do you just want to consider the girls you've slept with or include your fan base as well?" I glanced over my shoulder toward the café, but the woman had disappeared. *Crap.*

"I don't need this. I don't need more to worry about." Stress skipped through Cole's low voice.

"Hey?" I touched his arm as we entered the busy lobby. "We've got the situation under control. We're doing everything to keep you safe. Trust me."

"Do we need more security?" he asked as we headed for the elevators.

"We have more than enough staff and surveillance on you," I assured him. "We'll submit her photo to the hotel's and the venue's security teams. We'll make sure she doesn't come near you or cause any issues."

"What about the other guys? Are they safe?" He glanced around the people loitering in the foyer. I hated seeing him worried. His safety was my team's concern—not his.

"Yes, as much as anyone can be." I hated that I couldn't give him a 100 percent guarantee. "Let's get you and Charlotte back to your room until it's time to go to the venue."

"Thank you." He dipped his chin as he cradled Charlotte against his chest. "Next time I'll fucking call room service for pancakes and ice cream."

"It's fine to head out." Beckett pressed the call button. "We just need more warning so we can scope places out and ensure security is in place."

"Noted for next time." We stepped into the elevator. Once we reached his suite, Charlotte raced past Cole into the room, but the tension didn't fall from Cole's face. He leaned against the open door. "I'm sorry I can't provide more help on who could be following me. I've never had any issues before this tour."

"Let's hope it's just an excited fan." Beckett's calm tone never faltered. "We'll get Bruno to investigate further."

"Thank you." Cole took a step into his room. "I'll see you guys in a couple hours."

"See you soon . . . Cole." I dipped my chin and shuffled back a foot.

He nodded and let the door fall shut.

As I headed to the elevator with Beckett, I gave myself a stern reprimanding. Today had been a firm reminder. I couldn't let my growing feelings for Cole get in the way of doing my job. With my intuition in overdrive, I had to stay focused on my surroundings, protect the guys, and not let my emotions get in the way.

To do that, I had to stay away from Cole.

It was the only way I'd survive the rest of the tour.

My eyes were on my end game: getting Josh back. Nothing . . . absolutely nothing else mattered.

Not Cole. Not Charlotte. Not my heart, which wouldn't stop racing when he was near. Nor the want that fired in my core when he looked at me.

Shit!

Was I more involved than I'd originally thought?

Had I fallen for him?

No . . . don't go there.

I wasn't into Cole Tanner.

No, I wasn't. No, I wasn't. No, I wasn't.

Chapter 27

AVA

"It's a teacher. From Atlanta." I handed Cole my tablet displaying the intel we'd found on the blonde in the café.

I'd rejoined the tour in Orlando after my weekend with Josh. My team had called a meeting with the band after sound check in their dressing room to give them and their entourage an update. Bruno and our staff in LA had worked overtime to find out who the woman was over the past few days. *Melissa Whyte. Thirty-seven years old. Single. Elementary teacher at a school near Morningside.* But she had no online footprint. No Facebook, TikTok, or Instagram accounts. No work history on LinkedIn. Something in my gut didn't sit right. Why would a teacher want that much footage of Cole? Fans usually giggled, ogled, and wanted to meet their idols. This woman hadn't done any of that.

"So, it's nobody to worry about?" Leaning against a table, Cole scanned the report. Our findings didn't seem to alleviate any of his stress, nor did they alleviate mine.

"No, not at this stage." Unease crawled beneath my skin in slow slithers. "She just seems like a fan. But that doesn't mean we shouldn't remain diligent."

"Everyone wants a piece of your ass, bro," Slip teased, handing Cole a beer.

"I'll gladly give the psycho fans to you." He passed the tablet back to me and swiped the beer from Slip.

"This situation had a good outcome. Not all do." Wells folded his arms. "Ava and Beckett wouldn't have raised concern for no reason. It's better to be safe than sorry."

"So true." Cole nodded but his voice lacked any conviction. He took a sip of his beer then waved the bottle toward his band. "So let's forget about it and have a fucking good show?"

"Hell yeah." Flint clapped his hands. "We're gonna rock this joint tonight."

But the worry never left Cole's eyes, nor the nausea from my gut.

After Orlando, the band traveled north doing shows in Nashville, St Louis, Chicago, Indianapolis, and Detroit. There was no other sighting of the blonde, but more fans and photographers met us at every stop. It was hard not to get caught up in the fevered excitement. The guys' shows were electric, and they rocked up a storm every night.

Keeping my distance from Cole proved impossible. The spark between us flickered to life when we were in the same room. Our morning yoga, meditation, and running sessions in the hotel's gym ended in fits of laughter. At every after-party, he mingled and flirted with the guests but never disappeared with a girl or took one back to his hotel. His excuse had been that he was obeying doctor's orders and taking it easy. I didn't believe that. Not when his eyes were on me as much as mine were on him. I wanted him to enjoy himself. I had to be restrained—not him. He was Cole Fucking Tanner. He could be with whoever he wanted. He had to stop giving me heated glances. We couldn't be together, no matter how tempting it might be.

After their show in Cleveland, the band caught up with Lewis's brother, Lee, and his partner, Mateo. In a bar near the hotel, the alcohol flowed into the early hours of the morning. But each time Cole drank a shot of vodka, he'd pin me with his gaze. He licked his lips slowly, sexily, then raised one eyebrow. Every time, a jolt of heat shot through my core. I'd had that tongue between my legs. It had been three weeks since we'd slept together. He wasn't making this easy. But I refused to give in.

My court hearing was five weeks away; I couldn't afford to put one foot wrong.

But as the tour headed to Buffalo, a new alert arose. A Black, male photographer followed our route. Paparazzi were often locally based but this man tailed us to Toronto, Ottawa, and Quebec. He'd stayed at one of the same hotels we did and loitered around the bar in the next city. But after the band had a few rest days and I'd returned once again from seeing Josh, when we regrouped in Boston at the end of January, there was no trace of him.

Thank goodness.

Cole had received no threats, no crazed fan letters—nothing out of the norm. There was no link between the incidents. But something about this didn't sit right. I hated that I hadn't been able to work out what.

The guys' shows in Boston would be two of their biggest concerts on US soil. More than thirty thousand fans would see them each night. As we drove from the hotel to the TD Garden venue for sound check, the guys' energy was set to max. They jostled and joked and shoved each other around. It was hard not to be caught up in their high.

My team and I met with venue security and the police on duty and made sure all systems were in place. We double-checked CCTV feeds and made sure the gate scanners were working, and everyone walked around the venue and through the auditorium to check for suspicious objects, bags, or boxes. *All clear.*

As we gathered in the guys' dressing room, ready to take them to their meet-and-greet session, Hannah arrived with Charlotte. They hadn't been to any of the shows since Christmas, but Hannah had insisted on seeing this one in front of the huge crowd. She loved the guys and was one of their biggest fans.

Charlotte clutched onto Barney, ran over to Cole sitting on the sofa, and jumped into his lap. "Are you going to play the drums?"

"Yes. Later." He hoisted her higher on his legs. "Are you gonna watch the show tonight?"

"Yeah." She swung her feet back and forth. "But can we play

them now?"

"No, I have to go to work." He straightened her puffy jacket on her shoulders. "How about tomorrow at sound check we can have a hit?"

"No. Now." She pouted, thumping Barney into her lap.

"Char." He remained patient and soft. "Tomorrow."

Charlotte pushed out her bottom lip and pounded her fists against Cole's chest. "Now."

"Hey?" Cole caught her hands and pointed at her. "Tomorrow. I have to go meet some fans, and you have to stay with Hannah."

She slid off his lap, rushed to Hannah, and buried her face into her grandmother's skirt. She spun to Cole, poked out her tongue, then turned away again.

Cole's eyes glassed over. I felt his heart rip from where I stood by the door. I knew how much it crushed your soul when your child wanted to do something, and you had to say no. It was even worse when your kid said they hated you, wanted you to leave, and never wanted to see you again. Josh used to say those things to me when Luther and I'd first gotten divorced. Now, he cried and begged to stay with me and never wanted to let me go.

Soon, Josh. We'll be together very soon.

"Charlotte, that's not nice." Hannah pried Charlotte's face out of her skirt. "He has to work. You, missy, have to have dinner before we watch the band play. Okay?"

Slip jutted his chin at Cole. "Dude, it's not like you to leave a woman unsatisfied and upset."

"Fuck you." Cole stood, walked over to Charlotte, and squatted. "Hey? You be good for Ma. I'll see you before the show."

She just sulked and turned away from him.

Cole straightened but his shoulders slumped. "Kids, huh?"

"She'll be fine. You can't let them get away with everything." Hannah took Charlotte's hand and led her out the door.

"Ava?" Wells's voice filled my earpiece. "The guests have arrived for the VIP meet and greet. April and Blake have given the go-ahead. Can you and the team bring the boys, please?"

I pressed the button on my radio. "On our way."

The band held everyone captive as they talked to the fans and had photos, signed merchandise, and made some girl's dreams come true as they sang "Happy Birthday" to her. But no matter where Cole went around the room, his cool, charismatic charm held me hostage. Every time our gazes connected, my knees weakened, and heat touched my cheeks.

Only two and a half more weeks. I could survive that long. Then the US leg of the tour would be over. *I've got this!*

Three hours later, after the support band played, The Flintlocks hit the stage.

I stood in position beside Beckett, off to one side by a thick drape, watching the band perform. It was the prime spot to get a fix of Cole's ripped body covered in sweat as he hammered his drums. *God.* I hated that he was so good. Hated that I wanted him. Hated that I couldn't stop thinking about him.

Beckett chuckled. "You gonna focus on the job or Cole all night?"

"I don't know what you're talking about." I clutched my hands behind my back and straightened my shoulders.

"Yes, you do." His eyes glinted in the bright flashing stage lights.

"Yeah well . . . looking is all I can do." I took a deep breath, let it out slowly, and gave myself a fair kick up the ass. *Focus.*

The crowd waved and screamed and sang along to every song the band performed. The guys played their hearts out, making everyone—including me—fall for them more and more.

The high radiating off the guys as they rushed off stage at the end of the show tingled my skin. They jumped around and hugged each other and high-fived their crew. But just as we were about to take them back to their dressing room, Hannah came running toward us. Sheer panic paled her face.

"Cole?" She charged through the gathering of people. "Charlotte. I can't find Charlotte."

"What do you mean?" Cole caught her arms. The fear in his eyes sent a chill down my spine.

"She's gone." Hannah trembled all over. "We were in your

dressing room, watching TV. I'm so sorry. I drifted off. When I woke, she wasn't with me. I've searched everywhere. I can't find her."

I radioed all venue security. "All personnel. Charlotte, Cole's daughter, is missing." My breath shuddered through my lungs. Had security been breached? Had Charlotte been kidnapped? Hurt? *Oh God, no.* Nausea flooded my gut. Visions of blood and mayhem flickered through my mind. *Crap.* Was this LA all over again? "We're looking for a three-year-old. Shoulder-length, wavy blonde hair. Wearing black leggings, Burberry print dress, black puffy parka. Surveillance, scan the footage of the dressing room corridor, see who took her or which way she's gone. Becks and Sloane, get the guys back to the dressing room and make sure they're secure. Wyatt, get the road crew searching around the stage. Teams on the gates, restrict the exits and check every person that leaves. All eyes open, people. Stay alert."

"Ava?" Wells's voice crackled through my radio. "I'm leaving catering now and heading to the control room. I got this."

"No, I have." I didn't draw a breath as I scanned my cell phone for an image of Charlotte Cole had sent to me. "I'm texting a picture of Charlotte to venue security. *Fuck!* There are thirty thousand people trying to get out of here. She could be anywhere."

Cole caught my arm. "I'm not going back to the dressing room. I have to find her."

"We'll help." Flint clutched his shoulder. "We'll stay backstage and search."

"The gate crew are monitoring everyone leaving," Raymond, the head of venue security, said, vibrating my radio. "But the crowd is thick. If she's in the middle of that, we won't see her. She could already be gone."

Fear swallowed the light from Cole's eyes. "No. no. NO! Find her."

"We will." I placed my hand on Cole's chest. His heartbeat thundered against my palm. "But until we know if this is a threat or if she's just wandered off, you need to go back to the dressing room. It's for your safety."

"Fuck my safety. I don't care about me. Just her." Shock flitted across his face. Realizing that you'd do anything for your kid did that sometimes. Cole finally understood what it was like to be a parent.

"We'll do everything we can." I nodded. "You know that. Please, listen to me."

"I can't do that." He turned and spoke to the guys. "You can go back to the room if you want, but I gotta find Char."

"As if we wouldn't help." Slip stepped toward me. "The more eyes searching for her, the better."

I wanted to say *'stay in the dressing room'* but my priority was Charlotte. "If you're going to disobey orders, at least have one of us with you so we can radio the team. Stay with Becks and Sloane backstage. Venue staff has the outside of the auditorium and exits covered. Search everywhere. Let's go."

"We're on it." Slip nodded.

I spun to face my team. "Search every box, cupboard, closet, and corner."

"Will do." Beckett turned on his heels and rushed off with the guys.

Cole and I ran to the security office on the far side of the stage area. Wells hovered over a security guard sitting at the desk, scanning the video footage on one of the monitors. Another gentleman sat beside him; his eyes were glued to the other twenty-odd screens lit with live footage of the venue.

"Cole?" Wells snapped. "What the fuck are you doing here? You should be in the dressing room."

"No chance." His jaw tensed and twitched. "My daughter is missing. Have you found her?"

"Not yet." Wells's eyes flared at me. "Ava? Breathe. I'll take it from here."

My chest shuddered. He was my boss. He had authority. But Charlotte was missing. Her safety was all that mattered. Adrenaline burned through my veins. "Let's just find Charlotte."

The zooming video footage caught my eye. "Stop," I hollered and pushed past Wells. "Go back . . . there."

With her headphones on and Barney tucked underneath her arm, Charlotte had ventured out of the guys' dressing room . . . alone.

"Oh my God." Air shot from my lungs. "She's not taken. She's just wandered off. Lost."

"Where?" Cole wiped his hand down his sweaty face. "Where'd she go?"

But the next section of footage showed Charlotte walking out into the main corridor, into the sea of thousands of people. We couldn't find her again. We scanned the video surveillance recordings of the door exits, the gates, and people leaving. There was no sign of her.

"Fuck," I mumbled. "That's not good."

"What if someone recognized her?" Stress quivered in Cole's voice. "Covered her up? Stole her? What if some psycho fan has taken her and uses her to get to me?"

I didn't want to think about that scenario, but we had to be prepared for anything. "Cole?" I didn't want to give false hope, but I injected confidence into my tone. "We'll find her. Trust us to do our job."

Worry clouded his eyes, but he nodded.

It took thirty minutes for venue staff to clear the auditorium. Another hour to clear the corridors, check the bars, the restrooms, the merchandise stands, and the foyers. Cole and I joined in searching the food service areas, the storerooms, and the kitchens. There was no sign of Charlotte. *None.*

With every minute that passed, my panic levels rose. But not as much as Cole's.

With a team of security personnel, we formed lines and walked every row of seats in the complex, searching under the chairs and along the aisles.

Where could she be? Fear constricted my chest and seized my veins. "Charlotte," I called out. "Charlotte."

As Cole and I finished the section of seating in front of the stage, his breath rasped. Fear loomed in his eyes. "Ava? I've gotta find her."

"We will." But with every second that passed, those odds deteriorated. I radioed Wells. "Any update?"

"None. The gate crew has checked every small child that walked out of the place but none of them were Charlotte."

"Okay." My mind swam through what to do next. "Let's search the parking lots. The tour buses. The semitrailers. And every equipment trunk. Can you get a team on that, Wells?"

"Ava?" I didn't like the tension in his tone. "Yes. But—"

"Thanks." I clicked my talk button, cutting him off.

Cole clutched his gut, then pummeled his fist against his forehead. "This is my fault. I should've had someone watching over her and Hannah all the time. I should've organized a second nanny for the times Hannah's been tired. Fuck. Fuck. FUCK!"

"Hey?" I clutched his forearms. He shook all over. His focus, distant and distraught. "This isn't your fault. This place is covered in surveillance, and we have hundreds of people searching for Charlotte. We'll find her."

Agony rippled across his face. "I got mad at her before the meet and greet. She was upset. Angry. What if she ran away? Left me? I've lost too many people in my life; I can't lose her too."

Cole's fear and heartache slammed into my chest. The tears welling in his eyes pierced my soul. He'd hidden his anguish, grief, and heartache too much, brushing it aside to care for others. The reality of Charlotte disappearing had brought it to the surface with a vengeance.

"You won't, Cole." This was my job. We were doing everything we could. We'd find her. "Let's search the backstage area again. We'll reconvene with the group and make sure no place has been missed."

He scanned the huge auditorium "Where else could she be?"

"We'll double-check everywhere." I placed my hand on the small of his back and guided him toward the stage.

Weariness and worry remained embedded on his face. We'd been searching for more than two hours and found no sign of her. We walked up the steps, and as we crossed the stage to join the others, something shiny caught my eye. My breath hitched. A small patent leather shoe stuck out from behind Cole's drums.

I charged across the stage. "Charlotte?"

Curled up on one of Cole's sweaty towels, tucked in behind the bass drum, was Charlotte, asleep with Barney tucked under her arm and her headphones on. That was why she hadn't heard us calling her name.

"Cole? She's here." My hand trembled as I touched her softly on the leg and gave her a gentle shake. "Charlotte? It's Ava."

"Ava?" She wiped sleep from her eyes, then burst into tears as she rushed into my arms.

"Char?" Cole sprinted forward and took her from my embrace. He sank to his knees, cuddling her and covering her face in kisses. "You scared the daylights out of me. Are you okay? Are you hurt?"

"No," she sobbed. "I wanted to play with you. I got lost. I got scared."

"Shh." Cole closed his eyes, cradled her against his chest, and rocked her back and forth. "You're safe now. How did you get here?"

"There were lots of people. I fell over. I couldn't find you. I crawled through a big door and saw the stage. I wanted to play the drums. I waited for you. But you didn't come."

"I did. I'm here." He smoothed his hand over her hair.

I splayed my shaking hand across my chest. *She'd come to Cole's drum kit?* God, I just wanted to hug her for being so good. So smart. We'd looked everywhere but behind the drums at the back of the stage. I radioed the team. "We found her. Behind the drums. All clear."

Cole sat back on his haunches and wiped the tears off Charlotte's cheek with his thumb. "Good girl for staying somewhere where I'd find you."

"Are you mad at me?" Her big green eyes welled with more tears. Her bottom lip trembled. "Am I in trouble?"

"You can't wander off without Hannah. You can't do that again, okay?" He drew her into his embrace once more. "But we found you. You're my little girl. I don't want to ever lose you. I . . ." He blinked, and stared deep into her eyes as if she were the only person in the room. "I love you so freaking much."

My heart exploded, hitting the stage lights above. It was the first time I'd heard him say that he loved his daughter.

Charlotte just nodded and tucked her face into the small of his neck.

Wells radioed. "Excellent. Get the band back to the dressing room. Let's get them to the hotel."

Cole rose to his feet, clutching Charlotte against his chest. "Ava. Thank you." He cupped the back of my head and kissed my forehead, lingering for too many seconds. "For everything."

Tears stung my eyes. An overwhelming, emotional mix of relief from finding Charlotte, gratefulness for the successful outcome, and care for Cole and his daughter flooded through me. I sniffled and nodded. "Told you we'd find her." *Luckily, we did.*

The band rushed to hug Charlotte and thanked the team for our efforts. But Wells didn't look happy. I didn't care. I'd done my job. So had the team.

At the hotel, we escorted the band to their floor. They hung out in Cole's suite to have a couple of drinks to wind down after the scary ordeal. *Fuck.* I could do with one too, but I had to wait for Slip to finish and return to his room.

After an hour, Wyatt left with Lewis and Tia to take them to their suite. Five minutes later, Slip and Flint came out of Cole's room and called it a night. I was about to escort Slip down the hallway when Sloane grabbed my arm. "I got this. You look exhausted. Go to bed."

"I won't say no." I stepped aside. "Thanks. Night, guys. Thank you for your help."

"Any time." Flint nodded.

"You're the shit, Ava." Slip slapped me on the back. "Night."

But as I stepped past Cole's door, my heart ached. I had to make sure he was okay.

I knocked on the door. Beckett opened it.

"Is he alright?" My voice snagged in my throat.

"Why don't you ask him?" He held the door wider. "I'm calling it a night."

I peered into the room. Cole sat on the sofa, his head down. Hannah and Charlotte were nowhere to be seen, no doubt in their room asleep. A half-empty bottle of vodka sat on the coffee table. A full glass dangled from Cole's fingertips. I wanted to go to him. Comfort him. Be there for him. But I couldn't. My heart wasn't in sync with my head. "Becks?"

"Ava?" Concern softened Beckett's voice.

"I'm in trouble, aren't I?" I whispered.

"It's okay to care about someone."

My heart ached and burned. "It's more than that."

"I know." Beckett dipped his chin.

Shit. "Can I have five minutes with him. I just want to make sure he's alright."

"I'm off duty." He shrugged. "So are you. I'm going to bed. Take all the time you need." He eased past me into the hallway.

The heavy door slowly closed, but I caught it with my hand. My heart beat way too fast. "Becks? Will you stay?"

"Do you want me to?"

"No . . . yes . . . no . . . *Fuck.*"

Beckett threw me a warm smile and patted my arm. "You'll be fine. I've got your back, no matter what. Call me if you need me, otherwise . . . I'll see you in the morning."

"Okay." I managed to nod. "Night."

I tightened my grip on the door's edge. So much turmoil spiraled through my brain. I should leave. Walk away. Not get involved. But I was. I cared about Charlotte—and Cole—more than I ever should.

I sucked in a deep breath, stepped into the suite and let the door close behind me.

Cole looked up.

Our eyes met. He drained his vodka and rose to his feet, looking sexy as sin in his tight black T-shirt and jeans.

"Hey?" I tucked my hands in my back pockets and took tentative steps toward him.

The charge between us sparked.

In three strides, he'd closed the gap between us. He caught

the back of my head and crushed his lips to mine. *Oh, God.* His lips shouldn't taste this good after sweating it out for hours playing a show and searching for Charlotte. I splayed my hands against his chest, willing myself to stop but failing. Licking, nipping, and tasting him, I moaned against his onslaught. Our hot breaths entwined, tying us together.

Shit. I dug my fingers into his biceps and took a step back. "Cole. Stop."

"Fuck!" As he wiped his hand over his mouth, regret and fire flickered through his eyes. "I'm sorry."

I placed my hand against his stampeding heart. "Is Charlotte okay? Are you?"

"Yeah, thanks to you."

"And my team." I clutched his hand and gave it a squeeze.

"Can't you take credit for anything?" He linked our fingers and drew me closer.

"Not my style."

He brushed his thumb down my cheek and across my lips. "Your style messes with my head. In a frustrating, fuck-I-want-more kind of way."

I swayed on my feet. "You want more? Of me?"

"I'm tired of fighting this, Ava." He pressed his forehead against mine. "Nothing about us makes sense. But every time you're in the room, my head spins."

My heart raced against my ribs. "So what do you want to do about that?"

"I want to make it stop."

"How do you plan on doing that?" I slowly slid my hand up and down the sides of his waist.

His lips brushed across mine, teasing me with his breath. "I can think of several things that involve you, that wall, my bed . . ."

My eyes fluttered shut. "It's been a long night. I should go."

"You probably *should*. But do you want to?"

I clutched onto a handful of his T-shirt to ground myself. No, I didn't want to leave. "Cole, Hannah's in the next room."

"I gave her strict orders not to come out unless I screamed

murder."

"Charlotte?" I whispered.

"She's exhausted and asleep too."

Why did he have an answer to everything?

He caressed the side of my neck. Desire, want, and need burned in his gaze. "Ava? Stay. Stay because I want you to . . . because you want to."

My head swam with dizziness. My body ached for more of his touch. This man had cast a spell on me. I hated that his charm had become my weakness. My addiction.

All my reasoning went out the door. "On one condition."

"What's that?"

"We shower first." I poked him in the chest. "You stink of sweat."

He cupped the sides of my face, kissed my lips, and walked me backward into his room. He closed the bedroom doors behind us. "You can wash my back."

"As long as you go down on me."

Brushing his lips against mine, he growled, raspy and hot. "That I can do."

Chapter 28

COLE

Something about Ava dressed in uniform made me hard as fuck. Guiding her into the bedroom, I peeled the jacket off her shoulders. *Shit.* She still had on all her security gear. I ran my finger underneath the strap of her holster. "How do I get this off?"

"Let me. It'll be easier."

As I ripped my T-shirt off my head and tossed it on the floor, she undid her holster and placed it on the chair in the far corner, then unclipped her radio from her belt, unthreaded the earpiece from her shirt and tossed it next to her gun. She removed the items attached to her utility belt and put them on the chair.

"Shit, Ava. How much crap do you carry?"

She tapped the pockets on her work pants and pulled out her cell phone. "That's it."

"Not sexy . . . but sexy." Who was I kidding? Everything about her made my mouth water, my blood hot, and my dick ache to be inside her. I hadn't craved to be with any woman in years. I had a lot of sex, but most of the time, it was just for fun. *Feel 'em up. Fuck 'em. Leave 'em.* But with Ava . . . I burned for her. I wanted to taste every inch of her skin, take my time exploring her body, tease and taunt her until I made her come. Preferably more than once.

She pursed her lips and eyed my bare chest and stomach. "You, in nothing but ripped jeans . . . *damn.*"

"I prefer you in nothing." Grinning, I caught the bottom edge of her black T-shirt and tugged it over her head and tossed it on the chair. I pulled her belt free, then lowered the zipper of her work pants. Dipping my fingers inside them, I brushed the front of her wet panties. "Hmm. Are you just sweaty or hot for me?"

As she leaned into my touch, her eyes fluttered closed. "Sweaty, but keep this up, and it will change quickly."

I chuckled. She was always blunt and honest. In this world of bullshit and pretense, she didn't get swept up in the hype of who I was. She never spun lines to impress me, nor offered to do anything just to fuck me. I liked that. And every tease of her warm breath on my face intoxicated me.

Usually I took my time with a woman. I loved foreplay and fooling around . . . but not today. I needed Ava. After taking hold of her work pants and panties, I yanked them down her long legs. *Fuck. Boots.* I caught her around the hips and lowered her onto the bed. But pulling her clothes over her boots proved futile. The cuffs weren't wide enough. *Shit.* I grabbed the heel of her shoe. "Can these just pull off?"

She giggled. "No. They're double-laced knots."

I should've removed them first. Me and my dick were too eager to get inside her.

"Cole?" She leaned forward to undo her laces. "I'll do my boots. You do yours. And remove the rest of your clothes while you're at it."

I took hold of her chin and tilted her head back. As I glanced down at her, my heart hammered against my ribs. "What if I want you to take them off?"

She stole a quick glance at my crotch, then met my gaze again. "This way is quicker. When you're naked, you'll get my hands and my mouth all over you. So stop fucking around and undress . . . Mr. Tanner."

"Fuck." My dick doubled in hardness. I ripped my laces undone and yanked off my combat boots, followed by my clothes. As Ava kicked her boots free and eased her panties and work pants off, I scanned her long legs. My balls lurched. "We're not gonna make the shower."

"I'm amazed we made it onto the bed." She reached behind her back and removed her bra.

I stepped between her knees. She ran her fingernails up through the hairs on my legs. My raging hard-on loomed before her. It ached and pulsed and begged for action. I'd love her sweet lips around me. To fuck that pretty mouth of hers. But all in good time. As I leaned forward, she laid back on the mattress. I kissed her fiery lips, then made my way down her body, flicked my tongue over her nipples and across her stomach. *God.* She had a rockin' figure. As I fell onto my knees on the floor, a surge of heat flooded through my veins. I had to have her. Be with her. Taste her.

I glided my palm over the flat of her belly, across her hip, and down her thigh. Lowering my head, I teased my lips across her bare pussy. The scent of her spun my mind. Touching her lured me in. I flicked my tongue into her slit—just one gentle swipe. *Fuck!* Her hot arousal had never tasted so good.

"Cole." She drove her fingers into my hair and gave it a pull. "Don't tease me."

"Ava, I've craved you for three weeks. I'm gonna make you come, then fuck you, then we'll go from there."

"Good. Now stop talking." She wriggled on the bed, widening her knees.

Grinning, I claimed her with my mouth. Firming my tongue, I licked and swiped it over her clit. As I savored her taste, I buried two fingers inside her. Teasing. Taunting. Touching. The little murmurs falling from her lips and the pulsing of her pussy against my face had me close to coming undone.

She hooked her leg over my shoulder and clutched at the bedsheets. The heat between us scorched the air. I let go of all my restraint, fear, and frustration. The walls around my heart cracked. She'd gone above and beyond to save my daughter and help me. How could I not care for her? I lapped and licked her, unable to be restrained. I was a lost cause. As her breath quickened, her body tensed around me. My pulse surged, igniting my fire for her. I plunged my fingers into her wet warmth. Flicking my tongue, I circled and sucked her harder and faster. *Pure heaven.*

"Oh . . . there." She arched off the bed. Her core clenched around my fingers. With a moan, she cried out, "Oh, fuck."

Giggling and panting, she convulsed and shuddered. As I held her in place, I dragged and swirled my tongue over her as she rode out her orgasm. She clutched at my hair and wriggled to stop my onslaughts. "Damn, that's so good. But enough."

Oh, we were so *not* done.

I crawled onto the bed, and we shuffled up toward the pillows. Hovering over her, I eased between her legs. Tilting my hips forward, I teased my cock against her opening. A raspy moan rumbled in my throat. "See what you do to me?"

"Yeah." She drew my lips toward her and clutched onto my hair, tight.

Fuck, I loved that—the shivers shooting over my scalp, along my arms, and down spine, rushing toward my dick. Fire consumed me. I thrust my tongue into her mouth. Every touch of her lips and taste of her kisses was an overload. I hadn't been this lost in someone for years. Every kiss made me burn for more. Made me hunger to be closer to her.

I had to have her.

"Shit, Ava." I dragged my lips away. "Let me grab a condom before I blow my load."

I dashed to my suitcase, grabbed one from my stash, and rushed back to the bed. Back to kissing her, teasing her, touching her.

"Cole?" Fear flickered in her eyes as she placed her hand on my thundering heart. "I'm not gonna lie to you. I'm terrified of the way I feel for you. I'm worried about tomorrow. The future. But now, I'm here. Very here."

So was I. I didn't know if this was just one more hot moment or something more serious. But we needed this. Needed each other . . . for how long, I didn't know. She deserved to be happy. I wanted to show her I cared, thank her for finding Charlotte . . . and make love to her.

"Ava, I promise. I've got you." I kissed her eyelids, her nose, then her mouth. Kissing her did something strange to my heart—filled my chest with warmth and my veins with want. I owed her everything for helping me and my daughter. "I'll do everything I can to protect you. Anything to help."

"Thank you. I just want you inside me."

I smiled against her lips, then sheathed my cock. "Oh, you're going to have me. Here in my bed. Then, the shower. Again before we fall asleep. And, all going well, before breakfast too."

"You want me to stay the night?"

"Yes." I wanted to wake up next to her so I had to make damn sure she had no reason to leave.

"I'm not sure that's a good idea."

"Maybe not. But being with you now is." I ran my hand down her side and over her bare thigh, then drew her knee up toward my hip. "Okay?"

"Yes." She swept her mouth across mine, then nipped my lower lip. Clutching the back of my head, she crushed my lips to hers, kissing me, long and deep, stealing the air from my lungs. After a long night of playing my heart out and panicking over Charlotte, and the weeks of craving Ava, I couldn't take it anymore. I needed her. Wanted her. I took hold of my dick, nudged it against her opening, then pushed inside her. *Oh, yes.* My breath shuddered through my chest. Heat coiled up my spine. There was nothing like sex to feel better. But this was more than that. I hadn't felt like this about anyone since Priah. The future scared me. The American leg of the tour finished in a fortnight. We had a two-week break before we headed overseas. I'd be gone for six months. I'd miss Ava's smooth smile, her gorgeous laugh, the pull I had toward her . . . and her protecting me and my daughter.

Would she be open to the idea of seeing me again? When I got back?

Don't be stupid.

She'd want commitment. That wasn't me. *Was it?* I constantly traveled, lived in the spotlight, and had a kid. She had her own life, a new job, and a family to care for.

We lived close but were worlds apart.

But why did being inside her feel so good? Why did the void in my chest flare when we were together? Why was she everything I didn't want... but wanted? I buried deep inside her, drove into her, thrust long and hard. Her touch burned my skin. Her hot breath teased my face. Her kisses tapped on my heart.

She dug her claws into my shoulders and wrapped her legs around my waist. In a breathy pant, she whispered into my ear, "Fuck, you feel good. So good."

"Careful Ms. Matthews." I thrust into her as I braced my arms beside her head. "We might agree on something."

She rocked and pulsed against my cock. *So freaking hot.* "Can't have that, now, can we?"

"No. Never." I teased my lips against hers and ran my hand down her chest, cupped her breast, and tweaked the nipple. "Want me to stop?"

"Don't you dare." She murmured against my lips.

Her hot, hungry kisses spurred me on. I couldn't bury myself into her deep enough or drive into her hard enough. I wanted more. Of this. Of her. To fuck her again and again.

Sweat coated my skin. My balls ached. My dick throbbed. I ground my teeth together. My whole body climbed and clambered to find release.

Yes.

Fuck! "Ava..."

"Yeah. I'm... there!" Clawing my back, she arched into me, crushing her breasts to my bare chest. *Oh yeah.* Flush against me, she rocked her hips. She fucked me. Grabbed my ass and tugged me closer. Then the tension in her muscles snapped. Her quaking body sent me over the edge. I spilled into her, pulsing and throbbing, plunging and thrusting. Shivers shot up my spine and along my arms. That infuriating smirk curled across her lips. That sexy eyebrow of hers flicked upward. And goddamn it, I couldn't get enough of either.

Not wanting to move, I kissed her face, entwined our hands, and held them beside her head. Deep pulses thudded inside my cock. I'd be happy to stay inside her for the rest of the night.

As she panted to catch her breath, her eyes shimmered. "I like the way you fuck, Mr. Tanner."

I growled, low and raspy. "I like fucking you, Ms. Matthews." But as I pressed my lips against hers, a hot rush washed over me. I didn't want this to end. But the way forward terrified me. Was I willing to take the leap? *Was she?* I rolled beside her, discarded the condom, wrapping it in a tissue, then drew her against my chest. I kissed the side of her head. "Is that all this is, Ava?"

She propped herself up on her elbow and placed her fingers over my lips. "Shh. Not now." A gazillion doubts, questions, and concerns flashed through her eyes, reflecting my own. "Let's go have that shower."

Guessed the conversation about us could wait until tomorrow. That was a good thing, considering uncertainty still clouded my mind. Once this emotional day was over, I was sure the path would be clear.

We were there.

That had to count for something.

I followed her into the bathroom, caught her around the waist, and guided her into the shower. "We've done dirty sex—now you want clean sex?"

"Yes, please."

"If you insist." I turned on the faucets and let the steaming water cascade over our entwined bodies.

We took a long, hot, soapy shower, then fell back into bed. After tasting every inch of her body again, covering every space between her head and her toes, I made her come twice. I fell asleep somewhere around five a.m. with Ava in my arms.

Crazy dreams filled my head. Dreams of running down the beach with Charlotte and Josh, and Ava laughing as her hair blew in the breeze. Us with our kids, standing in my kitchen, baking chocolate-chip cookies. Singing and playing music together. Lazing on the sofa watching movies. Eating ice cream covered in sprinkles.

They were just dreams. Not reality.

When I woke at eleven a.m., Ava was gone.

I'd just had the longest and best night's sleep I'd had in years.
But my skin prickled. Something wasn't right.
The ache in my chest burned—burned hot and bright.
And I was terrified it would burn me to the ground.

Chapter 29

AVA

I made it down to my floor in the hotel without seeing anyone from my team or The Flintlocks entourage. I swiped my key and slipped into my room. But my boot kicked something on the floor—a large yellow envelope with my name scribbled across the front. I picked it up and headed toward the twin beds that hadn't been slept in. Ramona must have been with Wells. *Again.*

After taking off my jacket, holster, and comms gear, I sat on the end of my bed and let out a deep breath. Last night blazed behind my eyelids and spun through my mind. Being with Cole had been mind-blowing. Between my legs still throbbed and ached. But I'd panicked when he'd wanted to talk about us. The emotional day had derailed my focus. We'd had an incredible night together. We cared about each other. I couldn't contemplate anything more than that until I got more custody of Josh. Even then it was impossible to fathom a relationship with him. It was best to accept that Cole and I had no future.

I needed my son—nothing else.

My energy was homed in him, not Cole.

I slid my finger underneath the lip of the envelope and tore it open. As I shook the packet, a mass of printed pages fell onto the bed.

Photos?

I picked up the top picture. My lungs froze. My hand trembled, out of control. It was an image of me and Cole running near his home. The next one was of us at the park he'd taken Charlotte to. We were having coffee, but his hand touched mine. That few seconds of comfort he'd given me had been caught on camera. *What the fuck?* The following snap was at the *Angels in LA* after-party. The picture was of Cole and me dancing close together. My chin rested on his shoulder. His hands on my bare back.

The blood drained from my face. Nausea flooded my gut.

I sifted through more of the pictures. They were all of us. Us, dashing back to the hotel where we'd stayed. Us, leaving together in the morning. Us, in the café in Atlanta. *Fuck.* Going by the angle, this photo had been taken by the woman in the corner. More shots showed us in a gym, laughing as we did yoga. Us, outside Gabrielle's Boutique. Us, at parties after their shows, giving each other suggestive gazes. *Fuck.*

My pulse pounded in my skull as I scanned more of the images. The next shots were of the fan-filled crowds we'd encountered. Me, escorting Cole through a mass of screaming people. There were zoomed in shots of the cut on my face I'd gotten at the first photoshoot we'd taken the band too. Several pictures were of incidents where I'd shoved or blocked some girls and guys to get them out of the way.

The pile consisted of at least fifty photos of me with Cole. But something about the angle of the shots was off. They'd caught *me* laughing, blushing after he'd told me a dirty joke or brushing against him. They'd captured *me* focused, often scowling, when I was being diligent in my job, protecting Cole and Charlotte against the overzealous fans.

The last page was a note.

Ice prickled my skin, and shards stabbed my heart:

> *I've been watching you, Ava.*
> *You thought you'd get away with this?*
> *See you in court.*

The breath shot from my lungs. Tears burned my cheeks. As I

covered my mouth, my fingers trembled. *Oh my God. No!* I grabbed my cell phone and called Beckett. I struggled to draw in air to talk. "Becks. Becks. It's Luther. Fucking Luther's been following me. Not Cole. He's after me."

"What the fuck? You in your room?"

"Yes."

"I'm coming. Stay there."

I paced the floor as tears streamed down my cheeks. I'd played into Luther's hands. He was going to use my nonexistent relationship with Cole against me. He was going to use my job against me. *Again.* Fuck, Fuck. *FUCK!*

My chest crushed my heart. My lungs collapsed. My vision blurred. Was I going to lose Josh over this? I couldn't. I couldn't do that. *Oh no! Oh no. Oh God, please no!*

Four minutes later, there was a knock on my door. I charged over to let Beckett in. But he wasn't alone. Wells and Ramona followed him, piling into our room. Beckett wrapped his arms around me, and I cried against his chest.

"Ava, what's happened?"

"Luther has had someone following me everywhere. We thought these people were after Cole. But they weren't. They were after me."

"What? How do you know that?" Confusion flitted across Wells's eyes.

I pointed to the photos sprawled across my bed. "Every time I was out with Cole, he's had photos taken of us. Luther would've used the location services on my cell phone to track me down. He knew exactly where I was at all times." I pointed to the printed message. "Look at the note. He's going to make out in court that I wasn't doing my job. That I'm flitting around the country, partying, and sleeping with Cole. That I was in dangerous situations. He's going to make me look like an unfit mother again." *How could I have been so foolish?*

"Oh, shit." Ramona came over and gave me a hug. "Why would he do that?"

"Because he's an evil fucking asshole." Anguish tore through every cell in my body. "He's afraid I'll get full custody. Josh is the only thing that keeps me tied to him. He doesn't want to let me go." I sobbed and sniffled. "I can't lose Josh. What am I going to do?"

Wells sifted through the photos and picked out another one of us leaving the hotel together in the morning after the *Angels in LA* party. *Oh God . . . that night. Last night . . .* I still felt Cole all around me. *Fuck.*

Wells turned the photo to me. "So have you been fucking him?"

Taking two steps back toward the desk, I swayed on my feet. The throb in my head split my skull. I couldn't lie. I closed my eyes and nodded. "We have. A couple times. But never when I was on duty."

Wells scratched the tip of his chin. "So that's why you and Becks changed covers—not because Cole was an arrogant asshole?"

"You know I can handle smack talk."

"Oh, I know." Wells raised both eyebrows. "That's why I was surprised. But I never questioned your decision to swap." He jerked his chin at Beckett. "So you knew?"

"Yes." Beckett dipped his chin. "Ava did the right thing, changing with me. She loves this job and is damn good at it. Her situation with Cole has never affected her focus on duty."

"I never doubted that until last night when Charlotte disappeared." Wells's tone tightened as he tossed the photo onto the bed. "You were too emotional, Ava. You made some loose calls by letting the band help search for her rather than securing them in their dressing room in case it was a threat. You overstepped your position and took control of the op rather than letting me handle the process. You never left Cole's side when Slip was supposed to be under your protection."

"Slip was safe. He was with the others." My chest shuddered. I'd crossed the line in more ways than one. "I'm sorry. I just wanted to find Charlotte."

He waved his hand toward the door. "You put everyone in danger until we were certain of what we were dealing with. Being involved with the client is not allowed in this job. You know that."

Fire licked through my veins. "We're not supposed to be with fellow team members either, but you're with Ramona. Why is it okay for you to bend the rules and no one else?"

The whites in Wells's eye flared as he glanced sideways at Beckett.

Beckett puffed air threw his nose and shook his head. "It's obvious, dude. We're trained to observe and notice things. Don't stress."

Wells's shoulders sank, but then he tensed his jaw, diverting his gaze back to me. "Me being with Rommie is . . . different."

"How so?" I drilled him with a challenging glare. "If we were in a compromising situation, you'd do anything to save and protect her first, wouldn't you? You're fucking an employee. What is the difference between client and co-worker? You're emotionally involved."

"Hey?" Ramona held up her hands. "Don't bring us into this."

"Rommie's right." Hardness set in Wells's voice as he jammed his hands on his hips. "Yes, we're together. But we're never on shift at the same time. We're always one hundred percent focused on the client. Never compromised."

"Bullshit," I stood my ground. He was just pissed I'd overruled him last night. I deserved the reprimanding. I'd overstepped my position. But fuck him. He wasn't just my boss—he was my friend, too, and I needed to vent. "You're always texting her. Calling her. Why weren't you on the floor last night covering Blake and April? You were in the catering room when shit went down."

"Ava? Enough," Wells snapped.

Yeah. He'd been sexting Ramona. *Guaranteed.*

"Come on, man?" Beckett patted Wells on the chest and steered him over to the window. "Ava's upset, and rightly so, thanks to Luther. She's done nothing wrong. A few lines may have blurred with Cole, but so fucking what? She's your 2IC who's never put a foot out of place before. She has followed the rules. She hasn't been screwing Cole every night. They've actually stayed apart when they're fucking crazy about each other. Don't give her shit, man."

My heart pounded against my ribs. "Oh, I may be crazy, but

not about Cole. He's a fucking pain in my ass who's done nothing but get on my nerves and mess with my head. I fell in love with his daughter. Not him."

"Don't kid yourself, Ava." Beckett threw me a smug smile and shook his head. "You're so into him."

A tear trickled down my cheek. "No. I've stayed away from him. I've done my job. I've done everything right." *But . . . fuck*. I hadn't. The knots in my stomach cinched tighter and tighter. I sank onto the bed and wiped my wet cheek. "I've tried not to care for him, but I do. Now I'm going to lose the one thing I've been living for. Josh is everything to me. I fucked up." I picked up the photo of Cole and me in the park. I scrunched the photo in my hand. "Not one of these pictures are of me making out with Cole or fucking him. But Luther's lawyers are so powerful, they'll twist and turn every instance around. They'll make me look like a whore and . . . a bad mother." *Oh God.* Bile bubbled up my throat, threatening to spill across the floor.

"Ava, you're not a bad mom. Never have been." Wells lowered his chin. "But I'm sorry, I have to do *my* job and protect the band and the team. You're damn good at your job—I just can't have you on this one. I can't have you on active duty. Not like this."

As I wrapped my arms around myself, I trembled all over. "You're firing me?"

"No. I'm sending you home to the office sooner rather than later. Kennedy will cover Slip for now. I'll get someone from the New York office to help us out over the next two weeks."

Like a plummeting elevator, my heart crashed to the floor. Being pulled from this gig was just as bad as being fired. Not being 100 percent focused on my job crushed my soul. My involvement with Cole had gotten in the way of my clear thinking. My emotions had taken over. I'd disobeyed orders. I'd panicked, afraid that someone had taken Charlotte and wanted to hurt her—like that asshole had done to that kid in LA when I'd been on the force. *Fuck.* I'd thought I'd dealt with my past. I'd been through therapy, but maybe I wasn't okay. I wasn't cut out for this job. "I'm so sorry I let you down."

"You're lucky we had a good outcome last night." Wells stepped over and rubbed my shoulder. "You know all too well that's not always the case."

More than you realize. I nodded. "It won't happen again."

"I'll book you a flight home for tonight." Wells patted my arm then stepped aside. "I'm sorry Luther had you followed. You're a great asset to our team. You're a great mom. Josh is lucky to have you. If we can do anything to help, let us know."

"I will." But I doubted Wells could save me. Luther was too ruthless and played dirty.

"We've got a briefing about tonight's show in five minutes." He jutted his chin toward the photos on my bed. "We'll give everyone an update on this situation. After that, you can say goodbye to the team . . . and then the band. We'll call them and their entourage to join us and notify Cole of this outcome."

Say goodbye? Shit. How could I do that? "Um . . . thanks."

"We'll let ourselves out." Wells stepped toward the door. "We're in meeting room three on level two. See you there."

Beckett and Wells took off. I flopped on the bed and sobbed. I'd been such a fool. Luther had gotten his hold around my throat again and squeezed tighter than he ever had before. Would I ever be free of him? Would I ever get Josh away from him?

Ramona sank onto the mattress beside me. She draped her arm around my shoulders and gave me a big hug. "I'm so sorry, babe. I hate seeing you like this. I hate that you're leaving early."

"I broke the rules. I compromised the team."

"I feel awful." She rubbed my arm. "Wells and I are together, but you can't be with Cole."

"I'm not *with* Cole." I swiped a tissue from the box on the nightstand and wiped my eyes. "I know you and Wells do everything to keep work and your relationship separate. I love you both. I'm sorry for blurting about you two in front of Becks."

"It's okay, babe. Seems like he knew about us anyway. I don't care who knows. Wells is the one who worries."

"Yeah. Consequences suck." I twisted and scrunched the tissue in my hands, then pointed at the photos on the bed. "How am I going to fix this? I can't lose Josh."

"I don't know." She smoothed her hand over my loose hair. "But maybe something good has come out of this. Take out all the shit that's gone down—I haven't seen you laugh and smile as much as you have since we've been on this tour. Maybe Cole had something to do with that."

"Nothing good has come out of this. Not when it might've cost me Josh."

"You don't know that for certain."

"I know Luther. He'd sell his soul to fuck me over." Who was I kidding? He didn't have one to begin with.

I should've never fallen into Cole's bed. Or fallen for that charming smile and dirty talk of his. Or fallen for him and his daughter.

"Was he good?" Ramona threw me a sassy smile as she nudged my hip. "Cole? He's hot as fuck. He's got that quiet, mysterious sexiness going on but transforms into this captivating rock god when he's behind the drums. Is he like that in bed? Hot and dirty? I bet he is. Shit . . . don't tell Wells I said that."

Ramona had summed up Cole perfectly. But he was more than that. He had this incredible heart and uncanny desire to protect the people he cared about, and he wanted to make them happy. I clutched at the pain in my chest. "Cole is nothing like I'd expected. He's messed up like most people are. But God, he loves his daughter. His friends. His music. That was my downfall."

She quirked her lips. "Hot single dad. You could do worse."

"I've had the worst. Luther."

"True." She patted my hand. "We've got to get to our briefing. You gonna hit the shower first? I could smell Cole on you from across the room."

I sniffed my T-shirt. His cologne filled my head and tore my heart in two. *Shit.*

"I'd better." I didn't want to face the team or say goodbye to them and the band, but it was for the best.

After a quick shower, Ramona and I headed downstairs to the meeting room set up with platters of food for our lunch. As we ate sandwiches, Wells ran through the briefing and schedule for the evening. I slouched in my chair, hating that I wouldn't be a part of it.

At the end of his spiel, he gave me the floor. I told them about Luther and said goodbye to everyone, stating I had to leave for personal reasons. That wasn't a lie—I just left out the part about Cole. I'd see everyone again in LA before they headed overseas with the band.

Just as the meeting ended, Cole's voice shattered the quiet of the hallway outside. "Ava? Ava? Where the fuck are you?"

I froze in my spot. Doors opened and shut, no doubt as he searched the other meeting rooms. Then, our door flew open. Eleven sets of eyes swung from Cole to me and back again.

He rushed to where I stood at the top end of the table. Concern darkened his eyes as he clutched my arms. "You're leaving? Because of me?"

Shit. So much for not blabbing to everyone why I was heading home. "Not just because of you." With all my might, I took a step back from him. "Luther's the one who's been following us. He hired people to follow me—not you. He's concocting evidence to take me down in court. To keep Josh away from me."

"The fuck?" Cole wiped his hand down his face.

"Er . . . folks?" Beckett stood and pointed toward the door. "Let's leave these two alone to talk. Everyone out."

Cole paced the length of the window as my team left. Beckett circled past me and touched my arm on the way out. "Call me if you need me."

"You texted him, didn't you?" I lowered my voice so only he could hear.

"Yeah. Guilty." He nodded. "This will hopefully give you closure if nothing else."

He was the last one to leave, shutting the door behind him.

Cole rushed forward and cupped my face. "I'm so sorry. They're sending you home because of me."

I grabbed and lowered his hands. "Yes. We got involved. I've compromised the team. I can't do this job anymore."

"Then quit." Exasperation spiked his tone. "Work for me. Be my personal security."

I jerked my chin back. "You want me to be your paid whore? Fuck that shit."

"No." He closed his eyes and winced. "God. No."

"Cole, I'm not going to be a casual hookup whenever you're at home and feel like it. I'm not one of the supermodels, A-list celebrities, or fellow musicians who exist in your world. I have responsibilities. My son. And somehow I need a fucking miracle to erase the shit Luther's going to use against me in court."

"We'll work something out." He placed his hands on my shoulders. "But please, stay. For me. For Charlotte."

"Don't ever use your daughter against me." Pain rippled through my chest. "I've risked everything because I fell into your bed. Because I care about you and her. But Luther will go to any length to use the photos he's taken of us together as ammo in court. He won't let go of me. I'll always be his puppet on a string." Tears prickled my eyes as I jabbed my finger against his chest. "I won't ever be the same for you. We are over. You hear me."

"No. Stay with me until we get back to LA."

"Why, Cole? Tell me why?"

"So we can do this." He grabbed me and drew my lips to his.

His hot breath on my face made my head spin. Every muscle in my body cried. "Is that all?"

He pressed his forehead against mine. "And maybe a few other things . . . but yeah."

I wanted him in every possible way, but he just wanted me as a fuck buddy. He didn't feel the same way I did. "Then no." I slipped out of his hold. "I need more than fun in bed."

"I don't just want that."

"Yes, you do. I'm sorry. I can't do this, Cole." I splayed my hand across my chest. "I care about you. So much. And Charlotte. But we're not living in some fairy tale. You're . . . *you*, and I don't want to drag you into my shitty life. I can't comprehend being with you or anyone while Luther hangs custody over my head. Contemplating anything is impossible when a piece of my soul is missing. I want my son back. I want Luther out of my life. I want to be free. You can't give me those things."

"No, I can't, but I'll help in any way I can." He took a step toward me, but I braced my hand against his chest to keep two feet between us.

"Don't make this any harder than it already is. Being with you has caused me more problems and setbacks. You can't help me."

He grimaced like I'd punched him low in the guts. But it was the truth. "I want to."

"Please don't." A tear slid onto my cheek. "But can you do me one thing?"

"Anything."

"Say goodbye to Charlotte for me."

Tears welled in his eyes. "No. You."

"Don't ask me to do that." I needed to protect my heart. "She's a kid. She'll be okay. Just love her and tell her that every day."

"Is this what you want? To walk away?"

"Yes." It wasn't. But it was the right thing to do.

His shoulders slumped. "Fuck, you've messed with my head." His voice was barely audible. The sadness in his eyes nearly had me coming undone. But I had to be strong. I hadn't performed my job to the best of my ability when I was with him because my heart overruled my head. I had to protect him and his daughter from my messed up situation with Luther.

"And you with mine." I whispered. We were two tortured souls who couldn't be together. Life had dealt us a crappy hand and shitty timing.

I took one last look into his gorgeous green eyes, stepped forward, and brushed my lips against his. "Goodbye, Cole."

I dashed from the room and up to my floor. I let my room's heavy door close behind me and sank onto the floor. Tears rolled down my cheeks, so hot they burned my skin.

How had my life ended up in more of mess now than it had been at the start of this gig? *Oh, yeah.*

I fell for Cole Fucking Tanner.

Somehow, with all my strength, I had to focus on Josh. I had to find a way to get him back. Luther wouldn't get away with what he'd done to me.

And I was willing to sell my soul to take him down.

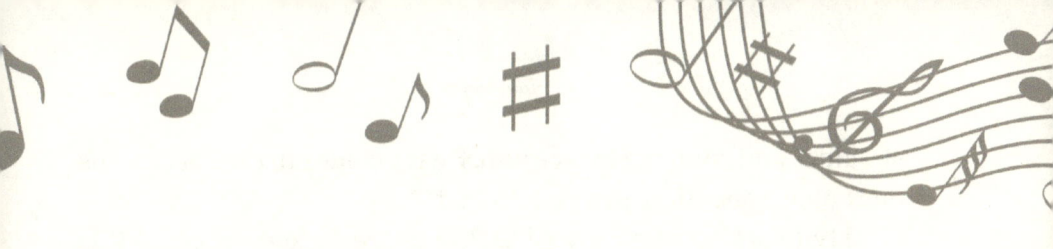

Chapter 30

COLE

"You're letting her go?" Beckett shoved me on the shoulder as we walked back to my hotel room. "Cole, what the fuck is wrong with you?"

Other than everything?

Ava was right. I'd caused her nothing but problems. We'd tried to stay apart. But I couldn't resist her, no matter how hard I tried. She'd weaved her way into the void inside my chest and ignited a fire that I hadn't thought would ever burn again. I hadn't wanted it lit again. But when we'd first met, one look from her, one slam against the wall, had struck the fuse. Now the blaze had caused irreparable damage to both of us. Nausea flooded my gut. If she lost Josh because of me I'd never forgive myself.

"Everything is wrong," I hissed at Beckett. "She doesn't want anything to do with me. She's pissed and upset about being sent home, but she's more worried about losing Josh."

"Of course she is. Luther's a sick fuck for following her and causing you and your band stress. Ava follows every rule, but seeing her risk it all for you is not like her. Josh is her life."

"I fucking know that. I care about her. I tried to stay away. But all I'm good at is fucking up people's lives. So keep away from me, or shit will happen to you too. And I don't want that."

"You just gonna do nothing?" At my door, he grabbed my

shoulder and spun me to face him. Heavy clouds drifted across his dark blue eyes. "How can you do that?"

My heart punched my ribs. How more fucked up could this situation get? "It's what she wants." I swiped my room key and pushed open the door. "Leave, Becks. I'll see you for sound check."

I stormed toward the kitchenette in my suite and grabbed a bottle of vodka off the counter. I cracked the lid and took a swig.

Hannah walked out of her room.

Charlotte came running toward me and crashed into my legs. "Where'd you go?"

"Hey." I placed the bottle down, swooped her up into my arms, and gave her a hug. Somehow that eased the turmoil in my mind . . . for one second. I slumped back against the counter as if the air around me weighed too much. "I said goodbye to Ava. She had to go home."

"Why?" Sadness flooded Charlotte's big green eyes. "When is she coming back?"

My heart lurched like it had been ripped backward on a bungee cord. But then I glared at Hannah. Too many conflicting emotions tore through my ribs. This wasn't her fault . . . but it was. Hannah was amazing with Charlotte, and a kind soul, but if she hadn't fallen asleep while minding Charlotte, Ava would still be here. We wouldn't have had hundreds of people scouring the venue, looking for my daughter. I wouldn't have spent the night with Ava. But she'd still be with us.

I swallowed the dry lump in my throat. "She's not coming back. She had to go home early to her new job."

The color drained from Hannah's face. "Oh no."

"Will we see her again?" Charlotte played with the zipper on my leather jacket, zooming it up and down.

I caught her hand and held it against the pain in my spleen. The truth was an uppercut to my guts. Ava and I were too messed up to be together. "Probably not."

"But I like her." Charlotte pouted.

"Me too." I put Charlotte down. "Go watch TV for a minute."

She took off into her bedroom and Hannah rushed forward.

"Oh Cole. What happened?"

I downed a mouthful of vodka. As I closed my eyes, I took a deep breath. "She got pulled from the team for overstepping her position last night when looking for Charlotte and . . . because we got involved."

"Oh, dear." Hannah's hand trembled as she fidgeted with the neckline of her sweater. "I'm so sorry."

"I don't want to hear it." The thudding boom inside my head offered little distraction. I didn't want to listen to anyone or think about anything. I just wanted to drink. *Fuck.* "Please watch Charlotte. I need a minute or ten."

I staggered out onto the balcony into the freezing cold and sank onto the damp ground. I wanted numbness to consume me. Feel nothing. As I leaned against the wall, I guzzled mouthfuls of vodka, trying to drown the sickening guilt that resided in the pit of my stomach.

I'd fucked up again.

I'd ruined someone's life again. Ava's life.

All because I cared, and what I'd thought was right was wrong.

It was Aidan and Shelby and Priah and Phil all over again.

Fuck.

I stared at the dull sky and muttered, my breath misting before me. "I didn't want this. I didn't want to get involved with anyone." I took another mouthful of vodka and laughed. I had to or I'd just end up more of a broken mess than I already was.

Fuck.

I never wanted to hurt anyone ever again. And that was all I'd done.

The doorbell to my suite chimed.

"I don't want to see anyone," I yelled out to Hannah.

But she didn't listen. Seconds later, my band and Tia stepped outside.

I rested my head back against the wall. "Guess you've heard, huh?"

"Yeah, we've just met with Ava and Wells." Slip came over. He squatted, swiped the bottle from my hand and took a swig. "They told us what happened . . . and she's leaving. You okay?"

I glared at him and threw him a smug smile. "I'm just fucking dandy."

"Crap. You're worse than I expected." Flint took the bottle from Slip and swallowed a couple of mouthfuls before he passed it to Lewis. "But that's why we're here."

"Women. Who needs 'em?" Lewis winked at Tia as he had a drink then gave her the vodka.

"You do need us." Tia nudged his arm and took a sip. "Sometimes it just takes you a while to realize that. But Cole"— she stepped toward me, bent down, and rubbed my shoulder— "it's awful Ava's ex had her followed, but I'm glad it wasn't some psycho fan after you. I was so worried about you and Charlotte. And everyone."

"Yeah, so am I." I caught her hand and gave it a squeeze.

"Sorry she's gone home, man." Slip tapped my knee. "Are you going to see her when we get back to LA?"

"Can we not talk about this now? Or ever?" It was still too raw. Still a mess. I was still trying to make sense of what had happened.

"Okay, maybe not now, but we are gonna do what we always do when we get messed up over a woman." A mischievous grin spread across Flint's mouth. "We're gonna get buzzed until it's time for sound check. Sober up and play our show. Then get fucking wasted at the after-party."

I grabbed the bottle from Tia and raised it to them. "Then you'd better catch up."

Lewis held out his hand, hauled me to my feet, and patted me on the back. "Here's to being fucked up by love."

I grimaced. I didn't love Ava. *Did I? . . . No . . . maybe.* I liked her a lot. I'd had my reservations about taking the next step to see if we could be something more. After spending the night with her, I knew I had to. I was convinced she felt the same way. But Luther had killed any chance we'd had. She'd walked away to be with her family just like Priah had. Family always came first. It did for me too—my band was my everything. Sometimes . . . some things just weren't meant to be.

I took a huge gulp of vodka and swallowed it down. "To just being fucked up."

By the time we ventured to the venue for sound check, everyone was tipsy. But we had a show to do. More drinking had to wait.

As we ran through a few songs, all the things I should've said to Ava slammed into my head: *'We're worth fighting for.' 'Luther won't win.' 'I want to be with you. Just you. Nobody else.' Fuuuuck!*

I poured all my frustration, anger, and heartache into pummeling the shit out of my drums, pounding my pedals, and striking my sticks.

We churned out one of our hits, "Forget You." Flint's voice filled my ear monitors. Each lyric speared my chest.

> *You're the devil in disguise*
> *I knew you'd be my demise*
> *I just want to be over you*
> *Leave what we had behind*
> *Not remember the way you kissed*
> *Or how we danced*
> *Not remember the way we laughed*
> *Or how we took a chance*
> *I just want to forget you*
> *I just want to forget you*

No matter how hard and loud I played, thoughts of Ava wouldn't stop hurtling through my head. I couldn't get the ache out of my chest. Nor the acid out of my veins.

After sound check, we showered, ate and met fans during the meet and greet.

We hit the stage just after nine p.m.

I needed the crowd.

I needed that rush of adrenaline playing gave me.

I needed to drum Ava out of my system.

The screaming fans fed the fire in my soul but not the one in my heart. That was dead.

At the end of the show, I summoned a big smile and waved to the crowd. I hooted and hollered. I'd never forget why I was there. I'd never take this tour for granted. I'd given the show my all.

But I was spent.

To a sea of applause and praise, I rushed off stage with Lewis, Flint, and Slip, cheering and riding the high. But the minute after we'd showered, changed, and hit the after-party, the crash hit, pressing down against my shoulders, building pressure in my head, and weighing down on my chest.

Was Ava okay? Had she made it home yet? Would she ever forgive me for messing up her chances to get Josh?

No . . . probably not. *Definitely not.*

I grabbed a bottle of vodka, sank onto the dirty old sofa, and drank.

Music blared. VIP guests laughed and bustled around us, taking photos. I smiled when needed, but my mind was elsewhere. I just wasn't in the mood to party. *Damn.* That wasn't like me. *I'm totally screwed.*

A sexy brunette slid onto the seat beside me, brushing her boobs against my arm. Her dress was shorter than a tank top. "Hi. I'm Kimmy."

"Kimmy. I'm Cole. Nice to meet you." *God, I'm not in the mood for this.*

"You shouldn't be sitting here by yourself. Want to come dance?"

"Maybe some other time."

"We could do something else that's fun." She slid her hand up my thigh.

I caught it and gently pushed it away. "Sorry. But I'm not feeling well."

"I'd be happy to make you feel better."

I bet she would. But not even my dick gave a shit. "No thanks."

"You sure?"

"Very."

"Oh." Disappointment and shock flitted across her brown eyes. It wasn't often that I didn't live up to my reputation, but I hadn't been with any other woman other than Ava for weeks . . . months . . . and I hadn't missed them. Kimmy threw me a saucy grin, as if she were intent on not giving up. "I'm over there with my friends if you change your mind." She took off, twinkling her fingers at me.

Change my mind? I'd lost my fucking mind, that was what. That chick was hot. Damn hot. But all I wanted was Ava.

Fuck. This. Shit.

I was out of there.

I gave Beckett the signal.

After grabbing a bottle of vodka, I veered toward the door. Without breaking my stride I passed the guys who were talking to some fans and waved. "I'm outta here."

"You want me to come with you?" Flint called after me.

"Nah. Stay. Have fun. I'll be okay." *Maybe. One day. Just not today.*

I staggered back to our dressing room to grab my gear. Almost everything in our changeroom had been packed away in equipment trunks and stacked against the wall, ready for transporting to our next stop, New York. I placed my bottle of vodka on the empty table and swiped my bag off the floor. But just as I stuffed my dirty clothes into it and zipped it up, Flint charged through the door.

"Cole? Are you feeling alright?"

I swayed on my feet. "I'm trying not to *feel* anything or think about anyone." Except that was all I did. *Ergh!* I wanted Ava erased from my head.

"How's that working out for you?" Worry slithered through his tone as he came over and leaned his ass against the table.

"I'll let you know once I drink this bottle." I picked it up and took a swig.

"How about telling me now?"

"There's nothing to tell. I'll be fine."

His shoulders sank two inches. "Fuck, I wish you'd stop saying that."

"Okay then." I slammed the bottle down next to him. Fire flared in my veins. "You want to know how I feel? I feel like shit.

Ava and I should've never been together because of her job and her son. But no, for some fucked up reason we couldn't stay away from each other. And now she's paying the price for my mistakes." I slapped my hand against my chest. "I fucking liked her, man. But I never meant to screw up her life. I'll never forgive myself if she loses Josh."

"Let's hope it doesn't come to that."

"Luther's out to hurt her. I've hurt her. I never wanted to do that."

"Cole, you didn't do it intentionally. This isn't all on you. Ava knew the risks. She fucking likes you too, bud."

"It should've never come to this. It's just another thing I've done that in the moment felt so fucking right but has turned out to be so fucking wrong."

"We've all made mistakes." He quirked his lips sideways as he took the bottle and had a drink.

"I've made too many." My palpitations doubled. My breath rasped through my throat. "So many I can't breathe. I can't sleep. I can't think straight anymore."

"What are you talking about?" His brows pinched together. "What mistakes?"

All my heartache and pain bubbled to the surface and erupted like toxic ash. "Aidan. Shelby. Priah . . . Phil. All I've done is hurt and kill people."

"Cole?" Flint shot to his feet and clutched my shoulder but nothing, no comfort, would erase the shudders coursing through my system. "We've all hurt people or have been hurt in the past. But you haven't killed anyone. Stop talking shit."

Tears burned the backs of my eyes. Nausea flooded my gut and scorched my throat. "I killed Phil."

Flint jerked his chin back. "Um, no . . . I was in the car. Phil was driving."

My chest caved and crushed my heart. "I gave him the pills that night. And a fuck load of cocaine. He was snorting blow and popping E like Tic Tacs on the pool table with Rici. When he asked me for more, we got into a fight over him using too much. I was pissed off at him for being so fucked up, an addict and a dick. He kept hounding me and hounding me and getting in my face. I gave him my stash just to get him off my back." I closed my eyes.

That night had haunted me for years.

It had plagued my nightmares time and time again.

Me, slapping the baggie of E into his hand. Me, tossing him my vial of coke. Me, handing him a bottle of vodka to chase them down with. Me, walking away. "I never saw the two of you leaving. I would've never let you get in the car if I'd known. It's my fault he was sky-high. I gave him the drugs." A tear escaped my eye, but I was quick to flick it away. "He died because of me. I almost killed you. It's my fault he's gone. Phil would still be here if it wasn't for me."

"Oh, God." Flint grabbed the top of my arms and burned me with an adamant gaze. "No. You're wrong."

"I'm not." I shoved out of his hold and shook my head. "All I've wanted to do is protect everyone, be a friend, do the right thing, but everything keeps backfiring. How can I take care of Charlotte when I keep messing up?"

"Because you're so good with her. You've changed. When was the last time you did drugs?"

I wiped my hand down my face and sniffled. "Um. The night Phil died." I hadn't even swallowed a party pill since.

"Me too," Flint whispered.

"I loved Phil." I rubbed the ache in my chest. "He was like a brother to me, and I killed him."

"No, you didn't." Flint's tone sharpened but held an undercurrent of grief and loss. "Phil was an addict long before that night. The three of us, you, me, and Slip, let him down. We should've pulled him into line sooner. We were days out from forcing him into rehab, but we never got the chance." He closed his eyes and lowered his chin. "I've never grieved like I did after losing him. It should've been me driving. I should've helped him sooner. I should've died in the crash too. I miss him every day. We all did things we shouldn't have done. You weren't the only one who fed him drugs and booze. Slip and I had a hand in that too. It's not just on you."

My head thudded under the pressure. We'd all borne too much. "How do you deal with it? The guilt?" *Because I'm not.*

"I didn't. Not for a long time." Flint staggered back a step and leaned against the table. "I kept drinking and drinking, hoping to stop hurting, but I never did. What I did with booze you did by going out to every event, partying at every chance, and screwing women. You're doing everything to avoid processing your loss. That's not healthy. So talk to me. Get help. Do something. You can't go on like this." He stabbed his finger toward my chest. "You gave me an ultimatum after losing Phil—now I'm giving you one. Get your shit together. For you and your daughter."

I clenched my hands and my fists. I didn't want to hear it. "I was okay before Charlotte showed up."

"No, you weren't. You just had more time on your hands—now that's changed. If we've learned anything out of all the heartbreak and loss we've gone through over the past few years isn't it to be honest with each other? Isn't that what we've always said? You've always been the first to help, the one to step up, the one we can always rely on. You've taken everybody's issues onboard and helped us through messed up times. But you forgot to take care of yourself in the process. I'm a shitty friend for not seeing it sooner."

Flint could never have been a shitty friend, not even if he tried. I just didn't want to burden anyone with my problems. "Everyone's got crap going on, Flint."

"Yes, but if you don't deal with it, you're going to keep spiraling." Worry clouded his eyes. "I don't want to see that happen. I've been in the gutter—it's not pretty. I only survived thanks to you and Slip." He slumped as he sucked in a deep breath and let it out slowly as if in pain. "There are times I'm still broken and riddled with guilt over losing Phil. But I've learned from my mistakes. I've learned to live better. Love deeper. Be true to myself. And most of all, focus on what is important. I treasure every moment I'm with you guys and Sutton, and playing music. Everything else is down the list. We're not teenagers anymore, Cole. Life is changing. Our family is growing. We're on our biggest tour. Take a breath and let that sink in."

"That's just it." I raked my fingers through my hair and paced the floor in front of the equipment trunks. "All I've ever wanted to do is play music, tour, and party, have fun and enjoy women. But it's not all going to plan."

"We're doing most of those things, but Charlotte has forced you to change. And so has meeting someone you like." Frustration embedded into his tone. "Stop fighting something that you've denied yourself for too long. Don't be foolish and let something that has the potential to be incredible pass you by. You don't just like Ava—you've fallen for her. Isn't what you had with Priah or Aidan worth taking another chance on?"

Ava was the first girl who'd made me consider that. I wanted her to stay, but she didn't. "She doesn't want anything to do with me."

"Fine then." Flint shrugged his shoulder. His carefree, so-be-it attitude didn't sit well in my stomach . . . or my chest. "Put her behind you. Forget about her and move the fuck on."

Fire ripped through my veins, and I punched the air. "I can't do that."

"Why not?" He shot to his feet.

"Because I fucking like her," I hissed.

"Then do something about it."

"What?" The thudding in my head pounded like an amphitheater full of bass drums. "What the fuck am I supposed to do when she doesn't want me?"

Ava wasn't the problem—I was.

I wasn't good enough for her.

I braced my hands against the top edge of an equipment trunk and dug my fingers into the cold metal. "Family comes first. So just like Priah, Ava left to focus on hers and I'm here with mine." I grabbed onto the trunk tighter and tighter. "I have Charlotte to take care of. She has Josh." I punched the trunk then marched over to the table and took a swig of vodka. "I'm not gonna waste another day caring about someone who doesn't want me in their life."

"Do you honestly believe she doesn't want to be with you? If you do, you're a fool." Flint swiped the bottle out of my hand and took a mouthful. "You've been into each other since the day you met. You've both been hurt before. She was horrified that Luther had her followed. She walked away to protect you from his crazy ass." He tilted the bottle and pointed his finger at my face. "You played your part in causing this mess whether you like it or not. The thing is, what are you going to do about it?"

"Nothing."

He narrowed his eyes and snarled. "Haven't you learned anything from the past or any of your mistakes?"

"Yeah." I grunted. "Don't get fucking close to anyone."

"No." He placed the bottle down and folded his arms. "For someone so smart, you can be fucking stupid. Use that head of yours. Tell me, why are we such good friends?"

I closed my eyes and tilted my head back. *What does that have to do with this?* Why had we been best friends for more than sixteen years? That was a no brainer. Everything I'd gone through with Charlotte reinforced why. "No matter what shit we're going through or do, we're always there for each other. Love each other. Trust each other."

"Yep. Always" He dipped his chin, then drilled me with a challenging glare. "Why were you with Shelby and so cut up over Priah?"

Why? As I lowered my chin, heartache stabbed my chest. I jammed my hands on my hips and sniffled. "I cared about them so much."

"Uh-huh." He leaned forward a fraction, adding a hardness to his tone. "Why do you feel responsible for what happened to Aidan and Phil?"

I rubbed at the nausea burning in my gut. "They needed help, and I didn't act soon enough."

"So don't make the same mistake again." The weight in his words rattled my soul. "Be there for Ava because you care for her. Don't ignore her when she needs you the most."

"It's too late." I didn't want to hear anymore. Guilt already riddled my bones. I didn't need to be burdened with anyone.

"Isn't the way she makes you feel worth fighting for?"

"All I've done is fight my feelings for her."

"Then stop fighting. If you want to be with her, find a way to make it work like Sutton and I have. "

The guilt of doing nothing would eat me alive. But the crater-load of bullshit that came with her ex wasn't in my capacity to take on. She may always be in custody battles with Luther. I had too much of my own crap to deal with. I had Charlotte to take care of along with my own health concerns and my band's tour to navigate over the months ahead. And what would be the point of being with Ava now? She'd eventually leave me.

"Flint, I beg you. Please stop. There's nothing to fix. Nothing to work out. So drop it."

Disappointment swam through his eyes. "You're just going to let her go?"

My heart clawed my ribs, but I pushed the agony into the pit of my stomach and locked it away. "I've hurt her enough. This is for the best."

"No. It's not." Fire flared in his voice. "Find a solution. You're the smartest person I know. Get that head of yours out of your ass and use it."

"Flint." I swiped the vodka off the table and staggered back a step. "It's been a long day. I'm drunk. All I want to do is finish this bottle and go back to the hotel. You got a problem with that?"

"No. But this isn't over."

"Yes. It is."

I grabbed my bag and my jacket, and stormed out the door.

There was only one woman in my life I had to care about—that was my daughter.

She was all that mattered.

Not Ava.

Chapter 31

COLE

My body rocked from side to side, then swayed and rolled like I was on a tiny boat being tossed about on a turbulent sea.

"Cole? This isn't your bed, silly."

Charlotte. Why couldn't she let me sleep?

"It's a great bed." *Not really.* My feet hung off the end of the sofa at an awkward angle. My cheek was squashed against the hard cushions. My head was hitting the armrest. I still wore the clothes I'd come home in from the venue last night, including my boots. I vaguely recalled that somewhere around three a.m., Beckett had carried my drunk ass into my suite and dumped me here where I'd obviously passed out. At least Ava used to make sure I'd gotten to bed . . . most of the time.

Now, she was gone. I'd drowned her out of my system with more vodka than the USA and France produced in a year. *Yep.* It was time to get on with my life. *Hopefully . . . maybe . . . Ergh!*

Charlotte tugged on my jacket. "But you're not in your jammies."

"Nope," I mumbled against the cushion.

"Can we go to a park? It's snowed."

Great. I rolled and shuffled onto my back. As I licked my lips, my dry mouth tasted like dead animal. The vodka fumes on my breath hazed the air before my tired eyes. I glanced at my watch.

Fuck! Six o'clock. "Yep. Later. When we get to New York, okay?" We had to leave at eight. *Ergh!*

"Yay!" She threw her arms across my chest, gave me a hug then dashed off toward her room.

A playdate sounded perfect. Charlotte had been cooped up in too many hotel rooms and I needed cold air to sober up. I shot a text to my friends in New York and stole a quick snooze before we piled onto the buses bound for the Big Apple. I scored another two hours of sleep during the trip. The only thing that made me feel better was the fact that the guys were more hungover than me. Luckily we didn't have a show tonight.

At two o'clock, rugged up in parkers, beanies, gloves, and scarves, I held Charlotte's hand as we entered one of the kids 'playgrounds in Central Park.

Since Ava had left us in Boston, Beckett hadn't stopped glaring at me. He took a seat on a bench off to one side of the playground and sipped his steaming coffee. Each breath misted the air like he was a dragon ready to douse me in flames and burn me to a cinder. I'd have wished he would . . . if it wasn't for Charlotte.

I swept and shook the snow off the toddler swing with my gloved hand, then lifted Charlotte into the seat. With a gentle push, I swung her back and forth. The squeaking chain was like a lumber saw slicing through my head, but the sun was shining, offering a tiny degree of warmth. It was good to be outdoors. The playground wasn't busy, with only half a dozen moms chatting in pairs as their kids played on the climbing fort.

But as a tall man in a navy anorak ambled toward the playground entrance with a small girl shuffling beside him, and his bodyguard matching his loping pace, a huge grin spread across my face. That stride, that hair, that physique would be recognizable anywhere across the globe. *Hunter. Fucking. Collins.* Everhide rock god. One of the owners of my band's record label. Phenomenal guitarist. Incredible vocalist. My friend.

He'd come. When I'd texted him this morning, he hadn't hesitated in accepting my invite to catch up. He was one of the only guys I knew who had kids. Kyle and Gemma, and Hayden from

Everhide did too, but they were traveling home today after a short vacation. They'd be at our dinner tonight and New York shows.

He opened the gate and his four-year-old daughter rushed toward me.

"Hi Ashleigh." I ruffled her beanie-covered head. "Is it too cold to play today?"

"Never." Ashleigh giggled; her azure eyes were identical to Hunter's.

As Mick, his bodyguard, joined Beckett, Hunter held his arms wide. "Cole. Good to see you, bud."

I gave him a warm hug, slapping him on the back. "Hunt. You're looking good, as always."

"I know. It's a curse." There was nothing wrong with his ego. Laughing, he shrugged then squatted beside the swing and wriggled Charlotte's foot. "And you must be Charlotte. Nice to meet you. I'm Hunter." He pointed toward his daughter. "And this is Ashleigh. She'd love someone to play with. Would you like to do that?"

Charlotte peered up at me with a can-I-please brightness in her eyes. "May I?"

"You sure can." I lifted her out of the swing. Ashleigh took her hand, and they ran over to the climbing fort.

"She's one cute kid." Hunter rose, dusting snow off his gloves.

"Life-changing." I kicked my boot against a clump of ice and stuffed my hands into my pockets.

"Oh yeah. They do that." He chuckled, low and soft. "I never thought I'd have one, let alone three."

"Where are the twins?" I tugged my beanie lower over my ears as we ambled over toward our kids. *Damn, it's chilly.*

"Levi and Louis have colds. Kara's at home with them."

"I don't know how you manage three. One has been daunting enough. I'm still adjusting." So much had changed in the past few months. Taking on Charlotte, commencing tour, meeting Ava, and my health all pressed like heavy weights on my shoulders. "How do you do it, Hunt? How do you manage everything? Making music. Playing shows. Running a label. Touring. Having a family. Going to events. Overseeing your charities and businesses. Is there such a thing as balance?"

"Yeah. There is." He scratched his stubble and nodded, but his eyes gave away that life hadn't always been set to a chilled beat. This industry was ruthless, demanding, and every moment either gave you the strength to keep going or had the power to break you. I never wanted it to ruin me. I loved music too much. He tucked his hands into his anorak pockets. "It took me a long time to find it. I wouldn't have done so without my wife, my friends, our team, and the people we trust. We're not just a band searching for our next gig anymore. We're a business, a bunch of friends who can always count on each other, and a family."

"The guys and I are the same. But we've just gotten on this bigger, better ride than we've ever been on before. I don't want it to stop. I love this life. I want to see where our music takes us."

"And we'll be here to help you." His tone remained calm, confident, and reassuring. "If you want to ramp things up or slow things down, we'll support you. But remember, you guys are in control. You set the pace. You're not contracted to a big corporation or under pressure to churn out the next album. You record, promote and tour when *you're* ready. We wanted to remove that stress off artists. This is your ride—we're just the engine to make it run."

"I like that. It's made the whole process so much fun." We had been in a pressured mindset to release a new album after Phil's death. But losing our contract with WestTyme Records had been the best thing that had happened to us. Signing with Everhide's EH4 Records had given us complete control over our career. We were in this for the long haul and wanted to enjoy every moment. Nothing happened without us all being onboard. So yeah, it'd be nice to have more time between album releases and space out touring even more. The guys would be down with that so they could spend more time with their partners . . . and me, time with Charlotte.

Ashleigh raced Charlotte up the chain ladder and helped her clamber onto the platform. A proud daddy smile curled across

Hunter's lips. "You've got to have a life outside of music. It took me a fucking long time to learn that. Music is still a priority, it's just not the only one anymore."

"Life changes."

"Yeah. It certainly does." He leaned against the fort pole and crossed his ankles. "The four of us still hang out nearly every day. We spend time with the kids. We're writing some of the best music we ever have. We want to be in this business for the rest of our days, so we're taking more time to produce an album and taking better care of ourselves than we used to. We learned we had to do that the hard way." Dark clouds drifted across his eyes, shadowing them, like each haze contained more than a million memories. Staring at the ground, he swallowed hard. "After Kara and I lost Ryan, Gem had a crazy stalker after her, and I had my throat surgery, we re-evaluated what was important to us. At the end of the day, we could live without being Everhide but not each other. Family comes first."

Shit! He was spot on. It'd kill me if I couldn't play the drums, but I'd survive anything with Flint, Sutton, Slip, Tia, and Lewis by my side.

"Do you ever regret it?" I asked. Kids had changed his life. His initial path was similar to mine, but I'd never want to lose my child like he had. I stubbed my toe into the snow. "Do you ever wish you could go back and change that night with Kara? Do you wish you never slept with her?"

He smirked and puffed air through his nose. "We've all made mistakes. I've slept with more women than I care to think about. But Kara wasn't one of them. I won't deny there were moments during the rough times and turmoil when I wish I hadn't, but now, looking back, no. She is who I'm meant to be with. She's my end game."

"I'm still in the making mistakes phase," I mumbled. But my gaze followed Charlotte as she giggled and ran across the fort's bridge. Her blonde curls bounced beneath her beanie. My heart flipped inside my chest. How could I ever regret sleeping with Shelby when I had the most incredible daughter? Flint was right.

Charlotte *was* the result of my friendship with Shelby—not a mistake. Yes, that night all those years ago had been messed up. But Charlotte was amazing. And I'd do everything in my power to honor Shelby's wishes and make sure our daughter grew up into a beautiful young woman . . . Well . . . as best as this fucked up musician could do. "But I'm trying to change that."

"What happened with your bodyguard?" Intrigue flitted across Hunter's eyes. "I saw something online about the two of you."

"Ava?" I winced. "That turned into a downright mess."

"They're the ones that leave the biggest mark." He chuckled. "Fuck, Kara and I didn't get along when we first met. Look how that turned out."

"Yeah, but I kinda fucked up Ava's life."

"How so?"

My breath misted the air. I tugged and tightened my scarf, still frazzled by what had happened. "Her crazy ex had us followed and photographed; now she could lose custody of her kid. He's out to make Ava look like an unfit mother and that she wasn't doing her job. He's out to prove that she jeopardized our safety and her team's. That she was always in dangerous situations or fucking me while on the job."

He raised one eyebrow. "Were you?"

I wished we'd been together more often. "No. The couple times we were together, she'd always been off duty."

Concern furrowed his brow. "So some crazy fuck has been stalking you, causing you stress, and plans to use that shit against her? Dude, that doesn't seem right. Isn't there some law against doing those things?"

Is there? Could we twist the situation back on Luther?

But my own concerns speared my chest. My stress levels hadn't come down since Ava had left. "I don't know. I'm afraid what went down could blow up in my face too. I have my final review with children's services when we get back to LA. I'm terrified they'll use what happened between Ava and me, along with the other gazillion things I've done wrong in my life, against me. That they'll rule me unfit and I'll lose Charlotte."

He straightened, taking a step away from the pole. "Then make sure you prove to them how good you are with her. Make sure they know everything you do for Charlotte"—he counted on his fingers—"the help you've got in place, the plans you have for her, and how much you love her. Show them every picture you've taken, document every place you've been to, and make a list of all the support you have around you." He tucked a long strand of flyaway hair back beneath his beanie. "I don't know much about custody, but isn't it about stability, safety, and security? You have money—not an issue. You have a great house and a security team—tick. But the most important element is yourself, your friends, and your family. They're part of your world and the environment that Charlotte will be raised in. They play a huge part in her life, right?"

"Yeah. Absolutely." Dare I let hope to fill my chest? I wasn't alone. I never would be. I may have been single, but Charlotte had a family who loved her. She'd always be around people who cared. "You make everything sound so easy."

Just as Ashleigh and Charlotte happy-shrieked and slipped down the curly slide, a young couple with their two young children entered the park. Their kids looked about the same age as Charlotte and Josh. My heart missed two beats. I'd always wanted Ava to bring Josh on a playdate, not just because I had no idea on how to be a parent, but because I wanted to spend time with her. Be with her. *Crap.* Could we be like that couple? Be together with our kids?

"Being a parent isn't easy. Trust me." Hunter grunted. "But it's also freaking phenomenal."

"Yeah. It is."

Crap. What am I doing? Ava and Josh had a toxic man hindering their happiness—a sick fuck who wouldn't let them be free. No one should live like that. She had her sister, dad, and work friends around her for support, but she could have so much more. Deserved more. As I closed my eyes, Ava's smile lit behind my eyelids. Just seeing her happy again would be incredible. But giving her a life full of laughter and fun and a family who adored her would be even better.

What if the way I felt for her fizzled out? But *fuck* . . . what if it didn't?

Shit.

I couldn't let her go—not without a fight.

I tilted my head toward Hunter. "Thanks, man. You've put a lot of things into perspective. I needed that." I patted Hunter on the arm and threw him a smug grin. "And here I was thinking you were just a pretty face."

"Fuck you." He laughed and nodded. "I have my moments. Life happens, bud. You've gotta be prepared to move with it or it will leave you behind."

"So true."

I'd been afraid to change and had resented the adjustments I'd had to make. I'd wanted everything on this tour to be the same as it had been when Phil was alive, but we weren't the same guys anymore. The others had moved on and grown up, but I didn't want to. Charlotte had forced me to do so. So had Ava. And that had been a good thing. If I was going to survive in this business and make this father thing work, I needed to make more changes.

It was time.

Losing Aidan had taught me not to ignore the people I loved. Phil's death had burned into me the need to step up when someone was in trouble. Priah had shown me how incredible love could be. *Fuck*, I'd loved her. But we hadn't been meant to be. It was time to move on. Charlotte was family. The band was family. I wanted Ava to be part of my world too.

I wasn't afraid to fight for her. I wasn't going to let her down.

I'd caused her issues, so somehow I had to fix them.

But how?

I sucked in the cold air and cleared my head. I couldn't do this on my own. I needed help. Luckily I had friends who'd do that. I'd always been afraid to ask them, thinking my problems were insignificant compared to theirs and they had enough of their own issues to deal with. I'd been even more afraid to lose them, disappoint them, but true friendship survived everything. Flint, Slip, and I were living proof of that. Lewis may have been relatively new to our family, but he had become embedded in our circle too.

We were stronger together. *Strength in numbers. Always.*

Skipping through the snow, Ashleigh and Charlotte came toward us. Their cheeks were bright red from running around.

Ashleigh jumped up and down in front of Hunter. Her glittery pink boots sparkled in the sunshine. "Daddy, can we make snow angels? Out there." She grabbed his hand and tugged him toward the gate and the snow-covered hills beyond.

"Us too." Charlotte raised her arms toward me. "Up."

How could I say no? I scooped her into my arms and we headed for the gate.

"The things we do for our kids." Hunter laughed, chasing after Ashleigh.

And the things we'd do for those we loved. "Yep. We're suckers. But I wouldn't have it any other way." That was the truth.

After Hunter and I ran around on the hills with the kids, made snow angels, and had hot chocolates with them at a nearby café, Charlotte and I headed back to the hotel. Beckett was always my shadow.

As I showered and got dressed for the dinner I had to attend, thoughts of Ava filled my head.

She wasn't my bodyguard anymore.

There were no rules and restrictions keeping us apart. If we were to work, we'd have to make sacrifices and compromises. Our life would be far from conventional. But that was what would make it fun, exciting, and worthwhile.

If she'd give me a chance, I wanted to be hers.

I had to make things right.

A crazy plan formed in my head. All thanks to Hunter.

First . . . I'd call my lawyer.

Second . . . I'd rope my friends into helping. I'd use every damn one of them if I had to.

Third . . . I'd call my former casual fling, Min. Ava may have followed the rules, but I didn't. If anyone could dig up information on someone in LA, it would be my supermodel friends who attended more parties than I did. Those girls knew everyone and everything that happened behind closed doors. And most of them would do anything for me.

I needed intel on Luther. No one that powerful was clean.

Fourth . . . I'd finish the US leg of our tour and get back to LA. To Ava.

If Luther wanted to play dirty over custody, he'd met his match.

Never fuck over a rock star and the woman he was determined to win back.

Chapter 32

AVA

"I want full custody—nothing less." My heart screamed as Wilson, my lawyer, lazed back in his big leather chair and glanced at me over the rim of his glasses. I clenched my fists in my lap. I wanted to shake the shit out of him, knock some fight into him, but he just sat there rocking like a content old man on a porch swing. *Ergh!*

"Ava." He grabbed one of the notebooks where I'd recorded every instance Luther had failed to meet our parental agreement conditions. "I've reviewed all your entries. It's great that you have documented the times Luther was late, changed schedules at short notice, and was inflexible. But the photos you sent of the bruises on Josh's arm could just be from playing in the playground or from sport. The stories you've told me about Luther's wild parties are irrelevant. We don't have enough evidence to go for full custody."

"What?" Bile pooled in my gut. *No. No. No.* This wasn't happening. My head spun as my mind sifted through the material we'd gathered for my case. "What about Josh's psychology assessment, reports from his teachers, or testimonies from my family? My reviews?"

Wilson splayed his hands. "I'm sorry. They'll help, but none of this information holds more weight than the damning evidence he can provide against you—your job was dangerous, and your time away from home on assignment could be construed as a lack of involvement in Josh's well-being. Your public behavior, drinking with The Flintlocks at parties, isn't favorable. Being swamped by crazed fans and the paparazzi is not ideal. You've been in your new role for less than two weeks. It's not a strong enough foundation to support stability. You don't have enough grounds to get full custody. Our best hope is to negotiate more time in your parental agreement."

"Luther can't do this to me." My breath shuddered and lodged deep inside my lungs, spearing pain throughout my entire body. "He can't use my work against me. I was doing my job as a security guard—now I'm in the office. There's no law against going to a party in my personal time. My short-term, less-than-casual, now nonexistent relationship with Cole has nothing to do with my ability to look after my son. I've passed every mental health assessment and met every criteria required by the law to get more custody. Luther's the one who should be judged. Not me. Why does my behavior matter and not his?"

"Oh, it will." Wilson shut the notebook and tossed it beside his computer. "But character history comes into play. You know that. The court will want what is best for Josh."

"That isn't Luther. You know that."

"I do. But we have to follow the law."

"Fuck the law." Tears burned at the back of my eyes. "What happened to compassion, and seeing through the bullshit to find the truth? Luther had me followed and provided an insane amount of stress on my client and his daughter, the band, and me. Isn't there something in that?"

Wilson sighed, slumping his shoulders. "It's not illegal to hire private investigators. He'll probably get a smack on the hand and be told not to do it again."

Fuck, I hated my ex with a passion. Fire raged through my veins. As I sat straight, trying to remain professional, my soul shattered and tore in two. I'd never win. I'd always be under Luther's hold. I hated that. I hated him.

There was a knock on the meeting room door. Bonnie, the firm's receptionist, entered and tapped her long, pointed fingernails against the door. "Sorry to interrupt, but Cole Tanner and his lawyer, Patrick, are here to join your meeting."

"Cole?" My heart scrambled into my throat. "What? Why? What are they doing here?"

Confusion flitted across Bonnie's face. "Um, Mr. Tanner says it's urgent and has important information for your case."

Wilson raised a questioning eyebrow at me. "Did you know about this?"

Does it look like I did? "No. I . . . I haven't talked to him since I left Boston two weeks ago." I didn't want to see Cole. It would hurt too much. But *shit* . . . if he had one more piece of evidence I could use against Luther, I'd take it. Even if being in the same room as him would pulverize my heart. "Please, let them in."

Bonnie spun on her chunky Mary-Janes and returned two minutes later. Cole strode into the room with his lawyer carrying a briefcase. As I worked my gaze upward from Cole's designer boots to his jeans, over his T-shirt, his shoulders, then his face, my pulse quickened. Those green eyes made my heart ache, made it difficult to breathe and impossible to think straight. How could I love him so much when we'd hardly been together?

Cole rushed forward and squatted beside me. Warmth and worry shimmered in his gaze as he cupped my face. "Hey? I've missed you."

"Cole? What are you doing here?" Anguish tore through my whispered tone. "How did you know where I was?"

"Beckett."

Damn him. "*Why* are you here?"

He tilted his head toward his lawyer. "We have something that might help you get full custody of Josh."

"Don't play with me." My heart had been tampered with enough. "Not after everything we've been through."

"I'm not. Trust me."

He rose to his feet and held out his hand to Wilson. "Sorry for the interruption. I'm Cole Tanner. Ava's friend. This is my lawyer, Patrick Lopez. We have additional information that will be useful in Ava's case."

"Wilson Brooks." My lawyer shook Cole's hand then Patrick's. He waved to the chairs for them to sit. "This is unusual. I've gone down every avenue for Ava, so what new evidence could you possible provide to help her case for full custody?"

A cunning glint sparked in Patrick's dark eyes as he undid the button on his designer suit jacket. *Shit.* He reminded me of Luther's lawyer.

Patrick settled onto the chair, grabbed a folder from his briefcase, and placed it on the desk. "From my understanding, Luther is refusing to negotiate a new parental agreement and is adamant on proving Ava is an unfit mother. Is that correct?"

"Correct." Wilson dipped his chin.

"Looking into her case via a colleague of mine. . ." Wilson opened his mouth as if he was about to protest with *how the fuck did you do that* . . . but Patrick held up his finger. "I am a family law expert, have my contacts, and methods, and have dealt with clients like Mr. Carrington before. He's a power-tripping narcissist who has manipulated and taken advantage of Ms. Matthews since their bitter public divorce. He's not concerned about the well-being of his son. Cole has hired me to assist Ava and ensure that the new evidence we have uncovered is handled with care and in the manner she sees fit."

"Hire you?" Wilson shot daggers at Patrick. "As in, take over the case?"

"Given that we're days out from the hearing, I am happy to work with you as co-counsel if needed. Mr. Tanner is covering my fees, so no form of payment is required. My sole purpose is to ensure Ms. Matthews gets custody of her son."

"Really?" My heart tapped against my ribs. I could just kiss Cole. But I couldn't get my hopes up. There was so much information Luther had at his fingertips that would be held up in court. "What have you found on Luther I don't already know?"

Sitting beside me, Cole clutched my hand and squeezed it. "What we have will hopefully not just get you more time with Josh but full custody. Patrick is confident."

I'd had too many setbacks to let belief spark inside my chest.

"How confident?"

"The evidence we have is damning." Patrick's reassuring tone never faltered. "Once we submit this information to his lawyer, I'm certain he'll do anything you want to keep what we have out of the courtroom. If he doesn't, we take him down." A low, simmering fire flared in his eyes as if he was begging me to let him take on the challenge.

"I just want to be free of him and get full custody of Josh." I wasn't a vindictive person. I didn't want to hurt Luther. He'd hate me no matter what I did, so if this information helped me get him out of my life . . . bring it. "So, what do you have on him?"

Cole took the folder Patrick had put on the desk and opened it. "I made a few calls to some friends around town. I've got my hands on photographic and video evidence of Luther doing a lot of shit he shouldn't be doing. I have written testimonies and several more contacts willing to testify if needed. Patrick thinks this information might even put Luther in jail."

"What?" The ringing in my ears exploded. It sounded too good to be true. "What did you find?"

"Some of this stuff came from Min, her friend Isla, and a couple other girls around town." Cole pulled out several printouts from the folder and fanned them across the desk. "These are just some of the photographs they've taken at several recent events."

"Min? Your supermodel hookup friend?" Stunned, I scanned the mass of party photos.

"Yep, that one. But most of this came from Zoe."

"Zoe? As in Josh's nanny?" Confusion stabbed my brain.

"Uh-huh. Isla is friends with her."

Holy fuck!

Cole spun one of the photos toward me. "This is Luther snorting cocaine at home in his office." He grabbed the next couple of printouts. "These are images of Luther fucking a hooker in the club Noir Nights." Then he handed me another picture. "This shot was taken at his birthday party at the studio that Isla and Min were at. In the background, Josh is playing on his tablet, but there are drugs and a shit load of alcohol on the coffee table. All of this was in reach of Josh."

"Oh my God." My breath shot from my lungs. The photo trembled in my hand. "Prostitutes? And drugs? Around my son?"

Was that woman in the back of Luther's car when he'd dropped off Josh a prostitute? Nothing would surprise me. I placed one hand on my stomach to settle the unease, but it didn't work.

"Unfortunately, yes." Cole grabbed a USB out of his pocket and held it toward me. "This is everything you need. Min is a good friend who'd do anything to help. Zoe's over covering Luther's ass and not delivering on his promises to give her a corporate job at the studios. The girls are willing to testify."

"This is amazing. I can't believe Zoe helped you." Tears slid down my cheeks. My mind spun. Cole had done this for me? *Why?*

"I just asked her, and she said yes." Cole entwined his fingers with mine, lifted my hand to his lips, and kissed my knuckles. "I have also gotten your entire security team and the band to provide character references validating your professional conduct . . . and I have written one too." He leaned closer, pinning me with his warm gaze. "Not once did we do anything while you were on duty. You'd kick my butt if I stepped out of line. You always put my safety, the band's, and my daughter's, first. You put Josh above everything else. You make me want to be a better father every day. If I turn out to be half the parent you are, then I'll be stoked. You're fucking amazing. That's why I fell in love with you."

My breath hitched and my free hand shot over my mouth.

Cole eyes glinted as he half-smiled. "You hear me?"

My heart beat so fast my head spun. "You . . . you love me?"

"Yeah, I do."

"You did all this for me?"

"Yes. I'd do anything for you, Ava."

"Oh my God." I curled my hand around the back of his head, clutched his hair, and pulled his lips to mine. God, I'd missed him. The taste of his lips. Their softness. Their warmth . . . *him.* "I love you. So much."

Wilson cleared his throat as he scanned the photos. "This is some serious evidence."

"Yes." With a hungry grin, Patrick reached for the photo of Luther's birthday party. "This is more than enough proof to show that Josh is living in an unsafe environment. Luther's illegal engagement with more than one sex worker and drug use, especially around a minor, are serious offenses. He won't get away with this."

A shudder coursed through my body, slamming reality into my chest. *But would he?* He had too much power. Too much money. Too many dirty tactics up his sleeve. I grabbed a tissue from the box on Wilson's desk and wiped my eyes. "He will. He always does."

"Not his time." Patrick's reassurance did nothing to loosen the knot in my stomach.

I stared at the photos. Once we submitted these to Luther's lawyer, he'd hate me even more than he did now. This information in the wrong hands could ruin his reputation and career, and the studio. I didn't want that. I wasn't out to hurt him. I just wanted my son. But Luther had done illegal things. He'd endangered my son. I couldn't let that slide.

It was time for justice.

Luther would no doubt try to keep a hold over me regardless of the outcome on Thursday at court. But I had friends and family who loved and supported me. I clutched Cole's hand. I'd survive the next round of shit from Luther as long as I had them and good souls like Cole by my side. "Thank you. This is hopefully what I need to get Josh." A new light flickered to life in my chest. I straightened my shoulders and nodded to Patrick and Wilson. "Let's do this. Send this information to Luther's lawyers. Please get me my son."

"We will." Patrick gave me a firm nod. I hated to think what Cole paid this guy per hour. But every penny was worth it. Patrick turned to Wilson. "Would you like to go through the legal submission for Luther's lawyer now? I've got an hour before I have another meeting."

Wilson didn't look pleased that Patrick had moved in on my case, but he didn't object. "Sure. Ms. Matthews, once we've prepared everything I'll send you an email for final approval. Is that okay?"

"Yes. More than yes." Standing, I wiped my sweaty palms on my dress pants, then shook Wilson's and Patrick's hands. "Thank you." Cole did the same.

"Let me show you out?" Wilson waved toward the door.

"It's okay. We'll manage." Cole took my hand and guided me toward the door. "You work on taking Luther down and let us know how it goes."

In a daze, I let Cole lead me down the hallway toward the reception area. But halfway along the corridor, he pulled me into a vacant meeting room and shut the door.

Now I was alone with him, and my head spun. My heart raced. My world blurred. No . . . they were just tears welling in my eyes. "Cole? How can I ever thank you? What you've done has been incredible."

He drew me into a hug and kissed the side of my head. "You don't owe me anything, Ava. I played my part in causing your problems—I had to help fix them. I couldn't let you walk away, hating me for what had happened between us."

"I didn't hate you," I whispered as I rested my cheek against his shoulder. "I was mad at myself for risking Josh."

"I never meant to hurt you."

"I know. I just want this fight with Luther over."

"I get that. I'm here for you. No matter what." Stepping back, he cupped the side of my neck. The warmth of his touch seeped through my bones and settled in my veins. No one had ever gone out of their way for me before. He smoothed his hand over my hair. "You said when you got custody of Josh you wanted to spend time with him. And I'm down with that. But I'd like to be part of the plan too. I want to be with you, Ava."

I swayed on my feet. "You really want to see me again?"

"Yes. I want to see you a lot."

Caution kicked in. "As one of your casual hookups?"

"No." He glided his fingertips down the line of my jaw and brushed the tip of my chin. "There's only one name I want on my list . . . and that is yours."

An ache shuddered through my chest. "Cole, you've seen what

Luther's like, who I'm dealing with. If I don't get full custody, he's always going to be in the background. I come with a lot of baggage." I didn't want to inflict my problems onto anyone.

"If you hadn't noticed, I have a few loaded suitcases of issues too. I'm not afraid of Luther. We can deal with him together. I care about you. I've made a lot of mistakes. Letting you walk away was one of them. Luther has treated you like shit. I want to treat you right."

I pursed my lips, holding back my tears. "Do you really want to get mixed up in my mess?"

"I already am."

"I'm afraid of getting hurt again." *Truth hurts.*

"So am I." He rubbed his palms up and down my arms. "But I don't want to fight how I feel for you anymore. I meant what I said before. I love you, for some crazy reason. I want to see where this road takes us."

"Cole? I . . ." I was so in love with this man. But I had to think about Josh. My life revolved around him. Nobody else. "I can't think of anything beyond my court hearing."

"Ava, that's fine. I'm not going anywhere . . . except on tour." He smiled as he took my hand, walked backwards, and leaned against the sideboard. Entwining our fingers, he softened his tone. "We'll go at your pace. I'm here for ten more days before I head overseas. I can come home once a month to see you like Flint is doing with Sutton, and Slip and Maddy."

He'd do that for me? *Wow.* I had messed him up. But he'd done the same to me. There was no denying we had an unexplainable attraction. We didn't have to fight it anymore. He'd gone out of his way to help me. All my skepticism about him had been shattered. He truly was a good and decent man. I couldn't rush this, but I'd be crazy not to give us a chance at being happy.

I circled my hands over his shoulders and threaded serious playfulness into my tone. "What about all your groupies and supermodels?"

"I'm sure they'll be okay. Flint was right. When you meet someone special, life changes. That happened to me when I met my daughter . . . and you. You've been in my head for months. I'm not gonna lie—I want you in my bed. I like a lot of sex." A cute smile curled across his lips. "But somehow, I think you'd be okay with that . . . and you'd be able to keep up."

Heat touched my cheeks. "How much is a lot?"

"You want to find out?" He snagged the bottom of my top and tugged me forward.

"Maybe." I linked my hands behind his neck.

"But it's not just about sleeping with you, Ava." He snaked his hands around my waist and held me with his hypnotic gaze. "I want to be with someone who gets me. I want our lives to be better together rather than apart. My priorities have changed since Charlotte came into my life. I want to be a good dad. You make me want to do that. You love my kid almost as much as I do. You understand this crazy life I live that has no routines and crazy schedules. Music is a big part of who I am—that's not gonna change anytime soon." But as he shook his head, warm contentment flooded his eyes. "But now, rather than hooking up with girls, I like coming home after a show and having Charlotte up, running around, excited to see me when she should be in bed. I go to a lot of events but also love being at home having a tea party on the floor with my daughter. She is my life, too, just like Josh is yours. You know who I am. You've seen my world; I'd like you and Josh to be a part of it. I'd like to be yours if and when you're ready."

"Tea parties, huh?" I combed my fingernails through the back of his hair.

"Yeah." Humbleness rippled through his voice. "Yesterday, she stuck all these glittery clips in my hair and fake-painted my fingernails. I freaking loved it."

I giggled softly. "I wish I'd seen that."

He sucked in a deep breath. "Yeah. I wish you were there too."

"Did you mean what you said before and in Wilson's office?"

He slid his hands onto my ass. "That I love you? Yeah. That okay?"

Butterflies danced through my stomach. *Cole Tanner loved me!* I could get used to him saying that. "Yes." I glided my hands onto his shoulders and fidgeted with the collar of his T-shirt. "I love you too. You've taken me by surprise, Mr. Tanner. So is it okay if we take this slow?"

"We can do that."

I brushed my thumb over his gorgeous lips. "That damn charming smile of yours works."

"It hasn't failed me yet." He caught my hand and kissed my fingertips. "But you were the most challenging."

Heat crept up my neck and settled in my cheeks. "I didn't want to make it easy on you."

"I pray you never do."

"So, drummer boy?" I skimmed my fingertips down the front of his T-shirt, then slid them around his waist. "Want to get out of here?"

"Yes. But can you confirm ... how slow is slow?" A sexy, heated smile crossed his lips. "I've come up with several ways you can thank me. Are you open to some ideas?"

Oh boy, I was in trouble. I was no longer bound by the rules of my job. No longer in denial. I wanted him. With every inch of my soul. He'd gone out of his way to help me. He wanted a life with me and my son. He'd threaded his way into my life and my heart. *Fuck slow.* "Yes. I have a few suggestions too. But none of them are appropriate to do here in my lawyer's office. My place is closest. Can we go there and discuss them? Preferably while naked."

A raspy moan rumbled deep in his throat. "Not sure I can wait that long."

"If you want me, you will."

He slipped his hand into my hair and crushed his lips against mine. Sweet sweeps of his tongue combined with the emotional day sent a wave of heat rushing through my system. God, this man could kiss. I eased back from his onslaught and licked my lips. "Not here. We might break the furniture."

"Damn, you drive a hard bargain."

Breathing Cole into every cell of my body, I let the hum, the spark, this crazy connection I had for him claim my heart. Hovering my lips against his mouth, I panted. "Let's go. Now."

Clutching my hand, he lurched forward from the counter and led me out the door.

Chapter 33

AVA

The drive back to my house in separate cars was a crazy blur. Was being with Cole insane? Was this too fast? *No*. I hadn't felt like this about anyone in a long time, if ever. I craved being with him without my job looming over me. In the parking lot before we'd taken off, Beckett had given me a big hug and said a prayer for me, hoping that my case went well, and he'd hollered a huge *hell yeah* to Cole and I being together.

I'd stipulated one more condition to Cole on the way out of the office . . . no sex around my friends. I wasn't shy—I just didn't want Beckett or any other member of my team listening in or witnessing us going at it. That'd be too weird. Cole had laughed and vowed to change my mind on that rule.

But not today.

Once we reached my place, Beckett took off. He'd return when Cole called him. In a flurry of hot kisses. Cole and I fell through my front door. As we tore off each other's clothes—jackets, shirts, pants, shoes—we veered toward the kitchen. My butt connected with the kitchen table.

"Shit." Cole dragged his lips from mine and rested his forehead against my brow. "Is your dad home?"

"No. He's at work."

A devilish smile quirked his lips. "I wouldn't care if he was."

"I didn't think you would. Neither would I." I caught the back of his hair and kissed him. Every touch of his hands seared my skin. Every taste of his lips sent fire skipping through my veins.

He moaned as he clutched my ass. After hoisting me up, he planted me onto the table and whisked off my panties followed by my bra. Lowering his head, he took one nipple in his mouth and tortured it with hot, wet kisses, licks, and sucks. Shivers and goose bumps dashed across my skin. *Damn, that's good.*

"What time do you have to pick up Charlotte?" Closing my eyes, I arched into him. *Fuck!* That tongue of his was incredible.

"Lewis and Tia are babysitting." He worked his way up to my lips and stole my breath. "I don't have to be home until whenever."

"And Hannah?" My voice came out a breathy pant.

"Catching up with friends."

"Hmm." I combed my fingers through his soft hair. "Did you plan this?"

"No. Good thing I'm spontaneous."

"Good thing I don't have to go back to the office this afternoon." I skimmed my hand down the smooth plain of his ripped stomach, then dipped them into his boxer briefs. As I lowered them over his thighs, his erection sprang free. *Oh yeah. That's mine.*

He caught my hand, yanked his boxer briefs off, and tossed them aside. Edging back between my legs, he teased his cock against my opening. He nudged and pressed it into my hot arousal. My core clenched and ached. I had never wanted anyone as much as I wanted him.

A saucy glint smoldered in the depths of his gaze as he swept my hair off my brow. "There's no one listening in. No one else home. No need to rush. You're so beautiful, Ava. I want to taste and touch every inch of you, but right now, I just want to fuck you. So is here okay?"

"Uh-huh." I wound my legs around him and pulled him closer, grinding and rubbing my pussy against his cock. My body begged him to enter me. "Here, then my bed."

"I can do that." He grabbed a condom from the wallet in his jeans and rolled it on. Stepping in close, he erased the gap between us and kissed me. He smiled against my lips and drove into me slowly. His rock-hard cock filled me as he thrust into my depths.

My insides clenched around him. Panting against his mouth, I whispered. "God, you feel good."

"You drive me crazy." He swept his lips across mine. "You make me hard." He rocked into me. "Blow my mind." He withdrew an inch, then drove into me, urgent and deep. "Turn me on."

Oh, wow. He could just keep doing that to me and I'd be happy forever.

As I snaked my hands around his shoulders, his hot flesh scorched my fingertips. Each touch, kiss, and connection embedded him deeper into my soul. We were different but alike. Messed up but cared about our families more than anything. We'd found each other when love had been the furthest thing from our minds. But now he was here, I didn't ever want to let him go.

"Ava . . ." My name fell from his lips in a hot whisper. His breath quickened. His grip on my hips tightened.

I rocked and pulsed, matching his every move. The tension inside me wound higher and higher.

Too much emotion spiraled between us. There was no holding back.

He moaned, then hissed through his teeth as he pounded into me harder and faster.

My need for release burned inside my core. Closing my eyes, I rubbed against him.

Oh yes. There. More. Just there . . .

My toes curled. I dug my fingers into his shoulders. "Cole . . . I . . . oh shit!" My head fell back. My orgasm shot through me, sparking jolts of electricity through my body, skipping up my spine, down my arms, and tingling in my fingertips. My pussy throbbed and pulsed. Every cell in my system hummed and screamed '*oh yeah!*'

With hard drives and deep penetration, Cole pummeled into me. "Fuck, I love watching you come."

"Careful, Mr. Tanner." I panted against his lips. "I might like you making me do that."

A sexy groan erupted deep in his throat. "I plan on it."

I wrapped my arms around him and crushed his body against mine. I tilted my hips forward, clenched my walls around his cock, and pulsed in time with his moves.

The breath shot from his lungs as he jerked, convulsed, and found his release. As we shuddered and quaked together, he grinned against my lips. "Fuck, you do it for me."

He kissed me, stealing my breath and my heart. Cole was mine, and I was his. We'd closed the door on one part of our lives and opened the door to a new chapter. But for the first time, I looked forward to the future. Now, all I needed was Josh.

***

Two days later, I ran out of the courtroom and rushed across the parking lot with tears streaming down my cheeks. I flung my arms around Cole, who'd been waiting for me. "Arrrrgh!" I screamed. "He's mine. Josh is all mine. I got full custody."

I couldn't stop shaking. Or crying. Or hollering.

"That's fucking awesome." He swung me round, placed me on my feet, then kissed me, fast and hot and fiery, all lips and tongue and total sexiness. "So when do you get him?"

"Today." I quaked on my feet. Even my voice quivered. "After school." I held out my hand. "I can't stop trembling. I can barely breathe. I'm so excited."

"So you should be." He rubbed my hands, holding them against his chest.

"I will never be able to thank you enough for helping me." So much warmth and gratitude flooded through my veins and exploded in my heart. "I couldn't have done this without you. Thank you."

"I was glad to help." He brushed a tear off my damp cheek. "And to see you happy."

"I can't believe this has finally happened." I jumped into his arms again. "I got Josh. Argh!" Nothing could make me come down from this high. Not ever.

I had a little less than two hours until Josh was mine.

"Would you like to celebrate? Or *how* would you like to celebrate?" A mischievous smile skipped across his lips as he raised a sexy eyebrow.

I'd had more sex in the past two days with Cole than I had in more than a year. So much for going slow. But right then, I was too wired. I was sure Cole wouldn't care if my mind was elsewhere, but when I was with him, I wanted to give him my undivided attention. That wasn't going to happen today. "How about some food? I'm starving."

"We can do that." Grinning, he rubbed my arms. "There's a little Italian restaurant near here. We can grab a quick bite to eat before we pick up Josh."

"We?"

"Ava, this is a huge day. I want you to treasure every moment with Josh. But so you don't crash your car with all those tears in your eyes, Becks can drive. We'll collect Josh, take you home, then leave you be."

Wow! "You keep impressing me, Mr. Tanner."

He stepped in close and threaded his fingers beneath my hair, dragging his thumb across the base of my neck. "If you keep calling me Mr. Tanner, you're gonna end up in trouble. We'll be celebrating, but it won't include Italian."

I played with the neckline of his T-shirt and lifted my chin. "What if I want some trouble?"

Hunger flared in his eyes . . . for me. God, that was crazy but so good. "I'm more than happy to cause some. My town car is right there. Should Becks go for a walk?"

I flattened my hand against his chest and giggled. "No. Not today."

"What about this weekend? Would you like to come to Big Bear with Josh? Everyone's going. I want to spend as much time with you as possible before I go overseas."

"Cole, I can't think about anything other than Josh right now."

"I know. Just putting it out there." He touched his lips to mine then wiped the corner of his mouth with his fingertips. *So sexy.*

"Let's go eat, then pick him up."

"I'd like that."

We joined Beckett by the car. After hugs and more tears of happiness, Cole took me to lunch. But I couldn't eat much. I couldn't sit still. I glanced at my watch every five minutes.

Then . . . it was time.

My heart raced at the speed of light.

For the entire drive to Beverley Hills, excitement somersaulted and backflipped through my stomach. Cole held my hand even though my palms sweated. Just after four p.m., Beckett pulled into Luther's driveway and parked outside the front door. Cole leaned over and gave me a quick kiss. "You ready?"

"Oh God, yes." This was it. Josh was mine. "I've waited for this day for more than two years. I can't believe it's finally here."

The second Beckett killed the engine, and I opened the car door, Josh came charging out of the house. With tear-filled eyes, I rushed toward him and fell to my knees.

He flung his arms around my neck. "Mommy. I miss you."

As I breathed him in, my world reset. "Me too. But you know what? Today you can come and stay with me. Forever."

"You mean that?" He sobbed against my knit top. "Is it true?"

"Yes." I held him close. Tight. He was mine. All mine.

"I don't ever want to come back here. I hate it."

"You don't have to." And I'd never have to see Luther again. I was finally free.

Thanks to Cole.

Cole stepped out of the car and tucked his hands into his jeans. "You need help?"

"No. We're good." I rubbed my son's arms. "Josh, do you remember Cole? He's a good friend of mine. Can you wait with him while I talk to your father?"

Josh ran over to Cole and high-fived him. Cole had the most natural instinct with kids. I couldn't believe he'd doubted being a good dad.

Luther stepped onto the porch with two suitcases and dropped them at the top of the steps. "I'll have the rest of Josh's things delivered to your house tomorrow. I'll have Brody finish packing his room."

His PA? Of course. Luther wouldn't do anything for his son.

"You happy?" he sneered.

"To have Josh? Yes. It's all I've ever wanted. This could've been so much easier if you'd been reasonable."

"I had you." Hate twisted his tone. "Right where I wanted you. Tied to me. But no, you had to play dirty again."

I shook my head. I should have pitied him, maybe even held an element of sorrow for him because he was losing his son, but no . . . I felt nothing. "I've never played dirty. I was just lucky people who cared about me uncovered the truth. You think you can control every situation, manipulate people and their lives, and think you're above the law. Well, you're not. I never wanted to hurt you. I still don't. What you did was illegal and put Josh in danger." I thanked God nothing awful had happened to my son. I sucked in a deep breath and drew my shoulders back. "I don't care what you do with the rest of your life—I just want you out of mine."

Shards of ice shot through Luther's eyes as he glared at Cole. "You shacking up with this guy?"

My life was no longer Luther's concern. "He's my friend. I care about him. If what we have evolves, it will be for the right reasons. For love and friendship, trust, and for our kids. Something you and I failed to do." I splayed my hand across my chest. "I am a good mother. Always have been. I love Josh more than anything. I promise to give him the best life I can, a home full of love and kindness and family. You are his father. When Josh is ready to see or talk to you again we can discuss catching up. But I wouldn't bank on that happening for a very long time, if ever." He'd destroyed his relationship with his son—not me. Not loving your child was unfathomable.

"If I can't have you, Ava, I want nothing to do with you or him." Spite hissed through his low, sinister voice. "I can promise you this: I won't follow you, contact you, or go anywhere near you or Josh. You're out of my life. I never want to see you again. But you keep your end of the deal." Warning blazed in his eyes. "Those photos of me leak, you tarnish my reputation, I'll—"

"You'll what?" He couldn't threaten me anymore. The moment my lawyers had sent the incrementing evidence and the request for uncontested full custody of Josh to Luther's lawyer, my ex had called me. After he'd cursed and called me every name under the sun, he'd begged me not to use the photos in court. But I wanted no tie to Luther, no hold over him—only justice to deliver what he deserved. I'd won! "If something happens to me or Josh or you hurt anyone associated with my job, Cole's band, or family, you will go to jail. You still might if other people involved want justice. But for now and hopefully forever, we are done. You live your life. I'll live mine. Deal?"

"Deal."

I turned, took two steps toward the car, then stopped. I swiveled 'round to face Luther. "At one stage, I did care for you, Luther. I wanted to make us work for Josh, but power and money went to your head. Maybe you can find a part of your soul that used to be decent and get help. I pray that you do."

"Who knows?" he sniggered. "Maybe someday we can be friends."

"Don't hold your breath." Hell would freeze over before that happened.

He glanced at Cole again. Defeat and surrender darkened Luther's eyes. "Does he make you happy?"

I glanced at Cole tickling Josh. My heart filled my chest. Warmth flooded my veins. What we had was new, exciting, and full of hope. I couldn't wait to see what we could become. So did Cole make me happy? "Yes. He does."

"I'm sorry I never did." With that, Luther walked into the house and shut the door.

A weight as big as Giant Rock lifted off my shoulders. The air became easier to breathe. Light filled my heart. *Yes!*

I rushed over to Cole, kissed him, and hugged Josh. I soaked them into my soul. No more drop-offs, exchanges, or goodbyes. No more Luther. I was excited about the future. I was in love. I had Josh. It was time to start afresh. "Let's go home."

Cole grabbed Josh's suitcases and put them in the trunk. We jumped into the car and headed to my house.

Tears filled my eyes—tears of happiness.

I could breathe.

I was free.

I was finally fucking free.

Chapter 34

COLE

One week after the US leg of our tour had ended, and the day after Ava got custody of Josh, I walked out of my review with children's services with Charlotte in my arms. Hannah, Ava, and Tia strode beside me. Charlotte was mine. All mine. No more legalities loomed over my head. It still blew my mind she was my daughter, but I'd promised to give her the best life I could.

After buckling Charlotte into her car seat, I caught Ava around the waist and kissed her until she moaned against my mouth.

She drew back a step. Heat flushed her cheeks. "What was that for?"

"I'm just happy and wanted to thank you for being here."

"You're welcome." She flattened her palm across my chest, but rather than pushing me away, she clutched my shirt and drew me closer. "So, I was thinking, if your offer is still open, Josh and I would love to come to Big Bear with you for the weekend."

"I'd love that." I tucked her loose hair behind her ear. "Would you like to stay at my place tonight? Save you going home after Hannah's farewell dinner."

"Mmmm," she murmured against my lips. "Yeah. I better go pack. We can come over once Josh finishes school."

"I'll be waiting."

That night, everyone gathered at my place. Tomorrow,

Hannah would head home to San Francisco. But I couldn't let her go without her knowing how much I'd appreciated her coming on the tour with us, minding Charlotte and giving me glowing reports to children's services when, at first, I didn't deserve them.

At my long dining table, my friends' laughter and chatter filled the air as we ate dinner and drank champagne and wine. Flint, Sutton, Tia, and Lewis sat opposite me. The kids were at one end. Slip and Maddy sat down from Hannah on my right. Ava was on my left. This was family.

I tapped my glass with my knife, gathering everyone's attention. Pushing my chair back, I rose to my feet. "Alright, folks. Tonight is about Hannah." I placed one hand over my heart and the other one on her shoulder. As I glanced down at her, gratitude flooded my chest. "Thank you for bringing Charlotte into my life. I know nothing will ever replace the loss of Shelby, but Charlotte hopefully makes the grief a touch more bearable. I can't thank you enough for staying and believing in me, that I'd come around in the end. Thank you for kicking my butt and pulling me into line as much as Ava did. You're amazing and the best grandma. Thank you for being a part of our lives, and I hope you had fun on the tour."

"Oh, I did. Thank you." She dipped her chin as she rested her shaky hands on her lap.

"I will be forever in your debt and grateful for what you've done over the past few months. Now I can't imagine life without Charlotte. She's adorable." I waved at my daughter, sitting adjacent to Ava. "Aren't you, sweetie?"

Charlotte shot her hands up in the air. "Yeah."

Fuck, my heart swelled every time she smiled.

"So, Hannah. . ." I placed my hand on the back of her chair. "As a thank you for putting up with me and the guys, I have a gift for you." I put down my glass and pulled out an envelope from my jacket pocket. "When you and Paul first came here, you said you wanted to travel together. So here is an all-expenses paid trip with a driver, accommodation, and anything else the two of you need to finally go see the Grand Canyon." I handed her the letter.

"Oh no." Tears welled in Hannah's eyes. "I can't accept that."

"I won't take no for an answer."

"Cole." With glassy eyes, she took the travel vouchers. "You shouldn't have but thank you."

"You're welcome." I grabbed my drink and raised it. "To Hannah."

She clutched the envelope to her chest. "Thank you. To everyone. I'll miss you. But don't be strangers. Any time you're in The City, come visit."

"We will after the tour," I reassured Hannah. "We'll catch up regularly. I promise."

"I'd like that." Then she waggled a finger at me and narrowed her eyes, only too much kindness shimmered in them. "Promise me you'll love your girls and everyone here. And take care of yourself in the process too."

"I will." I'd learned to say no and manage my time better. With the tour and our hectic agenda, life was still full on, but having Charlotte had changed my outlook. I looked forward to being with Ava and growing closer to her. My blood pressure had been good. I hadn't had any more dizzy spells. I was sleeping well. Our Flintlock family had grown and changed, and it would only get stronger.

The following morning, Hannah left after many tears, numerous hugs, and promises to visit her after the tour.

Just after ten a.m., my friends and I drove in convoy up to my parents' cabin in Big Bear. Everyone was excited to hit the slopes, snowboard, and chill out for the weekend.

As I parked Ava's Range Rover out the front of the lodge, her eyes widened. She stared up at the two-story place. "Holy shit. It's huge."

"Yeah. This is the first time we've been here in fourteen months. Last time was for a few days before recording the album when Lewis had just joined us." *Wow.* That seemed like a lifetime ago.

I hopped out of the car, opened the back door, and unclipped Charlotte from her car seat. Giggling, she slid down the sidestep and ran through the snow with Josh. He chased her around my friend's parked cars.

After an afternoon of sledding with the kids, building snowmen, and snowboarding with Ava while Tia and Sutton looked after the kids, I fell into the shower with Ava, had a hot quickie, then joined everyone in the living room on the big U-shaped sofa for some drinks.

A warm fire crackled in the hearth and filled the room with a soft light. I glanced around at my friends and our partners. I was truly blessed to have these people in my life. I couldn't wait to continue the tour. I couldn't wait to come home to Ava. But I hoped to change one thing. I wanted Ava with me. During the last two weeks of the tour, while I'd gathered information on Luther for Ava, April had struggled with her workload. She never complained, but the stress was etched into her face. So one night after talking to her, the guys and I had discussed a new plan. Now was the perfect time to bring it up.

I took a sip of my vodka and entwined my fingers with Ava's. "So, the guys and I have a proposal for you."

"Does it involve something indecent?" Cute wrinkles formed on the bridge of her nose as she took a sip of her red wine. "Like a girlfriend initiation ritual?"

Why didn't I think of that? "No. We'd like you to consider working for us and offer you a job."

She choked, spluttered, and coughed. "A what? A job?"

"Yes." Flint leaned forward, resting his elbows on his knees. "It's not security but involves privacy and protecting all of us. We need someone who is an exceptional coordinator. Ruthless at organizing people. Who can make things happen and work under pressure."

Bewilderment flitted across her face. "What do you have in mind?"

"We've gotten bigger than we ever imagined." A we're-fucking-good grin slid across Slip's mouth as he hooked his ankle up onto his opposite knee and draped his arm across the back of the sofa behind Maddy. "April is run off her feet. She wants to focus on our publicity and social media."

I curled my hand around Ava's thigh. "So we need someone to work alongside her to make our travel arrangements, coordinate our schedules, book appointments, manage communications, keep our team under control, get us from A to B, and kick our asses into line every single day."

Rubbing her brow as if processing everything, she glanced at each of the guys, then at me. "So you want me to be your personal assistant?"

"More like our executive assistant . . . yes." I shrugged, then gave her a saucy smile. "But I prefer the title of master drill sergeant, logistic officer, comms expert, and special ops manager."

She closed her eyes and pinched her eyebrows together. "Why would I want to do this?"

"You'd get to order all of us around—not just Cole." Lewis chuckled as he massaged Tia's feet.

"And you'd get to run every aspect of our life." I gave her thigh a played tap. We needed all the help we could get. Ava would be perfect. "This role involves a lot of field work—tours, events, meetings, photoshoots, album recordings, gigs, and more . . . It's a long list."

"Um . . ." She straightened and stared toward the fire. She hadn't totally freaked out or said no yet, so that was encouraging. "When did you expect this job to start?"

Questions were good.

"Monday." Chuckling, I nudged my elbow into her arm. "But we're flexible."

She sucked in a deep breath and shook her head. "I can't work for you. I have a job. I have Josh."

I swiveled toward her and held her hand against my leg. "Ava, one thing I know about you is that you don't want to be stuck behind a desk. You don't have to do that now you have custody of Josh. You can go back to being a security guard, but Wells won't allow you to work with us. As our EA, you can. If you come on the tour, Josh can come with you. Harper will look after the kids. She can tutor Josh when we travel, and he can attend school when we're home."

Excitement and worry swam through her eyes. "I don't know. What you're asking is a lot and has come as a shock. It's so different to anything I've done before."

"No, it's not." I shook my head. "You do these things for your team. We'd love you to do them for us. There's no rush to decide. We're just putting it out there and would love you to think about it." I squeezed her hand. "If you want to stay in your current job, that's totally cool. I'll come home once a month during the tour to see you, just like Flint and Slip are doing for Sutton and Maddy."

"You were serious when you said that the other day?" She searched my face as if doubting me. I wasn't joking around.

"Yes." I stroked my thumb over the back of her hand, loving how a small smile curled at the corner of her lips every time I did it. "This job may not be like your old security work, but you'd be coordinating our moves every day, and be looking out for all of us. We have a crazy schedule. You'll have to be prepared for the occasional shit fest, dilemma, and scandalous drama, media meltdowns, the odd wild party, and countless late nights. But most of our days are full of fun, music, and laughter. And every day you'd come home to this." I circled my finger slowly through the air, taking in my friends. "You're part of this now. I want to spend every day getting to know you better and falling in love with you more and more. I want us to be a family."

"A family?" Tears welled in her eyes. "Isn't that rushing things?"

"Anyone who becomes important to us joins The Flintlocks family. So sorry, not sorry, you're stuck with us. The option to work for the band is entirely up to you." I leaned in closer to her and arched an eyebrow. "But is there something I can do to convince you and leave you with no other choice?"

"Like what?" Her gaze softened as she pursed her lips.

"I will do anything you want." Pushing gently on her shoulders, I lay her down on the sofa, nearly crushing Tia's head. Hovering over Ava, I kissed and nuzzled into the side of her neck, licking, and nipping at her soft skin.

"Enough, you two." Giggling, Tia grabbed a cushion and smacked me on the back.

"See what I have to put up with, Ava?" I ruffled Tia's hair, then drew Ava upright, stealing another kiss from her lips.

"You deserved that." With a big smile on her face, Ava play-punched me in the arm.

Flint raised his glass toward her and bobbed his head. "Ava, we definitely need you around to keep him under control."

Shuffling on the seat, she straightened her sweater, then combed her fingers through her loose hair. "Okay. On a serious note, do you guys have an employment contract?" She glanced at each one of us. "I'd like to see an official job offer, including salary details and benefits, before I make any decisions."

"Absolutely." Flint nodded. "We'll get Blake to email you through the information on Monday. I guarantee we'll pay more than you earn now. You have to be compensated well for putting up with our crap." He took a gulp of his vodka and swallowed it down. "April was ecstatic when we discussed this with her. Blake's all for it. We know you love your security team; we'll continue using their services after the tour. But we'd love to steal you away from them."

"What if Cole and I don't work out?" She raised her questioning eyebrows at me.

Oh . . . we'll work out. I wasn't letting her go anywhere in a hurry.

Slip drained his vodka and placed the empty glass on the coffee table. "We'd still want you to work for the band. You're the right fit, Ava. Not just because you're with Cole."

"It's a lot to take on board." She stared into her wine. "Let me think about it."

"I'd be jealous if you went on tour with them." Sutton drank the last mouthful of her wine.

"Why don't you work for the guys, Sutton?" Ava pointed to the bottle of red wine on the coffee table in front of Sutton, silently asking for a refill.

"Me?" Sutton leaned forward and flicked her long ponytail over her shoulder. She grabbed the wine and topped up her glass, then Maddy's and Ava's. Tia was drinking bourbon with Lewis.

Flint, Lewis, and I were into the vodka. Sutton put the stopper back on the bottle. "One: I'm not qualified to do anything they need. And two, I love acting too much. I've landed my dream job. I'll be joining the band halfway through the tour now our filming schedule has changed. I'll be able to spend the last two months with them."

"What about you, Maddy?" Ava lifted her chin at Maddy, sitting opposite.

"I'm like Sutton. I love acting too much." Maddy glanced at Slip and smiled. "We'll stick to our casual, dirty weekend and romantic rendezvous for now."

Chuckling, Slip hooked his arm around Maddy's neck and pinned her against his chest. "I want more than our casual hookups. You know that." I didn't miss the low note of seriousness in his tone. They'd had an argument out in the hot tub over something earlier that afternoon. I hoped everything was okay. "What do I have to do to get you to trust me?"

"Put a ring on it." Sutton laughed, raised her wine, and jabbed her elbow into Flint's side, hard.

Oh boy. That was no subtle hint.

"On that note . . ." Flint jumped from the seat and grabbed his guitar. *Nice deflection.* "Let's play some tunes."

"Hell yeah." But before I grabbed my sticks, Charlotte and Josh came running down the stairs, Charlotte giggling and squealing as he chased her. She dashed around the sofa and collided with my legs. I picked her up, placed her on my lap, and kissed her soft round cheek. "Hey, sweetie. What have you been up to?"

"Josh is chasing me. With his dinosaur. But Barney and me are too fast." She held out her bear and patted his head.

Ava drew Josh into her embrace and tickled his tummy. "Are you playing nicely together?"

"Yeah." Josh giggled, hugging his plush T-Rex to his chest. "We made a cubbyhouse and played dinosaurs." He shoved the toy into Ava's face. "Roarrrr!"

Had they draped quilts and sheets over their bedroom furniture upstairs? Scattered pillows and cushions across the floor? I hoped so. Had to have some fun.

Charlotte wedged Barney between us then rubbed my scruffy cheeks. "Daddy, can I play your drum now?"

My breath shot from my lungs as I smoothed my hand over her hair. My heart exploded. Tears prickled my eyes. "W . . . what did you say?"

"Can I play your drum . . . please?" She pointed to the snare I'd brought with us.

"Before that." I struggled to find my voice. "What did you call me?"

She smiled, giggled, and fell sideways. "Daddy, don't be silly."

I hugged her against my chest and held her tight. Warmth flooded and filled my chest. *Oh. My. God.*

Ava gave me a strange what's-the-matter look. "What?"

I closed my eyes, buried my face into the small of Charlotte's neck, and breathed the smell of my daughter into every cell in my body. "She called me Daddy for the first time."

Sutton's hand flew across her chest. "Oh . . . that's so adorable."

Flint hooked his arm around Sutton's shoulders. "You can call me daddy any time you like, baby."

"Ew! That's not one of my role-playing fantasies."

I groaned, then laughed. "Too much information."

"Never and you fucking know it." Flint's ice-blue eyes glinted in the firelight.

"Hey. No swearing around the kids." I covered Charlotte's ears. "But I have no issue with you banging Sutton whenever and wherever you like."

"Good thing I'm happy to do that." Flint smothered Sutton with a big kiss on the cheek.

She blushed and giggled. "Later, baby. I wanna hear you play."

"I'm down for that." I lifted Charlotte off my lap and grabbed my drum and sticks.

After a few tunes, we had the casserole that Ava had made for dinner, and once we'd finished cleaning up, everyone re-gathered on the sofa. The guys strummed on their guitars. The girls drank wine. I cuddled Charlotte against my chest. Josh had fallen asleep next to Ava.

With a blinking, almost asleep Charlotte resting her head against my shoulder, I took Ava's hand. I stood and drew Ava over toward the fire. Snaking my arm around her back, I pulled her into me and Charlotte, and kissed her cheek. I had my two girls. Close.

Flint played a soft tune on his guitar. Lewis and Slip strummed along. The girls swayed in time with the music.

I circled my hand over Ava's back. "You know how I'm in this little band."

"Um, yeah." Ava moved in sync with me and the melody.

"Well, I wrote a song." I kissed her hand and cradled it against my chest, next to Charlotte. "But I can't sing well." I wrinkled my nose. "So is it okay if Flint sings it?"

"Is it about me?" she whispered.

"It's about everything. Everything that led me to you. That okay?"

"Yeah."

I nodded to Flint, then brushed my lips against Ava's. Holding her and Charlotte in my embrace, with a slow sway in my step, I lingered by the warm fire. Flint sang, low and soft.

I never believed in fate or destiny
But the world had something planned for me
There've been days when I've said too much
There've been nights where I didn't say enough
I wasn't the friend that I wished I was
I wasn't the lover she'd been dreaming of
I've made more mistakes than I care to count
Drunk my way through too much doubt
Didn't think I'd ever love again
But somehow you were heaven-sent

Some say we were a huge mistake
That I should've walked away
But after everything we've been through
Survived the weather, me and you
I know one thing to be true

You are . . .
The best mistake I've ever made

I've had my heart broken more than once
Lost my way, didn't know who I was
I should've turned away, not broken any rules
I hurt those I loved; never meant to be cruel
Just when I couldn't draw another breath
Or erase the darkness from my head
The angels sent me someone new
They sent me . . . you

I kissed Charlotte's curls. *My baby girl.* She'd fallen asleep on my shoulder. *So beautiful.*

One look from you across the room
I knew I was forever doomed
Your gorgeous eyes, so big and green
Just like mine, I could hardly breathe
As I hold you in my arms
And we dance in the calm
I know you are . . .
The best mistake I've ever made

I rested my cheek against Charlotte's head. The angels . . . and Shelby . . . had given me a gorgeous daughter and had brought Ava into my life. As our gazes locked, I hugged her closer and whispered the lyrics to her.

Nights together knocked on my heart
We tried so hard to stay apart
We defied all the rules
I crossed all the lines just for you
As I kiss you on the lips
My butterflies keep doin' backflips
I know you are . . .
The best mistake I've ever made

Some say we were a huge mistake
That I should've walked away
But after everything we've been through
Survived the weather, me and you
I know one thing to be true
You are . . .
The best mistake I've ever made

I cradled the back of Ava's head and hovered my lips two inches from her mouth. "You and Charlotte are the best mistakes I've ever made and have now turned into the best things in my life." I kissed the tear from Ava's cheek. "I love you."

I'd never known what I was missing until Charlotte and Ava came along. I'd locked myself away from getting close to anyone after being hurt too many times. But now I had found love again, I planned on never letting it go.

Ava nodded and sniffled. "No more mistakes. Let's just be happy. Together."

"I'd like that." I nodded to the guys. "Thank you."

"Any time, bud." Slip placed his guitar aside. "I'm stoked you two sorted your shit out and are together. But damn, Cole, I'm gonna miss you doing vodka shots out of girls' cleavages."

"It'll just have to be Ava's." I changed arms, holding Charlotte. She was growing too fast . . . and getting heavier. I shook my dead arm; it tingled from lack of blood circulation. *Worth it.*

"I'm down for that." Ava threaded her arm around my waist, then tapped my ass. "I don't mind if you do the occasional one on girls but only if I can do the same out of guys' crotches or waistbands or off their sexy abs."

"What?" My eyebrows shot skyward.

She tucked her hand into the back pocket of my jeans. A sexy glint skipped across her eyes. "Body shots are fun. As long as I'm the only one you make out with and fuck, it's fine."

"Wow." The breath rushed from my lungs. "There is a lot I don't know about you, Ms. Matthews. But damn, I can't wait to learn everything."

She rubbed Charlotte's leg. "How about we put the kids to bed, and we go test out that hot tub on the deck? I want a trial run of the benefits that come with the job offer to help me decide."

"Hmm." I brushed my lips against hers. "There might be some heated negotiations and bribery and corruption involved."

"I expect nothing less."

"Oh my God, I love you."

"Careful Cole. . ." Tia drained her bourbon and gave me a heartfelt smile. "You might have found your perfect match."

"I know I have." I swiped Ava's hair back off her forehead. "Why don't you get naked and into that tub. I'll put Char to bed, then Josh."

"The shit you'll do for a bit of pussy." Slip chuckled as he massaged Maddy's neck.

"Worth it." I kissed Ava's cheek.

Tia raised her fresh bourbon toward me. "Never thought I'd see the day you'd be a doting dad and all loved up again, but I like it."

"Me too. It's good. Real fucking good."

I was a father. In love. Ready for a steamy hot tub with Ava. And in one week, I'd continue touring with my band.

Life was good. No . . . it was fucking great. Every day got better and better.

Being a Flintlock rocked!

Bring on the next leg of the tour.

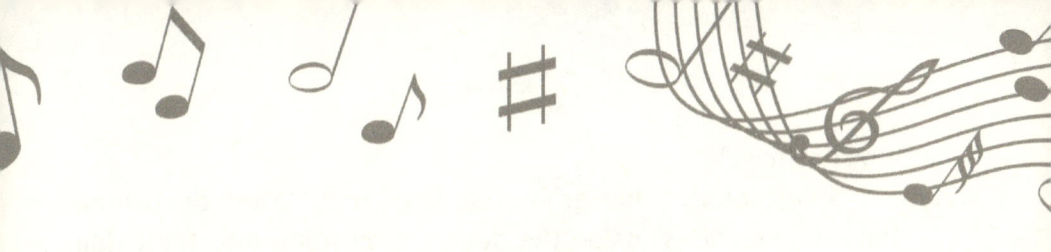

Chapter 35

COLE

On Monday morning, five days before we headed overseas, Harper arrived on my doorstep.

"Argh! Finally," I hollered and drew her into a big hug. Rocking side to side in my doorway, I kissed the side of her head. "It's so fucking good to see you."

"Cole." She stepped back and eyed me up and down, waving and shimmying her hand at me. "Baby cuz, you're looking good."

"So do you." I flicked the tips of her pixie cut with my fingertips. "What happened to the long dreads? This is . . . different. Stylish. Kinda sexy. It suits you."

"Thanks." She pulled off her crocheted Nepalese beret, then ruffled her fingers through the loose strands. "Time for a change. Gotta look like a nanny not a hippy."

"I loved your hair. But damn, this is sleek and professional."

She slapped her beret against my arm. "Can't have that, now, can we? I had my dreads for seven years. But they'd gotten too heavy, kept breaking, and weren't comfortable anymore. It was time for them to go."

"Fair enough." I shrugged, then tilted my head toward the hallway. "So, you ready? Would you like to meet Charlotte?"

She sucked in a deep breath, drawing her shoulders upward. Excitement and nerves flickered through her eyes. "Yeah. That's why I'm here."

"Awesome. Let me grab your bags first." After depositing Harper's suitcases inside the door and heading into the living area, I called out to Charlotte. "Char? Harper's here."

"Coming." From her room upstairs, footsteps patted across the carpet. Charlotte appeared at the top of the staircase and came scrambling down the steps. Her little feet struggled to keep up with the rest of her. She jumped to a stop in front of us and tilted her head back. Her eyes, big and curious.

I ruffled her soft, wavy curls. "Charlotte, this is Harper. She's going to look after you when I'm working."

Harper bobbed down and held out her hand. "Hi, Charlotte. Nice to meet you."

Charlotte gave Harper's hand a big shake, but her eyes widened even farther and her little mouth gaped. "Wow. You have eyes like daddy's. Big green ones."

"Yes, I do." She tapped the center of Charlotte's chest. "Just like yours too."

Seriousness set in Charlotte's tone. "Do you like coloring?"

"I do." Harper nodded. "And painting. And drawing. And cooking. And reading. What do you like?"

"Ummm." She tapped her finger against her cheek, then her eyes glittered and sparkled. "Playing Daddy's drums."

Oh!" Surprise spiked in Harper's voice. "He lets you play his precious drums?"

"He's teaching me to play."

Harper straightened. "Wow, Cole. You have changed."

"Yep. Kinda had to."

"Will you play toys with me, Harper?" Charlotte swayed her hips from side to side.

"Char, let Harper settle in." I rubbed the back of her head. "After lunch you can play."

She pouted and glared at me. Why did that always make me feel like a bad father? *Ergh!* Kids. This was a whole new level of guilt, but it was one that I was slowly learning to deal with—thanks to Ava.

"It's fine." Harper took Charlotte's hand. "Best start my new job right now. Let's go."

But Charlotte pulled her hand free of Harper's. She raised her arms above her head and flapped her fingers. "Up."

Wow! Maybe talking to Charlotte about Harper and showing her pictures had helped her warm to her straight away. Maybe they were kindred spirits. But Shelby had done the same thing, showing Charlotte photos and telling stories about us guys. It had made her settling into life with me easier. I'd take that as a win.

"You want me to carry you?" Harper grinned.

"Uh-huh." Charlotte nodded.

"I can do that." Harper scooped her into the air. "Where and what would you like to play?"

"Ponies and dinosaurs." She pointed upstairs. "In my room."

"Awesome. We can do that while your dad gets us some lunch."

"What would you like?" I grabbed my cell phone out of my jeans pocket. "Ava's coming over with Josh. I'll get her to pick up something on the way."

"I'd kill for a big greasy burger and loaded fries. It's been a long time since I've had those."

"Done."

"Let's go, Charlotte. Let's go play." Harper skipped across the foyer and bounded up the stairs with Charlotte in her arms. I laughed as warmth spread across my chest. Harper was a bigger kid than I was. She adored children and had a big heart, and I was glad she'd come home. She'd been gone for way too long.

After lunch, Harper settled into the guest room downstairs where Hannah had stayed. She'd insisted on some privacy and distance, and after the tour, she wanted to move into the guesthouse . . . once I cleared it out. I was happy with whatever she wanted to do. She was here. That was all that mattered.

That night, everyone, except Slip and Maddy, who'd gone to Las Vegas for a few days for some sexy time together before we left, came over for dinner and caught up with Harper. As the kids watched a movie, we sat around my huge sofa, drinking and telling tales about our tour. Harper's stories highlighting her travels, and teaching kids in remote places in Nepal, had everyone entranced. After putting the kids to bed, our catchup continued with laughs over exes and hookups. But no one brought up the topic of Harper and Slip's fling. *Thank goodness.* It hadn't ended well. Some things were better left dead and buried.

Just after midnight, Flint, Sutton, Lewis, and Tia left. I locked the door behind them, then hauled Ava off the sofa. I fist-pumped Harper good night. "It's good to have you home, Harps."

"Thanks, cuz." She cuddled her wine against her chest.

"It's been nice to meet you, Harper," Ava said as she snaked her arm around my waist. "You're great with the kids."

"I was born to look after children."

"I see that." Ava rested her head against my shoulder. "I look forward to getting to know you."

"Same." Intrigue sifted through Harper's tone. "The woman who has captured my cousin has to be someone special."

"She is." I tugged Ava's hand and led her toward the stairs. "Night, Harps."

Late Friday morning, we gathered at Flint's house. I was hyped, ready to continue the tour. We were just waiting for Slip to arrive so we could head to the airport.

I didn't complain about him being late.

Having Ava, pinned against the kitchen counter, pressing my hard-on against her crotch to let her know how much I wanted her and how much I'd miss her, helped pass the time. I kissed and moaned against her mouth. "Are you sure you won't join us earlier?"

"I like your negotiation tactics, Mr. Tanner." She wriggled and pressed her hips against mine. "But no. Josh needs to finish the school year. Summer break isn't far away."

Ava had accepted our job offer yesterday. April was more over the moon than me ... and I was fucking stoked ... and doing my best to convince Ava to start sooner than the end of May. Unsuccessful to date. She was the perfect fit to help run our band. She'd get to be with her friends, old and new. And our kids loved hanging out together.

"A spare bedroom isn't far away either." I slid my hand around her waist then down onto her ass, and crushed her against me.

Flint glided past, holding Sutton's hand, and veered into the kitchen. Sutton's eyes were red and full of tears. Neither one of them was looking forward to being apart over the coming month. But Sutton would be joining us at the same time as Ava. Flint wrapped his arms around Sutton from behind. He rested his chin on her shoulder as they leaned against the counter. He threw me a sly grin. "I have not missed you having a girlfriend. I thought I was bad, but I forgot how much of a horny prick you are."

"Hmm." I lifted Ava onto the granite countertop and edged between her legs. "Insatiable."

Ava blushed, covered my face with her hand, and pushed me away. "Okay, drummer boy. I love you, but enough."

"Never."

Flint's cell phone buzzed. He pulled it out of his jeans pocket and scanned the message. "That's Beckett. Slip is on his way."

Reality slammed into my chest. It would only be four weeks until I saw Ava again, but that suddenly seemed like a long time. I touched my lips to hers and breathed her in. We were taking things slow-ish, one day at a time. But every day, I fell more and more in love with her. I'd loved uncovering her element of fun and putting a smile on her face. She wasn't a hard-ass all the time. She was good for me. And I'd do my best to be the right man for her and treat her right.

The guilt I'd felt over losing Aidan, Priah, and Phil still lingered, but I didn't let it consume me. Rather than dwelling on my mistakes, or letting them darken my mind, I had an opportunity to make more people's lives better. People like Charlotte, Ava, Josh and Harper.

They depended on me. I'd never let them down.

I was in love and happy.

My family circle had grown. It humbled me that I'd been the glue that held and brought people together. My true family, blood or not, were my band, our partners, Charlotte and Josh, and my team. They had become my life. I'd always love and protect them with all my heart and soul.

We were The Flintlocks!

I was ready to tour.

The door crashed open. Slip stumbled and staggered inside. He slammed into the wall and sank onto the floor.

Fuck.

I rushed over and caught him underneath the arm. "Slip. What the fuck?"

My God. He reeked of alcohol, wasted and off his fucking nut.

"Let go." He yanked free of my hold. He clambered to his feet and wobbled a few steps into the living room. "Sorry I'm late. But I made it. Let's get the fuck out of here."

"Slip?" Flint raced over to join us. Concern charged his voice. "It's barely eleven in the morning. Why are you plastered?"

Pain and doubt and trouble swam through his eyes. He swayed on his feet, turned, and pointed a finger at Sutton. "This is all your fault?"

"Mine?" Sutton's eyes widened as she ambled toward us. "What did I do?"

"I should've never listened to you."

"What did I say?"

He tapped his fingers against his brow. "You got up in my head. That's what." He lowered his hand and closed his eyes. "Mads and I were happy in a messy but good way. Now it's all turned to shit."

"What's happened?" I asked, standing beside him.

"We went to Vegas. Got drunk. Then this happened." Agony speared his voice as he raised his left hand. A gold band shone on his ring finger. "We got fucking married."

"You're *married*?" Sutton shrieked.

"Wow! Congrats, dude. Crazy but awesome." I gave him a big hug but didn't get one in return. I stepped back, and my heart shuddered at the sadness looming in his eyes.

Tia and Lewis had woohooed, but fell silent as torment twisted across Slip's face.

"Whoa. Married?" Flint jerked his chin back. "I did not see that one coming."

"I just wanted to make things better. Not worse." Slip slapped his hand over his heart and hissed, "I fucking love her, man."

"So why aren't you stoked?" Worry wrangled my voice.

Slip glared at Sutton and shook his head. "So much for taking your advice, Sutt. It's fucked up everything. I put a ring on it. We had a few hours of being fucking happy. Then . . . it crashed like a ton of shit."

"Why?" Confusion clouded Sutton's eyes. "What's wrong?"

"Mads wants a fucking annulment." The anguish in his voice slammed into my chest. "We were married for less than six hours, and she wants to end it."

"Holy shit." I wiped my hand down my face. My ribs cinched around my heart. I struggled to say anything logical, too dumbstruck with shock.

"I'll talk to her." Sutton dashed to the sideboard and grabbed her cell phone. "I'll go see her."

"It's too late." Slip's shoulders slumped as he walked toward Flint's bar. "She's left, gone back to Vancouver. She flew out from Vegas." He grabbed a bottle of vodka and headed for the door. "I just don't want to think about or deal with this now. Let's drink and get the fuck out of here."

Slip never talked much about his relationship with Maddy. It always seemed the highs were high—the lows were like a bottomless abyss. Had they rushed into marriage after only being casual? *Probably.* Maybe she didn't love him. I didn't believe that was the case. So was it Slip's past or hers that had her running scared?

I guess we'd find out.

But fuck. Slip was married!

He loved Maddy. If he wanted to stay with her, he had one hell of a challenge ahead to sort this out.

I prayed Maddy was okay.

More so, I prayed for Slip.

Bring on the next leg of The Flintlocks tour.

THANK YOU

Thank you for reading TORTURED TONES, Book 3 in The Flintlocks Rockstar Romance Series. Cole and Ava found happiness together.

For TORTURED TONES BONUS SCENES and the next in series information, please read on.
More details are on the following pages.

Receive a BONUS BOOK, if you sign up to my newsletter.

PS. If you loved TORTURED TONES, would you kindly take a moment and leave a quick review on Amazon or Goodreads.
They are music for an author's soul.
Thank you.

NEXT IN SERIES

FRACTURED FRETS
The Flintlocks Rockstar Romance Series - Book 4
Available at Amazon.

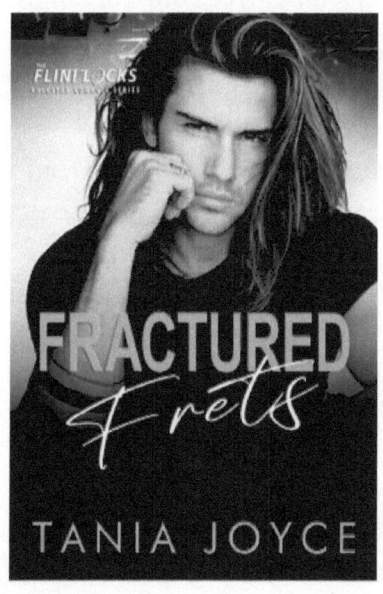

BEFORE YOU GO

Like Bonus Scenes?
Grab the TORTURED TONES Bonus Scenes for FREE via my website. Be prepared for some more steamy fun.

Visit: https://taniajoyce.com/torturedtonesbonus

- AND -

Find out how my world of rockstars started with the Everhide Rockstar Romance Series.

ROCKED – The Price of Dreams is the origin story of how the band met in high school and the foundation for the relationships that develop throughout the six books (3 x standalones, 3 x follow-ons – all happily ever afters, no cliffhangers).

From friends-to-lovers, enemies-to-lovers, accidental pregnancies, roommates to lovers and more, the Everhide Rockstar Series will have you falling in love, shedding tears and laughing out loud.

Read the prequel, **ROCKED – The Price of DREAMS,** for **FREE** if you subscribe to my newsletter.
Join at: https://taniajoyce.com/subscribe

BOOKS BY TANIA JOYCE

The Flintlocks Series

The Everhide Series

Billionaires and College Romance

NEWSLETTER

To stay in touch and to be notified about my new releases, sales, giveaways and more, please subscribe to my monthly newsletter. Join at: https://taniajoyce.com/subscribe

***

FOLLOW TANIA JOYCE

You can follow and find me on the following social media platforms.

Amazon: https://amazon.com/author/taniajoyce
BookBub: https://www.bookbub.com/authors/tania-joyce
Facebook: https://www.facebook.com/taniajoycebooks
Goodreads: https://www.goodreads.com/taniajoyce
Instagram: https://www.instagram.com/taniajoycebooks/
Pinterest: https://www.pinterest.com/taniajoycebooks
TikTok: https://www.tiktok.com/@taniajoyce
Web: http://taniajoyce.com

ABOUT TANIA JOYCE

Tania Joyce is an author of rockstar, contemporary and new adult romance novels. Her stories thread romance, drama and passion into beautiful locations ranging from the dazzling lights and glitter of New York, to the rural countryside of the Hunter Valley.

She's widely traveled, has a diverse background in the corporate world and has a love for sparkles, shoes and shiraz.

Tania draws on her real-life experiences and combines them with her very vivid imagination to form the foundation of her novels. She likes to write about strong-minded, career-oriented heroes and heroines that go through drama-filled hell, have steamy encounters and risk everything as they endeavor to find their happily-ever-after.

Tania shuffles the hours in her day between work, family life and writing. One day she hopes to find balance!

Visit www.taniajoyce.com